CASI'S GUESS

A NOVEL BY LAWRENCE H KUZNETZ

Paperback Edition published June 24, 2020

E-book 1st Edition published December 10, 2011

LIST OF CHAPTERS

BOOK 3. ANSWERS

IMPORTANT NOTE:

A TABLE OF FREQUENTLY USED NASA ACRONYMS CAN BE FOUND PP 558-562 FOLLOWING THE ACKNOWLEDGMENT

For AJ and mom.

And Astronaut Bob Overmeyer, my first boss at the Cape.
He perished doing what he loved.

Author's note:

There are two kinds of writers: those who can write and are looking for a story, and those with a story who want to write it. I'm the latter, not the former, and while it's your call if I can write, my story is a good one and may be the only one I'll ever tell so listen up:

The idea came in a flash, in less than a minute, on a plane ride back from the Cape on the occasion of *Return to Flight*, the first Space Shuttle launch following the *Challenger* disaster. The first draft took 7 months, was 750 pages long and sucked. I've been rewriting ever since, and the svelte 388 pages that follow are the end product to the best of my ability. It's a fictional story, and like most fictions, there are fabricated elements within it, but there are others based on fact. While the main characters portrayed do not exist, they are based on real people, icons of the space program whose names may be familiar. And the jobs these people do are very real and being carried out in the labyrinths of NASA, under the glass roof of Biosphere 2 and in countless labs and universities. The intent of this story is not to disturb. It's to awaken!

Mars

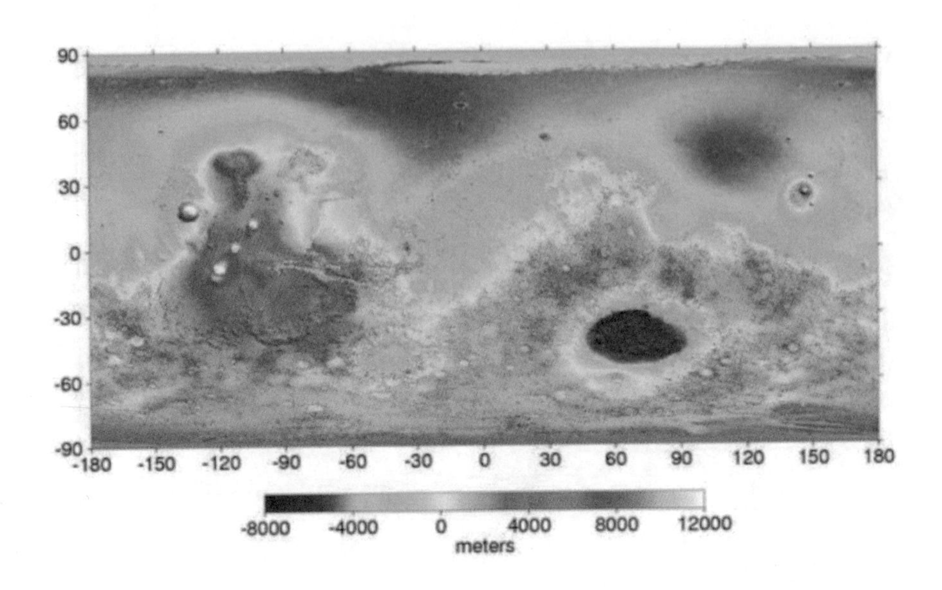

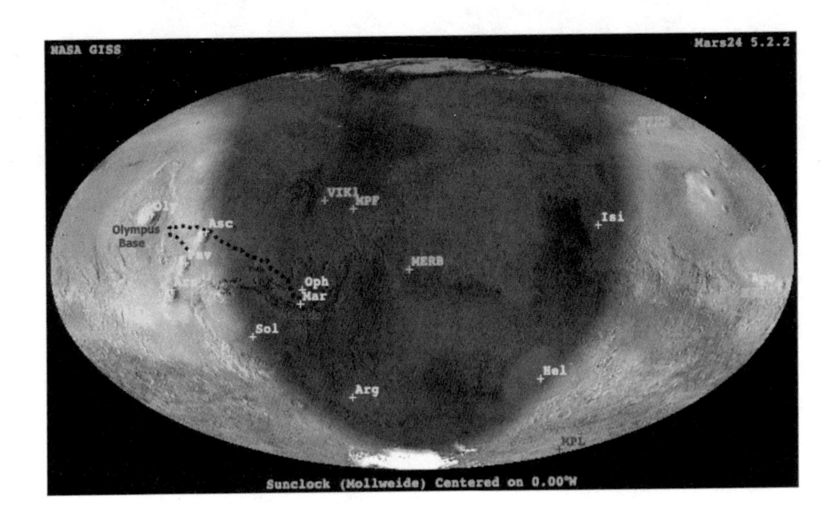

The road to Candor Base

Prologue

The little girl's world was oh so perfect. She lived in a perfect white house behind a tree she called Harry, on a perfectly clear lake. In that lake were all her friends, the frog she called Terrance, Lulu the lilly pad, Betty the bluebird and Goldie the coy. The little girl lived with her mother, her father and her Granny Green in the perfect white house, and loved to dress in orange, her favorite color. Her mother loved to prance about the house and preen herself, which the little girl thought odd. Her father was a scientist at the Cryon chemical plant and she hardly ever saw him, which she thought sad. And her Granny Green, who'd introduced her to Harry, Terrance and the others, was the most wonderful person in the world, she thought, a world of vibrant colors, smells and songs. A world where Harry the tree could rustle his leaves to sing a song of whispers or change colors from green to red-yellow to purple-orange all with the scent of mint. A world where Terrance could stare endlessly, daring you to blink, then stretch his tongue a mile, bellow like a trumpet or inflate himself into a balloon. A world where Lulu the lilly pad had magical power and Betty the bluebird would sing the happiest songs under the sun. Betty had even named the lake in one of her songs, according to Granny Green, Ling-a-loo. Goldie the koi loved to dance in Lake Ling-a-loo, especially when the little girl was about. She'd erupt in a swirl of orange, break the surface, and swim in circles.

The little girl's friends changed with the seasons, especially in winter: Harry's leaves would turn brown and he'd lose them; Terrance would croak lower and nestle closer to Lilly, who would dust herself with snowflakes.

And Goldie would stop dancing and hibernate in the cold. As for Betty, she didn't like the cold at all so like other bluebirds, she'd fly south to warm her feathers, always on December 22nd; then return in spring with a shiny coat and a host of new songs. That's how it was in the little girl's perfect world...until the day of the puff.

The first she heard of the puff was when her father got sick. "Lots of people are sick from it," she overheard him tell her mother. She found out later that it was a chemical in her father's factory that had "puffed out" through their chimney in an accident. Not long after that, a strange cloud appeared to the north above the chemical plant, a wispy, blue-black ugly cloud. Unlike other clouds, this one seemed to linger in the sky for a long time before moving south towards Lake Ling-a-loo. That was in June and after it arrived there, nothing would be the same. It took awhile to notice, until December 22nd, the day Betty usually migrated. Just like all the other December 22nd's, the little girl and Granny Green went down to the lake to say goodbye to her, and just like other December 22nd's, Betty said goodbye to them too, flapping her wings with great fanfare. But unlike the other times, Betty seemed confused when she got airborne, and flew north instead of south when she left.

There was a sadness to Granny Green after that. The little girl felt it throughout the long, cold winter where she'd stay inside playing with her orange toys. She couldn't wait for springtime to arrive when the warm sun would break the gray clouds, when everything would turn green again and Harry would burst forth with his colors and scents of mint.

The sun came out as usual that March, and the clouds broke to a clear blue sky. But the air smelled different, it had a tinge of sourness, and Harry's branches remained naked.

A sinking feeling gripped the little girl then and she ran outside to Harry, shaking his branches and scolding his broad trunk. "Wake up, wake up!" she yelled over and over, until she somehow knew he never would. What of her other friends?

Rushing to Lake Ling-a-loo, she found it murky instead of crystal clear and covered in a frothy foam like the soapsuds from a dirty wash. There was a rowboat on the shore, and she started paddling phrentically towards the clearing with the hyacinths and lilly pads. George and Lulu were gone and so were her other friends, Terrance and Goldie. Lake Ling-a-loo, her paradise, had turned into a eerie landscape of dying trees, silent birds and lifeless waters. That's when she noticed the pipe on the shoreline oozing slime into the water. She'd seen it before but had payed it no mind. The word CRYON was written on it, the factory where her father worked. CRYON, who made pesticides and caused the puff. In the aftermath of her perfect world gone mad, she searched out the only person who could make sense out of the madness. Granny Green took a long breath, shook her head and said:

"Soups of pollution are stirring, terrible things are being formed." She didn't know it then but those were the words that would shape the rest of her life.

BOOK 1 --- COLUMBUS

Chapter 1. Elephants and Microbes.

"V y ger requires the information."
"Who is V y ger?"
"Please provide the information."
"Who is V y ger?"
"You must supply the information,"
"Why does he need it?"
"It is not for you to know."

--Star Trek, The Motion Picture

It was a speck searching for another speck,
in a fathomless jet-black sea.
For thirteen months it had tracked its prey, speeding up,
slowing down and speeding up again,
like a bloodhound through the vastness.
Thirteen months through danger-littered paths
that had left it bent and broken but alert. Very alert.

As it probed ahead, its silvery body reflected a reddish glow,
the only hint of color in the otherwise ashen sea.
It came from the target, growing bigger by the second.
And now, 394 days after it began a 400 million mile
one way journey, fewer than a hundred remained.

Sensing the approaching moment, it slowed time down within it,
splitting seconds into milliseconds, milliseconds to microseconds,
each with a shred of information to help it chart its next move.
Across the void, its creators sensed it too,
and forty minutes later the signal KVUGNG they sent, arrived.
Following orders written long in the past,
it began a series of steps known as Approach Sequence.
From that moment on, the creators couldn't help it anymore.
From that moment on, it was utterly alone.

Preparing for the heat, it tucked long legs tightly in its turtle-like
shell and fired three tongues of flame in the opposite direction.
It fired again and again as an inferno arose,
but still the temperatures built.
Deep in its brain, calculations whirred at lightspeed;
computing commands to keep it on course;
staccatos of impulses at just the right time.
There could be no error now,
as it raced down the corridor of Final Approach.
Straying by centimeters meant incineration.

Forty two kilometers from target,
it maneuvered its shell to face the heat head-on,
then waited for a sign that would tell it it had peaked.
It came with twenty kilometers to go
and plasma gases licking from every direction.
A readout reaching 2800 degrees.
Suddenly there were clouds, winds and an outline
of something opaque below, closing at blinding speed.

It jettisoned its shell at 6 kilometers high,
before releasing its parachute at 5.
At 4, a splotch of terrain came in view,
but it was covered with canyons and gorges.
A flat spot at 3 seemed a good place to land in,
but boulders and craters confirmed it was not.
It scanned furiously for alternatives but realized there were none.

Hurtling down at 500 feet a second,
it was powerless to change things.
Its fate was in the hands of the chute, winds and luck.

At ten thousand feet, it unfolded its legs spiderlike
and began to brace for impact.

At five thousand feet, its engines ignited to cushion its fall.

At four thousand feet, the parachute unhooked,
and fell away like a rag.

By one thousand feet, it had slowed to 100 feet/second,
slower but still too fast.

Down it came, five hundred feet at 50 feet a second....
Two hundred feet at 20.
Fifty at 10.
Twenty at 5.
Ten at 2.

Small sense organs in its footpads touched something solid.
Time to stop! Time to stop! Shutdown! Shutdown!
Initiate arrival transmission!
Standing on the sands of a plain,
330 feet from the rim of a crater
in a place known as Chryse Planitia,
it then trumpeted a signal home.

It took twenty one and a half minutes for that signal
to span 200 million miles to a tomblike silent laboratory.
It appeared as a data blip on a screen and meant:
"I am here, I am safe, I am beginning my work."

It was July 20th, 1976, 5:34 AM Pacific Daylight Time.
Pops from champagne corks rang out in that room,
the aroma of cigars filled the air.
Viking 1 had just become the first human object
to land on planet Mars.

Viking had little time to waste on the sands of Chryse Planitia. Locking its cameras on the ground surrounding it, it dissected the scene a line at a time. Left to right the dissection went then the image was sorted, married with filters and transformed into pixels. It took long minutes to store those pixels on tape and minutes more to cast them back home to the Jet Propulsion Lab in Pasadena, California where a black and white mosaic began unfurling on a screen like a butterfly from a cocoon. A pitted stone came forth, sharply-focused pebbles; fine sand, the shadow of a landing strut that meant it was late in the afternoon. Viking began taking more pictures--panoramic scans of its landing site, 3-dimensional views from different angles, zooms to the horizon and close-ups. It passed black and white images through red, green and blue filters to get color, and used a color chart and an American flag on its body to true them. From there, it went to the data- gathering phase, switching on seismometers, spectrometers and samplers.

An alien starkness was revealed in the weeks that followed, striking yet somehow familiar: Windblown sands, rippling dunes and rolling hills; towering mountains; ancient riverbeds; ice-covered polar caps. Well-known forces could be seen at work: landslides and erosion; winds and clouds; storms and seasons; desert vistas that smacked of home. But some things were different, starting with the sky. It was salmon pink, not powder blue, from red dust suspended in the low gravity. There was a towering volcano 15 miles high and 24 miles across; a canyon that gashed the equator as far as North America was wide; yellow clouds, carbon dioxide frost, mysterious craters. And there was no sign of water. No rivers, no oceans, no seas, still or flowing. And most daunting of all because it so looked like it belonged...there was absolutely no sign of life.

But the creators of Viking remained undaunted; they knew not to trust first impressions. For Viking had been built to look deeper than the surface, to probe for life with two assumptions. First it should be based on the element carbon, and second, wherever large life forms roamed, small ones did too and would be far more abundant. If Earth was at all typical, a random plot of land wouldn't have a single elephant, but a thimbleful of soil would be teeming with millions of microbes. So eight days after landing, Viking began its real work. The equipment it carried--weather stations, laboratories, incubators and furnaces--would normally have filled a building, but the creators had done their miniaturization job well. On that eighth day, a small boom uncoiled and stretched ten feet to the ground. A scoop extended from the end of it, grasped a cupful of soil and placed it on the bed of a tiny railroad car. The car climbed up a track disappearing into Viking's guts and the first search for life on Mars, had, at long last, begun

.

Chapter 2. Chris

Imagine the ragged coast that no one knows,
How far the lands march inland, no one knows,.
Is there a northwest passage from the east?
No one knows....
Yet this I know, it must be tried....
to send our sailors out beyond all maps'

Stephan Vincent Benet

Twelve year old Chrisopher Elkay was no ordinary child; that was clear from the day he picked up a calculus book and read it cover to cover at age 5. He also could do things most children his age could only dream about: balance himself at impossible angles, ride his bike up and down stairs like it was an appendage and swing a soccer ball in a circle around his head *with his ankle*. His vision was extraordinary, with piercing evergreen-colored eyes that could focus the world at resolutions confounding to optometrists. His two biggest loves were airplanes and rocks, especially the cockpit controls of airplanes and rocks with flecks of bright minerals shining through them. With all of these gifts, he might have grown up arrogant had his parents not instilled a deep sense of humility and respect within him, and above all, an insatiable curiosity about the world around him, and other worlds as well. He had a soft demeaner and patience for all who came his way, including classmates who didn't absorb in a semester what he could absorb in a day. "He's a sponge," his teachers would tell his parents, "a supersponge."

Mr. and Mrs Elkay could have opted for advance placement private schools, but chose instead to send him to public schools and not jump ahead of his friends. He needed to experience the real world with all its blights, they thought, not the wealthy, sheltered, isolated world of Easthampton, Long Island where they lived until Mr. Elkay's business nearly failed, forcing them to move to Queens. Chris' mother was resourceful however, and bailed the family out. She would draw a laugh when she'd say she owed it all to a sack dress. Her husband's factory had made a good living for the family by manufacturing belts and buttons for designer dresses until the Chemise from Paris hit 7th Avenue, becoming an overnight sensation.

It looked like a sack, had no belts or button, and nearlwiped the factory out. To make ends meet, Mrs Elkay started picking up the neighborhood kids in her station wagon and the rest was history. Her little nursery school soon made it big enough to pay Chris' hefty tuition at Columbia years later.

Chris was closer to his mother than his father. She'd been his guiding light and without her, he might've fallen under the influence of his 2 closest friends, Jack Hart, who loved guns and ended up shooting his father with one, and Paul Rosenberg, who made pornographic phone calls from Chris' basement whenever he visited. But Mrs. Elkay knew how to overcome these influences. She'd been a child educator and could harness Chris' passion for science. When he was 7, she introduced him to LeMar Caidin, an ex-Navy pilot who owned several vintage warbirds. Caidin also hobnobbed with astronauts and was an expert in the nation's budding space program. He soon became Chris' mentor.

The day LeMar took Chris up in a P-38 Lighning with its video arcade control panel was the last day he hung out with John Hart and Paul Rosenberg. From that day on he couldn't get enough of airplanes, cockpits and spaceflight.

There was another side to that relationship, a side that ended up rocking Chris' life. His parents had worked hard to stay afloat, so hard that they'd barely had time for each other. So when they decided to take a quick getaway to Miami Beach, and LeMar volunteered to fly them there in his twin engine V-tail Beech Bonanza, they jumped at the chance. Chris heard the news from an uncle, his father's brother, who'd been watching over him at the Elkay household.

They'd gone down over the Everglades in bad weather and they'd never be coming back. Chris numbed out, refusing to believe it until reality settled in. He was an orphan at ten and his mom, who'd shaped his life, was gone.

As his nearest living relative, Chris' uncle became his caregiver and Chris was forced to move in with him. That was logical but unfortunate. The uncle, divorced twice and down on his luck, drank heavily and loved to tease and mistreat Chris. Chris would cower in fear whenever his uncle was around and rarely leave his room, an unkempt room with an unmade bed, a battle-scarred dresser and an ancient TV.

He would never know what made him switch on the TV the particular moment of that particular day when Discovery Channel aired a special on the Viking mission that had landed on Mars 35 years ago. Until that moment, he'd never really thought about Mars seriously but the images were spellbinding. Propping his lanky frame against the bedposts, he mopped back a wave of sandy brown hair and leaned closer. His evergreen-colored eyes, darkened in the pink sky's reflection, lasered in on an alien landscape trying to imagine what Chryse Planitia was really like. And then dreamt of a time when instead of imagining, he might touch the sands of Mars himself.

****

July 14th, 2020
Jet Propulsion Laboratory
Pasadena, California

Eleven years later, another pink light reflected off of Chris' green eyes, this one from the retinal scanner at JPL's security gate.

"You're cleared, the guard declared to the babyfaced kid coming through the scanner. "Keep this visitors badge on until you leave then drop in the box. Dr. Cochran's office is on the fifth floor, just to the right of the elevator."

Getting younger all the time here, the guard shook his head as Chris headed off.

"ENTER," Cochran bellowed through the half open door after Chris knocked. Cochran had read the boy genius' bio, but he'd had other child prodigys before and had sent them all packing. Why can't they send me a grownup instead of someone in diapers, he grumbled to himself as he motioned for Chris to take a seat. Chris had heard all about Ed Cochran too of course, the JPL lifer who'd fought every battle for humans-to-Mars and lost. Six foot four with a shock of white hair, thick glasses and a fat cigar clenched between his teeth, Cochran was intimidating. The smell of that cigar with its dense smoke wafting though the room didn't help. This was Chris' first job interview, the only one he wanted, and he was terrified, shaking in his boots.

"Wanna work on Mars do ya kid?" Cochran barked. "Okay, tell me why in ten words or less and I don't want a recitation of your PhD thesis. Shit, was that boring, couldn't you put in some gratuitous sex in there to spice it up?"

"Dr Cohran, y..you're one of my heroes," Chris mumbled taken aback at first. "The answer to your question is that Viking landed in the wrong place," he said quickly recoving, "and I know the right place. You should've gone where the water was, by the debris flows, fluvial channels and permafrost. I know you wanted to land in a safe place and didn't look beyond that but that was a mistake! Hire me and I'll show you where to land, and this time you'll find signatures of life--fossils, organics and other signs. And that's where we'll land people!"

"In Candor Chasma right?" Cochran shot back in a thick Brooklyn accent. "Cause you say so in your thesis? Well here's a reality check: Just cause you breezed through Columbia don't give you the cajones to tell me what we shoulda done! You weren't there then, were you?"

Chris worried he might have blown it with his brashness but unknown to him, that's exactly what Cohran had been looking for, be it in diapers or not. He wanted someone to stand up to him and shout back instead of the namby pamby liilypads they'd sent over from MIT or Caltech. He also wanted a real New Yawker to work for him, someone he could talk Yankees and Giants and Knicks with which he missed in the sticks of Pasadena. And most of all he wanted a deciple. He was 74 years old and in Chris Elkay, he saw himself the way he used to be, full of piss and vinegar for all things Mars until the politics, bureaucrats and assholes rubbed it all away like sandpaper, reducing him to one of them. "Okay son," he said, "we'll let you know about the job in a week or two. Before you leave, there's somethin you should know. Ya could bust your ass here, spend your whole life working for a Mars mission and never get it. Remember that!

Chris got the job, and soon noticed that the secret to Ed Cochran was shouting back at him though the cigar smoke and talking Giants, Yanks and Knicks. Once he did that, Ed was a pussycat and he soon found himself being invited to Ed's condo for home cooked meals where his wife Millie would prepare pastrami, kasha varnishas, blintzes, potato latkes and applesauce like his mother used to do.

The Cochran's took to Chris like a son when they found out he was an orphan, and he rocketed through the ranks at JPL rapidfire. It was just after another sterling performance bursting with creativity that Ed promoted him to be a subsystem manager, a title that came with an automatic pay increase and a perk-- round trip airfare and hotel to Cocoa Beach to watch a launch from the VIP stands of Cape Canaveral. It was the Gateway launch of the new Space Launch System (SLS) and it would be a landmark day.

****

Chapter 3. Tess

Parked in a long line leading to a guard shack at the Cape, Chris took everything in -- the bellowing of speakers, the sea smell in the air, and the towering rocket six miles in the distance, it's countdown paused at a built-in hold to allow the Ice Team to clear the last remnants of icicles away. People were everywhere, in cars waiting for their badges like him; in powerboats jockeying for a better view on the Banana River and on the sides of the road in makeshift stands. A small band of protestors was also there, chanting,

"Green not Black." They reminded him of hari krishnas.

The hubbub stopped abruptly as guards emerged from their shack to let a flotilla of vehicles through. Sandwiched between them was a polished aluminum Airstream Trailer with the blue NASA Meatball emblazoned on it. Within were 4 males and 3 females; 3 white, 2 black, 1 latino and 1 Asian. Seven astronauts, the American dream incarnate, waving at the crowd through the Airstream's small windows. Chris' eyes brightened in admiration as they passed through the gate on their date with destiny. The speakers suddenly shuddered to life with:

"This is KSC Launch Control. The flight crew is now on their way to Pad 39 B and the Ice Team has removed the last deposits. We are still GO for the launch of the first Lunar Gateway on the new Space Launch System at eleven thirty eight this morning. This is KSC Launch Control."

Brimming with excitement, Chris watched the guards lower then raise the gate again, dispersing passes to the waiting line of cars, and as he reached out to take his, the chant of the protestors grew louder.

"GREEN, NOT BLACK!"

"THEY'RE USING NUKES TO KILL OUR CHILDREN."

"GREEN, NOT BLACK."

"What are you talking about?" he shot back at a young girl bellowing at him through his open window. She seemed incongruous with an orange parka and hood that covered most of her face except for the wide sensual lips that hurled fog breath at him like weapons. "**Green, not black**."

He glared at her and she flipped back her hood and glared back at him.

He was only vaguely aware of the guard handing him his badge, and the horns behind him honking. All he could see was that face with the wide lips and oval eyes.

Time, the guards and a rush of announcements forced him to move on but he couldn't get the girl in orange out of his mind. He thought about her as he drove past the old Saturn 5 Moon Rocket; the iconic VAB (Vehicle Assembly Building) and the Launch Control Complex that would push the button. He thought about her through the wave of announcements from PAO and during the long meandering walk from the parking area to the VIP stands where he would sit. Only after he'd wedged his way into those stands among the crowd, a mere 50 meters from the big Countdown Clock and stared the 3 miles across the waters edge at Launch Pad 39B, did he pause. He was now as close as anyone could get to the launch.

"T minus six minutes and counting. The crew is now in the process of APU startup. The three Auxiliary Power Units provide pressure to the hydraulic system which moves the main engines and aerosurfaces."

"Four minutes and counting, this is KSC Launch Control. Flight Commander Scobee has just reported loading of the Backup Flight Computers...."

"T minus 30 seconds, T minus 20 ...."

A pale blue flame appeared beneath the craft's tail at minus 5, followed by a huge spray of water from the fire suppression tower at minus 3. A hail of white-orange that jounced the rocket against its moorings like a spring erupted at 2, until T minus zero with...

"Lift off. We have lift off of Gateway 1 and NASA's bold return to the Moon then Mars."

Fire overwhelmed the Sun, and it took seconds for the enormous craft to rise above the pad. At 8 million pounds and carrying the crew in a modernized capsule atop it, the 38-storey Space Launch System was the biggest rocket ever built. It had been controversial from the gitgo and Chris wasn't a fan. He favored SpaceX's Columbus program for deep space access because it would bypass the the Moon in favor of Mars and cut decades off the timeline. Nevertheless, it was mind blowing to see something that titanic locked in a battle against gravity to stay upright with each tick of the clock.

At first the battle was noiseless. The sound from its 4 RS-25 liquid fueled and 2 solid rocket booster engines would take 7 seconds to reach the VIP stands where Chris was sitting. All he could see was a noiseless inferno picking up speed, rolling right and arching upwards. And then the silence ended. An earsplitting crescendo of pops arrived first, quickly escalating to thunderclaps and followed by a shockwave that buffeted his jacket against his chest. It was unlike anything he'd ever experienced: the 4th of July squared, New Years Eve cubed. His senses reeled and he stood on his toes hollering "GO, GO, GO," with the rest of the crowd.

It all seemed normal at first, or nominal in NASAspeak, as if launching such a beast could be called nominal. Then suddenly without warning an off-nominal yellow flash lit up the sky at T plus 73 seconds and the trajectory split into two helter-skelter spirals. Faces outlined in shadows cried out and a grey dust began to fall like fine snow on cars, benches and roads. Some of that dust fell on Tess Elliot, the girl in the orange parka, the girl who'd grown up on Lake Ling a Loo, and though he didn't know it yet, Chris' wife to be.

****

January 29th, 2034 ....11 years later
CSF, Crew Quarters Building
Kennedy Space Center

Minus 00:16:00:00—Sixteen hours and counting

The only sound in the Crew Sequestering Facility (CSF) came from the flat screen monitor piping in CNN's coverage of the third attempt to get Columbus 11, the first human mission to Mars off the ground. Tess stared at her husband through the glass barrier separating them and placed her palm on the EQUALIZE button. No one was allowed access to that button other than key support personnel, flight docs and immediate family also under quarantine. She pressed it and waited for the tone and the hiss that would equalize the pressures and clear her to enter. She went to him slowly, enveloping him in her arms so tightly that the rise and fall of his breathing was impeded. He didn't mind. He wanted the suffocating closeness as much as she did. They might never be this close again.

She looked hard into his eyes, imploring him to promise what he couldn't—that he'd make it back alive. There were shadows under those eyes and his hair showed flecks of gray. He said nothing.

They'd been this close in the count before, and there could be another slip like the previous two, but Tess sensed there wouldn't be. The moment she'd long feared was finally at hand, one she'd share with less than a handful of human beings.

My husband is leaving for Mars. How do I handle that, what do I say?

"How do I reach you, when can I talk to you?"

"Tomorrow or the next day Adam Brady will call you. He's a Capcom at the MOCR. He'll give you the protocol."

"Anything else I should know, anything you'd like me to do?"

He stammered then grew silent again. She looked at him in that way of hers, knowing there was something. *What was it?* "This is no time for secrets."

"I've been thinking about Ed, that's all."

Ed Cochran, Chris' mentor and boss, had locked himself in his old 62 Falcon with the garage door closed, the engine running. A cryptic suicide note inside described a sabatoge plot.

"Sabatoge plot?" Tess asked with disbelief.

"Yeah. He was 88 and delusional at the end. Nothing he said or did made sense. I'm just sorry he didn't make it here to see this."

He cleared his throat nervously and pressed a small thermos bottle into her hands, cold and metallic. "Take this," he said, "call it a going away present."

"Wh…what is it?"

"My sperm," he whispered, barely audible. "Store it in liquid nitrogen when you get home, don't let anything happen to it."

She gazed at him dumbstruck.

"It's for our children …"

She placed a finger over his lips to stop the rest of the words.. *in case I don't come back.*

"So you can get a head start on our family," he said softly instead. She began to cry, something she swore she'd never do in front of him.

"I'm going to leave now," she said slowly, "you've got to get back in there and get some rest."

"I love you."

Every movement was a struggle now, unclinging from him; letting go; walking away. She felt leaden, each step towards separation like the tearing apart of 2 oppositely charged supermagnets. Finally the exit door was there and she leaned against it.

"Knock em dead, astroman," she tried to joke, then kissed him on the forehead, opened the door and was gone. He stared at the vacuous space that had been her with a numbness spreading down his body, then turned to the scanner on the inner door and reentered his quarters.

Royce Davies knocked briskly moments later. Chris grimaced at the intrusion then forced a smile. He couldn't stand any flight surgeon, and this guy in particular, but he had to be civil.

"You ready," Davies probed, "feel good, everything copasetic?"

"Yeah."

"That's all you got to say? First human mission to Mars and all you can muster is a 'yeah?'

"Got a lot on my mind, Royce."

"I imagine. Listen, I've got to get something off my chest before Launch. I wanted you to know that I've had your back from the onset. Ed Cochran was a loose cannon. Brandford knew it before I did. He had to be reined in. We were only trying to protect you."

"What about Joanna Hewitt, did she have to be reined in too?"

Davies brow curled into a frown at the thought of the woman everyone liked who he'd yanked from the mission and replaced with one they didn't. "Joanna Hewitt had a nori virus," he offered in a too-smooth demeaner Chris found hard to swallow. "We couldn't risk contamination. That's why we have quarantine procedures.

That's why we replaced her with Andrea. Speaking of which, you know the drill, right? You've got to maintain quarantine all the way from this room to Mars."

"Yeah, I know the drill Royce. The pressure's kept lower in this side of the building to keep bugs in the outside world from flying in and it's reversed when we get back to keep Mars bugs from flying out and contaminating the world with some horrific alien virus, right? You really believe in this bug stuff don't you?"

"Don't matter what I believe. The COPP, Committee on Planetary Protection, put the procedures in. I just enforce them."

Yeah."

"Well, good luck man. No matter what you think, you're still the right guy for the job. I firmly believe that."

"Thanks, Royce."

Sleep wouldn't come for hours, and when it did, it segued into the same disturbing dream he'd had for weeks now, a vision of his spacecraft bobbing up and down on a rolling green sea under rust-colored clouds. He was leaning out the airlock door as the clouds began to rain crimson, first in trickles then in torrents of blood until it awakened him with a start. He daren't talk to anyone about it, not the NASA shrinks, his crewmates, not even Tess for fear of being pulled like Joanna. He'd only be immune after Liftoff.

He decided to go for a run; that would calm him down, it always did. He'd have to be careful though, for he *was* under quarantine and as much as he'd love to stick it to Davies, it wouldn't do to break it. But he knew the back roads of the Cape blindfolded, and he didn't plan on bumping into any homo sapiens, let alone Davies, who'd shit a brick if he found out.

It was a clear moonlit night when he turned into the swampy path that led past two old hulks of the Mercury Program, the blockhouse and a rusted gantry used to launch Jupiter C rockets. He was devoid of rhythm at first, still preoccupied with the dream, but then, as always, he got into it, each step driving the other until the disturbing images receded to the background. It had taken less than 15 minutes and everything was back to normal when it occurred to him that normal on Mars would be a different kind of thing. And this might be his last normal run for a long time, a thousand days to be exact.

As the heat welled up in his body from the 6:30 pace he'd been clocking, sweat started pouring off his brow he decided to back off. He could see the headlines if he tripped:

Astronaut Breaks leg in Woods. Scrubbed from Mars flight

Maybe I should turn around now, he thought 25 minutes into it, when the unexpected happened, 5 round shapes stumbling and bumbling out of the brush in front of him, 2 wild pigs and their piglets, hilarious if they hadn't had tusks and a short temper. He visualized another embarrassing headline:

Astronaut Gored by Wild Pig hours before Mars Mission."

"That does it," he huffed, "I'm outta here." But just as he turned tail home for the CSF, he had another wildlife confrontation, this one with a tortoise.

Normally he wouldn't have given the reptile a second thought, they were all over the back roads of the Cape, but this one, fifty yards ahead to the right with its leathery neck extended to the limit staring forlornly at the other side of the road looked for all his worth like he wanted a hitch. Chris immediately regretted it when he obliged him. The tortoise thanked him by pissing all over his shorts.

"Yeccccch!" he bellowed, seeing the final humiliation:

Astronaut hospitalized with Urine Infection...

from Tortoise!

He fretted all the way back to the CSF until he got under the welcoming shower that washed away all traces of the incident. It was a shower that like his run might be his last normal one for 3 years. But he'd forgotten about the dream, which made it all worth it.

It was 4:37 AM when he donned his deep blue flight suit with the red Columbus 11 patch, and entered the CSF dining room. He'd hardly slept a wink but he was ready for the mission now, ready for anything.

Breakfast was steak and eggs served up by a master chef with great fanfare. It was followed by a message from Donald Vance Brandford, the NASA Administrator.

"We're with you, Columbus 11, those of us who've gone before and those who will follow. What lies ahead will be dangerous, and we know the risks well. But our team will be with you each step of the way, our voices and our images. This journey belongs to all of us, and the ages. You carry our spirit. Godspeed."

A chaplain came in next and delivered a prayer.

"Father, bless these travelers to another world. May their journey be safe and their greatest discovery the oneness of Your universe. One more thing Father. Please get them off this time. Amen. "

And just like that, the well wishing was over.

Just like that it was time for the Suit Room.

****

Nine hours and counting:

The road to the VIP press site with the big countdown clock at the foot of the green rolling lawn and the bleachers where Tess would sit was jammed with hundreds of thousands. She'd refused an escorted vehicle and would walk, just as she had the last time she was here, 14 years ago when she was a teenage eco-radical who could get no closer than an icy guard shack. That day she'd watched in horror as *Gateway 1* exploded to smithereens killing 7 astronauts, dooming the SLS Moon program and kickstarting SpaceX's Columbus to Mars, which could also kill him, with her secretly married celebrity husband aboard.

A highlight reel of their life together fast-forwarded as she wound her way on the 3 mile walk past the old Saturn 5 and the VAB towards the press site: the first time she's seen Chris on C-span, trying to sell the budding Mars program to a reluctant Congress; his first night at Biosphere 2 under a starstruck sky with Mars rising and her golden retriever Costeau baying at him, and the first time they'd made love, when he'd played her like a Steinway with those long, pianist's fingers.

So different were they. He'd come from the brink of poverty, his parents working their butts off so he'd never have to slave in a *shmata* factory like his father, ironic because his very first job after an Ivy League educaton and a Masters Degree was making space suits.

She, on the other hand, was a child of privilege. Her father, an executive of the Cryon chemical plant in Pittsburgh, and her mother, a runway model , who'd imbued her with a taste for life's finer things.

She'd grown up in a beautiful white house behind a white picket fence near heavenly Lake Ling-a-loo. If not for her Granny Green, she'd have followed in her mother's footsteps, preening about the house searching for mirrors to admire herself in. But Granny Green, who'd lived with them, had other ideas for Tess and became her role model. She'd introduced her to the wonders of nature and the threat to them by humans, a lesson that hit home the day everyone grew sick from a chemical spill at the Cryon plant.

Soups of pollution are stirring. Unspeakable things are being formed, her granny had said that day--words from the past that swept over her like a riptide. Those words, that warning, had become her mantra and led her to her life's work. CASI, her ***Climate Analog Situation Indicator***

It had been her crowning achievement at MIT, a PhD thesis for the ages, her professors said, because it could take the pulse of planet Earth. By carving the world into imaginary boxes of longitude, latitude and altitude, then adding more boxes for the oceans, rivers, and lakes; and mountains, valleys and plains, CASI could turn summer to fall to winter to spring and do winds, snow and rain.

While her looks could have scored her an anchor job on the Weather Channel, Tess wanted more. She wanted to work at the Biosphere 2 Project in Oracle, Arizona where CASI could be put to good use, where the action was in simulating Earth's eco-systems. She became an all-star there, using CASI to design and control their large-scale Closure Tests, month-long experiments where human "Biospherians" were placed within enormous glass domes to see how they interacted with miniaturized ecosystems.

But that was just a diversion for Tess. Her dream was not to predict Closure Tests, but the effect people had on the real world. Together with CASI, she wanted to run the same experiments on her simulated atmosphere that smokestacks were conducting on air. To strip simulated leaves from CASI's computerized trees the way insecticides defoliated forests and to leak toxic wastes into her prototype seas like her dad's Cryon plant did to Lake Ling-a-loo. And then she wanted to push CASI's buttons and predict the future. At that she'd failed miserably so far but it had led her to Chris Elkay.

She remembered him vividly the day *Gateway 1* went down but had all but forgotten him in the intervening years until his email arrived asking for a meeting. The subject was a NASA contract: an award to grow vegetables on the way to Mars, and to build a small greenhouse to test how they'd fare in Martian soil. But he was really after the dreamgirl he'd conjured up in his wildest imaginings and had finally tracked down. The meeting turned quickly to fiasco. "Glaciers are melting, the air is fouled, a thousand species a minute are going extinct and you want to go to Mars? "Are you smoking something?" she fretted at him.

"Let me explain," he'd responded patiently. "Mars is an object lesson for a planet gone wrong. It was warm once like Earth, had seas once like Earth and a thick atmosphere like Earth. They're all gone now. It's frigidly cold, barren and dry with a hundredth of our atmosphere. There's a lesson there. I want to know it and you should too."

"Come on spaceman," she persisted, "we can't afford it. Your caper will cost trillions. We need the money here; I need it for my research. Earth's in trouble, not some blasted sandpit a billion miles away that's already dead."

"Not quite a billion," he'd countered, "more like 35 million at its closest point. And the cost is less than a half a penny of your tax dollar spead over 20 years, the same budget NASA has now. More to the point, knowing what happened on Mars will help your research."

While his words sounded good, she didn't trust him. She didn't trust any man after what her father had done at Cryon. On the other hand there was something about this guy, a sincerity that was rare, a passion that was unsettling. And those green eyes.

"I don't buy it," she had dueled back, " it still sounds like a bunch of BS to me. Is that all you got?"

"I got plenty more!" he smiled, captivated by her expressive lips and floppy black pony tail swinging back and forth like a hammer trying to nail him.

He pulled his big gun out of the box, a machine he discretely urinated into, then drank the fluid that came out the other side without so much as a wince. Her eyes grew big as saucers. She'd been chasing the same idea for years, a urine recycler that could change urine to drinking water like an alchemist's genie.

"How...how did you, why did you?"

"Why…coz water's expensive and heavy on a Mars mission so we must recycle it. How…normally I'd have to shoot you if I told you but you're pretty so I won't. It works by vapor compression distillation. Anything else you'd like to know? I brought an encyclopedia of reasons why Mars will help your work, starting with money."

The magic word: money. Biosphere 2 needed it; CASI needed it; she needed it. Could she bastardize herself to accept it from a guy, an agency, a philosophy she couldn't trust?

It had been a gut wrenching decision but yes. Antagonists became partners and never looked back. Still, she pondered how she and Chris, as opposite and contrary as a couple could be, had stayed together: Ms Eco-rad feminist and Mr Astroman. And as she neared her seat in the VIP stands to watch him blast off planet Earth, all she could think of and exhale was the word, "wow!"

****

Chapter 4. The Suit Room

There's a myriad of ways to get to Mars.
Countless trajectories,
hundreds of booster types,
tens of mission plans.

Each must be carefully conceived
and its parts infinitely tested.

The cost isn't cheap; a dollar a nut,
five bucks a bolt, maybe more.
The price tag adds up-
50 billion, 500, a trillion?

There's no room for error in this high stakes world. You only get one shot at it.
And it might come once a century.

Five hours and counting:

The Launch Escape Suit was hot, the helmet's anti-fog coating useless. Each time he exhaled, Chris' faceplate misted up.

"Can't see a damn thing," he complained to the Tech working on him.

"It'll clear when your ventilator's hooked up," he was told, and became lost in thought about Ed Cochran again while he waited. He'd first heard the news from Millie, Ed's wife, at their Bon Voyage party in the midst of a conversation with H Buford Stone, his old buddy from the MVAB (Mars Vehicle Assembly Building). They'd just shared a laugh after he'd asked H for the umpteenth time what the H in his name stood for, and been told for the umpteenth time, "For me to know and you to find out snake," when Millie ambled in precariously and dressed in black.

"Ed's dead," she'd said zombie like. "Suicide. You were like a son to him you know." She then reached into her purse, handed him an urn and said, "These are his ashes. I'd like you to scatter them on Mars, Chris. It's what he would have wanted."

After he got over the shock, Chris wondered how he could do such a thing. The bureaucracy wouldn't like it, the ashes could outgas, maybe even tip the weight balance. But the urn and its contents erased the misgivings. Scattering his ashes was the least he could do for Ed Cochran.

Thinking back, he'd never properly thanked him for all he'd done for him: grooming him for management; giving him responsibility and most of all, being his surrogate father. He'd wanted to thank him, swore he'd get around to it, but then Ed had to go kill himself for chrissakes. Perhaps it was inevitable considering all the reversals Ed had suffered, starting with Viking when he'd backed the only experiment that seemed to find life only to be embarrassed by its detractors, who'd used graphs like shotguns to tear it apart.

The pattern had continued, with attacks on his plan to leave for Mars from ISS instead of from an outrageously expensive Moon Base, and on and on. Maybe it was his demeanor that turned them against him, the cigar, the barking, the perceived intimidation. He'd saved NASA's ass countless times as their *Chief Problem Solver* yet his final reward had been an unceremonious boot to retirement, brought on no doubt by his conspiracy theory involving NASA Administrator Brandford, who he claimed had given Andrea Beale, "the French floozie with the big tits," as Ed called her, a seat on the mission in exchange for blow jobs.

Some thought Brandford had taken it easy on Ed, giving him mental disability status and a pension instead of firing him outright. And it mattered not that the Moon Plan Ed so vehementaly dispised was eventually scrapped in favor of his own one to leave from ISS. He was long gone by then. The last Chris heard from him came in a delusional phone call in the midst of Antarctica training that he'd attributed to dementia:

"Sssssss... can't talk long, kid, they're onto me, That crew swap is a setup. They're all in on it, I tell ya, Brandford, Davies the flight surgeon, the moonies, all of em, especially Beale, the floozie. But I got em. They were so up to their ass in alligator shit they forgot to clean the pit. Watch out for em boy; don't trust any of em. Hear me?" "Remember the turtle, Ed had continued: "he gets in trouble when he sticks his neck out. Don't stick your neck out. Ssssss. Ssssssss."

‘Beware the turtle,’ Chris reflected soberly as his faceplate finally cleared. Ed had always stuck his neck out. Things might have been different if only he hadn’t, if he’d just once backed off. Ed’s parting words from that first job interview echoed through the years.

"Ya could spend your whole life working for a Mars mission…"

Ed’s never got his chance. Chris’ was about to unfold.

****

Four hours … and counting

"The suit automatically inflates in a decompression. You'll hear a snapping sound if the cabin pressure drops below 3 psi, then feel pressure in your ears. Don't mess with the zippers or you'll break sterility. One last thing: Don't pop your helmet till you hear three beeps. That's three beeps, got it?"

Chris memorized the Suit Tech's warning and followed him to the Mobile Quarantine Vehicle (MQV), the modified airstream trailer that would take them to the launchpad while isolating them from the germs of the outside world. He sat down between Roberto Diaz, the flight surgeon and Andrea Beale, the mission navigator or floozie, as Ed called her. The sexual tension between them could've lit the Superdome.

When the MQV started moving, hemmed in between a flotilla of security vehicles with flashing blue lights, they could see the hordes out the windows, lining the causeway to the pad for as far as they could see. Everyone was waving. Twenty minutes later their caravan passed the Vehicle Assembly Building and the old Saturn 5, then made the dogleg left for the final 3 miles to Pad 39A. The early morning sun lit up a swirl of color as they approached: white eddies against the blue ocean; misty haze rising from swamp grass; scrub pines blowing over sandy dunes. A startled swan rose up with a start, beating its wings in a retreat to the east. Chris followed it skyward towards the monolith awaiting him: Shuttle *Atlantis*. He smiled a knowing smile.

Few knew why *Atlantis*, a 35-year old relic of the 20th century languishing in an exhibit hall at the Kennedy Space Center for a decade had been hauled out for this mission. The goal to find cheap, safe commercial replacements for the shuttles had started like a gold rush but fizzled as one player after another--Sierra Nevada, Boeing, Martin, Blue Horizon, Virgin Galactic and the others—discovered that vowing to do what the shuttles had done was easier to promise than deliver, especially repairing and maintaining the International Space Station, from which the Mars mission would launch. At the end of the day, the only way to guarantee that Columbus 11 would get off to Mars at all was to resurrect, refit and modernize *Atlantis*, its gantry ever nearer, wisping vapor.

The entrance to *Atlantis* was at the top of the gantry known as the White Room, and the ferry pilots, Jon Overmeyer and Scott Musgrave were already there waiting. They entered first and climbed the ladder to the Flight Deck followed by Mission Commander Vadim Solodnov and Pilot Hirumi Yoshioka. Chris, Andrea Beale, Roberto Diaz and Astrogeologist Anna Vitale followed and stayed below in the windowless Mid-deck, where there would be nothing for them to see but white lockers and nothing to hear but checklists being piped in until they reached Space Station *Alpha* where their spacecraft to Mars awaited them. Then came the thud of the side hatch closing. They were sealed in, each lost in their own thoughts.

Andrea smiled as the count proceeded, thanking the heavens for Vance Brandford, the NASA Administrator who'd helped get her here. She loved him like a father though no one believed that. Everyone figured she'd fucked him then used him, the story of her life with men. Truth is he'd never once asked her to go to bed with him, and she'd gotten her seat *because she deserved it.* That especially, no one believed because she'd been swapped in last minute for Joanna Hewitt for health reasons when Joanna hadn't seemed sick. She took solace from the fact that what people thought would soon be irrelevant. That as *Atlantis* rose higher; Earth would get smaller, shrinking to a dot then a speck, to be replaced by another world with more meaningful things worth pondering.

Still, she had to be careful not let her guard down, that was unacceptable. There was little room for emotion if she was to be taken seriously, and she had to be taken seriously for her mission to succeed.

That meant putting men on the back burner, not easy because of the way she looked and the attention she got. There were times she wished she was motherly and plain like her crewmate Anna, whose physical traits wouldn't complicate things like they did for her. Still, she was happy in her own skin, ecstatic really, and adept at avoiding unwanted attention. But being taken seriously while not sending out the wrong signals was a tightrope she'd had to walk since puberty. And with the exception of those rare occasions when a certain kind of man would come along, she'd straddled that tightrope successfully. Fortunately not many men, especially men in the space business were capable of knocking her off of it. Unfortunately, two of them were on this mission, Roberto Diaz, the flight surgeon seated to her right, and Chris Elkay to her left.

She glanced over at Chris and recalled the first time they'd met, 14 years ago at the Johnson Space Center. Back then, JSC was something special: the place where astronauts trained, spacecraft were born and missions controlled. With its manicured lawns, meandering duck ponds and white-slabbed buildings under the vast Texas sky, the pulse of space could be felt there. It was also the place where some of the most storied decisions in the space program had been made, many of them in the Telecon Room at the top of Building 1. Chris had been in that room when she walked in and the scent of her Shalimar had reached him before she did.

He'd stared at her then, the way he was doing now, the way all men had since she was 15. For in the xy-chromosome world they populated, she simply didn't compute. A lilting french accent, perfect almond skin, inviting hazel eyes, wide expressive lips and long, long legs—someone out of Vogue, not the Sorbonne and Purdue Engineering.

The second time they met had been at the Nassau Bay Hilton on one of those rare Houston nights when the air reeked of excitement instead of humidity. She'd glided towards him in that catwalk of hers, as he'd later describe it, and order a bottle of vintage Pomerol, a prelude to picking his brain about the Mars mission. Then came the third time, at a NASA conference in Washington where he'd sought her out with war stories to tell her about funding struggles for the mission. The evening became a blur on wine after that and she'd ended up in his shower. She didn't remember much about that night, or the morning after, except for the note she left on her way out scribbled in lipstick on his bathroom mirror while he slept.

"Another time perhaps?" God, what was I thinking??

Emerging from his stupor the next morning, Chris had had a different take on the note and Andrea Beale. A line from Ian Fleming novel came to mind:

A first time meeting is happenstance, a second's coincidence, but a third is enemy action.

The thought would be amplified after she replaced Joanna Hewitt on the mission. He liked Joanna, the Systems Engineer and Navigator nonpareil. When Flight Surgeon Royce Davies yanked her for Andrea, citing stess and latent depression, it hit him like a ton of bricks. True, Andrea had all the right stuff: dual PhDs, fluent in seven languages and the creator of the NAV program that would steer their spacecraft to Mars. But there was more to her than a resume. And a bunch of it bothered him.

****

Chapter 5. The Others.

MEMBERS OF THE PRIME CREW OF COLUMBUS 11

Captain Vadim Solodnov--Mission Commander

Captain Solodnov, a 53 year-old veteran test pilot, made his first trip to space more than two decades ago. He has a Masters degree in astronautics from the Moscow Aviation Institute and has logged more than 4700 hours in various aircraft and spacecraft, including Russian Space Shuttle Buran and American Shuttle Discovery. He has also been a test subject aboard ISS, and has spent over 4500 hours in zero gravity. Captain Solodnov is single and resides in Star City, near Moscow.

Dr. Hirumi Yoshioka--Mission Pilot/Physician

Dr. Yoshioka became a pilot-astronaut the hard way after first becoming a medical doctor. A graduate of Kyushu University, she went on to get her MD degree from Tokyo Science University. The daughter of a well-known aviator/doctor, Dr. Yoshioka grew up flying and received her multi-engine, instrument and commercial ratings by the age of 18, a record in Japan. Following medical school, she went to work as a flight surgeon and test pilot for the JALTECH Corporation, helping to develop the JT-39 trainer. Her proposal on gravitational physiology earned her a seat aboard Spacelab 6, after which she was then selected as a pilot-astronaut for SpaceX on a Crew Dragon missions. She accompanied Captain Solodnov on the Expedition 47 mission to ISS, where she was part of the experiment that established the need for artficial gravity on the way to Mars. Dr. Yoshioka has logged 3900 hours in 36 different types of aircraft. She is 44 years old, single and resides in Tokyo.

Dr. Anna Vittale--Mission Geologist

Dr. Vittale, 39 years old, will be making her second trip into space. After earning a Bachelor's degree in nuclear engineering from the Polytecnico di Torino, she went on to study for a Ph.D at the Universita' la Sapiencza, Roma. Her doctoral work in geology--Utilization of Martian Minerals for the Manufacture of Oxygen, Water and Other Essentials of Human Survival--has been adapted by the Columbus Program as the key to long term self-sufficiency on Mars. Dr Vittale has been a staff member at the Max Planck Institute for Metals Research in Stuttgart, and later worked at the European Space Agency Technology Center in Holland before transferring to the Space Systems Group of Aeritalia in Torino. She first flew for ESA in 2024 as Mission Scientist on the third flight of the Hermes spaceplane Europa. Dr. Vittale was born in the village of Montalchino, near Florence, and currently resides in Torino. She is single.

\

Dr. Roberto Diaz--Physician

Dr. Diaz received his medical degree from the Guadalajara University and did his residency at Baylor College of Medicine in Houston Texas, specializing in orthopedics and aerospace medicine. Since that time, he has served on the Baylor faculty as an expert on osteoporosis and degenerative bone disease. He was a pioneer in the use of hyperbaric therapy to treat the debilitating aftereffects of long term exposure to low gravity, and the creator of the pinwheeling design of the Mars Transit Craft to prevent them. He is also the inventor of HUMMS, the Human Medical Monitoring System that will keep tabs on crew health during the Mars mission. Dr. Diaz has flown in space 3 times, first as Physician-in-charge on Expedition 11 on ISS and on Expeditions 14 and 17. He grew up in the small village of Aguas Caliente, in central Mexico and currently resides in Houston, Texas. Dr Diaz is 51-years old and single.

One hour and counting....

"Audio check!" Overmeyer intruded over the speakers, "how do you read?"

"Loud and clear, *Atlantis,"* answered the Orbiter Test Director in the Firing Room at KSC. "Ready for abort advisory check?"

"Affirm," Overmeyer rattled back.

Dr. Roberto Diaz, downstairs in the Mid-deck seated next to Chris, thought about his grandfather. Had he not been at death's door that fateful day when a doctor appeared to save him with his mysterious, magical black bag, Roberto might still be walking the dirt roads of Aquas Caliente barefoot. He was only ten at the time but that bag changed Roberto's life. The power of its contents inspired him to go to medical school where he'd learn about Space Adaptation Syndrome and pioneer the bone loss experiments that would lead to the rotating design of the Mars Transit Craft, then go on to create HUMMS, the Human Medical Monitoring System that would watch over them all throughout the mission. And yet, for all his accomplishments, he was insecure. He looked around the Mid-deck at his crewmates and worried what they thought of him. He'd sucked cactus, witched water, ate roots, and climbed mountains in space suits with them but none of that mattered when you hail from a village so poor that shoes are a luxury.

Had he shaken the image of the Mexican wetback so many gringos seemed to possess, even these gringos? He couldn't be sure, especially when it came to Andrea, sitting opposite him. There was something about her that made him uneasy, uncomfortable and nervous. He could never seem to read her and it was troubling. Perhaps it was the 'Sicilian thunderbolt' effect he'd read about in psychology, *an outburst of emotion for a person we hardly know which can turn the life of a most composed, well-organised and calm person upside down.* This thunderbolt had the force of a tornado and could destroy everything he'd worked for if he got too close to it. He knew this from "The Godfather" novel by Mario Puzo, one his favorites, when Michael Corleone, the lead character meets a girl who deconstructs his way of thinking. He had personal experiences too, in medical school, when the power of infatuation and sensuality drove patients to seek sex change operations when they were smitten beyond reason with someone of the same gender. Performing those operations early in his career when he needed the money was an embarrassment, a secret he'd protected with ferver. He wouldn't be here had anyone outed him, of that there was no doubt.

And yet he might be a victim of the same pheromonal storm from Andrea that had affected his patients so long ago. His readings said that the thunderbolt could strike irrespective of marital status; age; education; gender or temperament but had a greater effect on calm and reasonable people like him and that it was akin to a mental disorder.

The obsession could plunge one into loss of commonsense and predictability and could arrive unexpectedly, at the least appropriate moment, entering through the front door of the heart abruptly with a loud slam and without knocking. Asking neither for approval or readiness, before sucking you into the swirl of its emotions full force. Statistics said only every third person in the world was struck by the 'Sicilian thunderbolt' and only once in their lifetime.

Roberto hoped he was not one of those people because Andrea Beale had him by the short hairs. He recalled the day they met when the C130 Hercules skidded to a halt on the ice strip west of Ross Island at the start of Antarctica training. They'd been greeted by an unforgettable virgin white panorama, uninterrupted to the horizon. From there they'd gone by dogsled to McMurdo Station or Mac Town as everyone called it, passing Discovery Hut along the way, the tattered reminder of Scott's fatal attempt to conquer the South Pole. That journey had been a picnic compared to what they were about to attempt.

After over-nighting in the drab gray bungalows of Mac Town, they'd boarded helicopters the next morning and buzzed the Ross Ice Shelf, McMurdo Sound, and Blue, Piedmont and Ferrar Glaciers before descending into billion year old Howard Glacier and their destination, a rift in the Taylor Valley of Victoria Land that looked remarkably like the Candor Chasma canyon in Valles Marineris, their landing site on Mars.

Equally remarkable had been the four vertical, metallic monoliths of the MARS outpost (Martian Analog Rehearsal Simulator), as bizarre in Antarctica's white wasteland as they'd be on the sands of the red planet.

The 2 Habs, Rover and Power Modules--connected by an intermodule tunnel—had been alien yet welcoming, and Roberto had slowly lumbered towards them after landing behind Andrea, who seemed to sway instead of lumber. It wasn't the first time Roberto had wondered about her, and why she'd replaced Joanna Hewitt. Joanna had engaged him. Andrea, by contrast, would ignore, infuriate or tease him. But it was the way she carried herself that really uncoiled him, everything in place, every step orchestrated. Like the time she'd come to him complaining of headaches, and he'd suspected IDS (Isolation Dysfunction Syndrome), normal for Antarctica. Ignoring his diagnosis, she'd pulled a mirror from her purse, checked herself out and stared at him. Had she had sex in mind? Or the time he'd caught her reading a flyer from the radical environmental group, FirstEarth and she'd winked at him. What the hell was that about? What the hell was she about?

Forty-five minutes and counting....

"OTC to CDR," the Firing Room buzzed in to Overmeyer. "Proceed with cabin leak check."

"Roger that, in work. CABIN VENT to CLOSE on panel L2, VENT ISOL TO CLOSE. Standby for cabin pressure read, ok...seventeen point seven psi."

"Copy, *Atlantis*: seventeen point seven."

Anna Vittale, also downstairs in the Mid-deck, thought of Montalchino, Italy, the village above Florence where she'd been born and raised. In a place where the dream job was to work for the Brunello vineyards, her dream had been to become an astrogeologist astronaut, an unrealistically crazy expectation to all but her and her mother. She shed a solitary tear thinking of her mother, alone in Montalchino now and needing cataract surgery from the high doses of UV leaking through the ozone hole. The extraordinary mother who still made those fabulous dishes from the rarest of fungii that grew in the rich loam of the village, some of which she'd spirited aboard as a treat for her crewmates should things go well.

Her last obstacle for selection to the mission had been the MTA-1 Marssuit test, where she'd crossed through the world's biggest door, that slammed on the world's biggest "O"-ring in the world's biggest thermal vacuum chamber, affectionately called SESL (Space Environment Simulation Laboratory). Its door alone stood 40 feet high, 4 feet thick, weighed 7 tons and held ten to the minus five torr, a vacuum nearly the equal of deep space.

Within that door stood MTA-1 (Mars Test Article 1), the spacecraft that was a carbon copy of their Transit Craft and Lander awaiting them now at ISS *Alpha*. It spanned halfway to SESL's 12 story roof. There'd been two stated goals for the test that day: qualifying the spacecraft's systems prior to flight and checking out the brand new Marssuit. But for Anna there'd been a third goal, a far more challenging one. For as the gigantic cryopumps began sucking the air out of SESL; as its side shrouds began filling with LN2 (liquid nitrogen) and its xenon lamps turned aflame with an artificial sun; she'd have to get past choking claustrophobia.

Her first experence with claustrophobia struck like lightning, coming out of nowhere on a summer job at the Brunello vineyards before she started engineering school. She'd been working in a small office on a small desk tracking accounts and it all seemed fine until the manager brought in a second student to sit at the desk opposite her. The closed in feeling started within minutes, a suffocating, squeezing feeling that nearly caused her to faint. She'd blamed it on the tight proximity to another human being rather than to tight places because other than her mother, she wasn't used to being physically close to other people. The next time it happened though, she was alone, in a tiny study room at the *Polytecnico di Torino* preparing for final exams and blacked out. That's when she knew her goal of becoming an astronaut geologist for ESA would never happen without a major physiological intervention. That intervention came in the form of phobia behavioral modification or hypnotherapy. It was long, expensive and hard to find a doctor she could swear to absolute secrecy but it worked. For the most part.

Now and again the choking feeling would return to surprise her, yet somehow she'd managed to control it, all the way through grad school, ESA jobs and the biggest test of all, the MTA-1 test. She flashed back to H. Buford Stone's icy calm voice polling his team for readiness that day. There'd been 117 on that team, some manning the consoles, others the fluid flows and others the monstrous cryopumps, and not one would have an inkling of her body's attempt to betray her. The feeling started when the manlock door slammed behind her, as the pressure began dropping towards a hundredth of Earth's; the temperature started sinking to minus 110 degrees F and C02 flooded SESL. When she felt the Marssuit closing in on her, she immediately went into mantra mode.

She'd have to fight the suit's rectal probes that day, and the cumbersome weight-relief track that simulated Mars' gravity; and the exercise contraption they called "The Beast," but they'd be childs' play compared to that strangling feeling. Yet as the Beast quickened from 2 to 4 to 6 kilometers per hour, and its incline ramped up from 0 to 20 degrees, her resolve had stiffened with it. Until at the end of the day, she'd passed the hurdle. Just like all the other ones on her unshakable quest to stars.

SESL

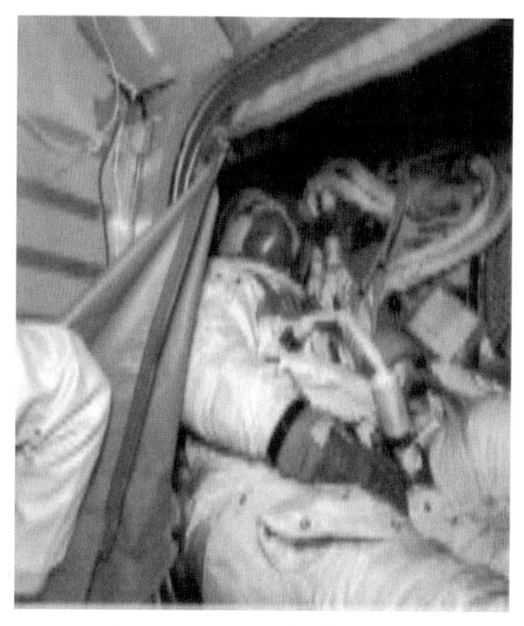

Stepping on The Beast

There was another hurdle Anna Vittale had to overcome, one even more challenging than the claustrophobia She was a lesbian. Not that being a lesbian in the 21st century was a show stopper (or being claustrophobic)—if you were landlocked. The first trip to Mars however, was another story. Either of those things, or even suspicion of them, would've disqualified her in a millisecond had anyone known and only supurb planning and sheer willpower sustained over decades had kept them hidden. The claustrophobia, she'd dealt with since her teen years. The lesbian thing was more recent, discovered by a process of elimination that began with a lack of interest in men.

She wasn't a knockout like Andrea or exotic like Yoshi, so it was no surprise men weren't that interested in her either. She was the earthy type that men preferred as mothers, not lovers, and if they weren't interested in her, she wouldn't be interested in them. Her career path hid the reality too, a minefield where women started as second class citizens and where the simplest misstep with sexuality could result in demotion, disqualification, pay reduction or worse. In this world, relations with men were to be avoided at all costs if you hoped to succeed. She'd never discussed it with Andrea or Yoshi but it was an unspoken given among the 3 female crewmates of Columbus Eleven.

Relations with women on the other hand, were more complicated. What started as a harmless shower in the NASA fitness gym opened her eyes to that. She'd always showered alone until she joined the gym, then suddenly there were naked women crisscrossing the locker room, many with interesting bodies. She found herself staring at some with feelings stirring in her groin that had never stirred before until someone stared back and said something. Embarrassed, she'd quickly left but the woman had found her the next time which led to a coffee, a meeting and a private shower. When she finally understood her sexuality, she had no regrets but knew she'd have to hide it like a blood oath, just like her claustrophobia. At least until lift off when no one could pull her, like they had Joanna Hewitt.

****

Thirty minutes and counting....

"OTC, *Atlantis*," Musgrave said briskly, "IMU alignment, 28 degrees, 36 minutes, 30.3 seconds north; 80 degrees, 38 minutes, 14.8 seconds west. Over. "

"Copy, *Atlantis,* alignment complete. Begin GPC loading starting with BFS transfer."

"Roger that," Ferry Flight Commander Overmeyer replied, "Loading BFS into GPCs."

Overmeyer clicked the icon for the Backup Flight System, SPEC 0 PRO, and began loading data into the 5 General Purpose Computers while Musgrave monitored him from the right seat. Vadim Solodnov and Hirumi Yoshioka sitting directly behind them on the Flight Deck also watched, and although they'd been here many times before, they'd never just been passengers. Vadim pulled a nitrogen-pressurized pen from a pocket on his launch escape suit and wrote a note in his logbook.

> *Waiting atop a rocket is nothing new for me; it's where I'm going that's different. And while I'm less tense because I've flown before, there's another kind of tenseness now from the enormity of our undertaking. I only hope I can honor the memory of Leoniv and Gagarin...*

Vadim, broad and powerfully built, stared at his words through steel gray eyes, and vividly recalled when Leoniv, Director of RSA (the Russian Space Agency) had taken him to Gagarin's Office. It had been a day of firsts. Leoniv, the first human to walk in space, had brought him to the office of Yuri Gagarin, the first man to ride a rocket into space. The things he remembered most about that office were the family photos and yellowed reports covering Gagarin's desk and the old government-issue wall clock above it, frozen in time at 16:30 on the day in 1968 when Gagarin died in a training flight. Leoniv had taken Vadim to that office because Gagarin was a true Russian hero and tradition called for cosmonauts to go there before their first flight.

A touch on the shoulder from Yoshioka jostled him back from the past. She was smiling. He shook his head slowly, knowing he had no business being in love with her. She was a flight doc, like Roberto, the bald Mexican with the hairy back, and he hated flight docs because they could disqualify him for flight. But Yoshi had compensating attributes. She was a damn good pilot and a *krasotka devitsa* (stunning young virgin) to boot.

Twenty minutes and counting....

"Cabin configured for launch," Overmeyer informed the OTC. "Ready for O2 enable."

"Copy, *Atlantis*, O2 XOVER SYS1 to OPEN, SYS 2 to CLOSE. Standby for first built-in hold."

As the early morning sun splayed a long shadow across the Flight Deck, Hirumi Yoshioka, or Yoshi as everyone called her, thought of her father, 3 miles away at the press site and his reaction when she told him she wanted to be an astronaut instead of a doctor.

"You've just finished medical school, are you crazy?"

He should have known better. Hailing from a nation where women were usually housewives, she'd always pushed the envelope. With pageboy-short, jet-black straight hair and a whisper-soft voice, she appeared submissive but it was a facade. She was bright, decisive and daring, her only flaw being a lack of confidence in her sexuality. It was a flaw no one but she ever perceived.

Yoshi had first flown when she was 5, in her father's twin Cessna 310. He'd sat her on his lap and she'd been hooked for life. Instead of a social life she'd gone aloft, in place of a boyfriend, she'd earned wings and ratings. From med school she'd gone to JALTECH, piling up the hours to qualify as their test pilot while doubling as their flight surgeon. Her big break came when NASA funded her proposal to test the effects of low gravity on the body. It flew on Spacelab 6 and she went with it.

That led to another Spacelab flight and more experiments—tests of fat, protein and carbo metabolism, blood, bone and immune system function; plasma, urine, hormone and enzyme chemistry. And though she'd designed many of those tests, as had Roberto, she never dreamed where it would take her.

"You'll be a guinea pig, nothing more," her father had told her.

He was wrong. It wasn't a ticket to Mars,
but it had put her at the head of the line.

****

Chapter 6. A Simple Cone and Cylinder.

All was ready. Everything had been done....
The work of more than 300,000....
Planning, testing, analyzing, training
The time had come...

As we ascended in the elevator to the top
we knew that hundreds of thousands
had given their best effort to give us this chance.

Now it was time for us to give our best.

Neil A. Armstrong
Commander, Apollo 11
First mission to the Moon

Five minutes and counting....

"APU startup checklist," the OTC requested.

"Roger," replied Musgrave, "APU CNTLR PWR 1 to ON; PWR 2 to ON; PWR 3 to ON. APUs 1, 2 and 3 up."

"We copy and confirm," said the voice from the Firing Room. "APUs 1, 2 and 3 up and online. You're on internal power, *Atlantis*. Coming up on four minutes."

Internal power, Musgrave thought, two words more than any other that meant imminent launch. He felt the muscles in his body tense when he heard those words, muscles honed by punishing workouts in gyms, pools and tracks. Suddenly he felt a cramp in his knee and straightened it. Vadim, watching, thought he'd brushed his leg against the abort handle. It had power to it now and Vadim gulped. He could see the headlines:

"MARS SHOT FALLS IN OCEAN--CREW MISTAKE.
Last transmission..."Oops".

Musgrave pulled his knee out of the way and checked the handle. Vadim smiled.

****

Two minutes and counting....

"Engine arming in work," Overmeyer rattled off to the OTC from his checklist. "On panel R3, MPS He ISOL A 1, 2 and 3 to OPEN; PNEUMATICS He ISOL to OPEN."

"Copy, *Atlantis s,* Mains complete. Load and initiate SPEC 9 PRO."

"Understand," Overmeyer tallied back, "keying flight plan SPEC 9 PRO."

Aerosurfaces on the spanking new 21st century shuttle began moving--the rudder, elevons, speed brake and body flap. Then the nozzles on the 3 tail engines began wiggling, another step in a checklist tracing its lineage back to the earliest Cessna. Outside, a pale blue flame appeared under *Atlantis's* tail to burn away excess fuel and Overmeyer marveled at the new technology, built on the shoulders of the giants who'd designed the original space shuttle of the last century.

A thousand miles west in Houston, echoes of acronyms ricocheted round the horn between lead flight director H. Buford Stone and his team at the legendary Mission Control Room or the MOCR as it was known by to its insiders.

"EECOM?"
"Go!"

"EGIL?"
"Go!"

" BOOSTER?"
"Go! "

"FIDO?"
"Go Flight!"

On and on it went until Stone was satisfied and someone said, “Good luck everyone.”

“Luck is what happens when preparation meets opportunity,” Stone shot back in a pre-launch ritual; then signaled their readiness to the Firing Room at the Cape.

"OTC, this is Houston, we are GO for launch."

"We copy Houston, how bout you, *Atlantis*?”

“We’re GO for launch, OTC.”

“Copy. GO for launch.”

The next voice everyone heard echoed everywhere, not just over the loop. It was the voice of the mission from the Public Affairs commentator announcing the final countdown. Billions of people heard her, from the Florida Keys to the Himalayas.

"Nineteen....sixteen......thirteen.....ten.....nine…eight...seven...six...."

Chris heard 3 bangs at "five" as the three main engines lit, then felt *Atlantis* rock from the force of the massive ignition. A crackling noise arose as the Mains gathered power, growing louder until they obliterated every sound but the comm through his headset.

At "two" the solid boosters ignited with six and a half million pounds of thrust. At one, they were consuming four tons of fuel a second with the power of 11 Hoover Dams. At zero he felt the jolt. It was a milder than he'd imagined. A shove, followed by a push right, then left from the steering rockets kicking in. He could hear the words, "Lift-off," as they rose, "lift-off of Shuttle Atlantis on the first leg to Mars."

Three-tenths of a second later they were rising past the gantry like a slow motion elevator, the power awesome yet smooth. They launched tail south, but had to arch over east, which required a turn. They could feel the engines doing it, with their pitch, roll and yaw thrusters. The forces began to build, pushing them back into their seats and they could sense blistering acceleration: Mach 1, Mach 3, Mach 5, Mach 7, and ninety seconds later they were 29 miles high. When the solids gave out and separated at 2 minutes elapsed time, there was a slight deceleration, like before an elevator stops, then the Main Engines took over. With the extra weight gone, speed, force and altitude escalated: 1G, 2Gs, 3Gs, Mach 15, Mach 17, Mach 20; 80 miles high in 330 seconds. Two minutes later, "Press to MECO," (Main Engine Cutoff) could be heard throughout the cabin and *Atlantis* pitched over. As it approached orbital velocity, Earth came into view again but no one had time to admire it, the ET (external fuel tank) had to be jettisoned.

Pieces of foam insulation drifted by the windows as they separated from the ET, and Vadim flashed how a chunk of it weighing less than a pound had brought down Shuttle *Columbia* back in '03.

It's the littlest things that bite you, he scribbled in his logbook, and underlined it before switching his focus to Overmeyer, who was preparing for the OMS burn. The Orbital Maneuvering System engines in the tail pod had to be programmed to kick them into an elliptical orbit with a 160 mile-high "apogee" and a 60 mile-low "perigee".

It happened fast; so fast that the first sign of it was the 3 beeps sounding that indicated it was okay to pop their helmets.

Musgrave undid his harness and pushed off his seat like a swimmer might do in a flip turn, then floated towards the aft bulkhead. Zero gravity had arrived! He hovered to the central panel, lifted a protective cover over the switch that would open *Atlantis's* big payload bay doors and flipped it. A whirring noise reverberated thoughout the orbiter when the doors jarred open and exposed the space radiators that would cool things off. That done, he floated back to help Overmeyer program the OMS engines for a second burn. It was obvious he'd done this before. He was comfortable without gravity.

The next step, rendezvous with ISS, had to be done exactingly. The station was orbiting 245 nautical miles above Earth at an inclination to the equator of 51.5 degrees in a circular path 40 miles above and ahead of them. *Atlantis's* elliptical orbit had to be matched to ISS's circular one gradually and precisely. It was gallactic ballet that could turn deadly. Too much delta V (velocity change) would put them above and ahead, too little, below and behind, either way out of reach. It would take hours but they seemed to pass like minutes in the intensity of concentrated effort.

Vadim was the first to perceive the glint of its trusses, keels and panels. With its segmented modules and gleaming solar wings, ISS looked like a dragonfly.

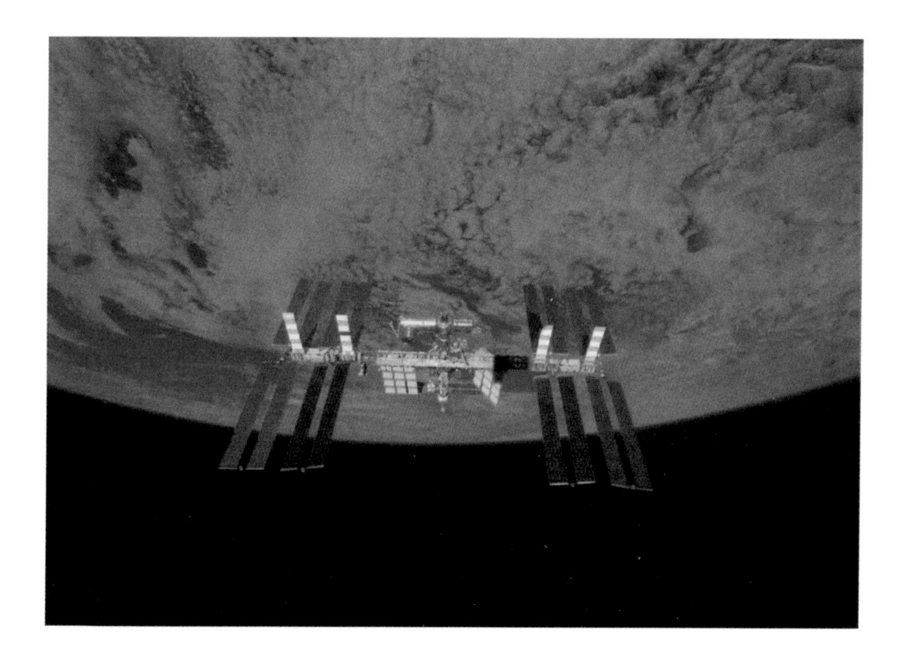

The official notice came when they closed to 1 1/2 kilometers.

" *Atlantis,* this is *Alpha* Control, we have you in visual. Closing speed 6 meters/second, go to proximity ops.

"Copy," Overmeyer shot back, "range radar, 1.5 kilometers, going to Prox Ops."

The OPS 202 Proximity Operations program on Overmeyer's monitor began blinking, "**MAN/AUTO?** Who should be in charge now, it was asking, you or the computer?

Like all astronauts, he hated **AUTO**, but the MOCR had been adamant. "Prox Ops are dangerous, use **AUTO**." Overmeyer punched numbers into the DAP (Digital Autopilot), turning the maneuver over to the bucket of wires he disdained. A palpable vibration followed as thrusters fired and *Atlantis* inched closer.

Musgrave checked their closing speed, 3 meters a second, and began lining up the probe in the shuttle's payload bay with the drogue in *Alpha's* docking port.

"*Ebat's pogonami*," Vadim whispered to him using the vernacular older cosmonauts taught him when he was a rookie.

"What's that mean?" Musgrave queried.

"Screw it like you're on shoulder straps," Vadim deadpanned. Everyone laughed but Yoshi who blushed.

At 10 meters, the computers pushed them back a tad then forward again, and repeated it until they were so close they could see the micrometeorite hits on the drogue ring. Then out of the silence came the soft clang of contact, followed by the noise of metal fingers extending into receiving holes. A green light illuminated, **HARD DOCK**.

Below in the Mid-deck Chris, Andrea, Anna and Roberto could only hear, not see because there were no windows. They knew they'd arrived and were within meters of their spacecraft but they'd have to go up to the Flight Deck to see it. Rising awkwardly in the zero gravity without nearly the aplomb of Musgrave, they floated up one at a time. Chris, last in line, fought the feeling instead of going with it like he'd been taught in the swimming pool, got momentarily nauseous and had to beat back an impulse to vomit, not how he wanted to start things off. Musgrave helped him up the ladder towards the aft workstation below the overhead windows where he inserted his boots in the foot restraints and stretched to look out. A hundred meters away nestled in ISS' robotic arms, Columbus 11 glowed in the void.

Columbia and *Eagle*, the 2 joined modules it consisted of were hard to distinguish at first, bathed in high intensity beams and flashing back reflections from the Mylar enveloping them. But as his eyes adjusted to the stark contrast of black, gold and silver in space, its shape emerged.

Christened in honor of the first spacecraft to the Moon, *Columbia* and *Eagle* formed a simple cone and cylinder, the most basic of shapes. In any other setting they would have been undistinguished, unexceptional. But in their element at last, they were unique in the universe, their purpose clear; their destiny self-evident: this was the chrysalis that would take humanity to Mars. How long have I imagined this, Chris thought that moment. How many times, in how many places? He pushed himself down from the windows to the ladder then; and from the ladder to the airlock towards the tunnel that led to ISS. Towards the dream that he'd had since Viking on that old Zenith: the dream of a thousand lifetimes.

****

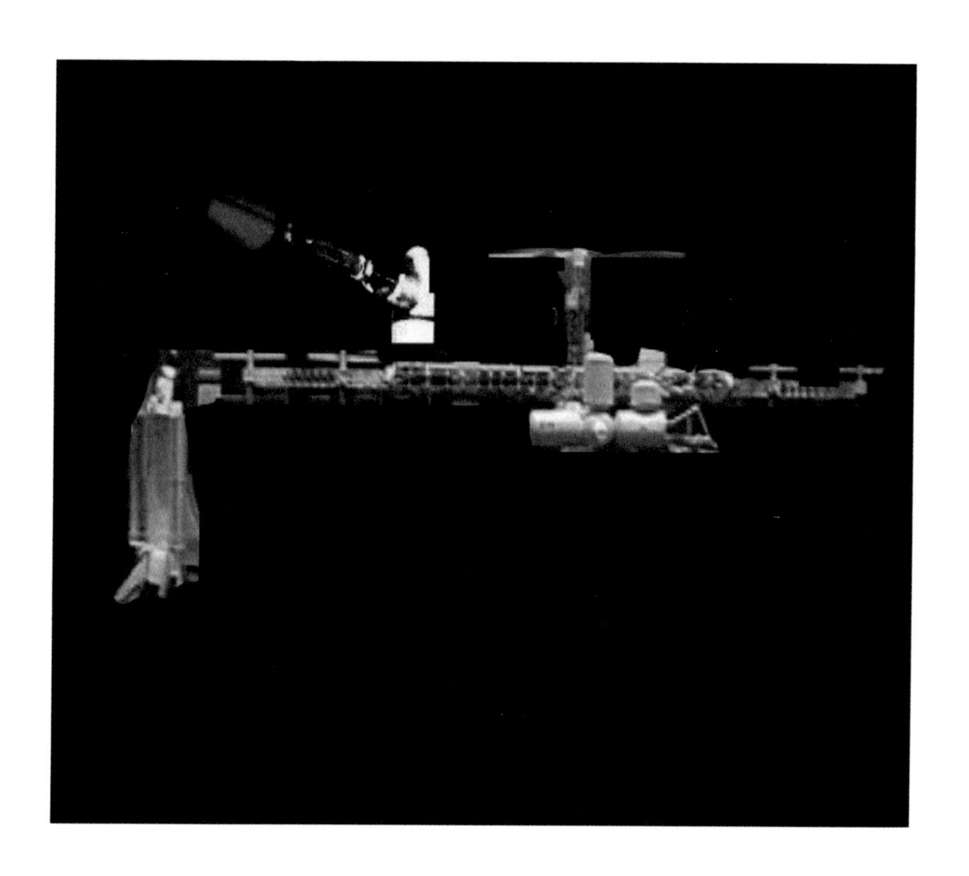

The dream of a thousand lifetimes

BOOK 2. JOURNEY.

Chapter 7. Checklists and Flashbacks

International Space Station *Alpha*, the first step in a billion-footstep journey, would be a mere pitstop. A place to catch a breath, review the disengagement procedure and fill up on squeeze-cupped coffee. Six hours and twenty seven minutes after transferring in through its docking hatch, the crew of Columbus 11 floated out again through the Refurbishment Bay in single file. Their spacecraft was waiting.

Entering through *Eagle's* airlock door, they took in the Lander's aura. It had come a long way from the half-finished frame of stringers and wiring harnesses they'd first seen years ago on the MVAB floor. Clusters of panels enveloped the flight couches; banks of instruments gleamed under fluorescents and the two pistol-grip hand controllers jutted out proudly with their red override buttons on top. The couches themselves radiated hammock-like from the central pillar to the conical walls, and like everything else, they were virginal and unsoiled. Resting on the floor in the space beneath each was a snow-white PLSS or Portable-Life-Support-System. If all went well, they'd breathe life into the MarsSuits before the first human steps were taken on the Martian surface.

After inspecting the Lander, the crew made their way to an access hatch in its floor that led to *Columbia*, the Transit Craft below. Along the way, they caught sight of a note dangling in zero gravity. Tied by a string to a bulkhead, it read:

Inkstain, Solidnuts and the rest of you:

We *busted hump for you.*

Don't fuck up or you'll answer to us.

Good luck. H Buford Stone and the Puzzle People

PS...This is for you, Inkstain. H stands for Hermayanee.
My folks wanted a girl.

Chris guffawed as the note took him back to the day he'd first met H. Buford Stone. He remembered the day well for 2 reasons. It was the day he first saw *Eagle*, and the day he *knew* he might actually go to Mars. Until that day, it had been dreamstuff for him, simply dreamstuff.

Images of the day flooded back in a torrent. It had started with a 4.4 mile run past the storied hangers of Edwards Air Force Base in the high desert town of Palmdale, California. He remembered it was 4.4 miles because he'd vowed to run a tenth of his age every birthday until that day, when aches and pains told him doing it at age 100 might be out of the question. He'd paralleled tumbleweed-littered runways packed with history on that run until he'd come to the MVAB, the *Mars Vehicle Assembly Building* where *Columbia* and *Eagle* were being built. Later, H's secretary, Jackie, had met him in Trailer One, headquarters for the Build Team, the team that was actually putting the crafts together. She took him to H's office, where a sign on the door read:

H. STONE—HEAD HONCHO FOR THE MGA

(*we do dangerous things to expensive people*)

MGA stood for Man's Greatest Adventure, Chris would learn, and H. Buford Stone was an ex-marine and blue collar practitioner of 4 letter words from the swamps of Louisiana. Stone, five foot ten and barrel-chested with a crewcut and bulging muscles showing through his jacket, loved whittling miniature wooden replicas of noteworthy firearms from the old west and was carving a Winchester 73 when Chris had walked in. He was sitting on an old easy chair with the stuffing popping out of it and his feet were propped up on his desk as he whittled. Aside from that, the thing Chris remembered most about H that day was his bright red nylon jacket. "Launch Fever, Catch It," it announced on the front, and had a very odd jigsaw puzzle emblazoned on the back. The puzzle was populated with acronyms strange even to Chris, which was saying something: FRSI, TPS, HRSI, OPF and the like. A caption at the bottom read, "Puzzle People."

"Them's my team," H had told Chris, catching him staring at it; "we're the ones who put the tiles on the kite. We're called puzzle people cause we gotta paste each one of them 16000 tile in exactly the right hole, only we call it a cavity. It's the biggest fucking jigsaw puzzle you ever saw and my people are at the end of the whip, so to speak, where the shit stops. You must be the nubie astronaut I been hearin' about, Doctor Inkstain."

"That's Elkay," Chris had said, smiling at the nickname he'd forever be known by to H.

"Yeah, like I said, Inkstain. Your Russki colleague, Solidnuts, was here yesterday. He didn't like his moniker either. Tough titties, I say, get used to it. You guys take yourselves too serious."

From there, Stone had taken Chris to get his retinas scanned, fitted for a tyvek clean room suit, and nursemaided him through security and badging before leading him through the imposing set of double doors that led into the 6-story MVAB. Extraordinary sights and sounds confronted him. Sound had been the first sensation: the rat-ta-tat of ratchets; the assaulting thud of pneumatic hammers; the whine of electric drills. Next came the air-con, a rush of man-made wind so forceful, it buffeted his tyvek suit against his legs. Finally came the floor, the size of a football field with 6 levels of scaffolding above it, a veritable jungle of metal. Human forms seethed everywhere on it, like bees on a hive. But instead of a queen they were swarming *Columbia* and *Eagle.*

H led Chris under the scaffolding after that, where they'd snaked their way to a mammoth lead ball suspended from above. Clusters of tiny engines protruded from it. "Acceleration Deployment Spinup System," H had sneered, "ADSS to you, Rube Goldberg piece-o-shit to me. It's attached to the kite's ass end and unfurls from a tether till it's taut. That's when them engines start pulsing to spin both ships around like a fucking baton. Four RPM will give us the same gravity as on Mars, I'm told, but I'll be a horse's ass if it actually works. Sonofabitch is trouble waiting to happen."

They'd moved further into the maze from there, to where a green-primed metal surface sat above them exposed. It was the surface of *Columbia*, the transit craft, though he'd never have guessed it with all the tooling and other paraphernalia surrounding it. The green primer was blanketed with inch-wide red strips affixed to each other in a matrix of squares that literally covered the vehicle. Each red square formed a cavity into which a tile would be set and ten digit codes were written on each. Scribed in yellow, they matched identical yellow codes of the tile waiting to be bonded into each red cavity.

“They’re all different," H had elaborated, "black tile for hot spots, white ones for cooler spots, big ones, small ones, thick ones and thin ones. We bond em to the kite with a superglue epoxy. That shit is strong enough to stick me to my ex-wife if I was ever dumb enough to get near her again.”

H led Chris to the deepest recesses of the maze from there, to an elevator that shot straight up. He’d been quiet as a church mouse as it scaled the fuselage of *Columbia* towards *Eagle*, enjoined to the top of it on the 5th story. His skin tingled as they passed in the flesh what he’d memorized in the blueprints: D-deck with the Galley, Command Consoles and Rec Area; C-deck, with the gym, med lab and computers; B-deck, with the life support system; and A-deck with the Crew Quarters. But it all had been a prelude to the emotions that gripped him when he stepped onto a gangway as the elevator stopped. There, under a makeshift tent, mercury vapor lamps played upon *Eagle’s* open airlock door, beckoning him inside. Hanging wires and exposed stringers greeted him then, and everything about the Lander was unique, even the smell, akin to a spanking new car but somehow different. It came from the six hammock-couches fanning out from a central pillar to the conical sidewalls, newly installed. And when he saw the fuel tanks through gratings in the floor, the parachutes in the apex above him and the 2 prominent hand controllers, begging to be gripped.

Emotions had overpowered him. Suddenly, all the lifeless, scattered parts came together in concert and magically transported him. He saw the plasma gases heating the tiles, heard the report of the engines and felt the jerk of the chutes until the final jolt of the landing legs upon the sands of Mars. He'd imagined those sands since the age of 12, when the images from that Viking show had poured onto his old Zenith. He'd taken a long and winding road from that Zenith to *Eagle*. Grad school, JPL, project scientist, marriage, astronaut, but never once believed he'd actually step on those sands until the day he first met H; the day he'd first seen *Eagle*; the day he *knew* he could.

****

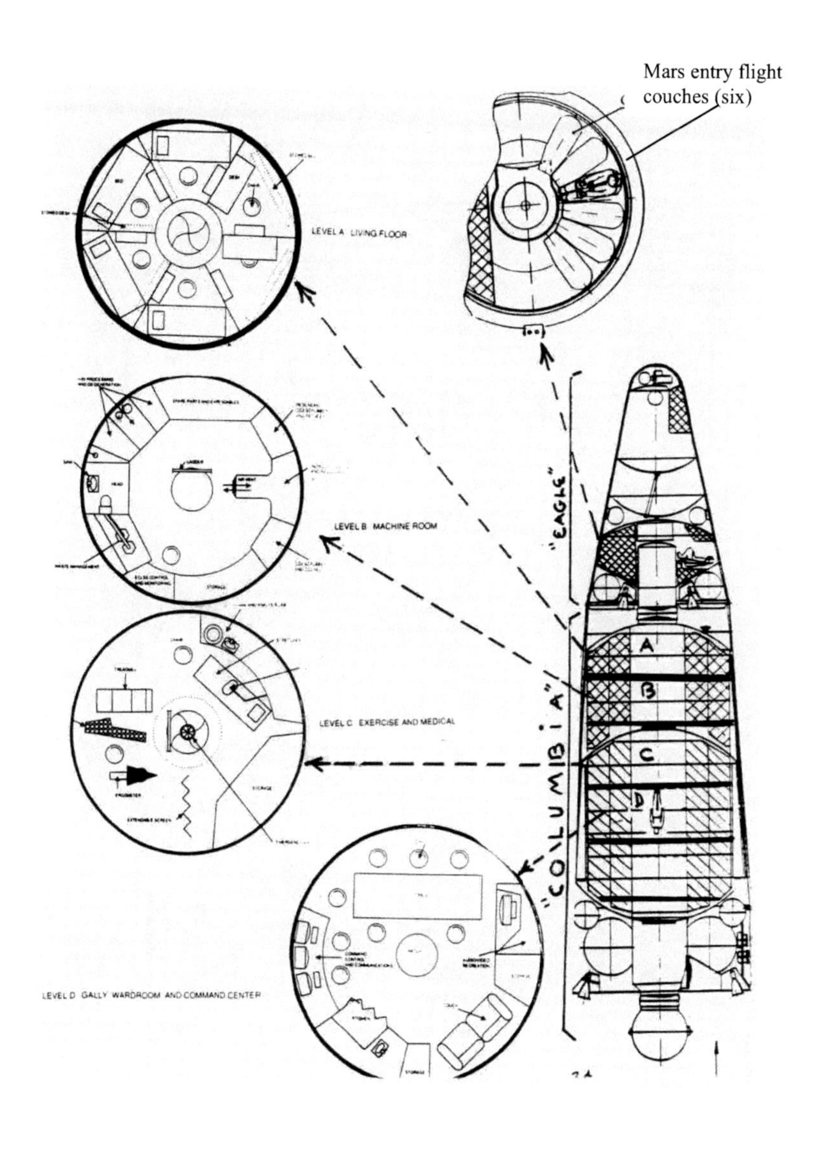

Columbia and Eagle

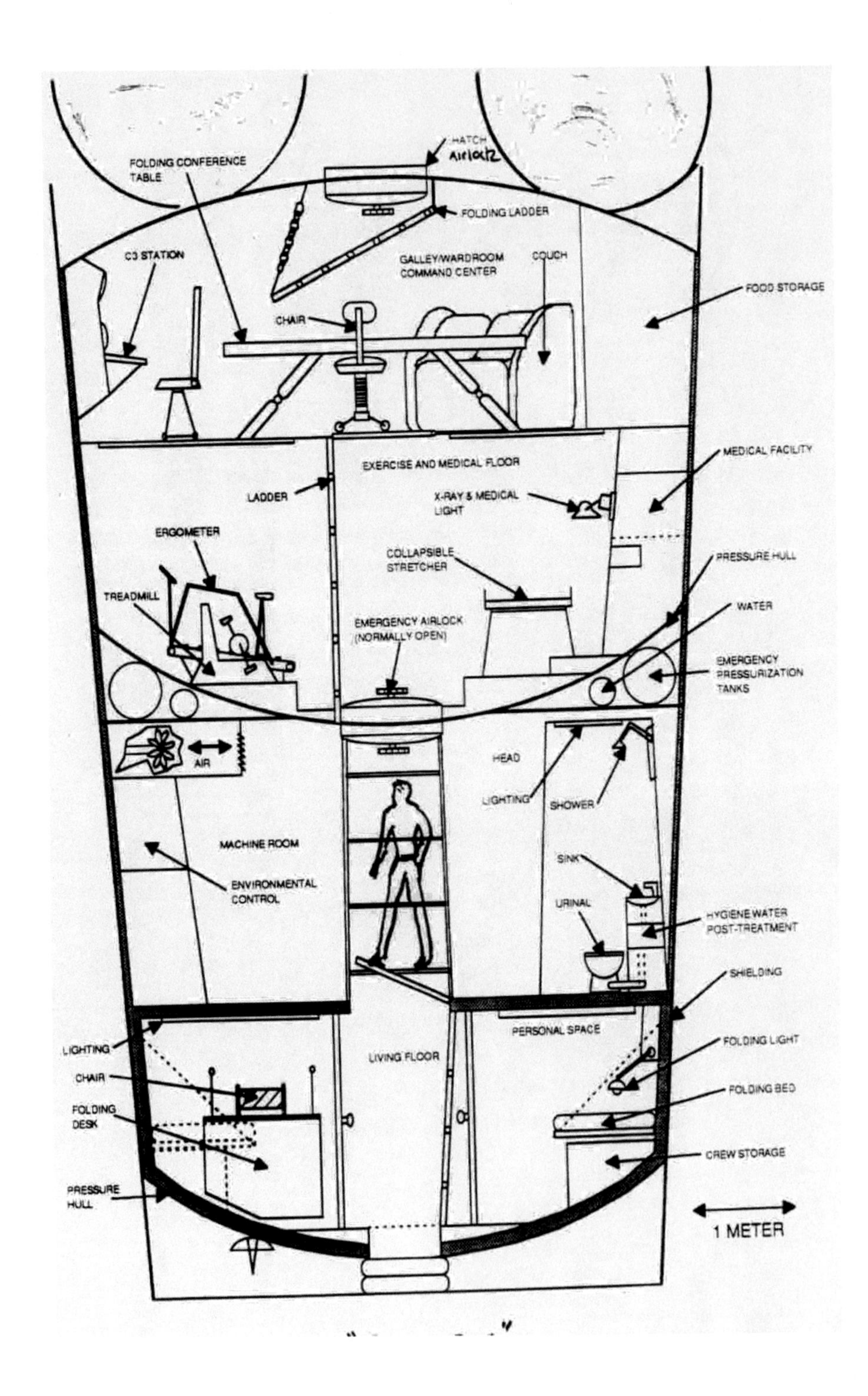

Columbia deck layout

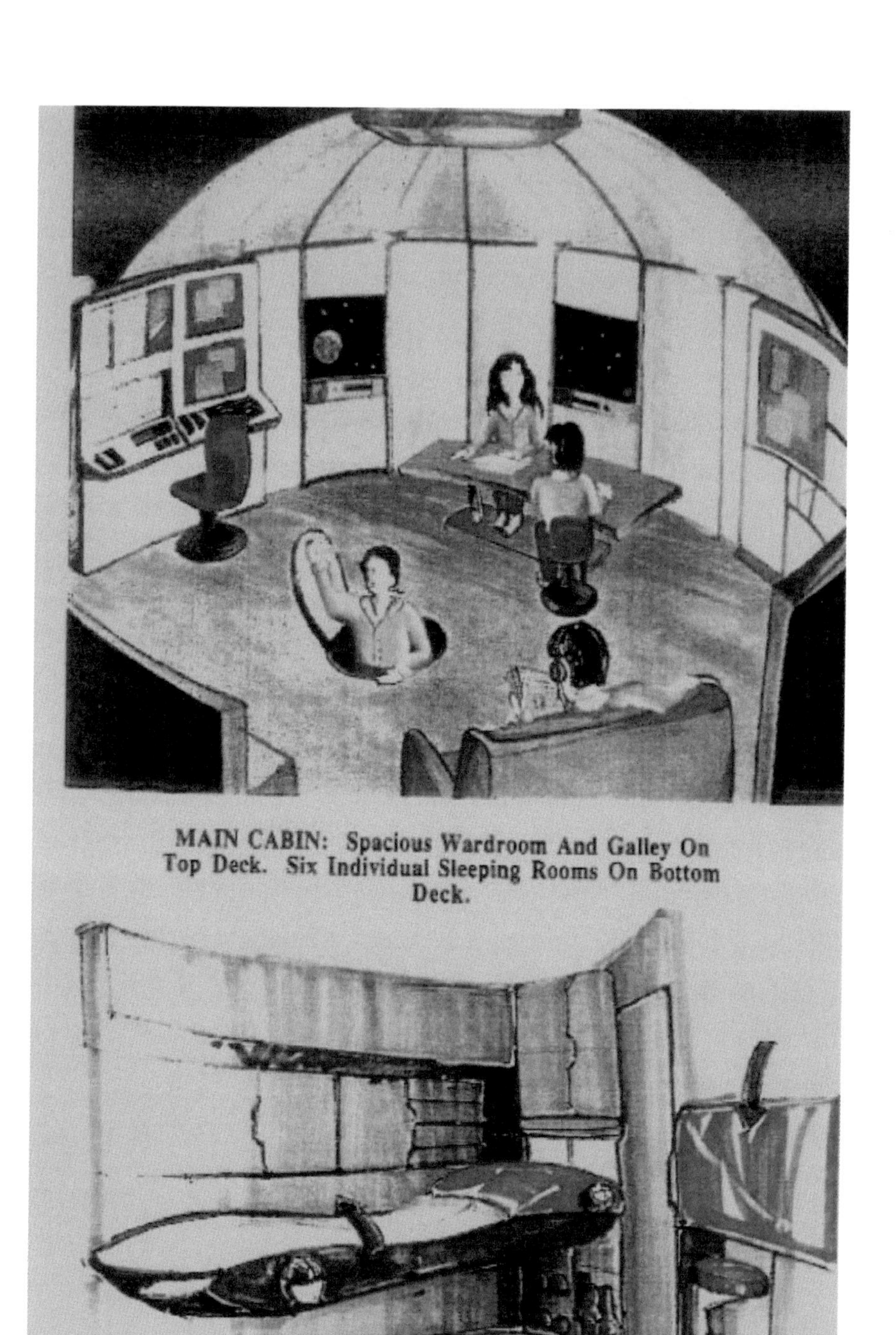

MAIN CABIN: Spacious Wardroom And Galley On Top Deck. Six Individual Sleeping Rooms On Bottom Deck.

Eagle had seemed like a toy when he'd first seen her, he reflected, and he a kid in a toy store. But now, 8 years later, as he prepared to leave everything familiar, he wasn't a kid anymore and *Eagle* was no toy. How many of its two million parts had to work perfectly to bring him back alive, he wondered. How many of *Columbia's?* How many failures could they withstand? 'It's the littlest things that bite you,' Vadim always said.

Don't go there, he chastised himself, proferring instead H's credo of luck, opportunity and persistence. Then he closed *Eagle's* airlock door behind him, maneuvered his body to the access tunnel in her floor, and with a flick of his fingers, propelled himself down towards *Columbia*.

His crewmates were waiting when he unceremoniously popped out the other side moments later and bounced off the 'ceiling' with his feet splayed out like a grasshopper. He'd forgotten that floors became ceilings and vice versa in *Columbia* because the artificial G would be induced from stern to stem and head to foot once the ADSS ball started spinning. Orientations swapped places. Up became down and down up. Floating above him on the 'floor', Vadim couldn't help but laugh at his grand entrance.

"Maybe try for Bolshoi next, Mr Ballerina?" he cracked.

A-deck, where they now gathered, was the crew quarters, arranged like pie slices around the central interdeck tunnel. And though each of the six wedge-shaped sleep compartments had about the livable volume of a VW bug, they'd been ingeniously designed to take advantage of it because of the low gravity. They contained beds, dressers and workstations, and while Claustrophobic to 99% of the human race under normal conditions, they'd be adequate because effective volume doubled when one can float. With two exceptions: to Anna they'd be another test of fortitude, and to Chris they'd be a delight. While she was claustrophobic, he'd sought out such places from the time he was a child, often climbing into boxes that he imagined to be spaceships. Even the medical tests where they'd zipped him into a fabric ball to rule out claustrophobia were fun. And though 6 months in a pie-room would be a challenge to Anna, Chris would embrace it like a cat in a paper bag. He loved tight spaces, he was claustrophilic.

After stowing his personal items, he left his pie room for the inter-deck tunnel that led "up" to Deck D where they'd all muster. Finger-pulling his body there was effortless, the best way to travel, so much so that he figured legs were really unnecessary here, and that space travel might be better suited to paraplegics than quadrupeds.

When he finally reached D-deck after passing B-deck, where the life-support systems hummed, and C-deck with its gym, medical lab and virtual reality trainer, it seemed Olympian. The Bridge, as everyone called it, held a conference table, gally, recreation area (the Rec), ultra wide flight couches and the Command, Control and Communication Console (the C3). The windows installed over the objections of the structures guys were especially welcome.

Vadim and Yoshi were already at the C3 when Chris floated in, loading numbers for the Disengagement program. Orange alpha-numerics highlighted their screens and one of them showed 33 minutes to Disengage and counting. The process would stay on Autosequence until just before Release, when control would shift to Vadim. Speakers crackled as Chris settled into his flight couch.

"*Columbia*, audio check," came a query from *Alpha.*

"This is *Columbia*," Vadim replied iron-voiced, "read you loud and clear."

"Copy that. Go to AUDIO SELECT to GND for Houston, over."

As the sequence moved through the same Comm, Nav, Abort and Leak checks he'd rattled through a thousand times, Vadim thought back to how close he'd come to being nothing more than a monkey on this flight. The battle between those who wanted the computers to run things and those favoring astronauts had been fierce. His old boss, Leoniv had saved the day. "If Armstrong hadn't been able to take over, he'd be buried on the Moon today," Leoniv had testified to the bigwigs, reprising the false computer alarm that nearly doomed Apollo 11. Vadim owed Leoniv for that and much more. Because of Leoniv and his pact with Chris' old boss, Ed Cochran, they were leaving from ISS *Alpha* instead of from the Moon. He still couldn't believe those idiots, Don Brandford and Royce Davies, pushing that plan to the brink of approval. The cost of a launch pad on the Moon alone would have bankrupted the program, let alone building the infrastructure. Vadim owed Leoniv for other things too; personal things like the kind Cochran had done for Chris. And like Chris, who'd promised himself to tell Ed how much he'd meant to him over the years but never did, Vadim had promised too until it was too late. A flit of shame surfaced but he quashed it. He was too Russian for such behavior. Let the Americans cry to their shrinks and paw to their mommies about feelings. Respectable cosmonauts wouldn't be caught dead with such groveling unless they had a shitload of Stolle to bolster them. Still, he felt a particular bond with Chris.

He'd risen from life's rubble, just like him, ending up in the all-time pinnacle of human adventure, or the MGA as H put it. Poker faced, bulletproof Vadim from Moscow with the steel-gray eyes and iron voice; sandy-haired Chris from Long Island, with his evergreen eyes and probing mind; outwardly so disparate; inwardly so alike.

As Autosequence approached Disengage, Yoshi, seated next to Vadim, stared at Earth through the windows, the last good look she'd have for nearly two and a half years. The colors were especially brilliant, even from 323 kilometers high. The cerulean expanse of the Indian Ocean; the greens and tans of Asia; the yellows of the Sahara; the reddish backdrop of Africa; the aquamarine splash where the Atlantic hugged Cape Canaveral. And as they spun around the planet going clockwise, a parade of vast oceans entered stage left, until Australia dispelled the notion that Earth was all water.

Tears welled in Yoshi's delicate hazel eyes at the sight of such beauty and coalesced into a single drop that began to float away from her porcelain skin towards Anna in the zero gravity. She quickly scooped it up, embarrassed, but thankful Anna hadn't noticed.

Anna, across from her, was in her own world. Using the blue-green shimmer of the Mediterranean as her guide, she was searching wide-eyed for Mount Etna, the Straits of Gibraltar and the Bay of Naples. Upon finding them she traced a path up the boot of Italy to the spot where she'd been born and raised near Florence. Emotions racked Anna too, but she was better at hiding them than Yoshi, far better. If they gave honors for hiding stuff, she'd have been Phi Beta

Kappa. She looked at Yoshi and whispered, "Mama Mia, *spettacolo.* Look at that!"

Sitting opposite them on the big, circular deck, Andrea and Roberto also took in the stunning scene below, while Chris narrowed his brow and started a SOTOL scan (State of the Ozone Layer). Rushing to complete it before Disengage, he noticed dark smoke rising from oil fires in Iraq, and patches of brown squeezing out the shrinking rain forests in Brazil. Eddies of gray bore witness to the Nile's erosion in Africa, and what used to be Mono Lake in California was but a shadow of its former self. Further to the south, the LA basin lay hidden in a veil of smog, and a hurricane was brewing in the Pacific. He then turned his instrument upwards to the thin, blue line where the edge of Earth met space, "*the only thing protecting us,*" Tess had preached at him a hundred times. Through the optiscope, he saw undulations in it now; ripples in the ozone layer: harbingers of disaster that would burden generations.

****

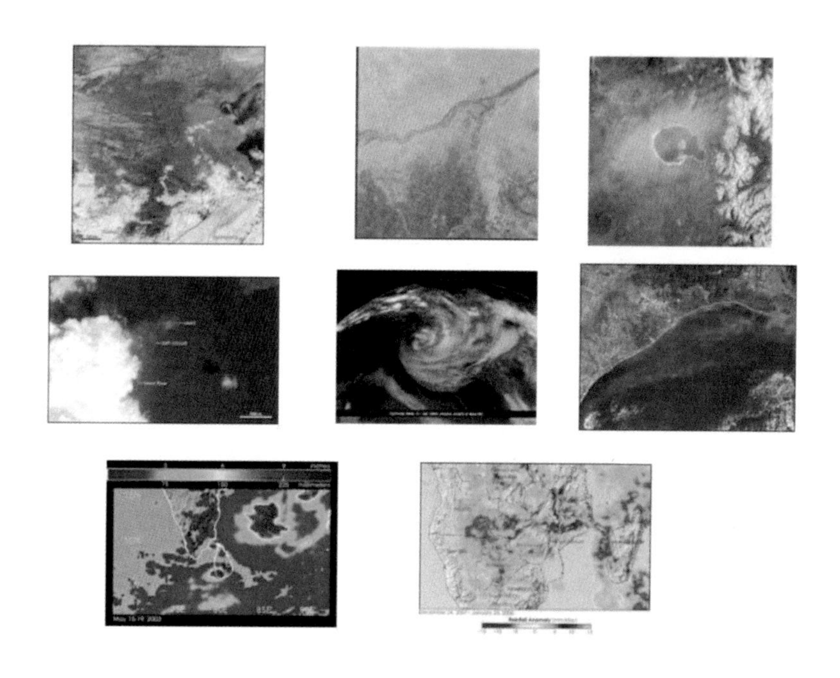

Harbingers of disaster that will burden generations

Chapter 8. Biosphere 2.

In January 1993, a single case of cholera broke out in Lima.
Within a week, 12,000 were infected.
By the end of February, it had spread to Ecuador,
by the middle of March, to Colombia,
by April to Chile and by May to Brazil.
Half a million people became infected.
Over 5000 died before the outbreak was halted.
Experts attributed the cause to accelerated algae growth.
Bred by global warming and shifts in ocean currents.

Soups of pollution are stirring. Terrible things are being formed.

Tess had known this since Lake Ling-a-Loo, and the fear of it had shaped her life. Fear was all she could think of after watching Chris lift off, the fear of all the things that could happen to him. She thought about this often on her flight home from the Cape to Tucson, and again from the airport to Oracle in her classic grass-green Triumph roadster.

It was just before dusk when she came to a stretch of fresh blacktop following 17 miles of stark desert road. A gate loomed, a security guard waved her through, and she took the right fork to a cul-de-sac and parked. Costeau, her golden retriever, shot out of nowhere with his tail wagging and his tongue flailing. He rolled over on his back; popped up again and followed Tess home.

Urns of flowering plants adorned the terra-cotta floor of Tess' adobe cottage, and Native American tapestries dangled from the high A-frame ceiling. Large picture windows framed panoramic views of the Santa Catalina Mountains to the east and the Biosphere 2 campus to the west, reflecting the last vestiges of sunset. Tess noticed none of this. All she could thing of was a shower and a bed. She was physically and emotionally spent.

She switched on the recycle pump in the bathroom, opened the gravity feed valve from the solar collector and luxuriated in the spray. She pondered lipstick when she got out, but with only Cousteau to look pretty for, moved to her hair instead, brushing it in long, swooping strokes until it dried naturally, rather than from the wasted kilowatts of an outmoded hair dryer.

Despite streaks of gray that seemed to pepper it in proportion to the stress tossed her way in ever increasing doses now, her hair still glowed with the look she'd embraced in her 20's, straight as an arrow from crown to below her shoulder blades. Was it that auburn hair that made people stop, stare and listen to her back then? Or the aristocratic nose that Michaelangelo might have chiseled; or the moon shaped brown eyes against her alabaster skin that Chris fell for in a heartbeat? Or was it the tall, lithe proportioned body that was envy of her girlfriends, or the wide expressive mouth with lips not too full or too thin but just right? She hoped it was none of those but rather the words formed by those lips instead that made people pay attention then and especially now, when getting them to listen was paramount. With so much at stake, hope sprung eternal.

A spot in the mirror froze her as she started to dab on some sun block, another new freckle to join the parade of others across her forehead despite the SPF 60 she used daily. More evidence, as if any was needed of the devastating effects of all the UV breaking through.

As much as she wanted to hit the sack, the glass domes' systems needed checking and she had to get off a new run for Biosphere 1. Modeling the real world was proving far more complicated for CASI than modeling Biosphere 2. Many things made it so and it started with Chaos -- the tiny changes that force a different outcome each time through a chain of events. Cigarette smoke breaks suddenly into swirls; drips from a faucet unexplainedly change rhythm; the jaggedness of a lightning bolt; the movement of the stock market; a butterfly beating its wings in Egypt stirring up a breeze in New Orleans.

Chaos Theory attempted to explain these things and Tess had hoped it might help CASI too. But after hundreds of backbreaking trial runs, she seemed no closer to success then when she'd started. Yes, she'd make progress but it had been snaillike, and the countless pitfalls reminded her of Ben Franklin's poem:

"For want of a nail, the shoe was lost,
For want of a shoe, the horse was lost,
For want of a horse, the rider was lost,
For want of a rider, the battle was lost.'

She was missing a lot of nails, Chris would say, and Chaos Theory was the least of it. But if she was anything, she was persistant, and she'd added a host of new tools to CASI's arsenal, AI, a Quantum Logic Board from D-wave, and the latest, a DNA subroutine. With one strand of DNA representing an "IF" command, and others for "OR", "TRUE", "NOT TRUE", etc, the latter had added raw, massively parallel processing power to CASI; a billion times more memory than the human brain. It begged believability that all she need do to get off a run was mix the DNA strands in a beaker with other strands representing climate data. The output would simply show up in the mix. As she neared Biosphere 2's glass domes, and the formidable gray airlock at the entrance, she was hoping this would finally get her over the "ten percent accuracy hump", the best she'd ever done comparing CASI predictions to planet Earth's history.

Biosphere 2

A cornucopia of color greeted her as she passed through the airlock into a cacophony of twitterings, moans and birdcalls exploding off the walls. A veritable jungle stretched out before her. Awestruck as usual, she descended the stairwell into the smoldering warmth of ECO 1, the Brazilian Rain Forest. She moved past the olive, fig and mango trees with a smile on her face now; through lemon grass lawns and coconut palms interspersed with guava, pineapple, papaya and orange groves. Regardless how stressed out she felt, the beauty of it all never failed to uplift her. It was her therapy: Freud, aerobics, yoga, meditation and great sex wrapped in one.

SOUTH LUNG
TUNNEL
LOW ACCESS
Your Head

The exit of ECO 1 led to the entrance of ECO 2, the tropical Savannah, where the clamor of twin macaws overhead heralded in a different kind of commotion. Spotted hummingbirds darted about and there were gardens of blue bougainvilleas surrounded by red impatiens and yellow heloconia. Other doors led to other Ecosystems: ECO 3, the Marsh, with its swamps and drooping willows; ECO 4, the Desert; ECO 5, the Farm; and ECO 6, the Ocean, with its 25 foot deep wave generator pulsating millions of gallons of sea water a day past live coral, invertabrates and vertabrates alike.

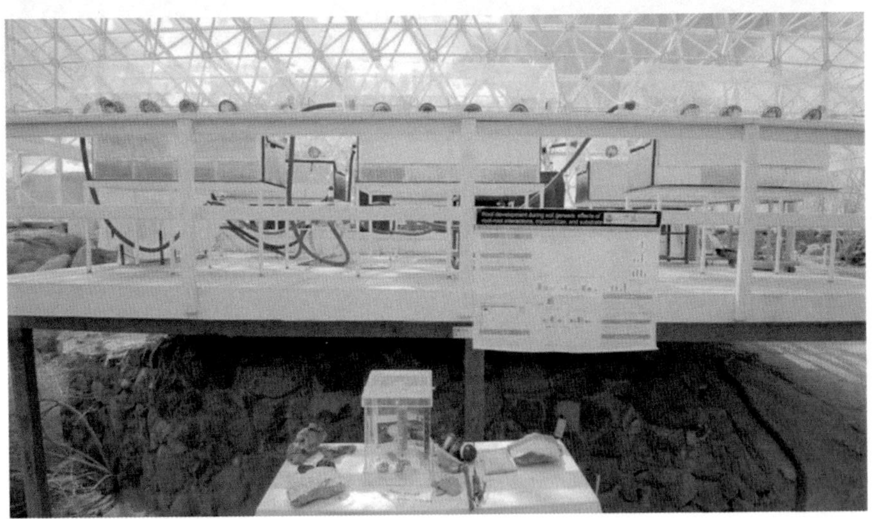

Passing through one last door at the far end of the complex, she finally came to ECO 7 and the BOCR -- the Biosphere Operations Control Room. Here was the nerve center that controlled everything, and the place where she'd tested CASI's mettle, hundreds if not thousands of times, each a false moment of truth. Would this be another?

Three thousand sensors from ECOs 1-6 fed the BOCR's computers, which in turn, fed two floor-to-ceiling flat screens in the front of an amphitheater. There were banks of consoles in the theater, and Tess sat down at one in the first row, switching on the power and entering commands slowly and deliberately. She knew the routine by rote, watching the left screen spring to life with wavy, black lines measuring the oxygen, carbon dioxide, temperature, humidity, PH and salinity in ECO's 1-6. Satisfied, she called up another set of lines, the organics: methyl chloroform, DDT, nitrous oxide, carbon monoxide, ethylene glycol, CFCs and PCBs. All measuring near zero, they meant CASI was doing her job of controlling pollution leak from the outside. This was a necessary prelude to Closure 4, the ultimate test where 8 Biospherians would stay locked under glass for as long as the system could keep them healthy. It was the long awaited *Indefinite Closure*; the one management had hitched their star to for funding and recognition. But it was their test not hers. She'd come for Biosphere 1, with stakes that made 2's seem puny and insignificant.

All business now, she switched on the right screen and watched another set of lines take hold. They formed under the heading, *MANU* for the Manu National Preserve, a 40 million acre rain forest in the eastern heels of the Andes Mountains of Peru. The organic lines leaped off the screen this time, mirroring waves of pollution carried in by the tradewinds from far away cities. It had to be so because only two known Indian tribes inhabited the Manu and they didn't pollute--they lived off the land. Tess prompted the system for a five-year history of the Manu's organics, and a bewildering splotch of lines peppered the screen in no logical pattern. If CASI could backtrack 5 years in time, then go forward and match that history, it would be a breakthrough of epic proportions. She'd never done better than a 10% match so far, her "ten percent hump". But she'd also never had a DNA computer.

Brimming with excitement, she typed in the code that would robotically drop DNA strands into sterile beakers brimming with the Manu's 5-year history. With the speed of the new logic, it wouldn't take long to get an answer, and red lines began playing out on the screen in less than a minute. At first they looked like all the other disappointing outputs she'd seen but then she caught the pattern. Red lines were scrolling over black ones in an obvious attempt at an overlay. The agreement figures leaped, to 34%. It wasn't epic, but it was a breakthrough.

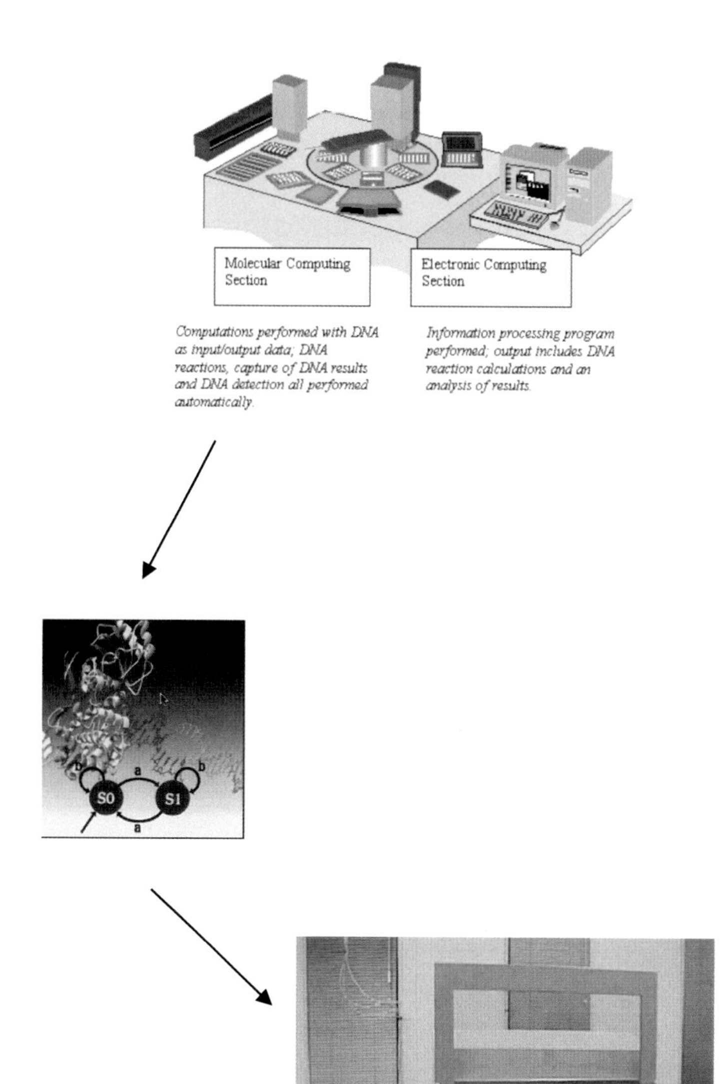

Climate Analog Situation Indicator (CASI)

Chapter 9. TMI

Strapped in his flight couch, Chris knew nothing of Tess' progress. Like Vadim and the others, he was focused on the C3, watching its orange numbers count down.

"*Columbia, Alpha,*" speakers intruded. "Disengage Auto-sequencing, 2 minutes, 13 seconds. Begin RMS deactivation checklist."

"Roger that, *Alpha,*" Vadim responded. "RMS ARM 1 and 2 to ON; COUPLE/DECOUPLE to DECOUPLE; STNDFF MAG to DEMAG."

"Copy, *Columbia*, you are go for extension."

"Affirmative, XTND/RECALL to XTND on my mark...5, 4, 3, 2, 1... mark!"

No one felt a thing when the standoffs holding them to the Space Station extended. Nor could they hear the low whine of electromagnets reversing polarity to push them away from the oppositely charged standoffs. Even their sense of movement was dulled by the crawling precision of the process until *Alpha* confirmed that they were floating free.

"Separation distance 20 meters, MAG PWR to OVERRIDE. RLS/ENGAGE to RLS."

The moment Vadim lived for had finally arrived: **Release**: the point where he could move an 82 ton spacecraft wherever his whim willed it. And though such moments paled between the pauses spent training for them, it was worth it. It was the sweetest joy he knew. It was who he was.

"*Columbia*, we'd like more delta R between us," *Alpha* interrupted, referring to the distance vector between them, "one zero zero in the plus z if you would."

After widening the gap between them to a hundred meters as requested, Vadim turned to TMI or Trans-Mars Injection--the engine burn that would fling them away from Earth for nearly 3 years if it worked…and to oblivion if it didn't. His entire life had been a prelude to it and loading the OPS 105 program that would start it, he considered that life. He'd had a lot of perks, prestige and pussy, especially in Star City where his exploits had become legendary regarding the latter. On the other hand, he'd loved no one, no one had loved him and he'd murdered his own sister. Accidentally to be sure, but murder nonetheless, and he'd existed on a diet of Stolle ever since. In the rarefied air of the cosmonaut core no one noticed because Stolle was akin to a membership fee as long as you didn't get caught drinking it above ground. But he was heading below ground before being selected for the mission.

The mission got him sober and getting sober was hard. He'd done it for Gagarin, Leoniv and the Motherland. Who knew what would follow, but for now, only the mission mattered. He stole a quick glance at Yoshi, thinking she mattered too. From her porcelain skin, to her silky voice to her understated brilliance as a pilot and flight doc, she was as different from the rest as borscht was from beets, and he knew borscht! Was it her exotic lineage, her calm, demeaner, her immunity to anger, her laugh, her attention to detail, her …her everything? Blinking numbers snapped him back. He gazed at them thinking this is the easy part. Just 40,000 pounds of methox fuel nudging just 82 tons of spacecraft against zero G. Piece o cake compared to a 5 million ton SLS launch with its mix of super-explosive propellants that had killed the *Gateway 1* crew. Still, there were risks. If the engines shut down early, they'd never make it to Mars; if they burned too long, they'd never get back; if a thruster stuck, they'd spin uncontrollably, and with a NAV vector off, they'd be wildly off course. Timing was everything, and the endpoint of bad timing could be fatal. Vadim didn't flinch as the burn approached, his attitude was *Harit*'-- get it on. This was *his* stage and he was ready for it. He double checked each number before punching it into the C3 and smiled with satisfaction at their acceptance.

TMI BURN PARAMETERS

Delta V x = 7.31 km/sec
Delta V y = 0.23 km/sec
Delta V z = 0.68 km/sec
PHI Angle = 0.03 degrees
Rmax = 1.02 x 10^6 R_0

Duration of TMI burn = 573 seconds
Thrust level = 105% of Max
Countdown begins in 60 seconds

"OPS 105 loaded and GO for Sequence Start in 60 seconds," he advised everyone on the comm loop. *Alpha* echoed GO, as did his buddy, Adam Brady, the Capcom from Houston who'd command the next Mars mission. Vadim's parting words to him were, "See you in a thousand days, *nastoyaschiy muzhik*," and then the methox engines lit.

Though he'd been told what to expect, Vadim had never experienced the kick of methox engines. All previous burns had been gradual escalations for him: slow buildups of acceleration from massive rockets struggling against gravity to get off the ground. *Columbia* and *Eagle* were a fraction of that mass and had no gravity to fight, a major reason they'd won out over the Moon plan. When the count hit zero, the result was unexpected: the Bridge shuddered and the force rammed him deep into his seat cushion. Earth lurched through the windows and was swapped for a mist of stars in a blink. "*Zdrastvui zhopa, novy gode, ohuyeviyusche!*" he proclaimed, "Jesus!!"

The velocity readouts on his screen were staggering, screaming towards escape velocity in an incomprehensible rush: 8 kilometers a second, 9.7, 10.3, 12.

Ten minutes later, the engines shut down to an eerie silence. The only movement in the Bridge came from the 4 big digital clocks on the wall reading:

MET=0000:00:10:30. HOU=17:46 CANDOR=05:07 DELAY=00:00

At 0 days, 0 hours, 10 minutes, 30 seconds Mission Elapsed Time, 5:46 PM Houston time and 5:07 in the morning at Candor Base on Mars, their landing site, they were now traveling nearly 9 miles a second. Adam Brady confirmed it from Houston: TMI was on the money. *"Ohuyeviyusche!"* Vadim replied, "Unbelievable!"

****

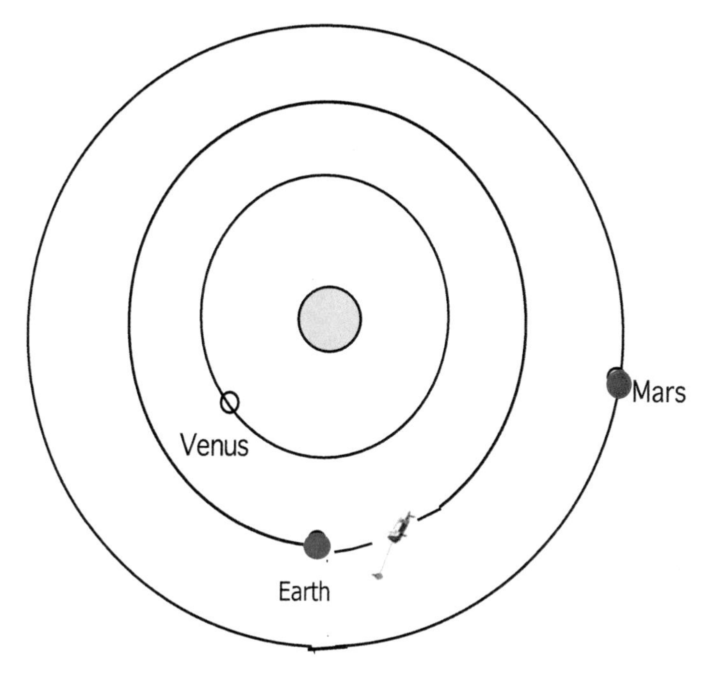

Earth, Mars and Venus at TMI

(Minimum Energy Conjunction Class Trajectory

(*Hohmann Transfer*) with Mars ¼ orbit ahead of Earth)

"Ohuyeviyusche!"

Chapter 10--ADSS

'ADSS to you, piece o shit to me,'

H. Buford Stone's words reverberated through Yoshi's consciousness as she prepared to set up artificial gravity, the first task after TMI. Everyone was antsy over it; the system had a checkered history and had gone through multiple redesigns. It had also been the last piece of hardware to pass QUAL (the Qualification Test).

Setting up the artificial gravity would be a 3-step process: Attitude Change, Reel-out and Spin-up. She glanced at Vadim. Step One would be the easy part, he'd said, all she had to do was pitch the ship's nose up to point it perpendicular to the direction they were going instead of straight at it, then release the big ball from *Columbia's* aft end. He winked at her and smiled. The ship came alive with thrusters once she keyed the 90 degree pitch change into the DAP (Digital Autopilot), a sound like the muffled report of howitzers firing from a distant shore. Yoshi eased her rotational hand controller back and Earth popped into view again through the windows as the nose began pitching up,. From 2000 kilometers away, it was a very different Earth from the one just before TMI. It had shrunk to the size of a blue-white beachball. Against the jet black pallet of endless space it had no hint of life whatsoever on it.

"AFT DOOR to OPEN," Yoshi read from her checklist, "TTHR PWR, ON. CTRWT to RLS on my mark: Mark."

The 5-ton ball that they would pinwheel around to provide a 1/3 G Mars-like gravity slowly released and floated freely behind them now attached to its composite chain tether. Yoshi's concentration deepened as she began setting up for step 2, the Reel-out.

The time she'd spent on the simulators did little to allay the myriad of things that could go wrong, starting with the tangle modes: the single, double or triple sine waves that could twist the tether up like a pretzel. This wasn't kid-stuff, this was five tons of lead ruled by Newton's law and there'd be hell to pay for violating it.

She gently wrapped her fingers around the ADSS joystick, a T-lever on the C3, and focused on squeezing it just so. Not enough invited the tangle modes while too much could over-pulse the ball's thrusters, yanking it against the tether to the breaking point. Her first try indicated underpulse and a possible Tangle Mode One. Uh-oh, she thought for an instant before feathering the T-handle forward. The ball responded as if hardwired to her brain, moving out slowly and steadily now. She checked its motion through the external cameras until they indicated full extension with no tangles. The C3 confirmed it. It was 211 meters behind *Columbia* with no tether slack. "We have Reel-out," she announced over the comm. "Step 2 complete, moving to Step 3." Another glance from Vadim who nodded his approval.

She needed that approval, not just because he was the Commander, but because he was her teacher, her sensei, her lover, her shining knight in armor, though he didn't know it. It felt good to get it but she steeled herself. The real fun was about to begin.

Step 3, Spin-up, the least forgiving of the steps had the smallest margin of error. So exacting was it that it couldn't be left to human hands. ADSS's voice cognizent computer had to do it. Voice-cognizant computers had come a long way since the days when directory assistance returned a request for Macys in Boston with a number for Sadie's Catfishhouse in Houston.

They still weren't perfect. They required painfully monotonic syllables spoon-fed in careful English and English was Yoshi's second language.

She recounted the uncountable hours she'd spent playing Eliza Doolittle to ADSS' Higgens, trying to conquer her demon—Received Pronunciation, otherwise known as perfect English. It wasn't easy. While her native Japanese alphabet had 28 letters to 26 in English, the similarities ended there. Japanese was really four languages in one: Romaji--the phonetic Roman (English) pronunciation of Japanese words; Hiragana--native Japanese words spoken in the Japanese alphabet; Katagana--non-Japanese words derived from the *gaijin* or foreigners; and Kanji--the pictogram language derived from the Chinese. As if not convoluted enough, Katagana had 48 syllables, Hiragana had no vowels and Kanji had over 8000 symbols and there wasn't an "r" to be found among them. Equilibrating this to English was tough enough. Doing it in Received Pronunciation bordered the ridiculous. But such challenges had defined her since childhood, and she hadn't backed off.

"ADSS, ID check," she started out slowly. She could almost hear the system resonating, digesting each word, its tone and pronunciation.

"This is ADSS." the computer soon registered. ***"Hirumi Yoshioka ID successful. Access granted. You may proceed with first input."***

"Rotational Direction Clockwise," Yoshi complied obediently.

"Clockwise confirmed. Next input."

"Reel-out length two one one point zero meters."

"Reel-out length: Two one one point zero meters confirmed. "Next input"

"Center of Rotation: One-one point zero meters."

"Confirmed. One one point zero meters. Next input"

"Mean gravity gradient zero point three eight G."

"Confirmed. Zero point three eight G. Next input"

And so it went like *the rain in spain goes mainly down the drain*, to the tick of an atomic clock instead of a metronome until a minute of uneasy silence followed by the words, *"Processing, standby."*

Computers were supposed be fast and instill confidence. Why *Processing, standby?*

Waiting, Yoshi wondered if she'd screwed up, if her ADSS-ji might not have been perfect enough, then chided herself for being so impatient. She knew ADSS was slow and finnicky so she willed herself to slow down with it and be calm. It was one of those traits Vadim most admired in her but one she could do without. She wished she was more like him, not giving a shit about perfection, calm or speed (or so he claimed). He was irreverant, impolite and jocular to the extreme and she loved it, so different from the way she'd been raised.

Even the Russian word for shit, *der'mo*, she admired, especially the way he said it, with emphasis and humor. It was part of his daily lexicon and she yearned to say it too—'shit shit shit, *der'mo, der'mo, der'mo*," a catharsis if only she could shout it out. She envied that attitude; so different from hers, as well as his twisted sense of humor. Like the time she taught him polite Japanese phrases oozing with the civility of *Ohaiyo Gozaimusu* (good morning); *Genki desuka* (how do you feel?); *Goshisumo sama* (what a delicious meal), or *oyasumi nasai* (good night), and he'd responded in kind with *escho nagnis', nizhe*; *drochit* and *chesat' yaytsa*, translations in Russian of the same phrases, he'd maintained. NOT. Little did he know she'd purchased the infamous *Pamphlet of Outrageous Russian Terms* in a Star City bookstore and knew that the English translation was "bend over lower, take the whole thing in your mouth,' and so on. Others might be furious at him but not her. That pamphlet and his use of it was a window to a world most Japanese couldn't fathom. Japanese, English, French, German, and Spanish, the other languages she was fluent in had no equivalent for *a fart too big for one's pants* or *a penis so huge it could murder a lover*. But the Russian language did because it didn't take itself so seriously. Which is precisely why she loved the language, the culture and Vadim. They were the polar opposite of the rigidity, obedience and homogeneity that had stymied Japanese women forever.

"Spin rate will be three point six six RPM," ADSS finally bubbled up, yanking her back to the C3. ***"Operation Complete will be in one niner five minutes. Are you ready to initiate?"***

"Yes," Yoshi snapped to, her words slow and steady again.

“Execution Start in thirty seconds. Standby for thrusting.”

The effect of the ball's tiny thrusters seemed nil when they started. The counter-thrusts from *Columbia's* bigger ones were not. They started spinning about the tether behind them and a floating cup began sinking to the floor, the first sign of artificial gravity. A wobbly view of stars out the window was the next sign, caused by the eccentric motion of the spacecraft as they rotated. Fifteen minutes later, the wobble had grown greater and their bodies heavier. There was no doubt about it now: Mars-like gravity was slowly but steadily being imposed. Twirling about itself like a baton, *Columbia’s* guages indicated a spin rate that grew from 0 to 1 Revolutions per Minute to 1.5 to 2, while the C3’s G indicators jumped from 0 to .1 to .2 G.

It would take three hours for the numbers to home in on where they finally needed to be: a spin rate of 3.66 RPM with a Mars Gravity level of 0.38 G. As suddenly as they started, the dueling thrusters of the ball and the ship ceased then, and Yoshi smiled in time to see Vadim’s thumbs-up. Spin-up had gone by the book.

As lead Flight Surgeon, it was Roberto’s job to test the newfound Mars gravity once he unbuckled and he was wary. The first few steps felt markedly different than the simulator but a few minutes of experimenting brought him to a sliding motion that felt stable. “It’s different than the NBL and POGO back home,” he cautioned, “you tend to bounce up higher and have less body control. Keep your feet on the floor, control your heel strikes and don’t push off!”

They marveled at the lightness of their beings caused by the shedding of 66% of their Earth-leaden body weight. It created a false sense of the superhuman. "Wheee," Andrea gushed, weighing barely 40 lbs now, as she leapt like a corkscrew nearly twisting her ankle.

"**Don't push off, I said**," Roberto grimaced, *"Tiene usted no cabeza?"*

She smiled back playfully. She was excited about this, who wouldn't be, why wasn't he? Because he was just doing his job or because he's fucked up? The latter she concluded, and readied for her next task at hand: getting the meal trays out for dinner. She decided to behave herself for now and be contrite.

The food storage lockers were one level down on B-deck, abutting the circular wall. There were seven of them, six crammed with prepackaged meal trays and one containing a sealed glass chamber fed by a phalanx of liquid nutrient tubes--Tess' salad machine. Though weeks away from harvest, it was already sprouting clusters of dense green shoots, and would be a treat when ready.

Twelve hundred meal trays had been crammed in the other six lockers, sorted by crewmember and mission week. Each had a B, L or D designation, for Breakfast, Lunch or Dinner and a T, R, I, AS, IM, NF or BE tag for Thermostabilized; Rehydratable; Irradiated; Artificially Sweetened; Intermediate Moisture required; Natural Form or Beverage. To assure each person got the meal prescribed just for them, the trays were individually color coded, a black dot for Vadim, green for Yoshi, yellow for Andrea, white for Anna, red for Chris, and blue for Roberto. These were the same color codes that had been placed on their utensils, spacesuits and everything else they handled in order to limit the spread of contagion.

"Thermostabilized chicken, veggies and lemonade," Andrea read off her tray in the Day 1 stack in Locker One, then grabbed Chris and Yoshi's trays while Roberto took his and the ones marked for Vadim and Anna.

Meals would be family-style, another of the routines planned by the Human Factor types to preserve a touch of home in a place anything but. Andrea and Roberto set the table with the color-coded place settings after they arrived at the Bridge, heated the trays in the galley's laserheater and liquified the lemonade powder with the pistol-like water injectors.

"Far cry from my first flight," Vadim mused as they sat down to dine, "everything tasted like plastic then. And laserheaters? Ha! A hot meal for us was lukewarm water on freeze-dried sausage." He looked at his fork and laughed again. "In those days, the forks clumped with twice as much food as you could put in your mouth from the zero G. Half of it would float off and end up in your underwear. We even had a Russian word for it, *shashlyk smonkya*, sausage-crotch. Today we know better, halfsized forks, normal sized bites: progress."

The dinner conversation was animated, seeped with the tinge of thrills yet to come and tempered by the marathon that had proceeded it--the last 24 hours, the last 24 months, the last 24 years. The marathon finally won out as they finished their meals and exhaustion set in.

Roberto and Andrea, completing their galley duties, stacked the utensils and trays in the Disinfectant Scrubber, the utensils for re-use, and the trays for use as radiation shielding. Roberto scanned the 4 digital clocks on the wall as he finished up; then read aloud

MET=0000:07:00:00 HOU: 00:36 CANDOR: 11:45 DELAY: 00:00

"Twelve thirty six past midnight, Houston time, everyone, time to turn in."

Time would match Houston time for most of the journey to minimize CRD (Circadian Rhythm Disorder, aka jet lag), and would coincide with the shift of H's Black Team at the MOCR, who were the most experienced flight controllers. But as they neared Mars with its 61 minute, 41 second hour and 24 hour 39 minute day, they'd transition to Candor Time, the time at Candor Base where they'd be landing. Getting used to it wouldn't be easy, as they'd learned from Antarctica training. They hadn't slept well there and this would likely be worse.

Before moving to their sleeping quarters, the urge to urinate suddenly erupted. They'd abstained since before TMI, and the combination of holding back and the reduced gravity, which overloaded the kidneys with an increased plasma volume sent from the lower legs towards the heart, prompted a signal that said NOW.

"*Nuzhda*!" Vadim growled when he got to the toilet on B-deck. He was last in line: Chris and Yoshi were already there, waiting on Andrea.

"It's the low gravity," Yoshi explained to him, "fluids shift to our chest and our thoracic pressure receptors misread it as excess plasma."

"I don't care what it is. I'm just pissed you all beat me here, even Andrea who was on cleanup duty."

Andrea emerged as if on cue: "It stinks in there. It's really foul!"

Vadim looked at her and grumbled, "It's a toilet."

After settling under the covers at his sleep station later, he was sure smelly toilets wouldn't be the last of Andrea's issues. Like Chris and Roberto, he was still dumbfounded over the swap orchestrated by Brandford and Royce Davies. It made no fucking sense to him, then or now. JoAnna Hewitt wouldn't have complained about space toilets.

In the pie-wedge sleep station next to him, Anna heard the heartbeat of *Columbia*--the rhythmic whirr of the glycol pumps; the sound of air hustling through heat exchangers; the hum of electricity bused from place to place, and it was like music to her ears. But there was another sound not quite so soothing--a barely perceptible *whum-whum* noise repeating itself every 16 seconds. It dawned on her that 16 seconds was precisely the period of rotation of the ship spinning about the big lead ball. Probably normal, she decided, but made a mental note to report it in the morning.

On the other side of her, Chris didn't notice the *whum-whum* noise in his sleep station. He was too preoccupied with his mattress, a wedge of foam only an inch thick as he prepared for bed. Anything to save weight, he fussed before crawling atop it, only to discover that it felt perfectly comfortable after all. That's when he recalled his body weight was just 52 pounds here and an inch thick mattress would do fine.

His thoughts returned to the strange dream he'd had in the CSF the night before launch, the one where *Eagle's* airlock had led not to *Eagle* but to a tossing green sea with red clouds. It had scared the hell out of him and he hoped it wouldn't return to disrupt the shut-eye he yearned for now. He needn't have been concerned. He was out in a blink. Before the fluorescent's afterglow had a chance to fade away.

■■

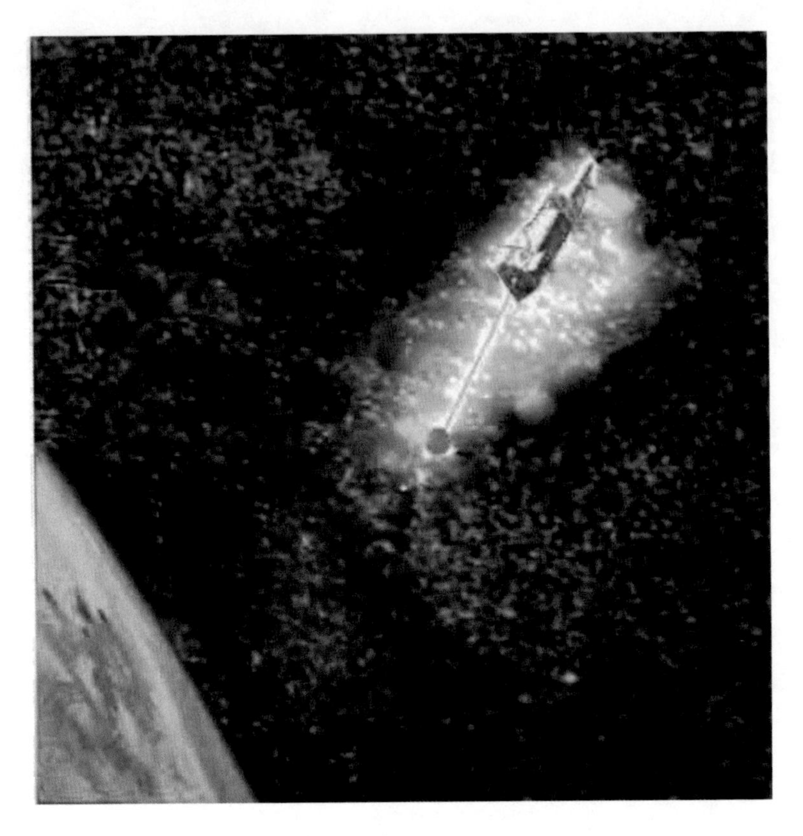

ADSS SPINNING UP FOR THE JOURNEY

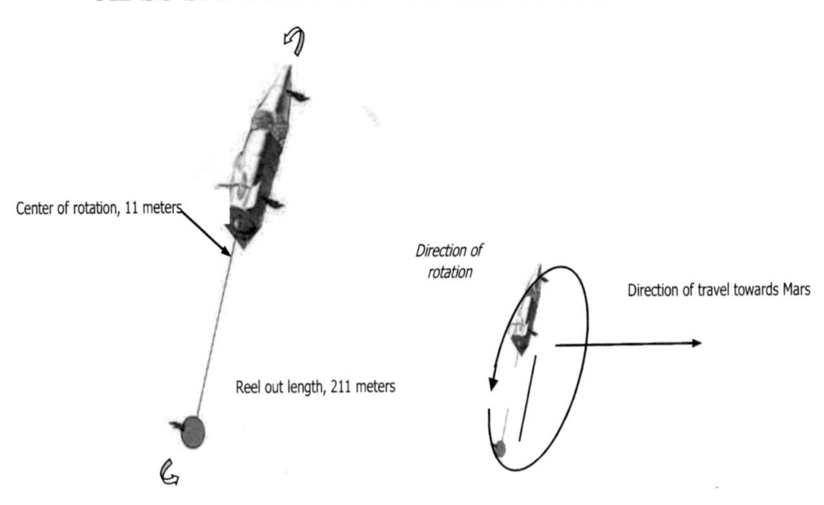

Chapter 11--Outbound

MET=0000:14:09:00 HOU: 07:45 CANDOR: 18:41
DELAY : 00:00

Strauss' Blue Danube blared through the speakers at 7:45 the next morning, followed by Adam Brady's resonant voice, easing everyone up. "Mornin', Columbus 11, it's a bee-yoo-tee full-day."

Chris rubbed the sleep from his eyes, un-velcroed his blanket and catapulted out of bed. "Uh-oh," he grimaced as he flew towards the ceiling knowing what was coming. "Schmuck," he yelped, banging his head.

"Remember the fucking gravity!" he repeated moments later, as he folded his bed out of the way to expose the floor bin. The linens and clothing inside it stored 100 sets of jumpers, socks and underwear, all color coded blue and protected with *bioshield* to extend wearing time to ten days before discard. "This better work as advertised," he mumbled to himself. Ten days in the same jumpsuit and he'd smell like that toilet if it didn't. Speaking of which, he needed a shower.

"*Val!*" Vadim crowed at him emerging from the steamy shower in B deck when he got there. "Leoniv would shit if he saw this, "a hot shower on the way to Mars!"

“I suppose so. It’s a lot warmer than where he is, six feet under,” Chris deadpanned. Vadim shot him a look. He didn’t like the joke obviously, and he made a mental note not to mess with Vadim’s hero again as he got in the shower and prepared to languish in it. He kind of got it. He wouldn’t want Vadim dissing Ed Cochran. Ed deserved dissing for some of the stuff he pulled, but not from Vadim.
Vadim was a friend. But a friend with a terrible sense of smell he discovered as the shower reeked from the same urine smell Andrea had griped about yesterday. To make matters worse it cut off after just 2 minutes leaving him chilled and unfulfilled. That at least was expected: everything had time limits to save energy and water, even the number of toilet-flushings, hand-washings and toothbrushings, but this stink was unacceptable. It could be the urine recyler and it would have to be dealt with.

His breakfast was grapefruit juice with peaches and scrambled eggs Mexican style at the Bridge. "Meaning chile pepper in the powdered eggs to kill the taste," Andrea cracked in her cute french accent as she dished it out to him before Vadim doled out the day's assignments.

“I noticed power fluctuations on the C3 last night,” he said, “so I’d like you in B-deck, Chris, checking the solar wing output; Anna, we’ve increased our heat load so you’ll also be there deploying RAD 2 to augment RAD 1; Yoshi and I will stay here in the Bridge for a C3 review, and Andrea, you'll stay here with us on NAV. That leaves you, Roberto, on C-deck. Have you got our countermeasure schedule?”

"Affirmative," Roberto nodded knowing how Vadim really felt about that. Countermeasures, psychology, and especially HUMMS, they were all the same to him: anathema from some flight doc that could only cause trouble. Engineering? You could fix things if they went awry. Physiology? Reasons to be disqualified if you didn't measure up. He'd heard it a hundred times but even Vadim must know that his stone age attitude was wrong, that the countermeasure protocols were the only ways to keep bone loss in check. Still, Vadim was the MIC (Man in Charge) so he'd have to hide his disdain for that attitude and the denigration of his profession accompanying it. But Yoshi's a flight doc too and he likes her. How does he deal with that, he wondered, unless its not the physiology. Unless it's me or my hairy back he doesn't like. Or the wetback thing. "As you know, we have p501

devices on board," he started, supressing the negative thoughts, "the TEVIS treadmill, the CEVIS exercise bike, the ARED weight system, the suit Impacter and the Versaclimber. Everyone will be on them equally at first, two hours a day in total, but I'll mod that as we go, based on your bone loss numbers and the HUMMS prescriptions. You've got to stick to it. As for today Vadim, you and Anna are on TVIS; Andrea and I on CEVIS; Chris you'll be on the Impacter and Yoshi on Versaclimber."

"Got that everyone?" Vadim underscored with a trace of sarcassam. "It's important. Hustle down to C-deck soon as you finish your tasks. Comments or questions before we break?"

"It's probably nothing," Anna chimed in, "but I heard this odd noise last night, a kind of a *'whum-whum'* keyed to our rotation rate."

Vadim's antennas rose. Unknown noises concerned him, the squall before the possible tsunami. He listened attentively then had Anna write it up in a squawk, which they'd upload to the MOCR. If they couldn't resolve it, it would go the next level up to the Sim Team.

The CWS, the Caution/Warning System on the C3 console of the Bridge was the eyes and ears of the ship. Hundreds of readouts in 3-set orange entries, organized in columns of current, high and low value which blinked at Vadim and Yoshi after everyone dispersed. Vadim had a penchant for these numbers, Yoshi, thought, almost feeling where they were going before they got there. He described it to her as a gift, like playing piano by ear or reading backwards, which he'd learned from Leoniv. Leoniv could bounce a golf ball off a ball-pein hammer with his right hand hundreds of times while reciting the alphabet backwards, then switch to his left hand and do the same thing. He'd also perfected the art of ambidextrousness, claiming it built the muscles and trained the brain to harness its unused neurons. He'd called it *Whole Brain Power* and Vadim used it at first instead of going to the gym (he hated the gym). When his muscles started growing and his mental skills with them, he knew Leoniv was onto something but couldn't keep it up. He didn't have the staying power when it came to exercise or boring drills and his gains all vaporized when he slacked off. All except his number sense. Aimless meandering versus meaningful move; nominal versus abnormal, he could literally sense it. He'd become so skilled at it that Leoniv challenged him to take a Wall Street job instead of flying rockets. There, at least, he could score a few mil before hanging up his wings broke. But money was never a priority to Vadim.

Flying a spacecraft was his Wall Street, and who better to teach it to than the best student he'd ever had, Yoshi, sitting next to him on the C3.

And what a *sensei* he was, Yoshi thought in synchrony, grateful for the special bond they shared.

Across from them unnoticed, Andrea worked NAV, the navigation system. With the stars as her map and the IMU (Inertial Measurement Unit) as her tiller, she would steer the ship like an ancient mariner. For the first part of the journey, the MOCR would back her up, but as the distance from Earth widened, the comm lag would widen and she'd be on her own. Her first moment of truth would come at Venus, whose gravity well would slingshot them towards Mars using waypoints she'd have to choose. There'd be help from her 21st century sextants of course, the IMU, Star Trackers and COAS (Crew Optical Alignment System) but it was still a humbling thought to do this alone. This was deep space, not near Earth where a GPS could help you out. To make matters worse, they'd be rotating, a complication that had dogged the GNC (Guidance, Navigation and Control) folks for years. Finding a star much less pointing at one becomes an issue when you're spinning. Everything blurs, especially the stars yet you still must lock onto them. The solution had been the IDF or Image Defocuser, a counter-spinning platform on *Columbia*'s aft end with corrective optics software to sharpen the image. Though elegant and ingenious, it was also fickle, just like ADSS, which was why she began her first fix that morning with the same anxiety that Yoshi had felt. But this was her pressure cooker, not Yoshi's and NAV was her baby.

She began by locking the solar sensor on the IDF to the Sun; then aimed one Star Tracker at Canopus and the other at Serius. From there she went to NAV and used the 2 stars to triangulate a position. She'd take a second fix moments later and get velocity and direction by subtracting it from the first. She would then double-check her numbers using the IMU--two black boxes containing gyroscopes and accelerometers held in 3 cages placed at right angles to one another. Each box could *gimbol* (pivot) in one plane only but taken together they could maintain a compass heading independent of movement and provide course or speed changes. The rest would be up to Andrea.

Only she could make the call which system to trust and which to correct; which engines to fire and which not, to get the ship back on course if it strayed. She had another option, of course, to give the raw data to Vadim and let him do it, but that would be the last option, one she'd never take. That's why her Star Tracker's "eyes", NAV's "brain" and the IMU's "nervous system" were so important to her. They'd prove to Vadim, Chris and Roberto that she belonged. She'd have to be perfect with her fixes though, especially at Venus. Only the fixes could do the talking for her now. Sexy and Shalimar might work for her on Earth, but the only thing that mattered here were the fixes. She stared hard at them when they popped up on the C3.

COURSE CORRECTIONS

Delta V x	**=**	**0.27 km/sec**
Delta V y	**=**	**0.21 km/sec**
Delta V z	**=**	**0.02 km/sec**

VELOCITIES

Vx	**=**	**7.53 km/sec**
Vy	**=**	**0.21 km/sec**
Vz	**=**	**0.02 km/sec**

ARRIVAL TIME NEXT WAYPOINT:

MET: 0004: 23: 12: 05

"Waypoint 1, no course change," she announced with a modicum of relief. Vadim simply nodded. If she'd been looking for more, a pat on the back or even a grunt, she wouldn't get it. It would take more than that to shake the notion that strings had been pulled to get her here instead of Joanna. That was fine with her. She'd been weaned on skepticism. "Go down to B-deck and see if Chris and Anna need help," Vadim added tersely.

Two decks below, Chris and Anna were struggling with their tasks, Chris with the solar wings and Anna with RAD 2. If there were any power surges, Chris couldn't find them, so he decided to go after the urine smell instead. First he tried the fuel cells, which combined cryogenic hydrogen and oxygen to make electricity for the ship but also produced potable water for drinking and non-potable water for hygiene as a by-product. It was supposed to be distilled, pure and odorless, and the water he took from its sample ports was normal. The fuel cell wasn't the problem. Next he crawled under the waste management cabinet to inspect the VCDU (Vapor Compression/Distillation Unit), which changed their urine to drinking water. One whiff said it all: the issue was here. He smiled at the memory of how his nearly identical VCDU *recycler* had bonded him to Tess decades ago. She'd been struggling to invent the same thing when they'd met at an ICES conference and her eyes had grown wide as saucers after he'd peed into a bottle, put it through his machine and drank it with gusto. That water had tasted fine, this clearly didn't. Eventually his nose led him to the overflow valve that diverted urine flow around the machine to control the pH. It was leaking, a simple solution. All he needed to fix it was a wrench and some washers.

"Ughh," Anna swore as he wedged his way out from under the waste management cabinet, "RAD 2's out." RAD 2 was the secondary heat pipe radiator that had to be deployed to help RAD 1 dump electrical heat to space, and without it, the cabin temperature was on the rise. Anna had already engaged the Flash Evaporator system when Chris wiggled out of the cabinet, but it was only a stopgap. If she couldn't get RAD 2 online, things could really heat up. She'd gone through the system in her mind, tracing the way the thing evaporated then condensed ammonia in never ending cycles to cool things off like a gigantic refridgerator, and that had led her to ECLSS, the *Environmental Control and Life Support System* computer for diagnostics. But the answers had come back in Z-base, the one language she didn't know, and that made her nervous. "You know Z-base, Chris?" she almost pleaded as he passed her on the way to A-deck for his tools.

"Nope," he replied, "but Andrea's our expert on that, I'll go get her for you."

He felt sorry for Anna as he started down the ladder; she looked overmatched in this contest, sweating and fretting as she was. He had a soft spot for her with her homespun tales about growing up in Montalchino. He also liked the way she tried to make others feel good about themselves; how she praised Vadim for his joystick prowess; Andrea for her brains and glamour; Yoshi for her tenacity and Roberto for his HUMMS. A quality like that was rare, especially for one as gifted in astrogeology as she was. He was glad she was here with him.

Anna was relieved to see Andrea once she arrived. "It's this Z-base," she said shaking her head, "I have as you say in English, too many cobwebs."

It took less than a minute for Andrea to trace the issue to T21, the 21st temperature readout on RAD 2. "The sensor is bad."

"How can you tell?"

"Because it's reading a hundred degrees colder than T22, T23 and T24 and its right next to them. Not only that but you see statement 1004?" she asked, calling up a string of equations on the screen. "It says the average temperature must be 180 degrees or higher for the flow valve to open. T21 is reading so cold that it's forcing the average to never get there."

```
1001    T21 + T22 EQ SUM Y
1002    T23 + T24 EQ SUM Z
1003    TAVG EQ (SUM Y+SUM Z)/4
1004    IF TAVG GTE.180, RAD 2 EXEC. <-------
```

"I see! So why not put a dummy in for it, make it read higher?" Anna asked brightening up.

"That's exactly what we're going to do, Anna but it's not so simple. We have to modify the program and I don't know if it will let us."

Anna tried to follow as Andrea homed in on the Z-base but soon lost her. She was in hypergear now, wrestling with the convoluted code until she saw the flash in her eyes and she knew she'd pulled the answer off the shelf of some long sitting dusty neuron. Mesmerized now, Anna watched her add a statement 1000 below the T21 reading and above the others, bypassing the bad sensor by fixing it at 180 degrees, simple and elegant.

```
1000    T21 EQ 180.0 <-------
1001    T21 + T22 EQ SUM Y
1002    T23 + T24 EQ SUM Z
1003    TAVG EQ (SUM Y+SUM Z)/4
1004    IF TAVG GT.180, RAD 2 EXEC.
```

Suddenly the RAD 2 LOCK message that had been torturing Anna for hours extinguished, and the temperature immediately started to drop. “Mama mia,” she exclaimed, “you are genius,” and she hugged Andrea.

But Andrea was in another world, the one where she'd first learned Z-base surrounded by the sexual innuendos of the white male establishment. Proving herself there should’ve ended all the questions, but it hadn’t. Anna noticed the mood change, only a brick wouldn’t. Andrea was a complex woman with a lot of issues. The kind she usually fell for.

****

Chapter 12—Hissss

MET = 0002:00:11:00 HOU: 17:47 CANDOR: 00:49 DELAY: 00:01

When the MOCR called in for status the next day, an empty hiss preceded them. Even before he looked, Vadim knew the DELAY clock had moved. They were 185,867 miles from Earth now--the distance light traveled in 1 second. The 00:01 on the clock said it all. Voices would take a second to reach listeners' ears now, likewise for video and data. One second between an event and awareness of it, and two seconds or more before answers came to questions. The delay would get worse the further away they got. By the time they reached Mars, it would be 40 minutes. Responses would be from the past, not the present.

"hissss.....okay, *Columbia*, before we get on to the press conference, what have you got for us?" Adam Brady began.

"RAD 2's deployed," Vadim responded. "It was a bad sensor. We also diagnosed the odor, a blockage in the upstream side of the VCDU causing urine build up. The valve is leaking and it's not too accessible. Chris figures he can get to it though."

"hisss....tell him fixing toilets are part of his job description. "What else?"

"Power fluctuations, but they seem to be gone for now. An-end to-end solar wing check was negative. You guys see anything?"

"ssss…..the Red team didn't report it at the shift change this morning. Might have been a temporary surge. We'll take another look and get back to you. Other squawks?"

"Noise from the aft end last night. Anna describes it as a *'whum..whum'* kind of thing. Says it's keyed to our spin rate. Most likely from the ball mechanism."

"ssss…..can you hear it now?"

"Negative, but there's lots of background noise with all systems up during the day."

"…..keep an ear out for it tonight. We'll pulse the contractors for an explanation. That it, Vadim?"

"Pretty much, Adam. Everything's in spec on the CWS. We're on trajectory with two healthy spacecraft."

"sssss…..we concur. One more thing before we get to the media. We'll have to limit the privacy calls to one a week, 30 minutes. We'll be needing the bandwidth for data."

"Copy, I'll pass that along. They'll be disappointed."

"…..sorry. We'll try and make it up later. Okay, now for the press conference. Let me read you PAO's advice. They say the public pays the bills so they've got a right to see what they're paying for.

And no jokes please or funny business. Give them a tour of the decks and answer the questions short, straight and to the point."

"Copy that. Andrea wants to know what we should say if they ask SST questions?"

"----SST?"

"Yeah, sleeping, sex and toilets."

"----She would think of that. Suggest you keep it clean," Adam laughed.

The very first question, however was an SST: "What about your beds?" queried a USA Today reporter, "there's not much to them."

"They're fine," Vadim jumped in first. "They only have to support a third or our body weight."

"sssss.....But what if you've got two bodies, as in romance?"

"Every minute of our day is accounted for," he shot back unblinking. "Romance is not on our timeline."

Listening in from Houston, the Black Team guffawed over that one

****

MET = 0005:00:52:00 HOU: 20:28 CANDOR: 04:15
DELAY: 00:08

Five days out, 1.5 million miles from Earth

While a rotating ship solved one problem, it invited others, like corrupting the view out the windows. While everything inside appeared normal, outside was another story. Stars and planets seemed to wobble, including planet Earth, which tracked a path of crooked spirals. That's why Roberto hated the windows. They invited fixation hypnosis, dizziness, SAS and disorientation. To him, their threat outweighed their benefit. If a view was required, they could have pasted one on the telescreens.

Not so for Chris. Seeing a real, live Earth, even a wobbly one, was essential. It was home and they needed to see it. But it was so small now that he could blot it out between his thumb and forefinger in the window and it looked so vulnerable, a point Tess would surely make if she could be here with him to see it. She soon would be, at least her image would. Her first patch-in from Oracle was imminent.

He closed the door to his quarters and punched in her security code, then watched as the video materialized on his laptop. At first it was disappointing: ghosts intermingled with shadows. The voice was even worse, a collision of throaty rasps, high-pitched whines and no discernable words. Communicating like this will be pointless, he thought, just before the aberrations corrected, and Tess suddenly sprung to life.

"…..h...how are you?" she quivered, "is everything ok? What's it like there? Oh just talk to me. Say something...anything."

He gushed in the joy of the contact, so busy beforehand, he'd barely had time to think of her.

"Hi, beautiful," he crowed.

As they talked, the ever-present hiss reminded him that she was not next to him after all, but a million and a half miles away. He suddenly yearned to touch her, but that wouldn't happen for three years now. He'd have to be smart with his words until then, for the lag had grown to 8 seconds now and getting worse. Conveying information this way was one thing; expressing unequivocal love was another. He decided to compose his words beforehand so he could pack all the things he wanted to say into the limited time he had, the next best thing to a love letter over the airwaves. But there was so much to say and so little time to say it, could he really do it? Antarctia training had prepared him for a lot of things but not this.

"How've you been, what's new at Bio 2?" he asked still unsure how to comport himself in this offset world. "Everything's been A-OK so far, launch, release, spin-up. No complaints, even the meals are good and I'm exercising. Oh, I got your optiscope results, honey. There are gaps in the blue band like you figured, bad news. The pattern's widespread. I'll uplink it on our next data dump. Tell me about you...Closure 4, CASI?"

He chided himself for babbling, and losing so much track of time that her words could cross his and he might never hear them. Sixteen seconds round trip, he told himself, talk for 8 listen for 8 next time but then he grew anxious when nothing came back after 45.

Only the hiss could be heard, with her image still frozen at the last cycle nearly a minute ago. Another minute passed before her lips began moving again, an interminable wait in this anxious state. They carried a hint of a frown with them this time. Was it from the same sense of separation he was feeling or something else? Should he waste precious time even asking?

"sssssss.....Let's see, better get business out of the way first," she said. "We've had more fish kills around the Sea of Japan; I'm knee deep in Closure 4 buildup, it starts next month and as for CASI, I'll save that for last. More relevant to you, I checked the duplicate Mars greenhouse today. I do it every day actually, kinda like that guy in *Silent Running*, your favorite film--the one with the last forest on the spaceship. You remember it don't you? Don't end up like him, pleassse! Anyway, the optimum soil mix ratio has changed. You'll need to alter it when you set your greenhouse up. Add more nitrogen to get things moving. Adam has the data and he'll uplink it. As for personal stuff, you'll be glad to know I stored your you-know-what, you know where, at minus 320 like you told me to. And no, I haven't given kids a second thought. Anyway, I don't want to talk about me, tell me more about you. How's artificial G, ECLSS, my salads, your bed?"

"The gravity's easy to adapt to," he responded quickly this time, "It was weird at first, not like the training, but we've all got it down now. We had some nausea in the first 3 days, but it's abated as expected. As for ECLSS and your salads, you should be proud. ECLSS helped solve our radiator problem and your salads are on their way. It'll be a few more weeks till we can harvest them, and we're all looking forward to that..."

As they chatted on, he thought about the things they usually did back home together, only instead of together, they were doing them in parallel universes now, separated by much more than distance. The muscles on his forehead furrowed knowing their only real contact from here on in would be through this wormhole in the S-band connecting them. He tried to put the thought aside, rubbing the palm of his hand against his forehead so she wouldn't see the lines but it hardly mattered. The comm gap passed even more uneasily now, with hisses of wasted seconds spreading to minutes. When her video motion resumed, Tess seemed almost sad. Had she figured out what he'd figured out? That their actual conversations would amount only a fraction of their 30 minute budget? That it had been stilted, contrived and contorted from the git-go and there was less than six minutes of it left now.

"ssssss…. I know we're low on time so I saved the best for last. Something's happened with CASI."

He sat riveted to the laptop as she described the jump in CASI's accuracy, finishing with a smile. There was barely 2 minutes left now, barely enough for advice.

"I'm proud of you baby, but remember that CASI's only a model," he said softly. "You'll need 70, 80, 90 percent agreement, not 34 before anybody believes you. And you'll have to have it for a lot more places that that rain forest, major cities for one thing. I've been there sweetie, and I've made the mistake every model-maker makes.

I've taken my predictions too seriously. You're too smart for that, Tessie. Remember Sagan. 'Extraordinary claims require extraordinary evidence.' "

Listening across the chasm, it was what she wanted and needed from him: firm, wise and reassuring guidance. He was absolutely right about that accuracy. She'd only clocked 34, a failing grade in high school. Still it was progress, and she was proud of it. She started to thank him when his image began fracturing. She flashed on their marriage as it did so, wondering how it had survived with more commitment to career than each other it seemed. Passion was the answer, hot-wired, primeval, irrational passion. She wanted to tell him that but it was too late. Only a disintegrating jawline remained of him on her screen.

****

Chapter 13. HUMMS

"A journey to tomorrow, a journey to another world:
A manned mission to Mars.
Why Mars?
Because it's our destiny to strive, to seek and to find.
And because it's America's destiny to lead."

Those had been the President's words. They'd been Chris' lightning and he'd been their rod, but they rang hollow for Tess now after that first patch in. *Is this it for the next thousand days?* She couldn't dwell on it, it was just too depressing, so she clicked on the news to distract her, and a story about ELF, the Earth Liberation Front, popped up. They were one of many eco-terrorist groups that had sprung up as the environment declined while the White House played Nero.

"The fire at Joe Romania Chevrolet targeted 30 SUVs," the story began, and went on to say how the ELF specialized in burning SUVs. There was also a piece about the TRA or Tree Rights Army, who'd poured kerosene on golf courses; and the GLR (Green Life Rights), who'd burned a field of genetically altered peas leaving a note, *"You can't control what is wild."*

\

Tess shook her head in disgust. With their vows to blow up *the power structure*, these guys were hurting not helping their cause. What if they were all linked, like Ed Cochran had warned, in a bizarre conspiracy to take over the government? After all, FirstEarth, the most dangerous of them all, had gone mainstream with a Green Party and was winning votes in Congress. She went to the mirror to chastise herself. "Get a grip, woman, your husband's on a spaceship. Stop imagining things!"

****

MET = 0015:16:00:00 HOU: 09:36 CANDOR: 10:35 DELAY: 00:24

--two and a quarter million miles from Earth--

At fifteen days, sixteen hours Mission Elapsed Time, Yoshi and Vadim were in the middle of their morning CWS check. Chris was in B-deck, resetting the valve that finally stopped the urine leak, and Anna was in C-deck getting HUMMS-scanned for her medical update. Andrea, still on a high from her last trajectory calculation, was about to perform another. Her waypoints had been flawless so far thanks to NAV. But just she was congratulating herself, NAV rudely interrupted:

> ***IMU ALIGNMENT REQUIRED. The gyroscopes in the IMU must be realigned to prevent precession. Failure to do so will lead to false headings. To realign, position Star Trackers to a fixed reference while using COAS and Doppler Shift as backups. Input the weighted average into PRGM 112. Repeat...IMU ALIGNMENT REQUIRED.***

"Okay, my friend," Andrea frowned as if the program could understand (it couldn't, it wasn't voice-cognizant like ADSS). "Don't blow your fuses."

Alignment was the task she liked least. Yoshi had to help her because it was so tedious, sighting the Star Trackers on Serius and Canopus while she targeted the COAS on two other stars. Then she'd have to enter the coordinates into NAV, get two lines of position and extend them until they intersected at a point.

Then she'd have to do a Doppler Shift, using the change in frequency of radio signals sent by Houston to verify the position. Despite the complexity, it turned out to be worth it.

"Miniscule correction," she bragged to Yoshi,

"I could get used to this."

"Shi shi," came the reply,

"I'm superstitious. If you talk about a no-hitter you may lose it."

"What's a no hitter?" Andrea asked."

****

MET = 0027:22:00:00.... 27 days, 22 hours out.

Vadim made his way to C-deck for his medical or "HUMMS-scan" as it was called. Once a week, Roberto's *Human Medical Monitoring System* would do bone, body chemistry, neuro, blood, cardio, pulmonary and psychological scans on him and the rest of the crew. The worst part was the MAT or Memory Acuity Test, a series of questions designed to see if exposure to the GCRs (Galactic Cosmic Rays) that were pervasive is space and on Mars could cause memory problems. It was already known that their 3 year mission constituted a career dose for cancer, raising the odds to a 1 in 10 probability and eliminating them from consideration for future spaceflights, but memory loss was a real possibility too. Vadim hated these tests; only bad outcomes could result. They'd screwed some of the most famous astronauts like Al Shepard and Deke Slayton, so why not him?

Shepard had been undone by an inner ear infection and Slayton by a heart murmur and while neither of their problems had been serious, they'd been grounded anyway. Only a relaxation of the ground-rules had enabled them to fly at the end of their careers, Shepard to the Moon on Apollo 14 and Slayton on Apollo Soyez, but their grounding had been unfair and their reinstatement late and arbitrary. Vadim was so convinced that these decisions were made by *huy marinovanniy* (limp, marinated dickheads) that he'd employed tricks to hoodwink them thoughout his career, such as the Orthokeratology Ruse an old optomologist comrade had taught him. By wearing an overly-curved contact lens prior to his annual eye exam he could pass the test even if he couldn't see well.

He wouldn't have gotten away with it had the exam been unexpectedly scheduled but knowing the date in advance
had enabled him to endure the ill fitting lens long enough for it to temporarily nudge his visual acuity back to the 20-15 mark then pop it off just before walking in the door for the test with no one the wiser.

Vadim was thrilled he could fool the flight docs with tricks like this, exacting a measure of revenge for Shepard, Sleyton and the others but HUMMS wasn't so easily fooled. On the other hand he could care less now because it was too late to ground him. He was on the way to Mars and HUMMS couldn't stop it even if he failed its tests. That was a comforting thought as Roberto's machine began putting him through the ringer:

"This updates your psychological health profile.
Please answer to the best of your ability

:

On a scale of 1 to 5, what are your feelings about each of your crewmates?
1. very warm 2. warm 3. neutral 4. anger 5. hostility

How would you judge your performance this week?
1. above average 2. average 3. below average

Rate your sleep:
1. need more 2. adequate 3. need less

Rate your meals:
1. tasty 2. average 3. foul

Rate your exercise program:
1. strenuous 2. adequate 3. deficient

Rate your attitude:
1. very positive 2. positive 3. Indifferent 4. Poor

A Rauscharch Test in which HUMM's displayed ink spots on its screen came next:

The color best describing your feeling about spot A is:
1. white 2. orange 3. red 4. green 5. blue 6. black

The time of day best describing your feeling about spot B is:
1. sunrise 2. noon 3. dusk 4. night

The type of sky best describing your feeling about spot C is:
1. very sunny 2. sunny 3. overcast 4. cloudy 5. Dark

The output that HUMMs gave Vadim at the conclusion of the scans contained his nutritional, exercise and psychological prescriptions for the week. It recommended 7 hours of sleep with 1 hour of recreation daily and an increase in his caloric intake of 200 calories to offset the weight he'd lost. That part was fine. It was the output HUMMS didn't provide that galled him, medical ammuntion to make his life miserable at Roberto's whim. Should he so choose.

****

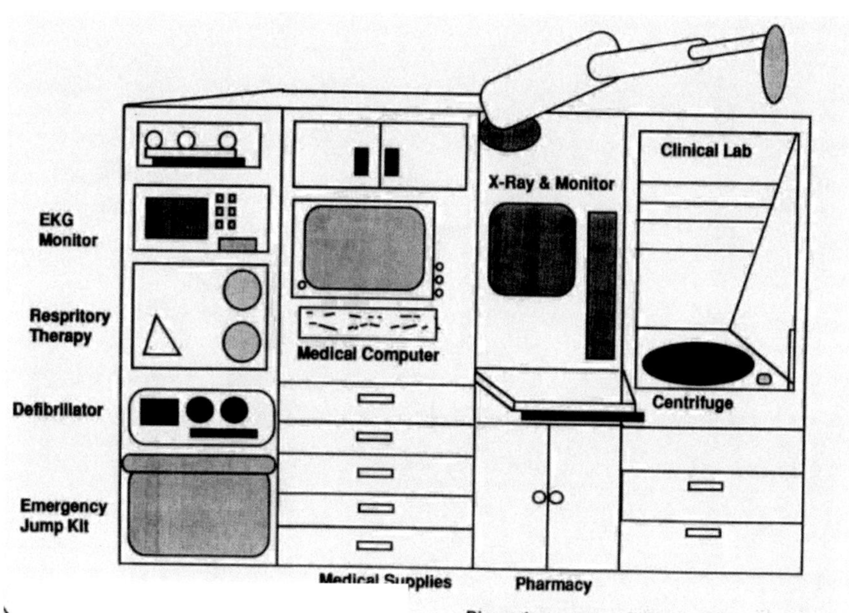

HUMAN MEDICAL MONITORING SYSTEM (HUMMS)

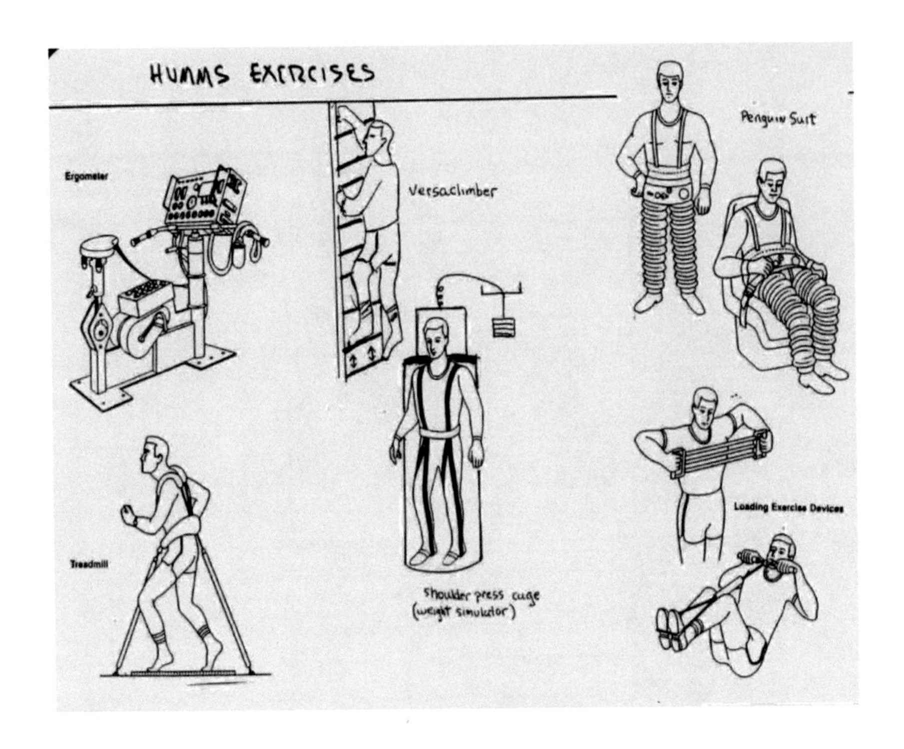

HUMMS Exercise Countermeasure Protocols

MET = 0042:15:00:00.... 42 days, 15 hours out

Anna was in C-deck in the middle of her workout, perspiring profusely with a pained look on her face as she labored against the bungee cords anchoring her to TVIS, the Treadmill Vibration Isolation System. "I know what you think, "she wheezed at Andrea, cycling next to her on the CEVIS (Cycle Ergomer Vibration Isolation System). "No pain, no gain, right?"

"Pain I can take, abstinence I can't," Andrea cracked in the midst of her Tour-de-France simulation.

"*Non capisco* abstinence. I don't understand."

"Use your imagination, Anna."

Anna didn't think about this until her pace and elevation slackened, when it dawned on her that Andrea was talking about sex again. She took a hard look at Andrea's body then, from head to toe, taking in each part starting with the swell of her sports bra. Avoiding her gaze, Andrea huffed, "Do you have any secrets, Anna," "anything you'd like to share?"

Anna felt herself turning red with embarrassment, then snapped into the protective cacoon that served her so well. Looking askance, she replied, "I have no secrets. I have a mission to do and avoid distractions. Is good advice, yes?"

"Is good advice, no!" Andrea huffed at her. "Secrets make life exciting, but only if you share them. I know that sounds strange, but it's really about friendship. A friend is someone you trust and can tell everything to. Do you have someone like that, Anna?"

"Only my mama. And even she doesn't know everything."

"Not good, Anna, especially here. The stress can drive you mad, you know, like it did to that astronaut who kidnapped the other one."

"Which astronaut?"

"Elaine Novis. She had an affair with this other one—Bill something or other--but she was already married so she decided to break it off. Only Bill didn't like it. He went loco I guess, and kidnapped her to Mexico."

"*Mio Dio!* "

"Yes, and he ended up in a mental hospital, where they diagnosed his problem as *Astronautitus* something or other, a funny medical term, which I loosely translate as no one to talk to. The lesson is, if we let our secrets out, we could be grounded but if we don't, we could go crazy. That's why you need to share your secrets Anna."

"And you?" Anna asked with mounting curiousity.

"Me? I'm the queen of sharing. I keep nothing in. So I have a proposal for you. Let's exchange some secrets. I'll go first; then it's your turn. I'd like to sleep with Roberto. I think he's very sexy."

"If you like hairy backs," Anna replied, not knowing what else to say.

"I do, *mes ami*, I do."

Anna raised her eyebrows. This wasn't going as planned. Andrea was weaving a web of captivation around her, threatening to break the ironclad concentration that protected her.

"Be careful who you call Mister Hairy Back," Andrea cautioned, "he's the one who will treat you if anything goes wrong. But as for me, if we're going to be gone 3 years you have to pick someone. Chris is taken and faithful, ugh, while Vadim doesn't like me, and even if he did, he's got Yoshi. That leaves only Roberto."

Anna nodded, adjusted her bungees and considered all that Andrea had said…and her proposal. Being her friend was a risk. It meant compromising herself, revealing things she'd never revealed. On the other hand, Vadim had said it best: "*They can't ground us now, it's too late for that.*" That did it. There *was* nothing more to lose. "There are other possibilities," she said softly.

Now it was Andrea's turn to be *non-capisco*, as she pondered Anna's words until their workouts wound down and she finally got it. She suspected this, of course, with those looks and body signals. They'd been there since the training, before even, but she'd dismissed them then. She couldn't now, and the idea of sleeping with a woman had of course occurred to her. Still, as many lovers as she'd had, she'd never actually done it. If she did, who better to do it with than Anna: wholesome, giving, warm and sexy in that cute Italian way of hers. But could she actually do it, sleep with her, could she really make love to her? Her brain said no, but there'd been tingles when Anna's eyes had probed her body on the CEVIS. Maybe yes, maybe no came the answer and with words failing her, she could only burst out laughing at the question she'd raised with her "secrecy" discussion.

"Something I say?" Anna asked.

"No," Andrea fibbed, "I was just thinking of all those tests they used to select us, the perfect crew. A Mexican, Italian, American, Japanese, French and a Russian. Four Caucasians, an Asian and a Hispanic."

"Yes, and three males and three females of questionable sexual preference."

"Oooh, very good Anna, that's a sophisticated English expression."

"It was in the magazines I read."

"And what kind are they?"

"Maybe I tell you some other time. But you are right about us. Instead of the perfect crew, we now have Vadim the Russian control freak; Chris the abstinent monk; Roberto the hairy backed gorilla; Yoshi the pure; and you and I: the only normal ones."

They looked at each other with a giggle that grew to a belly laugh as their workouts ended, Anna on the TEVIS and Andrea on the CEVIS, standing there revealed in their mutual distaste of all things judged normal.

"We're in a bell curve with us at the front or the tail but not the middle, three sigma if you know what I mean," added Andrea. "No one is who you think they are. When we get home and close our door, maybe we watch porno movies or don't clean our dishes or our underwear. Our last French chancellor was a pickpocket."

"The worst I ever did was masturbate in public at the Cappela Sistena under Michelangelo's fresco."

"No, you didn't. Really?"

"Si, Andrea, when I was on a school trip, age 9. Under my skirt hidden by a guide book."

"We're all really animals, aren't we? Chimpanzees I think. Picking us was a territorial choice, one monkey each from six different tribes."

“But there must have been some logic,” Anna said turning serious for a moment. “There are 4 space agencies represented--NASA, ESA, NASDA and RSA. That meant at least one American, Chris, one European, me, one Japanese, Yoshi and a Russian, Vadim. The other two: you and Roberto? Roberto, with his hairy back, perhaps you are right about the monkey theory Andrea.”

“And me?”

“You, well there are many theories on that. We can talk about them later. But I will leave you with this thought, which is also my secret. The touch of a woman is more than you think.”

****

MET = 0050:09:00: 50 days, 9 hours and fourteen million miles out.

Everyone was sleeping when the ship entered Venus' gravity well--the place on the star map where the cloud-shrouded planet began tugging at them harder than did Earth. It was called the Libration Point, and prior to it, Earth had had the greater pull. Now it was Venus' turn and if the calculations were right, they'd begin hurtling towards her at nearly 2 million miles a day and whip around her backside like a yo-yo on the end of string. The maneuver was called a Swing-by and Venus' gravity would "sling-shot" them on towards Mars with it, adding delta V (speed), cutting trip time and saving fuel, mass and dollars in the process. The only minus was timing, it had to be perfect. Like a trapeze act requiring two artists to arrive at exactly the same spot and moment in a high wire handoff, a Swing-by required a unique alignment of Earth, Venus and Mars at launch, and a near perfect trajectory to a precise point in space. Like most trapeze acts, there would be a safety net, a backup trajectory called Conjunction or Opposition if they messed up the timing, but no one, least of all Andrea, wanted to resort to that. It would be embarrassing, expensive and dangerous.

Not that a Swing-by wasn't. The DELAY clock read 1 minute, 14 seconds when they crossed the Libration Point to begin it, and aside from Anna's *whum-whum* and Vadim's on-again, off-again power surges, all systems were go. The crew felt nothing when they passed the point. They were moving 20 miles a second but felt absolutely nothing.

****

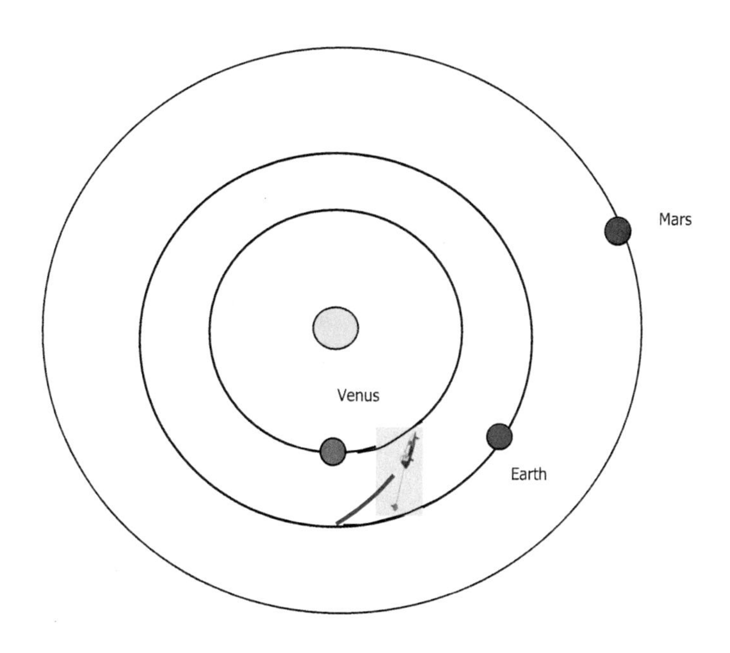

COLUMBIA AND EAGLE: 50 DAYS, 9 HOURS FROM EARTH
(orbits and sizes not to scale)

Chapter 14: Humphrey

They had tested the airlock many times in trial runs. This time was for real. At 8:15 AM on a bright, sunny morning, the eight of them bid farewell to hundreds and ducked in.
The airlock was the size of a cargo container,
with gray, stainless walls and two doors that had portholes like a ship.
One opened to Earth, the other to Biosphere 2.
After the first one slammed shut,
the 8 pushed down the lever on the second and went through.
Everything changed when they stepped through that inner door.
Their restaurants and grocery stores shrank
to an incredibly small plot of mother Earth.
It's one thing to grow food,
quite another to live off food you grow.

Excerpted from *Life Under Glass*

March 29th, 2034….Oracle, Arizona.

The long awaited test was about to start, Closure 4, the *Indefinite One*, the one where 8 people would lock themselves into Biosphere 2 for as long as they could take it. As Tess watched the Biospherians, 4 men and 4 women trundle up to the airlock and pass through, she wondered how anyone could commit to such a thing. Chris and his crew would only be gone a thousand days by comparison, but these guys had signed on indefinitely. And though she knew it would take as much to prove Earth could be duplicated under glass, she couldn't do it. She liked the smell of real air too much, the warmth of real sunlight, the touch of people she cared for. Most of all she liked her freedom. And though Biosphere 2 was the size of 3 football fields, it would be like a closet after a week inside to her….with 8 caged-in humans she might not like as closet-mates. Thankfully, none of the crazy 8, as Chris called them, shared her views, which was fine, because if they did, there wouldn't be a test and she wouldn't be getting paid to do what she really wanted to do: steer CASI down the road to credibility until everyone believed her warnings. That was just one of the thoughts she wanted to share with Chris as their next contact loomed tomorrow, Valentine's Day. Another was the blossoming of her little Mars greenhouse, now exploding with fruits and vegetables.

The greenhouse, a prototype of the one they were carrying to Mars, had been the acid test of their relationship, the kind of project many couples embark upon that either makes or breaks them. This one had nearly landed them in jail. Tess smiled at all the missteps: Chris granting her a sole source contract to build it; getting caught doing the nasty on the floor of the first prototype by a jealous co-worker; the embarrassing conflict of interest investigation that followed it and so on. Barely escaping the clutches of the IG (Inspector General) only underscored what seemed obvious to all but them. Chris was a square peg to Tess' round hole and their lives would be far easier spent apart. But passion was their credo, and they could no sooner be apart than space and time. That's why it was hard for Chris to leave Tess to sink or swim on her own, something he knew he had to do to for her to make a real contribution to the mission. She blossomed when he finally figured out how, especially with the greenhouse. Unfettered, she'd tinkered with the pressure and temperature till she finally hit upon the right combination (1/3 Earth pressure (5 pounds per square inch) and 50 degrees Fahrenheit).

Next, she'd fiddled with the parts per million, coaxing the right level of cleanliness for max yield (antiseptically clean of trace contaminants). And so on with the other variables until everything clicked as it seemed to be doing now.

If the production of the Mars greenhouse was anywhere near what Tess' was getting on Earth, it would feed Chris and his crewmates for years. She could hardly wait to tell him. And she'd look sexy when she did, she decided, tussle her hair the way he liked it and not give in to her emotions like the last time. That had been a disaster. Tomorrow would be different though, because she'd practiced control.

She'd practiced in front of a mirror and a voice recorder, monitoring her facial expressions, her voice fluctuations and most of all, her tears. She'd even added a simulated Comm hissss for realism. And just to make sure, she'd prepared an outline of things to discuss besides the test and the greenhouse. A crib sheet of topics to keep the conversation moving. A prop to avoid letting him know how she really felt. So desperately alone without him. But 24 hours later when the call was about to come in, she received another call, this one an urgent message from her boss, Leslie Forbes. Chris would have to wait. There was something more pressing to attend to.

****

April 2034: The Arctic Circle

The changing of the leaves had been a ritual of the ages in New England. For as long as anyone could remember, the greens of summer had turned flame-red in fall. It didn't happen that way in the year 2034. It happened in winter.

Other things didn't happen the way they were supposed to that winter either. There was a Hosepipe Ban in London; cherry blossoms bloomed in DC; sparrows flew north; acid snow fell in India and chunks of the polar ice shelf calved away.

Then there were the fish kills, with species disappearing daily. That's why Leslie Forbes had cut off Tess' call to Chris. As nuts as she could be sometimes, with her prophesies of doom, there was no better Climatologist on Earth. That's what it would take. Someone had to get to the bottom of this fast and she was the one!

From the onset, Tess suspected the ozone hole. With so much UV-B pouring in through it now, it could mutate DNA. Phytoplankton, at the microscopic end of the food chain, would go first. If the mutated versions multiplied fast enough, they'd overwhelm the normal plankton that fish fed upon. But the hole was over the Arctic and the kills had started in the Sacramento River Delta. Why would they start there?

That was the question as she crisscrossed the Delta in search of explanations. She could find only one, and it was far-fetched and tenuous. A humpback whale named Humphrey had been stranded in the Delta two winters ago. The kills had started within months at the same spot. Could that be it, she conjectured as she boarded her flight for the Arctic?

The route took her first to Fairbanks, then to the Arctic Circle for detailed ozone mapping. The numbers there were worse than she'd feared. The hole was growing twice as fast as expected. From the Pole, she boarded a helicopter to the Aleutian Islands, home of the vast krill grounds where the whales fed. Her first day out in the chopper drew a blank, and the three that followed turned up nothing more than subzero temperatures and lurching yanks from one glacier to the next. With his ears ringing from rotor buzz, the pilot was getting annoyed. She hadn't told him what she was searching for--the whale equivalent of a needle in a haystack.

The chopper's heater went out over Unimak Island, and by the time they reached the coastline they were shivering. Tess tried every trick in the book to keep warm: hunching over in a ball; wrapping her fingers around a hot coffee thermos before gulping cup after cup of it until it ran dry. Nothing helped. Cold and disgusted, she was ready to abort when a lake at 2 o'clock grabbed her. It was one of many with narrow outlets to the sea, but decidedly different with a dark crimson color instead of the usual glacial blue.

She'd seen that color before, from algae gone mad in the Delta. And there was a pod of beached and decaying whales surrounding it.

It took a month and a half for the autopsy report to come back from the Roger Payne Marine Laboratory:

"The surrounding waters had no trace of Euphasia Supurba. This species of brine shrimp, commonly known as Krill, is the exclusive food source of humpbacks. Conversely, there was an overabundance of the unusual strain, Zooplankton A in the upper respiratory tracts of the whales. So much so that it caused the surrounding waters to be tainted red."

That did it for Tess. The ozone hole was behind the fish kills as she'd theorized. Radiation pouring through it had caused Zooplankton A to grow unchecked in the Arctic, and enough had hitched a ride south on Humphrey two years ago to set off the domino effect. One well-placed snort through his blowhole in the Delta east of Sacramento had started it. Warmer temperatures and faster replication rates had sustained it. It all made sense. And she had no idea how to stop it.

****

Chapter 15: Encounter and Swing-by

A Swing-by is a maneuver that gets you to a planet faster and cheaper. Instead of rocket fuel and engines,
it uses the gravitational force of one heavenly body (like Venus) to "slingshot" you on towards another (Mars).
This elegant ballet is not without cost..
Careful attention must be paid to the planet you're swinging by.
Too close an Encounter could slow you down,
defeating the entire purpose.

Or kill you.

MET = 0070:19:00:00.....70 days, 19 hours, outbound.

Meal 070D: Dinners of rehydratable shrimp cocktail, thermostabilized beef with broccoli, rehydratable peach ambrosia and freeze-dried lemonade. It was accompanied by the first harvest from Tess' lettuce machine, the hot topic of conversation on night 70. Awash in the joy of fresh salad, the usual guards came down and the talk soon drifted to what everyone had snuck onboard without telling the big boys from Headquarters.

"Fungi from Montalchino!" Anna admitted proudly, "my mama's special recipe. I am excited to make it for you."

"I took lipstick and birth control pills myself," Andrea quipped, looking teasingly at Roberto, who took the bait and rolled his eyes. "Andrea, Andrea," he responded. "You have a three track mind and the S word is on all three."

"If you mean sex, that's presumptuous of you, Dr. Diaz."

"But true, I suspect."

"If so, why not? It's at least as important as some of the other things your HUMMS asks us about. I don't want to tell you how to do your job, but I could think of much more interesting questions for it to ask us then about some silly ink spots. How about this one: On a scale of one to five, one being dead, five being ravenously horny, how would you categorize your attraction towards breasts?"

Roberto's mouth twisted uncomfortably as Vadim looked on with a grin and newfound respect for Andrea. Anyone who made Roberto squirm couldn't be too bad. But when she persisted in her teasing, he decided to intervene in the name of crew harmony. "Let's return to the question, Roberto. What did you bring aboard?"

"Me? *Nada*," he replied dismissively. "I don't believe in breaking rules."

"Stretching is not breaking,"Vadim said dryly, thinking what a humorless pompous ass the guy is, like all flight surgeons. "What about you?" he said turning to his friend, Chris.

"I wasn't sure I should say," Chris hemmed and hawed, "but I will since no one can do anything about it now. I brought Ed Cochran's ashes in an urn. His wife, Millie gave them to me at our Bon-voyage party. I'm going to scatter them in the Martian winds."

"Admirable," Vadim nodded, "I would have brought Leoniv's but the old reptile is a national hero buried in Star City."

"What did you bring then?" Roberto said to Vadim, suddenly feeling left out.

"Three bottles of vodka, doctor, three bottles of vodka."

Roberto's jaw began to drop until he saw Vadim wink and realized he'd been had. A flicker of recognition came over him then that maybe he was too much of a hardass so he feigned a laugh to counter it. "Okay, break my chochones if you must. I apparently deserve it."

"No comment," said Vadim, "but it's progress you're aware of it. Ok, I'll tell you what I really brought: an old photo of Yuri Gagarin. I keep it on my workstation to give me inspiration. Not that I wouldn't have preferred the vodka. And you, Dr Yoshioka?" Vadim pressed on, addressing his second-in-command, and lover to be, he hoped.

"Nothing so dramatic," Yoshi smiled, "just an iPod nano with my favorite songs on it."

“I hate to get back to business,” Roberto intervened, “but can we discuss your QCTs, DEXAs, and ultrasounds?”

“Must we?” Andrea fretted until Vadim waved her off, realizing they’d have to deal with it sooner or later.

“In summary, everyone’s doing fine. Our bone loss is averaging a half a percent. My scans are the worst, down one. Say what you will about ADSS but without that artificial gravity, we’d be in trouble. I thought you’d want to know, especially Yoshi, who has such concerns about ADSS. And on that note, I will take leave of you. I’ve work to do.”

A collective gaze followed Roberto as he left, but Vadim’s soon swung back to Andrea. "You like giving him a hard time, don't you?"

"I’ve no problem with Roberto,” she answered back coyly. “In fact, I like him. And he’s just reminded me that I also have things I need to attend to. Personal things.”

Again eyes followed as she moved down the tunnel in that way of hers. Even in the artificial gravity she sashayed. Vadim shook his head. “They deserve each other.”

****

MET = 0080:21:00:00: Probe Ejection, 22 million miles outbound.

Earth was but a shimmer in the Milky Way ten days later on Day 80, and Venus loomed large. With 25 days to Encounter, the timeline called for probe ejection: the deployment of 3 science probes from *Columbia's* cargo bay that would intercept and land on the shrouded planet in time for Swing-by. The first probe would descend into the southern hemisphere, the second along the equator and the third in the northern hemisphere. Their assignment--imaging the terrain, mapping the topography and analyzing the atmosphere—wouldn't be easy. There'd be much to contend with, 450 G entry forces, thousand degree surface temperatures and pressures no previous probe been able to withstand.

If all went well, however, if these were to be the exception, the probes would hit Venus' atmosphere on MET:101, twenty one days from now. Even an hour of clean data would make the scientists back home ecstatic. For the probes had been built to pierce long-standing mysteries, conundrums that had confounded geniuses. Atop the list was why Venus had gone so wrong while Earth had gone so right. And next in line was that question about Mars. Why hadn't it gone as wrong as Venus…or as right as Earth?

****

MET = 0092:17:00:00—13 days to Encounter.

Each of the sleeping quarters had a multipurpose laptop that could be used to watch movies; listen to music; read e-books or training manuals; record log entries or communicate with Earth. They also had another function--voice-transcription of intimate thoughts on dedicated *diary-discs*. Chris had yet to do that, since his thoughts hadn't reached the intimate stage yet, but on day 92, he did use the training system to bone up on Venus:

Venus Review.
This information was up-linked March 31st, 2034.

Venus is now 47.8 million nautical miles from Earth in an elliptical orbit around the Sun with eccentricity .0416. Aphelion is 71.7 million miles and Perihelion is 64.8 million miles. The planet's rotational speed is one revolution every 243 days and it completes one orbit around the Sun every 248 days making it solar geocentric. The atmosphere is largely carbon dioxide with average density and pressure 90 times that of Earth. As a consequence of greenhouse gases and solar proximity, surface temperatures exceed 480°C. In size and internal composition, Venus most closely resembles Earth. It is 95% as large and 80% as massive. Unlike Earth, there is no evidence of water, tectonic plate movement or a magnetic field. Topography probably arose from volcanism and surface features have little relief.

The most prominent surface feature is the Beta Regio double shield volcano located at 27 degrees north, 285 degrees west. Occupying a land mass 10.03 kilometers long, 15 kilometers high and 3.55 km, wide. Beta Regio is......"

Chris finished the briefing knowing much of it was guesswork. The planet's clouds were so thick, only radar could penetrate them and the only radar data in existence was nearly 4 decades old from Magellan. He switched off his laptop and thought about the Venus. The probes they'd sent out would be arriving there in 9 days, and it would be on him and Anna to read their signals. He got a buzz contemplating what he'd soon be doing. Answering questions heretofore unanswerable.

****

MET = 0101:21:54:00: Probe Lock.

The days had passed quickly, a delicious anticipation honing their already sharp edge. An hour prior to the first probe's parachute deployment, Chris sent a command that would plunge it towards Venus' southern hemisphere. Anna sat next to him at the C3 console, listening and waiting, waiting and listening.

"Think of it," he said to her, " it's nearly there."

Anna said nothing, lost in thought.

"On your toes, Anna, are you ready?"

"Sorry," she replied with a start, "I was just thinking of my mama. They finally got me patched-in to her last night. She didn't look so good."

"The resolution isn't the best, Anna, it makes everyone look bad."

"It's not that, Chris. She hasn't been well. The ozone hole is over central Italy now. She needs cataract surgery from all the UV, and more, I'm afraid. I just hope she lives long enough for our return. I so want to share it with her. What about your parents, Chris? I never asked, I must confess."

"They died in a plane crash when I was young."

"Oh, I'm so sorry. So then, is Tess the only one you speak with? How come you never married, you've been with her such a long time. Oh, I'm being, how you say it, nosy. Please forget I asked."

But he couldn't forget. Should he tell her the truth, that they were married, tell them all the truth like he yearned to? Or keep the damn secret another thousand days?

Why not tell them, he asked himself? After all, they couldn't yank him off the mission now even if they wanted to. On the other hand, it was nobody's business but his, and he had promised Tess to keep it quiet. He flashed back to the event that had prompted the subterfuge in the first place, the day he got the notice from Code AHX. It had come in a thick, not a thin envelope, unexpected: He'd held it a full ten minutes before getting up the nerve to open it, and his heart had skipped beats as he'd skimmed the lines until....
"Report to the Johnson Space Center, training begins February 10th."

His first reaction was disbelief. His second had been, how to tell Tess?
Unbeknownst to him, she already suspected. While he was dallying, she'd heard a hint from the internet:
"Space agency officials today selected the Columbus 11 prime crew who will attempt the first human landing on Mars. Also chosen were the members of the Columbus 12 crew, who will serve as backups to the prime crew and journey to Mars themselves on the second mission. The mission will commence in January 2034 if all goes as planned and...."

Of course, he'd told her he'd applied, but he'd couched it in Mission Impossible terms. There were 60,000 applicants vying for 12 positions on the first two missions, he'd said. And not just any 60,000. These were multiple-degree savants who could solve the Shrodinger equation backwards while playing Mozart on the harpsichord.

As if that wasn't enough, only 2 of the 12 slots would be reserved for Americans and 46 astronauts would be applying for them. And if he somehow made the cut, it would only be the first of many.

There'd be water tanks to conquer, and jungles, and isolation traps. There'd be Failure Sims to pass and tests that would made med school seem like kindergarten. He'd have to memorize ten of thousands of gauges, switches and codes and…

It mattered not. She knew he'd be chosen. She had premonitions about such things and they usually panned. Besides, he'd been an architect of the program, and few had his skill-mix. They would have been crazy not to select him.

She'd listened in silence when he finally came and broke the news, even then trying to pooh-pooh it by saying the money could falter, support could crumble or a hundred other things. Choking back tears, she'd just looked at him and said, "I'll miss you terribly."

That's when he'd burst out with, "Let's get married."

He'd proposed before of course, but she'd demurred because she believed Earth's ecosystems were in shambles. There were 15 holes in the dyke and only 10 fingers to plug them, she often told him. More to the point, if CASI's forecasts were correct, the world would be unfit for children. And with Antarctica melting and some coastlines under water, she believed the predictions *were* coming true.

This was different though, because it wasn't about her or CASI but him and where he was going: two hundred million miles into space with a 50/50 shot at getting home alive at best. And in the awkward silence that followed this proposal, issues she'd postponed forever reared their ugly head--commitment and family, children and grandchildren, homes and stability. She'd been a dreamer, she realized soberly, living in a pretend world under a glass dome. A silly girl. The only things she'd ever confronted had been green plants.

"I can't think about marriage now," she'd started to say as before, then stopped herself. suddenly crying out, "okay, okay. But we mustn't tell anyone. Marriage could disqualify you, They want single people. It's obvious. You mustn't tell a soul. Promise!"

He hadn't but, here and now, did it really matter? He would tell Anna the truth, he decided, when a warble at 1.6 Gigahertz on S-band interceded. Probe 1 had entered Venus' atmosphere and locked. Signals would follow shortly.

****

MET = 0104:21:05:00 HOU: 14:42 CANDOR: 15:61
DELAY: 02:37

Encounter Minus One

Three days later, Yoshi was getting nervous again. She had changes on her mind, the kind she would soon be executing. The Let-It-Be rule was weighing heavily on her mind: If a spacecraft system failed, it usually did so during changes.

There would be four at Encounter.

First, de-spin. She'd have to halt their spinning to maximize Venus observations. The radar and telescopes worked best without rotation.

Then, zero G. The de-spin would put them back in floating mode. This only days after they'd finally acclimated to .38 G.

Then an MCC burn, She'd have to execute a course change if Swing-by didn't go perfectly.

And finally the re-spin. She'd have to Spin-up and resume .38 G again, using ADSS.

Yoshi wasn't the only one antsy over Encounter. Vadim disliked ADSS as much as he did HUMMS; Anna was still distressed thinking about her mother; Andrea had had a mood swing and was feeling sad and isolated, and Roberto was battling a migraine headache.

Only Chris felt excited and unfazed. Until the night before Encounter, when his unsettling dream recurred, the same red and green nightmare that had yanked him from sleep before launch. The dream with the raining blood. What does it mean, he asked himself once again. ***What the hell does it mean?***

****

MET=0105:05:00 HOU: 06:42 CANDOR: 07:34
DELAY: 02:39

Encounter

Venus' day/night terminator line tracked rhythmically through the Bridge windows early the next morning. It rotated in sync to the 3.66 RPM spin rate like a slowly turning baton, hypnotic and alluring, like a flame to a moth. As Yoshi loaded the de-spin coordinates into ADSS, the clouds below seemed close enough to touch, so pillowy, so peaceful, so innocent and so deceptive. There was hell under them, she guessed: soil at lead's boiling point; volcanic eruptions, unimaginable pressures. And with a single miscue on her part, they could plummet headlong into it.

"Time to harness up!" she commanded the others as the drama built. The stress showed in her voice as it briefly cracked. She wasn't good at hiding it. Unlike Vadim, she was the antithesis of the steel-coated astronaut. More like Anna, she'd use every ounce of will-power to hide her fears. But as Vadim well knew, she could hide them but she couldn't run. Paradoxically, he was glad. He didn't want an automaton for a lover. He wanted someone who could complement him. Someone as smart as he, but with imperfections he lacked. He cherished those imperfections. He wanted someone who *needed* him.

"If you want my input," he whispered softly in her ear. "I'm here for you."

"Then where's the MOCR?" she asked with a hint of tension. "I need their go-ahead."

“They’ll be along, he responded calmly. “The lag is just about ..”

"sssssss----*Columbia*, Houston," the speakers buzzed on cue. "Got your uplink and you’re go for de-spin. We concur with the entry angle of seventeen twenty niner. Your LOS (Loss of Signal) time will be 64 minutes, 17 seconds as you pass around the backside. See you at AOS (Acquisition of Signal) on your way out.”

Overly anxious now, Yoshi blew her first voice command to ADSS, rushing her words and causing the computer’s drool voice to prompt her for a repeat. Sheepishly, she mini-meditated, thinking of a rain falling gently in a Japanese rock garden of white pebbles with perfectly round shrine stones. She closed her eyes, and repeated the command.

"Five minutes to de-spin" ADSS' metallic voice responded this time.

The dropping elevator feeling soon revisited everyone’s gut, followed by the sense of a merry-go-round slowing as ADSS timed the De-spin. Yoshi felt better. She could hear opposing sets of thrusters firing at the nose and the ball. The cameras confirmed they were slowing, and in the correct direction.

As the frequency and intensity of the thruster reports built, the dancing ellipse of the terminator line out the window danced less, and as it did, the reports lessened with it. ADSS was working perfectly, negative feed-backing everything. There was no cause for concern. The pulses grew shorter and softer until they ceased altogether. Three hours after they'd begun, microgravity reasserted itself. De-spin had been accomplished.

"Commencing reel-in," a more confident Yoshi announced. With the sense of her body weight abandoning her again, she began gathering in the tether, initiating the steps that would cause the great lead ball to methodically draw closer to *Columbia's* aft platform. A slight shudder shook the ship as it arrived, and concern momentarily displaced comfort. Vadim's raised his eyebrows ever so slightly. "*Yolki polki,* what was that?"

Yoshi was too busy zooming the platform camera in for a closer look to respond at first. "The mechanism is intact," she finally said with relief. "Everything looks normal."

"It didn't sound normal."

"Perhaps it was a tether kink or a hitch as I drew it in. We'll report it to the MOCR, and see if they have inputs."

"Affirmative, madam. How many more times do we have to use this *dryan huyesocka?"*

"Four," she answered in control again, then half smiled. ADSS *was* a *worthless cocksucker*. But even though she agreed, she would never use such nasty words. She did consider letting him know she knew what they meant, however, but stopped herself. This was no time for small talk. She had to reorient the ship so the SAR (Synthetic Aperture Radar) could penetrate the opaque clouds to gather the data from the probes. She began by blipping the thrusters, and Earth, ping-pong sized out the window, moved slowly in an arc until it disappeared completely. A wave of sadness spiked when she realized they wouldn't see it again until they neared Mars, but it was soon overwhelmed by a mammoth, cream colored Venus backlit by the Sun. She gaped at the rare solar Conjunction, an alignment that could only be seen from her vantage point in the universe and might never be seen again.

Vadim, looking on with approval next to her, imagined them together in his sleeping quarters, cuddling under the sheets of his pie-wedge bed. He'd be gentle; he'd be sensitive…if it killed him. She smiled back at him, uplifted and happy, her tasks for the moment complete.

Now it was Andrea's turn to take over. They were brushing the fringes of the atmosphere now, 15,000 kilometers above the surface, and it was her job to compute their entry angle through it. Wide-eyed in the dimly lit cabin, she scanned the gauges tracking Encounter until they sprang to life. The Slingshot Maneuver was starting. And as they descended behind the dark side of the now-still terminator line, Andrea reaffirmed the 18 degrees 28 minute angle she'd programmed into the DAP (Digital Auto Pilot) from NAV.

Looming menacingly on the SAR radar screen, Aphrodite Terra appeared. It was half the size of Africa, and approaching at 2.8 miles a second. Now it became Chris and Anna's turn to work, to gather up the terabytes that would soon be arriving by the busload. But as the cabin lit up in white light when they emerged around the dark side, their pupils didn't react fast enough and they couldn't see their screens. Anna was the first to put on sunglasses and realize they'd lost signal strength. She acted quickly, narrowing the frequency bandwidth of the returning echoes. "Got it, hold it!" Chris shouted as they reappeared. The rift valleys of Aphrodite morphed into the wrinkled-peach dune fields of Lakshmi Planum on their screens, with Chris whispering into Anna's ear, "Look at that, look at that!"

The crests of the Danu Montes mountain range followed, with multiple troughs radiating everywhere. One in particular, stood out from the rest, its dendritic mouth tapering to an axon-like body filled with lava that meandered spider-like for 30 kilometers. The last image returned was the Lavinia crater field, the most memorable of all. Field was an oxymoron, Anna thought, it looked more like a planetary war zone. And as they swung out from the backside, she was left with a lasting impression. The goddess of Love was a cosmic joke. Venus was a tortured cauldron, the home of the devil, incarnate.

****

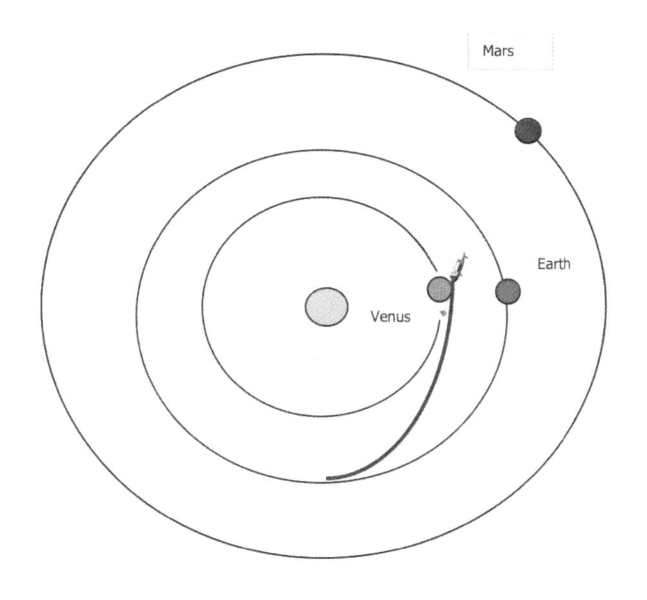

Columbia and Eagle at Venus Encounter, 105 Days Out
(orbits and sizes not to scale)

Chapter 16—The Day the Earth Stood Still

May 11, 2034. Researchers today announced what may be a breakthrough in the cure for cancer. Scientists at Rhongmass labs, a joint venture between MIT, Massachusetts General Hospital and Harvard Medical School released the startling results of a new clinical trial with a large group of patients suffering from small or oat cell lung carcinoma, an expecially virulent type of cancer that is usually fatal within 6 months of diagnosis. All 54 patients on a protocol of a new drug called VSA have gone into remission. The drug, based on an antivirul approach used successfully against HIV, attacks the honeycomb substructure of the cancer cell wall, causing it to lyse or break apart.

Earth: Oracle Arizona—56 days after IC (Indefinite Closure) Startup

The numbers said it all when Tess returned to the BOCR following her Arctic trip. Two months after IC start-up, key parameters were spiraling down. The Indefinite Closure was in trouble. An **UNSTABLE RESONANCE** alarm had already sounded, and she'd have to act fast or the 8 Biospherians would have to be evacuated and the IC would fail. It was only then she realized just how much she'd been neglecting the Closure. Fish kills and the Mars greenhouse had consumed her and now she was paying the piper. With the oscillations widening, and a host of alarms with it, Tess' normally unflappable confidence was flagging.

"I'm not sure I can save it," she told her boss, Leslie Forbes apologetically. Forbes kicked her butt.

"We had 12 crude equations, now we do a trillion calculations a second, thanks to you. So quit bellyaching, get on it and fix it."

The pep-talk drove Tess to CASI, and the RMT tool she'd been adding ever since she'd read about the lung cancer news. Her reaction to that breakthrough had been unbridled optimism.

As capable as humans were of wonton acts of terror; disdain for their fellow and sub-species, and for Earth itself, they were also capable of incredible acts of intelligence and kindness. *A cure for cancer*: the very words had inspired her. She'd been searching for a way to reinvigorate her quest with CASI and the research behind this "cure" had been it.

At first she was struck how VSA, the new wonder drug had succeeded where others had failed. It led her to something else entirely, something that wasn't even a drug but a mathematical tool. RMT or Random Matrix Theory had been around awhile, originating in the world of particle physics in the 20th century but making its name in the stock market by explaining some of its maddening variations. The tool, a statistical approach, was capable of finding hidden correlations within groups of data. Oddly enough, the known relationship between auto stocks and auto parts stocks had been its first success. If RMT could correlate these stocks amongst a phalanx of thousands that were all over the map in a volatile market, then maybe it could also ID not so obvious stocks that moved together in hidden ways. When that happened, RMT became a mainstay of market analysis. A decade later it was used to cure HIV and now it was being heralded in the fight against lung cancer.

Like the HIV virus it had cured, cancer cells replicated billions of times a day, Tess discovered, and shape-shifted in the process to render drugs obsolete. It was theorized however, that also like HIV, some parts of a cancer cell were not involved in the replication process since they had to have a fixed structure somewhere in the body to survive. RMT had found those "sectors" in the HIV virus, and now, a decade later found them in the lung cancer cells. When the drugs delivered to those sites were effective, Tess grasped the significance immediately.

If CASI could use RMT to pierce the cloudy veil of pollutants in the atmosphere and uncover which ones were changing in concert with each other, it might lead to a similar "cure". At worst it might supercharge her accuracy. With less garbage in, there'd be less garbage out. She'd been folding the RMT code into CASI slowly but surely since she discovered it, adding it to the DNA, the Chaos equations and the other things. There was so much in the mix now she was also beginning to wonder if all the tweaks were working together or against each other.

CASI responded on the first run with the new code, finding two obscure gases being generated in ECO-2. A simple filter was all it took to bring the IC back to normal the next day. Tess was so shocked at the speed and effectiveness that she began to believe CASI could handle anything now. Lulled by success, she decided to try another run on Biosphere 1. Just one, she told herself. Just to see if she'd gone past that 44% mark from the last one. Chris wouldn't approve, of course. But Chris wasn't here and he might never be again.

Just like the last time, she started with the MANU, prompting the system for a five-year history. And as before, the same bewildering splotch of lines peppered the screen in no logical pattern. Only this time when CASI's red prediction lines began playing out over them, they scrolled in a mirror image. Her heart to skipped a beat. She repeated the run, a second, third, and fourth time with the same outcome, then clicked for an overall and a lump formed in her throat when it came back 97%. It's an anomaly, she thought; it *must* be an anomaly.

But even with the memory of dozens of duds from past runs harnessing her excitement she couldn't contain herself. The only way to know if this was real was to do what Chris said to do. Try it on the cities, the other places.

She did Sydney first, with a 93% match; then Cairo with 88%; then New York, Los Angeles and Chicago, all between 80 and 90 percent. Her mind raced. ***No One will believe this***, especially with Biosphere 2's tainted reputation: rumors it was a cult, rumors they fudged their data; even rumors it was for money laundering. *Hold on*, she caught herself, *don't carry this too far. Stick to the science, not the scandals*.

But the science demanded conservativism; eliminating all other possibilities--its answers the explanation of last resort. She had no patience for that now. Tomorrow she'd do that but not tonight. Tonight she'd take a step she'd never taken before, something so preposterous, she'd only dreamt about it. If CASI could predict the climate of the past with a 90% accuracy, what about the future? There was no question of next steps now. Tess knew what she had to do: fast-forward in time.

It would be twenty past midnight before she could muster the courage. She'd heard all the warnings of course, from Chris and everyone else: *Models are just models; GIGO rules the day*. Still, she couldn't resist. She simply *had* to do it. Wasn't that the whole fucking point, wasn't *this* what her *entire life* had been about?

She started in San Francisco and moved east, programming CASI to run 1, 5 and 10 years into the future. The first 2 sets looked as expected, showing an upward trend in pollutants, but the 15-year prediction was curious. All the indices of pollution went to zero in 2049. It stood her on her heels. Would the ozone hole somehow close; would we fix the mess we've been making or would it somehow self-correct? But when she called up the air quality index to check, there was no air quality. CASI showed no air. Oxygen and nitrogen had flat-lined. *Like the EKG from a dead man.*

There must be some mistake, she thought, **a silly internal error.** She scoured the logic looking for it until exhaustion set in and she crawled back to her bed for some sleep. Sleep never came that night. Under the covers, a foreboding intruded. What if there is no error?

****

Chapter 17. Let Me Play Among the Stars

MET = 0106:04:18 HOU: 06:00 CANDOR: 06:52 DELAY: 02:45

Everyone breathed easier after Encounter. They slept like babies. Houston awoke them the next morning with a Jerry Lee Lewis tune.

"----you leave me buh-reth-less-uh," the refrain wailed out over the speakers. "Time to get up, guys," Adam Brady added, "lots to do today, lots to do!"

As he continued talking, it was obvious the comm protocol had changed. The lag time was nearly 3 minutes now and growing. The MOCR had decided to compensate. Their sentences were longer, packed with more information just like the ones between Tess and Chris.

"The SAR images were fantastic," they reported. "Venus is incredible, the SCIENCE guys are thrilled. We've scheduled your debriefing with them for later this afternoon, at MET:0106:08:30, after they've had a chance to do some enhancement.

We've also been working your trajectory numbers and they're good but not great. You came into Swing-by looking for an 18 degrees 28 minute path bend and we clocked you at 17 degrees, 16 minutes. It's only a degree, 12 off but you'll need an MCC burn to correct or you'll miss Mars by two million miles. GUIDO thinks the error's due to Masscons, variations in Venus' subsurface mass. He figures they biased the local gravity gradient. Bottom line--you didn't slingshot as much as we wanted you to but tell Andrea not to sweat it. The burn's 3 days away and we'll help her hone the delta Vs.

Concerning that shudder you reported at reel-in, the experts we pulsed say it was a tether kink. They duplicated it in ground sims. The way to stop it is to keep a tighter rein on tether slack. Apologies to Yoshi but she'll need to work closer with ADSS.

Next on the list is R&R. SURGEON wants you to take it easy for the next couple of days and we've decided to back off on the timeline. Good news, eh? You've got 60 hours to do whatever you want, kick back, relax, have a party. By the way you'll be glad to know ssss....... flight...sss.., the files.....sssss, craaaack are rear...sssssssss...hisssss, which makes it easy for the black shift to help you do your IMU align. Copy ?"

"Repeat if you would," Vadim replied, "we missed the tail end of that, Adam."

As he waited for Adam's response, Vadim scanned the CWS readouts. They were clean. Whatever had caused the comm. drop wasn't coming from his end. It was either the MOCR's fault or the weather, and after hearing about the big electrical storms back home, he suspected the latter.

It was weather, Adam confirmed after the lag, but not the kind he'd imagined. "Disturbances in the ionosphere. We'd blame it on sunspots if the Sun wasn't quiet but it is. Whatever it is, the deep space network's been affected. NOAA says more of the same could be expected but not to worry. It's rare and shortlived

Later that day at MET:0106:08:30, Chris and Anna gathered at the Science Console and prepared for their debrief. They were peppered with questions:

"-----did you observe active volcanism in Levinia?"

"-----you think the striations in the Navka region are genuine or anomoly?"

"----Please confirm the sun angle at Encounter?"

"----the ejecta blanket on the kidney-shaped crater at 21 degrees south, 334 east, does it look like a recent impact?"

They handled the questions with aplomb, despite not wanting to handle them at all (a SCIENCE debrief was like an appointment with a dentist). Thankfully for them, the static returned and forced an early end to the session. Back home in the MOCR they weren't happy over it. Comm degradation was cause for concern. Real concern. It was written in the Flight Rules and Flight Rules were god.

****

MET = 0107:02:30:00---Party at Midway: 200 million miles to go

A hundred and seven days out with Venus behind them. They'd gone 200 million miles with another 200 million to go. It was the midpoint of the transit and time for a break. 'So said the surgeons, so who are we to question,' thought Anna. And what better way to relax than with a party. Adam had suggested it and it was a brilliant idea. What kind of party, she thought next. I'll make my Fungi treat, she decided for starters but then she frowned. How can you party in zero G moving 25 miles a second?

Andrea was on CEVIS and Yoshi on TVIS when Anna floated into C deck to ask that question. The difference in the women was stark. Yoshi wasn't breaking a sweat, while Andrea was drenched, the perspiration drawing her nipples taut through her blue in-flight T-shirt. Anna mulled the other comparisons: Yoshi's dark straight hair to Andrea's brown curls floating every which way in zero g; Yoshi's pale yellow skin to Andrea's golden brown; Yoshi's unremarkable stance to Andreas straight-as-a-ruler posture; Yoshi's childlike body to Andrea's curvy soft and lithesome one. None of that mattered, she decided, as much as softness. She was drawn to Andrea because she was soft and feminine and Anna loved it. Yoshi was harder and stiffer, understandable since she was a pilot and a space doc, occupations of discipline. And more masculine, just like her. Yes, in spite of her best efforts to hide it, Anna had always felt masculine and had always preferred women. She wondered for a moment if Yoshi might be gay like her but dismissed it. No, she was crazy for Vadim, that was obvious. If she didn't know it she was fooling herself. Andrea, on the other hand, she couldn't figure out at all.

Unabashed, she dwelled on the shape of her breasts embarrassingly long before finally asking the question she'd come for.

"I'm thinking we should have a party. I would make my special recipe, *funghi al diablo*, a gift from the gods of Montalchino. Is good idea, no?"

"Is great idea, Anna," bubbled Andrea, "but would Vadim approve?"

"I will make him," Yoshi added gleefully as she spun the TVIS down.

"How?" both women asked simultaneously.

Yoshi considered the question for an instant, then answered, "I will tell him he's confined to his quarters if he doesn't agree," she laughed, "that he'll never see mine."

The three women agreed and broke into more grins. They'd breach the topic over dinner tomorrow night.

****

"Think smart," Roberto complained first, dumping his particular brand of icewater on the idea. "We're back in zero G and you want to dance around in it, perhaps hurt yourselves. This is not smart, this is mucho stupido."

"I hadn't thought of dancing," Andrea rejoindered quickly," but that's a wonderful idea, Roberto. *Merci* for that, it should be fun."

Consumed with visions of flailing bodies bouncing off ceilings and walls, Roberto replied sourly with, "I'd call it irresponsible."

"We can velcro our socks to the floor if you're worried," Anna offered gayly.

"Why not?" Yoshi giggled, "to prevent injuries."

"Once again you make me into the bad guy," Roberto grumbled. "It must be Andrea behind this crazy idea, *verdad*?"

"I confess," Andrea smiled. "I'm the guilty one. I need to be spanked. Would you like to do it?"

"Do not believe her," Anna interrupted. "It was my idea, I am responsible."

"No," Vadim cut in. "It was Adam's idea, we all heard it. But velcro-tipped socks across a velcro-dabbed floor? Only a woman could think of this." The Russian laughed heartily. "I like it. And, Roberto, try and have some fun, will you? You've been working too hard. All of us have."

If they were going to have a party, they'd have to clean house so the next day began with housekeeping. It was a task no one relished as they worked, for the amount of dust and dirt had become staggering. It hadn't been noticeable heretofore, since the artificial G had kept it on the floor or behind the cabinets. But with de-spin and microgravity, dust and the like had risen from nooks and crannies, coagulating into "fluffballs," as Anna called them, and getting into everything. There was only one vacuum cleaner to handle the load, and when it broke down they were forced to 'attack' the fluffballs by hand, a job Vadim likened to spearfishing minnows. In the process of doing so, he noticed that all of it seemed to be made of the same stuff, an amalgam of whiskers, food crumbs, lint and hair. The hair, he especially worried about. There was so much of it. Was he going bald?

He rushed to a mirror to check himself out but all his follicles seemed intact so it must be Roberto. The guy reminded him of a gorilla with his hairy chest but nothing atop his head so it must be him. He hadn't been that bald in Antarctica though which made Vadim wonder what other changes the mission had wrought. Perhaps Roberto's other body parts were changing too, maybe his *huyisko* (teeny weeny prick deserving of contempt) had morphed into a *hoy murzhoviy* (giant walrus prick)? Even if it had, he was not deserving of respect. With the exception of Yoshi, no flight doc was. Suddenly he was distracted by reflection in the window, Anna's, and he turned around.

"Look at you!" he marveled, "you look beautiful.".

" I've had a makeover."

Indeed she had. Relieved of the force of gravity, her wrinkles, furrows and creases had all but disappeared. Her stature seemed taller, her breasts perkier. "We should package this zero G," she told Yoshi and Andrea later after observing Vadim's reaction. "We could call it Instant Facelift."

Later that night, as the party got underway, the changes were even more startling. The men were left speechless, even Roberto, when the women floated into the Bridge wearing Andrea's lipstick; cleavage (courtesy of a scissors operating on their unisex coveralls) and fluffy, dangling hair. An atmosphere of expectation ensued. It was most welcome.

The evening began with wheat thins and cheddar cheese appetizers, garnished with apple slices and carrot sticks from the contingency pantry. A receding Venus bathed everyone in Venusbeams through the windows, adding a touch of romance. Yoshi matched it with a tune from her iPod.

"Fly me to the Moon and let me play among the stars," the haunting melody reverberated, *"Let me see what spring is like on Jupiter and Mars..."*

"*Dunque*!" Anna proclaimed, "*Che, cos e*? What is that!"

"Tony Bennett, 1958," Yoshi replied, "It's from a CD called, "If I Ruled the World."

"*Rabile*, how wonderful!" Anna responded. "**Let Me Play Among the Stars**. That's what we are doing, isn't it. *Roso!* We are very fortunate, no?"

"We are very fortunate, yes," said Andrea, "*C'est magnifique*! Don't you agree, gentlemen?"

Vadim, Chris and Roberto, who'd moved closer, forming a loose circle around the women, nodded.

"The 50's were a simpler time, I understand," Chris chimed in self-consciously.

Andrea looked expectantly towards Roberto. "*Et si tu m'emmenais danser ce soir*? Shall we dance?" she asked.

Even more ill at ease then Chris, Roberto began easing away but Andrea pirouetted around him and took him by the hand. He resisted at first but with all eyes on him, he had no choice but to give in.

As promised, the women had placed patches of Velcro in the center of the Bridge floor, and everyone was more or less glued to them. Standing in place was not really dancing though, so they soon moved off to the side. First Vadim and Yoshi, then Anna and Chris pinwheeled from floor to ceiling attempting to do the twist. Every movement of their bodies, from hands to feet set a spin or whirl in motion, like pairs of gyroscopes gone mad. It was great fun, except for Roberto who went off and brooded in a corner. Andrea, spying him, came closer. She had him to herself now and began making small talk.

"What do you know about the 50's, Roberto? The music seems so romantic."

"The cars, I know about, the romance, I don't," he replied brusquely.

"Souriez! Roberto, that means smile. Try to act like you're enjoying yourself. Just this one time. For me, *s'il vous plait,* please? What kind of cars?"

"A Chevy Bellaire, a Ford Crown Victoria, a Plymouth Fury," he said, noticing her lapses into French. He'd noticed all the women reverting to expressions in their native language lately, in fact, and concluded they must be very relaxed to do so. He would never do that-he'd fought too hard to learn perfect English-but it did behoove him to try and loosen up like the others. Perhaps Andrea was right for a change, he admitted. Besides, being the bad guy all the time was tiring.

"Where I grew up, ancient, old cars like this were the only ones we could afford," he began. " I came from a very poor village in Mexico."

"I know, Aquas Caliente, but I didn't know it was poor."

"*Pobrecito*, Andrea, poor and tiny. But it didn't stop us from dreaming. Back then, I dreamt of owning a Ford Sunliner hardtop convertible, vintage 1957. The hardtop would fold into the trunk at the push of a button. I even had the color picked out: two-tone, cameo-orange and crème-white with a cameo leather interior. Someday, if we return alive, and I have the money, I'll find one and restore it."

"That's a nice dream, Roberto," she said her eyes as wide as opals, "I hope it comes true."

In another corner of the Bridge, Yoshi was telling Vadim about her childhood as well. "Yoyogi Park was our place," she described. "It was so big, like a forest in the middle of Tokyo. But, of course it was a park and had grand trails and fields and theaters and ponds. Most of all, it had boys. I went to all-girl schools, starting from cram school at age 8, you know, and Sundays at Yoyogi was the only time I could mix, Vadim. Our parents would drag us there, then stand back and watch like it was entertainment. Goodness knows what they thought. The boys would come in black leather motorcycle jackets and pointy-tipped shoes. They were imitating American rebels. The girls were too. I would wear red high-topped canvas sneakers, a red and white, checkered dress and a big, white bonnet that hid my entire face. We would dance the *hop-san*, as we called it, bouncing around all day long.

We really had no idea what we were doing but we had fun. My parents were certain I would marry a Hell's Angel instead of the businessman they had picked out for me. I did neither."

"Lucky for me," Vadim interjected, and Yoshi smiled.

In their corner of the Bridge, Chris and Anna weren't discussing childhoods, but separations.

"It's hard for us, of course," lamented Chris, "but it's always been that way for Tess and I. More time spent on videoscreens than in person."

"*Spiacente*, I'm sorry, Chris."

"You know how it is, Anna, it's our choice. We choose these careers, not the other way around. It's a sacrifice we'd make all over again."

"Si, but careers do not touch your skin softly. Or speak with passion. Or say *spiacente* when something bad happens or you feel ill. Careers don't take care of you like Tess, or my mama."

"Well said, Anna. Well put!"

"Didn't she say anything about your, oh, how you say in English…ah, chastity?"

"What do you mean?"

"That you were going to be gone three years with three single females on your crew?"

"Oh, that," he laughed. "Of course, yes. That's why she decided to keep our marriage a secret. She was convinced that I'd be pulled from the mission if the space docs knew. Like Joanna. One married person and five singles would disturb the mix. The compatibility would be off, the critical balance disturbed"

"That's none of their business."

"Yeah," he laughed, "and they can't do anything about it now, can they? "

"*No.* Good for you."

"As for the three years with the three of you, you're right, Anna. It will be tough, it already is. Especially the way all of you look tonight."

Back in the center of the Bridge, that was precisely what Roberto was thinking as Andrea tightened her web of seduction around him. Unbeknownst to her, he'd long ago vowed not to be taken in by it.

"You're such a lovely butterfly," he whispered in her ear, almost melodically "and I know what you really want. *Tu es malaventurada*."

"*Que ça*, and what may that be?"

"Why to make love to me, of course."

"You are arrogant and presumptuous, Doctor Diaz."

"Nothing of the kind, Doctor Beale, your intentions are transparent."

"Am I to assume then, if I hid them better, you'd be sneaking into my bed?"

"Not at all. Don't take it personally, though, it has nothing to do with you."

"I'm pleased," she said hiding her rising anger. She was angry because he was playing with her, treating her like a child, the one thing she couldn't countenance. "*Volgaire salaud* (asshole)," she started to say before invoking her oath not to let him get to her and throwing up her hands in the air instead. Don't let him get to you, *don't let him get to you*. She smiled and kissed his forehead. "I know there's a real person in there, Roberto, you can let him out, I promise I won't bite."

"There's much you don't understand," he replied disarmed, "things I don't want to burden you with."

"Burden me."

That's when he ran his thick hands over his scalp, then looked at her, then out the window, then back to her, as if questioning the wisdom of revealing even a fraction of what he was contemplating. She could see him vacillating, drifting between letting his guard down and lashing out.

Then unexpectedly, he bent over close to her ear, and the words poured out like floodwaters. By the time he finished, everyone else had gone and Andrea couldn't believe what she'd heard. *How could this be*, she asked herself, *how could it?*

What had began as a lovely evening being couples instead of crewpersons, turned into something far different with his revelation, a mystery that began haunting her from his first to his last word. She suddenly couldn't bear it and had to leave him, seeking out the only person she could talk to about this, Anna. Anna, consumed with her mother's health and awake in her quarters, forgot all else when Andrea knocked and floated in disheveled. She listened in rapt fascination as the story was retold.

"He began with a nervous laugh," Andrea related, "telling me about a woman, Lilly, a lover he'd had in medical school. She was Thai, a virgin and very naive, he thought at the time, so naive that he didn't question why she never let him touch her or even see her naked. After a year of it, though, it was enough. He got suspicious and demanded an explanation."

"*Che, cos e*, what was it?"

"She told him she wasn't an original woman."

"*Cos'altro c'è di nuovo*," Anna joked. "So, what else is new, neither am I."

"It didn't mean she wasn't a virgin," Andrea clarified. "It meant she'd had a sex change operation, that she was transsexual."

"Ma che diavolo !" Anna exclaimed, "What is this? I don't believe him!"

"I don't know," Anna. I was looking at his eyes as he talked, his hands, his body language. I usually know when someone is lying, and I didn't think he was."

"What else did he say?"

"That was just the beginning. He told me he nearly hit her after she told him but she suddenly undressed, right in front of him. He was hypnotized, shocked, he said, because when he looked at her, she was a perfectly normal woman, anatomically correct, and beautiful.

He couldn't stop looking and then he started laughing. He laughed louder and louder and she started laughing with him until they were sick with laughter. And when they finished laughing, they made love. He said it was the most passionate love-making he'd ever known."

"*Di testa, pazzo*!" Andrea, this is crazy!"

"It gets crazier. After that she started bringing her transsexual friends around, and then her friends who wanted to be transsexuals but couldn't afford the operation. They dressed like women, acted like women and told him they were women in men's bodies, and he believed them. And because they were so desperate, and he was so in love with Lilly, he did it. He performed many of these surgeries once he'd graduated. He thought he was doing society a favor, making them normal."

"*Normale*, ha! And then?"

"The next part is the worst, Anna. He said that the more operations he did, the harder he found it to separate the sexes. That after turning so many men into women, their sex organs began to merge in his mind, and that sex itself became an illusion. He said something snapped after that, and he lost all desire, all sexual identity."

"*Non so cosa dire*,"Anna said warily, "I don't know what to say."

Part of her sympathized. As a lesbian, she'd struggled with her sexuality since childhood and had hidden it. It had taken a toll and she could easily see that happening to Roberto. And the shock at discovering his lover was a he, not a she would have been devastating. *If the story was true.* If it wasn't, on the other hand, Roberto was as sick an individual as she'd ever known, capable of extreme deception.

A glare crossed her face, and her eyes darkened at the many questions. *Is this true? How could he have hidden it, how could he have made it here?* He's lying, she finally concluded. He concocted this story to hurt Andrea. She shook her head sadly and a tear formed under her eyelid. It slid from her face, and floated off in a perfect sphere towards Andrea, who watched it and waited for guidance.

"He hates women, Anna said sorrowfully. "It's the only explanation. Keep away from him, Andrea. He will hurt you and that will hurt us."

Andrea was confused, her emotions befuddling her judgment for one of the few times in her life. She respected Anna's opinion but Anna hadn't been there. She had, and when Roberto told his story, she'd hung on every word. At that moment in time, she'd believed him. Now, she didn't know what to believe or why she should even give a damn. One thing she did know was that she couldn't take a chance. She'd follow Anna's advice because the alternative could jeopardize the mission. She began shedding tears too, as reality sunk in. With Roberto off limits, and the other men committed, a fantasy of hers had been dashed, Instead of having sex in space, she'd be sexless for 3 years. A smile crossed her face at the absurdity, and her tears became giggles. Anna's did too when Andrea told her and the women shared a laugh that led to another and another.

They'd been many such laughs lately as their relationship had grown, Anna realized, and Andrea had become the friend she'd always longed for, the person she *could* tell anything to. "I'm a virgin," she suddenly admitted, "I've never been with a man and never wanted to."

Andrea blushed, something she rarely did, and blurted out, "what about women?" Shit! she thought as the words escaped, why did I say that? It was almost a reflex, and she turned even redder, but didn't regret asking.

"Yes, I liked women," Anna whispered tentatively, hunting for the right words. "But I was very selective. My career would have been over if anyone found out, so I had few experiences and they were *segretezza*."

"Secret, right? Okay, Anna, no more secrets between us from now on. Okay?"

"*Dunque*, okay. And since I've told you one, I'm going to tell you another. I like you. I want to make love with you."

Andrea didn't blush this time. She'd expected this, in fact had asked for it. But *could she actually do it?* The alternative was masturbation, she knew- the triumph of stimulation over inhibition- her old standby. Three years of that wasn't very appealing though, and all she'd have to show from it at the end would be blisters on her fingertips. Pondering that thought, her inhibitions suddenly melted. She began removing her clothes and was amazed how liberating it felt. She giggled at the sight of her panties and bra dangling in space exactly where she'd placed them, and swam towards Anna's waiting caress.

The bed was tiny, of course, but it mattered little in zero G, for which she was grateful. As she ducked under the covers, Anna massaged her back, her arms and her inner thigh. She imagined she was someone else at first, someone who only looked liked Andrea but wasn't really her. Until the touch of Anna's fingers between her legs made it perfectly clear it *was* her and she was loving it.

"How wet you are," Anna whispered, "let me taste you."

"I can't believe I'm letting you," Andrea tried to whisper back until Anna cut her off with a hard kiss on the lips, then moved her mouth lower, to her neck, her breasts, her nipples and lower still. And as her body began moving in rhythmic spasms to the tip of Anna's tongue, she clenched the bed to keep from moaning and was struck by how easy this had been.

The sound of sex, though muffled, was unmistakable to Chris through the paper-thin adjoining walls. He'd been stirred by it before, from Vadim and Yoshi on the other side, but now it was coming from Anna's room. It moved him to masturbate. And for the first time since departure, he imagined making love to someone other than Tess.

****

MET: 108

Diarydisk Entry, Day 108,
Roberto Diaz

Last night I almost did Andrea, but thought better of it. She expects everyone with a cock to worship her and I won't. Tempting though, very tempting. HUMMS says she's predisposed to IDS (Isolation Dysfunction Syndrome) so I told her this story to test that. I need to know! She's overly sensitive, forgetful, and clumsy-an accident waiting to happen. Just what I need. I thought she had IDS in Antarctica, but I didn't reveal it then because we'd already lost Joanna. I couldn't, we couldn't risk another delay. Something else happened there too, which could bode trouble. A FirstEarth journal slipped from her bag while we were talking and she froze. When she recovered her explanation was ridiculous, full of nonsense. I will watch her every move now. Too much is at stake, the success of my, our entire mission. The story I told her was a good first step. We'll see how she reacts.

MET = 0109:11:21:00—MCC Burn, 109 days out.

The MOCR uplinked the delta V's for the Midcourse Correction burn early the next morning after the wake up call. Following breakfast, Vadim programmed them into the DAP (digital autopilot), and ordered everything secured. Someone failed to take note of a lemonade packet on the ceiling, however, and it smacked against the floor when the burn started. There must have been a tear in it, as lemonade splattered on Andrea's feet as she worked the NAV numbers.

"1 degree, 12 minutes," she reported, ignoring the lemonade. "Engine shutdown in 13 seconds and we're back on the money."

Yoshi performed the spin-up in record time following the burn. She paid excruciating attention to the tether slack, and there was no hitch like before. Even ADSS sounded better, more human, less metallic. She still kept her fingers crossed throughout the procedure.

Everyone welcomed the return of the 1/3 G after that, It brought feet back to the floor and slide-walking instead of floating, which they all preferred. Still, there was something about the zero G Yoshi would miss and she struggled to put her fingers on it. Was it the disappearance of wrinkles that took ten years off her face? Or the freedom of moving like a bird, in 3-dimensions instead of 2? Or the sheer joy of lightness of being? They were all part of it, she concluded, but not the most memorable part.

That had been lying in bed with Vadim. The very idea of it brought a smile to her face.

****

MET = 0112:17:00:00--Power fluctuations, 112 days out.

The power output had been nagging Vadim since Day 1. The readouts indicated surge, but it was sporadic with no pattern to it. He was convinced it was related to the comm drops, but couldn't prove it and the CWS didn't show it. No blinks, no numbers exceeding limits, no cause and effect. And because there'd been no consequence, the MOCR had played it down as well. "Westinghouse thinks it's the xenon-silicon chips on the solar panels," Adam had reported. "They say there can be power drift under high operating loads."

It had nothing to do with drifts, Vadim knew deep down. Drifts happened slowly, this had been step functions. But they'd been intermittent and fleeting step functions. Too fleeting to get a fix on.

"It's external," Vadim told Chris on the 112th day after another brief episode. "It's not coming from anything on our end, I'm convinced. It's from the outside, albedo, or something like it."

"Next you're gonna tell me sunspots?" Chris retorted.

"It's possible."

"Possible but not likely," Chris added quickly. "We both know the Sun's in Solar Minimum--the low point in its SPE cycle (Solar Particle Events). Those cycles last eleven years. They planned the mission for the lowpoints."

"Yeah, yeah, I know all about it. But that's just an average. There are out of family SPEs just like out of family stock market years. Never trust an average, that's what I say."

"Okay, I'll check the Particle Event Counter, if it'll make you feel better. I'll do a data dump and get a history."

"It will make me feel better. And while you're at it, get the GCR history too."

"C'mon, Vadim. Galactic Cosmic Rays have a constant flux. You're seeing a surge, not a constant."

"Maybe so, but they're heavier and have more energy than SPE's. It wouldn't take much drift to cause what I'm seeing."

"Alright, I'll do it, but it's a stretch."

"Maybe so, but do me a favor, as you Americans say, humor me."

****

Chapter 17--FirstEarth.

Science and politics are forces that don't mix.
Science depends on repeatability and peer review,
politics on the rule of the majority.
Long before the planet's systems buckle,
democracy will disintegrate under the stress of the two.

From the Heat is On

Tokyo, Japan

Jiro Hosokawa had had no need for school. Anything he needed to know, he taught himself. Some said he was a genius, others an idiot savant. The former cited his patents, the latter, the detritus he'd accumulated over the years: yellowed copies of Asahi Shinbuns crowding every corner of his home; mounds of electrical parts atop the Shinbuns like anthills; rusted out cars; mold growths in his refrigerator and overflowing garbage bags in his bedroom. The flotsam and jetsam of his life on the edge was everywhere, and with shadows under his eyes and a scowl etched on his lips, he was a social misfit. A samuri-style *chunghei* (ponytail) and teeth clenched in perpetual anger didn't help. His was an intimidating presence.

Even as a child, people steered clear of Jiro because of that presence. *That*, he could tolerate. Dismissing his intelligence, he couldn't. And so, he'd compiled a list of the worst *dismissers* who'd affronted him, both individuals and institutions, and vowed revenge. At the top of that list was the Japanese space agency, NASDA and its big brother, NASA. NASDA, he hated, because they hadn't even had the decency to respond to his employment inquiry years ago when he was still a naïve simpleton. NASA was far worse. They'd dissed not only him, but the rest of the world as well. They were at the forefront of the rebellion of the technocrats, a secret movement to overthrow the elected leaders of every industrialized state. Humankind was divided in two, the way they saw it, Those who made the technical breakthroughs, and everyone else who reaped the benefits.

The technocrats were smart, generous and kindly, while everyone else was stupid, stingy or evil. And since stupid, stingy and evil people reproduced with reckless abandon and elected stupid, stingy and evil leaders, they would always be a majority unless drastic steps were taken. Enter NASA's radical plan: to rid the planet of this human refuse and bring technocrats to power.

The process had already begun. Their mission to Mars was the first step, a misnomer if ever there was one. It should really have been called The Resettle Earth Movement and it was a disguised a form of ethnic cleansing. Not the Third Reich-kind based on extermination, but a kinder, gentler form where everyone who didn't fit would be sent as far away from Earth as possible. Jiro called it intergallactic busing, and everyone either looked the other way or laughed nervously when he brought it up, as they did with his other fantastical ideas. Never mind, he'd told himself from the outset, and buried his fury deep inside--fury at the technocrats, so condescending and dismissive, and fury at the others who wouldn't heed or follow him. It was that fury, the fury he couldn't bury, that eventually drove him to form FirstEarth: The party of environmental fanaticism. *His* party.

To an outsider looking in, FirstEarth seemed a force for good, a key to a greener planet. On introspection, its methods were Machiavellian.

To achieve its ends, Hosokawa would spare no means. His favorite was to stage environmental catastrophes and blame the "techno-scum" for the chaos that ensued. He smiled at the thought of his most insidious schemes: The acid rain of 2028, when he'd peppered rush hour traffic with sulfuric acid from a high flying Cessna; the nuclear panic of 29', when he'd polluted a public reservoir with pellets of nuclear waste; and his most recent, the nerve gas scare at the 2033 Japanese World Series in the Tokyo Dome. Instead of being reviled, however, he'd been elevated to hero status by these incidents, first by discovering" the threat, then by catching the "fiends" in the act. What the public didn't know was that they were *his* fiends. Martyred operatives, silenced with blind allegiance.

****

May 21st, 2034

As she walked past her Mars greenhouse to check for new growth, Tess was stopped in her tracks by dark spots on the lettuce leaves. She groaned and rifled through possible causes. Soil nitrogen was the first that came to mind. Nitrogen (in the form of potash and other minerals) was essential for photosynthesis, and the amount in the Martian soil would be critical. Tellingly, the 2012 Sample Return Mission indicated that the entire topsoil layer might have been baked into a dead zone by unrelenting radiation pouring through Mars' thin atmosphere for millennia. If true, the topsoil would be devoid of useful nitrogen and nothing would grow in it at all! To combat that possibility, Tess had labored mightily to create a startup mix using a soil substitute, and was working to refine it. As she guessed they would, the first seedlings from her lettuce plant had grown strong enough in the startup mix to send their root emissaries down through the dead zone to a nitrogen-rich layer beneath it and thrive there. Assuming such a sublayer existed on Mars, plants grown for food should thrive there as well. The mixture that Chris and his crew were carrying with them might have to be tinkered with based on her latest findings, but she derived great satisfaction knowing it would make them self-sufficient. A*ssuming that the sublayer existed.*

Tess chose lettuce for her first test crop because it was hypersensitive to soil nitrogen. Like the canary test for toxins, the slightest drop in Nitrogen levels would cause the lettuce leaves to turn brown. That was why nitrogen was such a good first guess for what had gone wrong. But it turned out to be the wrong guess. The spots didn't clear when she upped the levels, as they should have.

The next culprit could be the air, she suspected, kept at the same makeup as the air on Mars--95% carbon dioxide, 3% nitrogen, 2% argon and the rest trace gases. At the low pressures to be used in the Mars greenhouse, the plants would be especially susceptible to contamination in this makeup. Tess doubted that was the problem though. She prided herself on cleanliness and was obsessed with proper procedures. So as she prepared to analyze a greenhouse air sample, she did so skeptically. The results stood her on her heels. Her mass spec showed with a spike in carbon tetrachloride, cleaning fluid!

.

Starting with the door and windows, she began methodically inspecting all the seals that could have let it in. As she proceeded, it occurred to her that a tear in an O-ring, or break in a supply line that isolated the greenhouse from the outside world would only have let *outside air* in, not *carbon tet*. For that to happen required *both* a rupture *and* a carbon tet source. The odds of them occurring simultaneosly seemed impossibly low.

Hours later, after checking for leakage with no success, Tess turned to her old reliable, Herbert, the Helium Sniffer. Herbert was a device that could find even the tiniest leak by injecting isotope-labeled helium on one side of a source line, then looking for helium seepage on the other side using an isotope detecter. She usually used Herbert when all else failed, and in the miles of underground lines carrying gases or fluids through Biosphere 2, she'd used him often. But that was in Biosphere 2, not the Mars Greenhouse, which she'd personally designed and built almost singlehandedly.

The greenhouse was far smaller, cleaner and more reliable and should have been impervious to leaks. She shook her head sadly with delayed awareness. Wasn't it just like her to think that? That her greenhouse would be foolproofingly perfect? That was her dad and mom's thinking, not hers. Before that chemical spill had disabled him, her father, a scientist at Cryon, had done everthing just this side of perfect. And her prima donna mom was no slouch either, having started and sold 3 successful businesses: a nursery school, an antique shop and a line of women's lingerie. Yes, both of her parents were geniuses and she'd been raised thinking she was too. "There's nothing you can't do, if you've a mind to," her mother had drawled at her in that charming Louisiana accent for as long as she could remember. The reality had been more pedestrian. Yes, she'd accomplished much, but she'd done it through grit, perseverance and stubbornness, not genius. And though deep down in her gut she knew that, her first reaction on completing any project, be it hardware, software, a technical paper or even poetry, was the same as her mother's. "Suburb job," a little voice would whisper, "a truly suburb job". Fortunately, her parents had also given her a healthy sense of humor. So when supurb became good, fair, or even poor, as her piano playing had been, she learned to ignore that voice, and laugh at herself. It had served her well. It had kept her from becoming arrogant, and helped her to accept failure.

It was mid-day when she began working with those thoughts in her head, and with Herbert in her hands. She slowly worked her way downward from the shed that contained the Mars atmosphere canisters towards the greenhouse 200 meters away at the bottom of a hill.

The canisters fed the greenhouse through a tortuous, underground line that had to be inspected inches at a time. By dusk she'd covered less than half of it and realized she might be on a fools errand. For unlike her simulation greenhouse, the real one on Mars would leak *out*, not in because the pressure in it would be so much greater than the air outside. Even if carbon tet was there, which it couldn't be, it couldn't have gotten in!

It was precisely that moment, the moment she was about to pack Herbert up and leave, that the Sniffer's counter went off. Even if this couldn't happen on Mars, she decided to follow the chirps anyway because the detective in her--all scientists are detectives—wouldn't have it any other way. The chirps drove her onward, accelerating and tugging at her curiousity until they peaked at a barely visible clump of freshly packed dirt. She clawed at it with her spade, knowing the supply line would be less than a meter underneath, until she hit metal, then grabbed her flashlight. The soil, unremarkable to the naked eye at dusk, suddenly glinted with metal shavings under the beam. She continued to dig, more slowly now, until she exposed a section of the supply line. A closeup inspection revealed a tiny pinhole in its side, and less than a foot away, partly buried in soil, was a 5 cc syringe. Even before extracting the plunger and bringing it close to her nose, she knew what she would be sniffing. Cleaning fluid! Someone was deliberately poisoning her greenhouse! It was all the more shocking because of the senselessness of it. How dare they, she fumed as she began hatching up a plan. Whoever they were, they hadn't finished their job. She figured they'd be back and that's when she'd catch them.

The plan would work to perfection. Retreating to her lab, she concocted tiny capsules of fluorescene and placed dozens of them in the ground by the exposed supply line, then replaced the syringe, and repacked the soil. The intruder would never see the tiny capsules in the dark and when squashed underfoot, they would leave an indelible trail of purple footprints when lit up by blacklight at night.

Three nights later, the trail was as clear as a psychodelic poster, and led straight to Pete Drummand's laboratory. Drummand, a lab tech who fancied Tess and had once pursued her doggedly, had never forgiven her for rebuffing him. But to go to such extremes because of infatuation turned sour? Could it all be that simple? When Security grilled Drummand the next morning, and they found out it wasn't. Before being led away, Drummand sneered at Tess. "We've got other things in mind besides you, silly girl. Much more important things."

What did he mean by "we?" was her first reaction. Less then 24 hours later, she'd be sorry she asked.

MET: 114—Earth.

Oracle, Arizona, 6PM.

When her videophone chimed with no caller ID later that afternoon, Tess ignored her better judgement and answered it. The face on the other end froze her. It was Jiro Hosokawa's, a demon if ever there was one. She'd first met him at a conference when he was taking FirstEarth mainstream and she'd been impressed. She'd also been incredibly naïve back then. Shortly afterwards, he'd invited her to a fundraiser at a VFW hall in Phoenix. She'd accepted because she thought he could be an ally. She thought all environmentalists were allies in those days, but his event changed her mind. The sights and sounds of it had been eyeopening: Musty corriders; yellowed World War 2 posters, aging metal folding chairs, worn out curtains flanking a worn out stage, and she hadn't seen that much cigarette smoke in one place since the pubs she used to frequent as a teenager. But it was the mood that really unsettled her, somewhere between a religious right protest, a political rally, and a KKK march, replete with camouflage garb instead of white hoods and sheets. In keeping with that mood, the crowd reeked of revolution: armbands, badges, tattoos, pins, buttons and other paramilitary paraphernalia. The only thing missing were their AK47s.

Most unsettling of all was Hosokawa. Tess bore witness with eyes wide open as he played them like Casal's did his Cello, using smoke and mirrors to convince them that the world was being torn asumder.

The Pacific Ocean would rise 10 feet in the next ten years forning new coastline and beaches where inland cities used to be. The Sea to Shining Sea stanza from America the Beautiful, would have new meaning and Hosokawa had everyone sing it to underscore that message. Earth was in trouble, he had said again and again.

She hadn't disagreed with the message, but even back then, she saw through the halftruths, and there were many. And the solutions proposed--compulsory solar; forced public transport and unreasonable waste and water limits were dictatorial. But, "Something had to be done," he'd bellowed, "and fuck the rules if they got in the way," ?

To do that would take a lot more followers, however, an army of them, a country of them. More than he could possibly muster, Tess recalled thinking at the time.

But that was 9 years ago and he'd duped many people since then. Firstearth had grown in stature, and Hosokawa had become a major figure. And though he hadn't won an election yet, that was his ambition and he was shifting the balance of power. Republicans and Democrats alike were brokering deals with him and his influence was on the rise. It made his unexpected videocall all the more alarming. Why now, why me, Tess asked herself when she saw him on her screen.

His features had changed dramatically; he'd become more presentable with his increased notoriety. The scowl on his lips was gone, replaced by a soft smile; his *chunghei* had melded to a Jay Leno-like, salt and pepper coiffe suitable for a politician; his teeth were no longer clenched; and his skin was no longer pockmarked and rough. He seemed like a comforting, not an intimidating presence at first glance. But he couldn't hide the thinly veiled stare from his laser-focused eyes, the same disturbing gaze that had so unnerved her when they'd first met. It was the gaze of someone barely under control back then, and despite the massive makeover, it was unmistakeable now too.

"Nice to see you again, Dr Eliot," he smiled smoothly, "thanks for taking my call. I see the years haven't taken their toll on you as they have on me."

He went on making small talk, deliberately avoiding the bombshell he was about to drop for what for what seemed like forever, until …

"We're both very busy, so I'll get right to the point, Dr. Eliot. I've called to alert you to a problem you may soon be confronted with, a serious one. Now you probably know my attitude towards that Mars flight—a waste of precious resources. That said, I'm deeply concerned for the crew's safety, especially since one of them is your husband."

Tess could feel her heart pound, how did he know Chris was her husband? "What do you mean, their safety?"

"I have heard through my network that there's a saboteur onboard. That someone wants to make sure they fail."

"Y...you have evidence for this?"

"Such a thing could be easily arranged," he went on ignoring the question. "There are those fully capable of it. An eco-terrorist band such as the ELF, the Earth Liberation Front, for example. They would do something like this just to discredit me and FirstEarth. Think about it, Dr. Eliot. You remember Joanna Hewitt, who was removed from the mission last minute?" Well I happen to know she'd been infected with a biological agent. And the same people who did that also arranged her replacement, I suspect."

"I repeat, do you have proof of this?"

"Let's just say I have a big network. For example, I also know your greenhouse was infiltrated recently."

"H...how could you know that?" she said with growing anxiety.

"That's not important. What is important is that Mr. Peter Drummand is an ELF operative." Tess flashed on Drummand's words as he'd been led away from Biosphere 2.

"We've got other things in mind besides you, silly girl."

"Sorry to be the bearer of such news," Hosokawa went on, feigning concern, "but you might want to alert the authorities. I'd do so myself but I'm in a sensitive position now, you understand. I must appear to embrace this Mars cause for political reasons, even if I don't believe in it. I've got to go now but the rest is up to you. Goodbye, Dr. Eliot."

As Hosokawa's image faded, Tess first response was disbelief, then doubt. Sabotage, killers, eco-fanatics? It sounded like a bad sci-fi novel. Then she remembered some of the things Ed Cochran had said before his suicide, that there was a sabotage plot, that Brandford was in on it, and so was Andrea Beale. She began to feel faint. Her mind lurched to Chris and Columbus 11 and what to do

MET=0115:03:11 HOU=20:47 CANDOR=15:32 DELAY=03:00

Deep space: 33 million miles outbound

The midcourse correction burn had transformed the star field. Libra, Scorpio and Sagittarius, pillars in the intergalactic sky for weeks, had disappeared, swapped to the backside of the ship in exchange for Gemini, Taurus and Aries. Still, it took until Day 115 before anyone spotted the reddish blur out the windows. Anna saw it first, a vague pattern of crimson obscured by the ship's rotation. An unmistakable pattern, nevertheless. Target Mars had at last shown its face.

Chris couldn't wait to tell Tess. Sitting at his workstation while his downlink was being patched in, he hoped they'd stay locked this time. That he wouldn't have to walk away feeling cheated like the last three times when comm drop had frozen her words.

At her end, Tess waited anxiously too, the gaps in their video routine playing on her mind. They'd grown all the more frustrating for there was so much to say now that needed saying.

She flashed on their marriage again, thinking of little else since Hosokawa's call. Crazy and electric, it was, with more time spent apart than together, the touch of video screens replacing fngers, skin and lips Even their vows had been whimsical, and now he was off to Mars of all places. What difference would it make, she'd fooled herself into thinking beforehand? After all, a videocomm call is a videocomm call...be it from 3000 or 300,000,000 miles away.

She must have been delusional. The idea versus the reality was getting harder and harder to swallow. He was further away than any human being had ever been, and going to a hollow valley in a dead land. To a place barely a red twinkle in the evening sky.

And the interviews and the publicity; the unendingly asked questions; the rumors and inuendos had filled her world with turmoil since he'd left. The moment of launch, everyone wanted a piece of her. Wanting to know who *he* was, who *she* was, who *they* were. Ugh!

Then there'd been the signals:
The wave of blindness under the ozone hole, threatening to become pandemic. The escalating outages in the power grids, worldwide. The change in the Northern Lights, both in color and size. The disappearance of the cockroach, seemingly invincible

All that was in the background now after Hosokawa's call and the immediacy of addressing it. Columbus 11 had a sabateur aboard, he'd said, but what he hadn't said was far worse. Was only the mission's success in jeopardy or their lives? Or was it all just BS meant to sow disharmony. She'd had time to digest all this before Chris' comm call but uncertainy still riddled her. On the one hand there were too many holes in the sabatage story. Too many people had to be involved, too many to keep it secret.

On the other, Hosokawa could have paid Brandford off or blackmailed him; they could have recruited Andrea long before the selection process. Could those three alone pull this off?

No, that was a James Bond novel, not reality, she decided. Disruption, dissention, lies and halftruths were Hosokawa's calling card and that call fit his profile. He knew that if she told Chris, he'd tell the others and they'd all suspect each other. Suspicion caused conflict and the history of space travel was rife with such conflict. ISS Alpha and the Russian station *Mir* before it had been nearly undone by astronauts or cosmonauts stretched to the limit. Hosokawa would know all this, of course.

But did he actually think he could cause a mission abort with this cockamamie story? And why would he even try? To kill funding for space and divert it to his own schemes; to discredit technology and its consummate symbol? It was anyone's guess. Hosokawa was a nut case and nut cases were illogical. Regardless, dissention was more plausible than sabotage or murder, and far easier to execute. That was believeable, easier to fathom. It was also why she *wouldn't* tell Chris about the call until she'd hacked into FirstEarth's website. There might be clues there --perhaps Andrea would be on their membership roster, or evidence that Brandford was a donating sponsor. They'd be crazy to post such stuff, of course, but isn't that what they were? And if she did find something, shouldn't she alert the authorities before telling Chris, didn't that make more sense? But with his patch-in imminent, nothing made sense except: *How can I possibly hide such a thing from my husband*?

When his image appeared, it was rock-steady stable for a change. Decision time!

"Great to see you, honey," Chris began, "you look beautiful as ever. Sorry about the comm loss last week. Houston still thinks its weather related. I've something special to tell you.

We saw Mars tonight. The rotation makes it look more like a smudge than a planet, but it's got everyone's adrenalin going. We had a bet. Whoever spotted it first would get a double portion of your salad. Anna won.

Speaking of Anna, she asked me to ask you about the hole over Italy. Her mother's ill and she's afraid the UV might worsen it. Can you look into this for her? I really like Anna. We took a break last week after Encounter. Had a party to celebrate and she made me laugh. We even tried dancing in zero G if you can imagine that, but fell all over ourselves. There was hanky-panky afterwards. Not me, but, everyone else, I suspect. Not that I'm sorry, not even for a second. I'm married to the foxiest ..ssss...you've no idea how I miss you, baby. Things will be different when I get back, promise. You know that farm in Wyoming you've always wanted? It's yours, complete with chickens, bean sprouts and vegetables. Kids too, if you're willing. Still got that thermos on ice, don't you? You look a little tense, Tessie, everything ok? Can you hear me?" Better shut up so you can get a word in. Over."

Tess steeled herself to mask what she was thinking before she responded. Don't give it away, act normal; act happy, she told herself.

"I've had to get my news of you through Adam since the dropouts," she began, relieved he still looked healthy. "He keeps me posted, says you're doing fine. I do have a thought on the comm loss. I think it's from sulfate particles in the troposphere, not weather. They act opposite to greenhouse gases by scattering incoming radiation instead of absorbing it. Comm is electromagnetic radiation so there you go, that's my theory. As for Anna's mom, I'd get her out of Italy fast. The hole's really bad there and the UV is gettting worse. By the way, I am going to hold you to that promise about the farm, Elkay, I don't know about the kids but the thermos is on ice.

Watching the clock, she began rushing her words as if a scissors were about to cut them. She chattered about Closure 4 and how it was still going strong; about CASI and the new visitor's center at Biosphere 2, then the dead zone in the Gulf; the massive hurricanes; the droughts; Cousteau and the cockroaches, but her heart wasn't in it. Her mind was on that cursed call, nothing else. He'd surely notice if she didn't brighten up coz her anxiety was through the roof. She forced another smile and babbled on about the Red Sox, his favorite baseball team, kissed the screen and waited for his return volleyj, spending the intervening time watching the clock tick down and thinking what to say next?

There'd be 3 minutes of lag time before he'd come back to her, three tormented minutes to wonder if he'd seen her falling apart. Three minutes of pulling at her hair, tearing at her fingers, clasping her hands so tightly they ached. How could she not tell him about the call? On the other hand, what harm could come from waiting a week while she dug into FirstEarth's files? Over and over, the persistent and agonizing question circled her mind, what to do, what to say.

When his image came back, he looked so upbeat, his eyes, so alive and dancing, his smile, like a sunbean; even his hair, floating in reduced gravity, playful and carefree.

She would tell him how much she needed and missed him; and yes, about that damned call. She knew when she did, she'd surely bring him down, ruin his obvious joy. Yet as he started talking, she knew she had no choice. There was no way she could keep this from him. He was her soulmate. Static did the job for her. His image jerked suddenly to pieces. He was gone!

****

Thirty-three and a half million miles away, Chris fumed at the LOS. He'd been in such a good mood, wanting to douse her in his highs, reassure her, flirt with her. Instead he'd been cut off again. Disgusted, he made his way to the Bridge, where he found Vadim, who already knew about the problem.

"This drop out's different this time," Vadim informed him somberly. "The S-band just quit, *yolki—palki*, we've lost high-gain! "

Chris looked at him incredulously. "What do you mean, lost it?"

"The antenna's lost steering lock, we can't train on Earth. The 1.6 and 2.4 gigahertz frequencies are useless, *der'mo*."

"What about the other antenna?"

"We've got 1.6 on the low gain but there's static."

"Static?"

"Yes, intermittent, like some kind of interference."

"From where?"

"I don't know but not from Earth. It's omnidirectional and coming in waves, like from a pulsar or quaser."

"Maybe it's from Mars," Chris snapped sardonically.

“This is no time for jokes, Chris, the 1.6 is a telemetry-only channel and there’s no S-band."

"What's that all mean?"

"It means no voice, no video, it means we’ve got a problem, a big one. Scramble everyone, I need them up here right away."

Vadim was soon repeating the news to the rest of his crew as they gathered around the wardroom table. "High-gain's lost steering," he reiterated. "We can't lock on Earth, we can’t transmit or receive high bit rates. Low-gain's ok but jammed with static, meaning we’ve effectively lost all comm. Loss of comm is grounds for abort, it's a mission rule. I need ideas and I need them fast. Roberto, you first."

"Maybe I’m naive," he responded sarcastically, "but if the high gain's stuck, I say we go unstick it. Anna and I have been trained for EVA. Let’s just go do it."

"Negative!" Vadim snapped back. “In-flight EVA's are risky. As our medical officer, you should know that. We’d also have to de-spin and I won’t do that unless I have to.”

"I agree,” added Anna. “Unlike Roberto, I'm not anxious for an EVA. We should wait, maybe the antenna will free itself. "

"Anna’s got a point,” Chris broke in, “and there may be a way to help it. That antenna's been in shade since the MCC burn, it’s probably near absolute zero. We can reorient the platform to face the Sun and heat it up. If temperature’s the problem, heat will free it."

“Good idea, I like it."

"Yes, but we’d need an attitude change,” Yoshi countered, “and for that we'd have to de-spin anyway."

"Aren't you forgetting something?" chimed in Andrea. "The static on the 1.6 low gain is intermittent. That means there's got to be a calm period when we can send a message. I can digitize one with the laser scanner and transmit it to Houston as telemetry."

Vadim looked at her puzzled. "I'm not following."

"Think of a bar code. I can make one up using light/dark lines that our scanner will read as ones and zeroes. All the MOCR needs to read it is a scanner on their end. And if they can read it, there's comm. No?“

“And the mission rule's not violated,” Anna interjectedk “Brilliant, Andrea.”

"You think they'll decode it," Roberto wisecracked, “by reading your mind? Even if they could, what good would it do? They can't beam themselves up here to fix that antenna, only we can do that.”

"This buys us time for that,” Vadim countered. If it doesn't work, we'll do the attitude change, de-spin and barbeque. If that doesn't work, it's EVA. If that doesn't work, we'll get Houston involved. That's it, that's the game plan! Go to it, Andrea!”

In less than an hour Andrea's bar code was complete.

```
 1              2      3        4          5          6
 |'|||  |'||'  ||'''  |'|||
 ||'''  ||||'  |'||'  |'''|
 '||''  '|'||  ||'|'  ||'|'  '||'|  |'||'
 |'''|  ||'''
 |'|'|  ||||'  |''|'  |''|'  ||'|'  ||'||
 |''||  |''''  '|'''
 ||'''  ||||'  |'||'  |'''|
 '||''  '|'||  ||||'  '|'||  |'||'  |||''
 ||||'  ||'||  '|''|  |'||'  '||''  ||'|'
```

With its sensitivity adjusted to see only the short, stubby lines but not the long, thin ones, *Columbia's* scanner would convert the long lines to zeroes and the short ones to ones. Taken in sequence at their end, the MOCR would read the matrix as:

01000 01001 00111 01000
00111 00001 01001 01110
10011 10100 00101 00101 10010 01001 01110 00111
01010 00001 01101 01101 00101 00100
01100 01111 10111
00111 00001 01001 01110
10011 10100 00001 10100 01001 00011
00001 00100 10110 01001 10011 00101

Hopefully they'd know the code was in binary and that 00001 meant 1; 00010 meant 2, 00011 meant 3 and so on. That it was an alphabetic code and that 1 stood for "a", 2 for "b", 3 for "c" through the alphabet.

Translated properly, it would read, "HIGH GAIN STEERING JAMMED, LOW GAIN STATIC. ADVISE."

Translated properly. If they were smart enough.

****

Chapter 18--Storm and Storm

MET = 0118:00:00:00.

Two days later there'd been no reply to the message, forcing them into fallback position 1-- de-spining and facing the Sun. That didn't work either. It not only failed to free the S-band antenna, it aggravated matters. The static on the 1.6 low gain went from sporadic to constant. EVA became the last fallback option, the only option.

EVA or Extravehicular Activity had been performed many times in the past. In the 60's on the Moon; in the 80's to fix broken satellites, in the 90s to save the Hubble Space Telescope and in the first decade of the new century to build Space Station *Alpha.* Walks in zero G space were still risky, however. They required cumbersome spacesuits with limited dexterity and complex systems, systems that could fail. Anna and Roberto knew this full well as they reviewed their suit-up procedures. Just as they knew they'd been chosen for the EVA because they were the ones most expendable. The journey could go on without them. If something happened, they'd be least missed.

Vadim, as prime pilot, commanded the mission.
Yoshi backed him up and doubled as ship doctor.
Andrea was prime navigator and knew the computers best.
Chris was prime astrogeologist and could also back up Andrea.
Whatever Anna and Roberto did *could be done by someone else.*

Their suits were waiting for them when they got to B-deck, hanging from the donning station with their rear entry openings agape. Chris and Andrea had already charged them with 8 hours of life-support and were nearby to assist. The sight of them hovering in the microgravity that had returned with de-spin did nothing to allay Anna's fears. Neither did the countless hours she'd spent in training. As many times as she'd rehearsed in the NBL (Neutral Buoyancy Lab); the KC-135 Vomit Comet; the Link Simulator called Murphy's Module; and in JSC's SESL, she still knew it had been gameplaying. Games conveyed how space felt, not how it was.

Her suit's aluminum-composite torso beckoned as she neared, with its swingaway back wide open. The innards of that back held tubes, pipes and heat exchangers that would keep her alive once in space. It was called the PLSS, (for Portable Life Support System), and stared at her as if to say, *"let's see what you got"*. All she could think of was another impending bout of claustrophobia.

Before getting into the suit, she put her Liquid Cooled Garment (LCG) on. It would control her body temperature with the turn of a knob, like a personal air conditioner. Without it, her work capacity would be crippled, a lesson learned from the old Gemini Program when air-cooled suits had pushed astronauts to the brink of hyperthermia. The LCG's water circulating tubes pressed deep against her skin after she slipped the bio-med sensors under them and zipped it up, making her feel like a pin cushion. Next she placed a conformal cup over her vagina and hooked it to a urine bag on the leg of her LCG.

She did it shyly and tentatatively while Roberto made a similar connection to the condom on his penis almost brazenly. No place for modesty here, his actions announced.

With their their undergarments in place, they floated above and into the rear-entry openings but needed Chris and Andrea to direct their feet through the leg holes of the lower torso. As tight as they were, the upper torso entry rings were even harder. Their heads had to be squeezed through the neck rings while their arms had to be snaked through the shoulder rings. Again Chris and Andrea helped them, taking care not to pinch, push or crimp skin or hair. Finished, they then connected their water, air and electrical lines and placed the Snoopy Caps on their heads. The caps, honoring Charley Brown's cartoon character, would keep their hair out of their eyes and contained their microphones, sensors and food bars. A silver Snoopy was one of NASA's highest awards and a good luck charm, Anna recalled. She hoped she wouldn't need any luck, but her claustrophobia told her differently. It was already surfacing. *Take deep breaths,* she told herself*, take deep breaths.*

The LCG

SUITING UP FOR A SPACEWALK

A spacesuit weighs approximately 280 pounds on the ground (nothing in space) and it takes 45 minutes to put it on. The astronaut must spend a little over an hour breathing pure oxygen before going outside in order to adapt to the lower pressure maintained in the spacesuit

1. Put on **liquid cooling** and **ventilation** under-garment.
2. Put on **lower torso** (trousers).
3. Prepare **upper torso**.
4. Climb into **upper torso**.
5. Make sure **under-garment thumb loops** are properly adjusted.
6. Connect cooling **water umbilical** to backpack and join suit halves.
7. Put on **communications carrier** also known as a "snoopy cap."
8. Test and adjust **oxygen flow** in suit.
9. Put on **gloves**, snap and lock connecting rings.
10. Put on **helmet** and start oxygen breathing adaptation.

Thumb loop

Conecting ring

Oxygen regulator

Sources: NASA. The Space Shuttle Operators Manual

ALBERTO CUADRA : CHRONICLE

Take deep breaths

Anna glanced at Roberto, suspicious of him as always. What if something goes wrong out there, *could she count on him?* Andrea had the same thought as she led his 500 pounds of flesh, suit, and cables towards the Bridge as one might lead a dirigible, as did Chris, towing Anna, who wished he was going out instead of Roberto.

The airlock was visible when the entourage floated into the Bridge, exposed at the end of a short tunnel Vadim had uncovered by removing a hatch in the ceiling. Vadim looked on in silence as Chris and Andrea rotated the red capture latches clockwise on Roberto and Anna's gloves to lock them to their wrist rings, then filled their in-suit drink bags with electrolyte punch; secured the TV cameras to their helmets, plugged one end of their life support umbilicals into a suit connector and handed them the free end.

"Don't plug it into the airlock wall until the door's sealed," Yoshi piped in dryly. "Don't wait too long either or you'll go hyperthermic. Once you're on umbilical life support, stay on it till you're sure the PLSS is working. I want full comm at all times, is that understood? Call out every step in the Depress Sequence until you're disconnected and out the door. Let's review the checklist."

"Plug into the panel for umbilical power and oxygen," Roberto shot back from memory. "Next we put on the helmets, lock them to our neck rings and verify comm with each other and you. INIT on our DCMs tells the suit to initiate the Depress Sequence. We monitor pressures, flows, temps and caution warning to verify normal operation. When the display reads zero pressure, we cross-check it against our cuff gauge and the airlock indicator to verify hard vacuum.

We don't unplug the umbilicals until the READY light flashes, then it's unlock the door and out," he finished.

"You've got to be in the airlock at least 30 minutes for nitrogen washout," Yoshi added, "not a second less."

"Of course," he retorted, "I know about the bends, I'm the flight doc."

"*Volgaire salaud* (asshole), listen to her," Vadim responded. "She's just making sure. And one more thing, both of you. Keep your chatter active and your cameras on. I want to see and hear you at all times, is that clear? That's it then, watch yourselves."

The rest of them shared the same concerns as the two floated up into the passageway. Roberto *was* an asshole and Anna looked petrified.

"PLSS ONE umbilical to 02 CONNECT," Roberto sounded off over the loop after he'd closed the airlock door behind him moments later.

"PLSS TWO umbilical to 02 CONNECT," Anna repeated dutifully.

There was no voice contact for minutes after that, only a series of beeptones and hisses, accompanied by rhythmic breathing. When chatter resumed, it chronicled each step in the depressurization sequence culminating with Roberto reporting, "Zero pressure, door open." Forty minutes after they entered the airlock, they stepped out into "el negro del negro," he whispered in awe. "The blackest black I've ever seen."

"TV!" Vadim scolded him as only a fuzzy likeness of Anna appeared on his monitor. "Do you have your helmet light on, we can't see Anna."

"Negative," he said sheepishly, "standby…is that better?"

"Affirmative, how do the suits feel?"

"Warm," Anna complained, "and I can see steam coming off the top of my PLSS. There's a cloud of it around me. Is normal?"

"Is normal, Anna," he reassured her. "That's feedwater dumping through the porous plate and sublimating. It's how you keep cool." She should have known that, he worried, and that it would disappear when the ice layer built up. More reason for concern. "Crank your cooling up if you're warm Anna. How about you, Roberto?"

"I'm fine, A-OK. We're heading towards the platform now, can you see us?"

"Affirmative. How's the movement?"

"As advertised, just like at the NBL. The visibility's bad though, hard to see the footholds. We're coming up on the engine pods…huff. Got to flip around to.. huff…get past them. Standby. You might lose us for a minute."

Hearing accelerated breathing, Vadim looked to Yoshi for input. Glued to their bio-meds, she counted breaths for indications of hyperventilation while checking pulse and blood pressure.

"Anna's high," she reported to Vadim, "18 BPM to 12 for Roberto; her pulse and BP are also high, 110 and 140 over 85."

"Should we be concerned?"

"Not yet. It's psychogenic, stress. Let her get used to it. Her EKG's normal, no PVCs. Try to relax her, I think she'll be ok."

“How you doing, Anna? Doctor Yoshioka thinks you need calming down. That so?"

"Okay, a little nervous, that’s all."

"Don’t worry, the best flight doc in the universe is watching you, right Yoshi? Where are you now, video's blurred again."

"By the rear pod, in back of the ball,” Anna whispered barely audible. Roberto's coming out from behind the engines now."

"We see him. A little louder on the comm. please, Anna. How about a PLSS status check?"

Anna reached for the DCM (Display Control Module), the little box on her chest that she’d have to program to get the numbers Vadim sought, and ran through the sequence on its keypad. But she failed the first time through when her bulky, pressurized, gloved fingers fumbled across its keys, hitting two instead of one. Embarrasssed, she wished it was like the Mars suits, which provided the status by voice response instead of keys but knew such technology couldn’t be justified on a transit suit that might only be used once. Summoning up the patience of Job, she repeated the sequence a second and third time until her HUD (Heads Up Display) finally sprung to life. Numbers projected across her inside of her faceplate in irredescent orange, and she read them off one by one.

“Okay, suit pressure, 8.1 psia; pCO2, 6 millimeters; vent flow 6 cfm; battery, 14.9 volts; leak rate, 75 cc/minute, LCG temp, 16°C.”

“How does the suit feel?” Yoshi cut in, guessing the last number, the Liquid Cooled Garment inlet temp, which controlled her body temperature, might be too high.

“I dunno,” Anna replied, “this suit still feels warm.”

"Where is your diverter valve set?" Yoshi asked. "If it's not in AUTO, I suggest you turn it there."

"Copy, going to AUTO," Anna responded, and a few seconds later added, "***Mi Dio***, that was it! Reading 9 degrees C. *Sciocco*, I'm not warm any more. Grazie, Yoshi."

"Are you at the platform yet?" Vadim interceded.

"Si, yes, almost. Roberto's already there, working. Standby, I snagged my lifeline, trying to huff, clear it...huff."

Rustling noises followed and once again, Vadim glanced at Yoshi.

"High 02 flow, tympanic core at 38.8," Yoshi grumbled.

"What's all that mean?"

"Her met rate and heat storage are up."

"What do we do?"

"Wait for that LCG to cool her off. She's not in performance impairment yet."

"OK," Anna came back shortly, sounding more at ease, "It's free. It was caught on the engine pod. I'm at the platform now with Roberto. He's at the S-band antenna. Can you see him? He's found something."

Robert's voice suddenly pierced through the TV images, which remained dark and shaky. "*Ay caramba*, there's mylar in there," he exclaimed excitedly. "Mylar tape is caught in the swivel housing... hisssssssss in the steering motor."

"Say again," Vadim queried quickly.

"There's a ribbon of mylar wound around the drive motor. You're not going to believe this, but it's from *Eagle*. There's a long strip of it dangling down from her. It must be at least 20 meters long. "

"*Novy gode*! Are you sure?"

"Affirmative. It must have popped out a bulkhead, then found its way to the swivel housing."

"How the hell could it have done that?"

"*No lo se*, I've no idea. Maybe someone left a door open."

"No one left a door open, Roberto, but *someone did something*. How much life support do you have left?"

"Stand by, let me query. Okay, I read 7.2 hours, feedwater, 6.9 oxygen, 8 power and 6.8 on the scrubber."

"How long will it take you to climb up to *Eagle* to check this out?"

"Hmmm. It's a guesstamate but I'd say hour to climb up there, an hour to find where that tape is coming from, an hour to climb down and an hour contingency. That makes four. That's plenty of time. I've got nearly 8 hours."

"I'll give you 4, amigo. I want you and Anna back in the airlock at four thirty five on the EVA clock, comprende?"

"Okay, Capitan, you're the boss. I copy. What about Anna, where do you want her while I'm doin all this?"

"Untangling mylar at the housing if she can. Do you copy that, Anna?"

" ssssss…"

"Say again, Anna, we've got dropout on the loop."

"...sssssss Si, I copy."

Vadim turned his head to Yoshi and shook his head at the static. As if we don't have enough going on."

****

Roberto scaled *Columbia* towards *Eagle* using the strategically placed handholds and footholds that had been placed there for just such a contingency. He followed the mylar trail as he proceeded, knowing a single misstep could send him into the abyss that surrounded him and swallow him up like a black hole. As he ascended, Anna tore mylar from the S-band housing, thinking she could lead it out in a single strand, like fishing line from a reel. She was wrong. It kept breaking off in shreds.

"There's meters of this tape in here," she puffed at Vadim, her frustration evident.

"Don't rush," he cautioned her, "we'll do another EVA tomorrow if we have to, and one after that. Can you still see Roberto, he's out of camera view again."

"Ssssst....sssst...."

"You're breaking up, Anna."

"I sssssss, he's ok, fine!"

Roberto made quick progress. He'd been a mountaineer in his younger days, and had climbed El Capitain at Yosemite during mission training, He made to *Eagle* in only 51 minutes, ten minutes ahead of schedule, and was proud of himself and wanted to brag, But he couldn't because the comm. was even worse up there and he couldn't get through. He ought to stay put, he knew, since Vadim had *told* him to do so, but that would waste valuable time, life support, and the outstanding job he'd done at getting there so fast. Besides, he couldn't raise Vadim so what the hell difference would it make if he went on, he reasoned. Vadim felt otherwise. When nearly an hour passed with no word from either of them, he'd had enough, and prepared to don a suit and go after them. He'd just started towards the airlock when the static suddenly cleared and Roberto rejoined the loop with a flourish.

"*Mierda, el diablo*! I know where that tape came from!"

"Copy," Vadim sighed scrambling back to his seat with relief.

"*Yo no creo*! A tile's popped off *Eagle*. There's an opening smack dab in the middle of the cavity it left behind. The tape's coming out of that hole."

"**What?**" Vadim shot back.

"It's an access hole. There was a plug meant to be in it but it's gone too. At least it's just a hole and not a puncture. Guess we should be grateful for the small stuff."

Vadim flashed on a scene at the MVAB upon hearing this, where H had demonstrated the strong and weak points of aerogel tile years ago.

"They'll keep you from becoming toast during Mars entry," H had said, "and they're superlight, good to 3000 degrees and easy to replace. But, the fuckers are fragile as eggshells," he'd added, and with that, he'd poked a hole in one with his index finger to prove the point. It was a point Vadim had never forgotten. And if this missing tile was in a Criticality 1 spot, the aluminum skin cavity exposed by it would be vulnerable. If the temperature reached 3000 degrees *there*, in fact, the skin could melt causing a burn-through, an explosive decompression and, in H's words, 'a very bad day.'

"**Is it Crit One**?" Vadim nearly shouted over the loop to Roberto. "**Is it Crit One**?"

"How the hell should I know?" came the defensive response. "All's I can tell you is it's a six by six cavity in the A128 quadrant."

Vadim's heart sank. The A128 quadrant *was* a Crit One region, meaning an area of maximum heating. And a six-inch square cavity in that region *would be vulnerable indeed.* Thankfully they had a tile repair kit on board. The only question now was would it work?

"Pick up Anna and get back here ASAP," Vadim ordered, rolling those thoughts through his head. As he did so, he could only speculate how the tile had been knocked off: vibrations at Encounter; a poor epoxy bond; crappy QC? He'd probably never know. As for the tape, a roll of it must've been left in an external bulkhead by some careless tech and when the plug in the middle of that access hole became dislodged, maybe from the same vibrations, the free end of that tape had been sucked through the access hole like soda through a straw. The rest of the roll must've unraveled like a ball of string from there, magically finding its way to the S-band antenna and jamming the housing. It was a crazy, illogical sequence of events and it might have killed them, as that small piece of foam had killed the Columbia astronauts 15 years ago. That had been a freak accident from a freak chain of events that had gone undetected. But this, they *had* detected, thank goodness, and he was relieved and proud of his crew, even Roberto. He smiled momentarily at the string of seemingly unrelated events that had occurred, smiled again at the cleverness of his analogy, strings of mylar, strings of events, then felt his muscles tighten up. Unrelated, they might be, but the events were nothing to smile about.

****

Oracle, Arizona

Three days after Chris' image had vaporized, Tess blinked at the sunrise yet again with concern. She hadn't heard a word from anyone, not even Adam Brady. This was unusual. The Capcom nearly always called after comm loss, maybe not that day, but the next at the latest. Something was amiss, she knew, something serious. At first she felt helpless, like the other times, but that quickly turned to guilt, then shame. She'd kept that call from Chris, that fucking stupid call. Why, for what, she kept asking herself. She tried to take her mind off it by playing with CASI, checking reports, dealing with the Closure but nothing worked. Finally, after cleaning up her lab and checking on Chris' *sperm bank*, as she jokingly called it, she decided to do something constructive: scour the Firstearth website, debunk the conspiracy theory as she'd planned on doing in the first place. It might be pointless but at least it would make her feel better. But where to start, what to look for? Andrea Beale on their membership roster, Brandford, an active sponsor? They'd be crazy to post such stuff, but isn't that what they were? Wearily, she made her way to her computer and punched FirstEarth into Google.

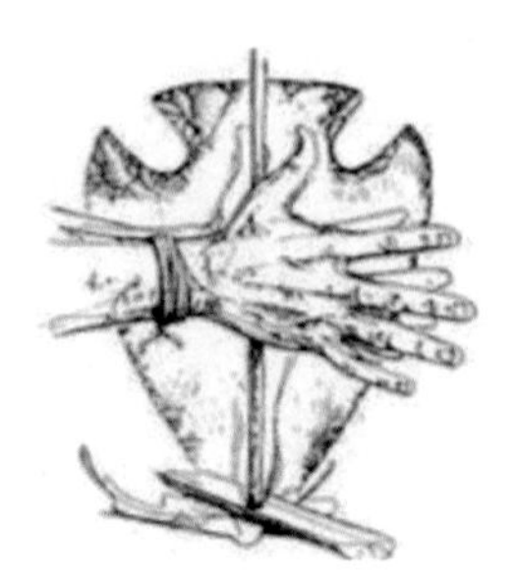

First Earth,

The name First Earth represents a time when humankind walked in balance with the earth, as a member of the natural community instead of its master. Modern civilization's indifference toward nature in pursuit of wealth and "progress" has resulted in an environmental legacy that may prove to be globally disastrous in the near future, and if we are to survive as a species, we must develop a sustainable culture that doesn't consume the planet for material gain. Learning the ancient ways can re-awaken our awareness... Recognizing the sacred gift of our food plants and animals...and sleeping under the stars can re-aquaint us with the miracle of "the spirit that moves in all things."

The website surprised Tess: There were courses on survivalship with funny names followed: Rabbitstick, Wintercourt and Bois D'Arc Rendesvous; and pictures of people sitting around camfires with Indian medicine men (Hosokawa wasn't among them). And there were no membership lists, radical policies or signs of ill intent. Must be the wrong site, she figured, so she went to a second website, then a third, fourth and so on with similar results. She was blown away, there was nothing!

At first she felt relieved. Hosokawa's story had been nonsense, and she'd done the right thing by not troubling Chris with it. But doubts set in again when she thought about Firstearth. Would an operation its size led by a madman with Hosokawa's ego have piddley ass websites like the ones she'd just seen? Of course not! It would be impressive, convoluted and angry. Unless that madman wanted to hide his motives because they were so nefarious! Now she was back to square one, vacillating and mindfucking herself again. She should have told Chris when she had the chance. she shouldn't have; the call was a bluff, it wasn't.

She understood then that this wasn't about Chris at all, it was about her. It was her job to protect him, no one else's. And no matter how far away he was, that's what she would do.

****

MET = 0119:00:00:00. Thirty four million miles from Earth

A printout of bar lines arrived while they slept, on the 1.6 telemetry channel, the only one working. It lay on a tray begging to be noticed, until Andrea finally saw it, well after breakfast. She jumped at the sight of it.

"It's from the MOCR," she yelped excitedly at the others. "They got my message, they replied to it."

"*Ohuyeviyusche!*" Vadim proclaimed, "We can communicate!"

But he grew anxious when he saw the odd pattern on the paper, the response to their query that Anna might not be able to decode. "Not a problem," she reassured him, "it's the same code I used." He still had his doubts. Roberto had clued him in to a strange habit Andrea had when she was unsure of herself—her eyebrows arched—and they were half moons now. His concern grew further when she sat down at a console with the note. She began playing with her hair, braiding and twisting it in knots then flipping it in a cadence that bordered the obsessive. He pondered his backup plan again, the one he dreamt up when Roberto was up at *Eagle*: they'd fabricate a cavity plug and replacement tile from the onboard repair kit; then do another EVA with Roberto installing them, and Anna extracting the mylar from the antenna to restore S-band. It was a good plan. They'd be whole again and could press on. It was such a good plan, in fact, that he began not to give a shit about the message from the MOCR. After all, the only thing those guys could do was bless his plan or send them home. Home would mean going all the way to Mars before turning back since they didn't have enough fuel to simply reverse direction. It would mean getting close enough to almost touch and smell the surface without actually doing it, then arcing around in a painful turtured swing back to Earth. He couldn't handle that. No way. He'd come too fucking far to abort and be a laughing stock the rest of his life. The man who got close enough to Mars to taste it only to be sent back home by fucking *muzhiks*. On the other hand, those guys back home were pretty smart, smart enough to come up with another option he may not have considered. Maybe he should give them the benefit of the doubt, at least this once. *What the fuck's with Andrea*, he suddenly thought, and went over to bug her.

She stood when she saw him coming, dangling the note in front of him, almost, teasing him with it. But it wasn't a tease, he realized soon enough, it was hesitancy born of defeat. She handed it to him and he was perplexed. It was a hodgepodge of words with missing letters, a senseless anagram.

SOL F A E. EX R E Y DA GE S. G T ST M HELT R

"Some of it must have got cut off," she apologized sad-eyed. "I did my best, but English is my second language. Maybe Chris can do better, you should give it to him." She looked like she wanted to cry.

Vadim tried hard to look disappointed, but couldn't carry it off. He'd wanted this. Deep down, he wanted Andrea to fail because he wanted to be in charge, not the MOCR. The good soldier he was though, he did give the anagram to Chris, crossing his fingers that he'd have no more luck than Andrea. Chris didn't. It was official. They'd have to execute *his* plan now. Their fate *was* in his hands.

The EVA started smoother this time, shaving nearly 20 minutes off the time to reach the platform. "Step One complete," Anna reported brightly over the loop after hour one. Her voice, unimpeded by static for a change, sounded loud, clear and triumphant. "The tape, she is out, the antenna, she is clear."

" *Zdrastvui zhopa*, well done," Vadim replied. "Now back off and get out of the way, Anna. I'm going to activate the drive motor."

She watched the dish jiggle and begin tracking a slow arc towards a patch of stars moments later, until it stopped at a small bluish orb near the edge, barely discernable- Earth. Anna suppressed a smile, certain they'd be raising the MOCR soon, then trained her helmet cam on Roberto, still ascending towards Quad A128 on *Eagle*. But he was in the shade and she was in the sun so she couldn't pick him up. Her job mostly finished, she decided to sit down on the platform, dangle her knees at deep space and bask in the moment. Inside her earpiece she could hear Vadim querying the MOCR, "Houston, *Columbia*, how do you read, how do you read? We've fixed the problem." The certainty in his voice resonated through her helmet, confidence personified. Most of her life, she'd been saddled with doubt and longed for such confidence. But in the aftermath of success, she'd found it, here, in deep space, on the platform. She calculated the minutes to the expected return volley, six and counting and decided to meditate. Take in the stars, exhale, enjoy.

Inside the Bridge, Vadim fidgeted next to Yoshi, waiting and watching, watching and waiting until 7 minutes came and went. Two more passed in dead silence with the pinprick of excitement sequeing to the dull ache of disappointment.

He was about to say something when the clicking of static made him jump, the same static that usually preceeded contact. He readied to hear Adam, but more static came instead, followed by a sustained burst of clicks. They had a timbre of their own, he realized, a frequency and amplitude like none he'd ever heard. As more minutes passed, their nature changed, becoming higher pitched and whistle-like. "**Sssst....wsssst.....whesssst. whesssst.... whesssst......**"

Anna heard them too outside, and tried to call in but couldn't. The whistles were so intense, she could hardly hear herself think, much less talk. She began to sense concern, but breathed easier when Roberto's voice suddenly pierced the loop, loud and clear.

"Ufff...I'm here," he said proudly, "I'm at *Eagle* at the Quad. The cavity looks uff...okay. Got the...huff...tape out of the hole, snipping it off and...ufff, sticking it back in. Okay, hole's clear now. Proceeding with...huff...plug insertion. Squeezing epoxy around...huff...perimeter, inserting repair plug. Okay, it's setting up and holding.

Step 2 complete, going to Step 3."

The report riveted Vadim's attention. *"Ohuyeviyusche!"* he chimed back overjoyed and relieved. "Fucking A good job, Roberto."

"Muchas gracias," said Roberto, crystal clear and huffing, "how's Anna doing?"

"Anna, you copy?" Vadim queried in response, "Give us your status."

Anna heard "copy," but not the rest of it due to static. The whistles had returned with a vengeance, even louder.

Yoshi yanked her headset off. The bursts had become so loud they were nearly deafening her. She waited ten minutes before putting her headset back on, whereupon Roberto came in again asking after Anna loud and clear. Its either the transmitter or the location, she began to suspect about Anna's comm. issue, then homed in on the platform. Roberto, too, had been muffled there before his ascent. Now he wasn't.

"The trackers, gyros or motors, any one of them could be causing this," she told Vadim. "That's got to be the source of it, the platform."

"Maybe," he replied admiringly. "I'll have her move away to test that. If you're right, she should come in clear, right?"

"Unless she can't hear your request. Roberto should try. He might have better luck reaching her."

"Good thought, I"ll ask him."

Anna copied nothing when Roberto complied, only the whistling, ever louder. Her eardrums ached so, she decided to mute her comm. knob, and wait it out. The interference would abate sonner or later. Sitting on the porch of the platform, space's vastness suddenly struck her, its trillions of stars buttering an infinite slice of black toast as far as she could see. She felt naked out there, the majesty before her humbling everything she'd ever known. Feeling tinier even, than an amoeba on the head of the tiniest pin, Anna saw nothing and everything on the brink of the porch, until a new burst of static assaulted her. Her ears rang from it, even with her volume muted all the way down. How could that be, she asked herself?

Another sensation soon followed, a warm pulsing inside her suit, localized around her torso.

Anna on the brink!

Reflexively, Anna reached for her LCG cooling knob to dial in more cooling. It was already maxed out, with 42 degree water surging against her skin. *I should be freezing, yet I'm hot, she thought. Maybe the suit's failed.* She quickly checked the DCM readouts and all systems were normal. A premonition overcame her then. Something else might be wrong, Something terrible.

The claustrophobic feeling that had cursed her all her life resurfaced, worse than yesterday, worse than ever, palpable. It was crushing her chest, making her gulp air, and jumbling up her words until all she could get out was a plaintive cry, "Can you read me, Vadim? Come in, please, Vadim. Come in."

It was then that she glanced at her glove and noticed an indigo iridescence. It emanated from her wrist ring and was pulsing. How pretty, she thought first, then saw the pale blue aura also coming from her camera. She turned around to look at the platform then and noticed the same glow around the Star Trackers, the telescope mount and the antennae. Two plus two reached four when she saw it surrounding every metal part. Only then did she suspect that the stifling heat she felt was related to the glow. She suspected it the same moment Yoshi realized Anna was in sunlight and Roberto in shade. The moment she knew that the source of the static was the Sun, not the platform. The moment an ECLSS alarm suddenly triggered with a piercing wail and an on-screen warning:

SPE--3000 REM: SPE--3000 REM: SPE--3000 REM:

"***No sankyu, iesu erai,***" Yoshi shrieked, **"Solar Particle Event, Get them in here, get them in here!"**

Vadim, taken aback by two things Yoshi never did, screaming and cursing in Japanese, was set on his heels. He didn't know what 3000 REM meant but he sure as hell knew it couldn't be good. He rammed the C3's Push to Call button and started to yell, but his pilot instincts took over. Yelling would unsettle, yelling would cause panic, yelling was futile.

"External alarms," he said calmly instead, "we're reading external alarms. We need you back in the airlock immediately, both of you. Do you copy?"

Yoshi knew two things that instant. First, they couldn't copy, their comm was wiped out, and second, they weren't the only ones in danger. SPEs were devastating. The particles could penetrate metal like butter and were flooding the ship. The only protection was the storm shelter on A-deck, a radiation-toughened safe haven.

"You can't reach them," she said sternly, jostling Vadim. "We must get to A-deck. All of us, NOW."

The look on her face said it all. He wouldn't argue. He was unprepared for this. Until it passed, she'd be in charge.

Outside on the platform, it continued to rain protons, a rain fiercer than Earth's surface had ever known, fiercer than the force of all its hurricanes and earthquakes combined. Deluged by one of nature's most violent and epic events, all the more unspeakable because of its rarity, Anna didn't even know it. She suspected something, of course, from the glow and heat, but Vadim's transmission had failed to reach her and the only feeling she had was that strange, bathlike warmth against her skin.

The low mass protons were invisible at first, but as they struck her suit, careening off metal parts, higher mass particles shot off like billiard balls, secondary radiation. The warm feeling turned to a burning sensation as it drenched first tissue, then bone. When Anna's arms, chest and legs began to ache, she knew she had to break protocol, get to the airlock, NOT wait for orders. She tried not to think the worst as she moved away from the porch, that she was being immersed in deadly radiation, but the ache became sharper and her suit became her enemy. Everything inside her was exploding, every organ, every body part, especially her brain, now revolting against reality. "GET THE SUIT OFF," a voice from inside her head told her, "GET IT OFF, GET IT OFF." It took every resource she had to fight it, not to give in. She'd been through worse, she kept telling herself, but she hadn't. Convulsed, anxious and queezy, she somehow managed to steel herself and push on past the platform; around the engine pods, towards the airlock. At one point, she slipped and nearly fell into the abyss but managed to grab a handhold, drag herself back and hook a lifeline to the railiing. Superhuman effort inched her onwards, the same kind she'd marshaled her whole life against the odds of being who she was, a claustrophobic lesbian, a label she'd never live down had anyone known it.

It took her an hour to retreat the distance to the airlock, sixty minutes, thirty six hundred seconds with every second in fear. Miraculously, unexepectedly, the door was wide open when she arrived, and Roberto was inside. It's a mirage, she thought, the entire event is a fantasy, a dream. She knew it wasn't when Roberto reached out and grabbed her, slammed the airlock door, twisted the handle and hit the REPRESS button.

Torrents of air suddenly buffeted her body, knocking her against the wall with such force that her vision dimmed and she began to pass out. Roberto counted his lucky stars once again as the pressure built up. The back of the ship, where he'd been working had acted as a shield. He'd climbed down in the shade, minimized his exposure and escaped, he thought. In fact, he'd had no clue of the SPE until Anna's desperate call finally reached him. Even that had been luck, Shielded as he was, the signal had somehow gotten through.

Anna, poor Anna, on the other hand, had had no such luck. The blistered face behind her plexiglass helmet made that all too obvious. He had to get her out of her suit and fast, he knew, but how? *How can I do it without exposing myself,* he wondered with the image of cooked flesh nearly consuming him. But then he remembered the man with the little black bag in Aguas Caliente where he grew up, remembered who he was and what he'd trained for. Remembered the Hippocratic Oath and the vows he'd taken.

Should I keep my suit on while I doff her, he thought first, since it could protect him from the radiation. If he did, it would shorten the doffing process and increase her odds. On the other hand, his suit could already be contaminated and drilling him. If so, he had to get out of it first and fast. That could save him but *comdemn her.* He wrestled with the thought for an endless 15 seconds before deciding. He went to Anna with his suit still buttoned up.

When he undid her wrist rings and removed her gloves, her fingers were discolored and starting to blister. He called out to her but she didn't answer because she'd fainted. She was in a bad way, he knew, but just how bad he wouldn't know till he checked her D-patch.

The D or dosimeter patch, a leftover from the old days, was crude but effective. Unlike the microchips on their MarsSuits, which kept a running tab on radiation, these simply changed color. He struggled to recall the mnemonic the rad guys had taught him. What were they?

"White for No dose; Gray for Low dose; Brown for High dose; Black for Die dose.

Anna's D-patch was black when he pulled her from her suit and unzipped it from her LCG, **Dead** was his first thought, what's *mine*? his second. He gagged at the brown hue, a 50 % fatality rate.

It took hours for the ship's readings to stabilize after that, and hours more before Yoshi would let the others exit the storm shelter. She left nothing to chance as she emerged from A-deck with a hand-held RAD counter, scanning her way towards the other decks slowly. The counter read normal when they finally reached the Bridge. All the video monitors seemed quiet. Save for one that suddenly flickered with a trace of movement. It was the airlock monitor and Anna and Roberto were in there. Alive!

MET = 0120:22:06:00--Day 120.

"*Columbia,* Houston," came the calm voice over S-band. It was Adam Brady's and he spoke as if he had no idea what had transpired. He hadn't. Listening to him, Vadim soon surmised that he and the others at the MOCR assumed all their warnings had gotten through, that the crew had been tucked away like bugs in a rug riding out the storm in the safe haven of A-deck. "The flare was type AL, Anomolously Large," Adam went on unknowing, "3-Bright, X8 in flux and out of cycle. Hell of a thing, the way it surprised us coming out of cycle the way it did. Damn near took out comm. over the entire planet. We're back to normal though now, and assume you are too. How'd it go then, Columbus Eleven? We're standing by for status, copy?"

"*Standing by for status*," Vadim mimicked derisively towards Yoshi. "I'll give you status. Anna and Roberto are practically dead, how's that for your fucking status."

He wasn't angry at Adam, or the MOCR, how could he be, they'd done their job. They'd sent their warning.

Minutes later in the uplink he would learn that:
SOL F A E. EX RE Y DA GE S. G T ST M HELT R, was meant to be:
SOLAR FLARE. EXTREMELY DANGEROUS. GO TO STORM SHELTER.

He was furious with himself. He'd foisted the anagram on Andrea and Chris when he should have done it himself (he was a champion riddle-solver).

He was also angry for being such a pompous ass. Wanting to be Mr Czar-in-charge of this trillion dollar kahuna and shunning all help. Most of all, he was upset because it brought back terrible memories of what he'd done to his sister.

"How do I explain ***that*** to them," he asked Yoshi, "how do I tell them ***that***?"

"You don't," she whispered. "You did what you thought best then. This is now and our concern, everyone's concern is Anna and Roberto, *Wakarimasu?* Do you understand? She touched his arm softly, then said, "Vadim just give them the status."

He nodded and did so. Their response took considerably longer than the six minute lag time it took to get to the MOCR and back, basked in a silence thicker than pea soup. It was short and shaky when it came back. "Jesus, Vadim, standby. We're polling our team for guidance. Just give us some time, we're going to need time."

The orders that came back an hour later were not shaky but concise. One person, Vadim, was to enter the airlock just long enough to place a RAD counter in it, then exit quickly. When the scans in the airlock dropped below 5 RADS, Vadim would re-enter to get Anna first, then Roberto. During this time, he, and anyone else who came in contact with Anna and Roberto were to wear a lead apron over their chest and back, to be found in Drawer 4 of the Med lab in C-deck. While Vadim was in the airlock, the others would set up a sickbay in C-deck, including infusion lines and provisions for CBCs and blood gas analyzers. Vadim would transfer Anna and

Roberto to the sickbay one at a time, whereupon Yoshi would take over and everyone else would evacuate. She would hook up catheters, do the blood tests and other workups and transfer their data to HUMMS for analysis and transmission to the MOCR. She would also perform a workup on herself, to verify she wasn't being contaminated. HUMMS would be set to AUTO TRANSMIT, to telemed the life-signs every hour. An elite team of flight surgeons would be on hand to dissect it once received. More instructions would come.

It took the remainder of the day for the RAD levels to get below 5, and even then Vadim hesitated before going in. He had good reason, Roberto was puking and Anna looked lifeless. When he finally did and transferred them to the sickbay, Yoshi was the only one there. The others had already left. He thought about ordering her to vacate as well, taking care of Roberto and Anna himself, even if he wasn't a physician. There was a certain logic to it. If Yoshi fell ill caring for them, they'd lose a pilot and a doc. Same with the others--if it was Chris, they'd lose the only healthy geologist; and if Andrea, the only navigator. Only he could afford to be lost now, quite a jolt to his ego. "The mission can go on without you," the little voice in his head said, "you're expendable big boy, it's the ROE (Rule of Expendability)."

Yoshi was having none of it when he tried to sell the idea. "What do you know about radiation sickness?" she said angrily. "Or any sickness. So please leave and now!" He couldn't argue with her. She was right and he knew it. Besides, he found it irresistible when she talked tough, and he'd already caused enough trouble so he nodded and left.

After he'd gone, she reviewed everything she knew about heavy particle radiation and it was just north of nothing. The only true countermeasure was to avoid it in the first place and it was too late for that. In fact, after 50 years of studying the human body in Skylab, Mir and ISS, medical treatment was still a crapshoot in space, and no one could tell her otherwise. Everything was either an unknown or a compromise, especially in microgravity. Without gravity, IV fluid lines wouldn't even drip, and while she'd anticipated this problem and solved it by enclosing the saline bag in another filled with pressurized nitrogen, the drops that came out were now almost twice the size as on Earth. It was bad enough that the affect of drugs in space, ie., their pharmacokinetics, was poorly understood even if the dosages were the same, but with the drop size off, it was anybodys guess. Double the drop size and half the drip rate, she decided. Then she decreased the nitrogen pressure, moved on to the blood work and settled in. There'd be nothing to do but wait now, until the HUMMS analysis was complete. And then do it again, wait some more and repeat until guidance arrived. It could take days or weeks for something to change, and the change could be subtle, drastic or fatal.

Two decks above her in his quarters, Vadim was rewinding his blunders again. Accidents were the result of a chain of events, always a chain never a single link and *he* should have seen the chain coming apart. There'd been power surges and funny readouts, comm drops and static, and he'd missed all of them. It didn't matter if the others had missed them too. He was the one in charge, Mr. Left Seat, Mr. Pilot-In-Command. He flashed again on his sister, the other catastrophe he'd caused in his life.

They were only kids that cold Moscow night, he ten, she six, when he'd attempted to fire his first rocket motor, an engine the size of a soup can pieced together from a chemistry kit he'd borrowed from a friend. All he'd really wanted that night was a tiny controlled explosion, a second or two to prove his engine worked. He got much more than that. It lasted 20 seconds, long enough for a spark to catch the wads of papers his mother had stuffed along the walls to insulate their tiny flat and keep it warmer in the subfreezing winter. The place had erupted like a roman candle. He managed to get mother out, but not his beloved sister, Tatiana.

"*What the fuck were you doing lighting matches to chemicals inside our apartment*?" he was sure his mom wanted to ask him but never did before she sunk into a depression she never recovered from. He had no answer, then or now. The fact he was only ten years old then didn't matter. Just as it didn't matter now that the flare was out of cycle and he hadn't gone by the book in handling the events leading to it. Once again, he kicked himself for agreeing to the EVA, it was a stupid and regrettable decision. And while others might say he'd tried everything else first, barbequeing the antenna, sending the code and the other things, they didn't know what he suspected, that Anna and Roberto were either claustrophobic or incompetent. Others might say they were the logical choices, no, the only choices for the Extravehicular Activity due to the ROE. Fuck the ROE and fuck them. If anyone should have gone outside, it should have been him. He should be the one lying there in sickbay now, not Anna and Roberto.

****

Yoshi stayed with them 36 hours straight before meeting the others in the Bridge. She looked exhausted when she floated in. "I've done what I can," she said straddling a console. "My assessment is that Anna took a lethal dose of alpha and secondary radiation, Roberto less. Anna's white count is triple normal and rising, Roberto's is high but stabilized, a good sign. I've given both of them 5 units of plasma substitute, which wasn't easy because of the drip issue. And we don't have a lot of it onboard. We never anticipated this kind of emergency."

"Are you saying you need blood?" Andrea burst in fretfully. "Chris and I are both O-negative, universal blood donars, let us help!"

Yoshi considered the offer. "It hasn't come to that yet and I hope it doesn't. Transfusions have never been done in zero G before and I don't want to be the first to try. If we need one, we'll do it after re-spin and gravity, which I want to do as soon as possible."

"But they're weak and in stretchers," Vadim objected, roused from his well of remorse. "How can we spin-up with them like that. They're not in flight couches, they're not even restrained."

" We'll restrain them then, we have no choice. The zero G will create other problems if we stay in it, worse ones."

"Is the MOCR okay with this?" Vadim asked tentatively. Once he didn't give a shit about their buy in, now it seemed crucial.

"I sent a request for spin-up starting zero nine hundred day after tomorrow. I plan to do it over six hours instead of the usual three to ease the stress."

“Okay then, assuming they approve it, we should work on a restraint system for the sickbay.”

"I concur, Vadim.”

“Can’t we see them?" Andrea suddenly interrupted, close to tears. “All of this is happening so fast and we’re all just…”

"Of course,” Yoshi said softly.

“What about contamination, what about the RAD count?” Vadim cut in. He had to assert himself, he’d realized gradually, He had to show strength now, resume command, inspire confidence. “Those orders were explicit. No breaking quarantine.”

“It’s okay,” Yoshi answered. “The count’s down and I’ve cleared it with the SURGEON team. They're awake and resting comfortably. You can go in but don't stay long."

****

They went to Anna first. She had IV lines in her veins when they floated in, wires connnected her to HUMMS and bottles of medication surrounded her: Valium, xylocaine, demerol and morphine; sulfacetamide, epinephrine, atropin and neosporin. Her face--the parts of it not covered by ointment-saturated bandages--was grotesquely swollen. Clumps of hair were missing. Andrea, suppressing an urge to vomit, attempted to look at her without giving her feelings away. She couldn’t.

"How do you feel?" she asked unnerved.

"Not so good," Anna whispered weakly.

"Is Yoshi taking good care of you? She's the best doctor in the world, you know."

"That's right," Chris added. "If anyone can get you through this, it's Yoshi."

"I don't think anyone can get me through this."

"Sha," Andrea broke in, "I don't want you talking like that. I won't stand for it."

"Is there anything you'd like?" Chris interjected trying to break the tension. "Some music, a video, an email to someone?"

"Maybe you can beam my mom up," she said forcing a smile. "She always made me well when I was sick."

"We'll see what we can do," Chris said trying to stay upbeat.

"I feel very tired now, so tired."

"That's enough," Yoshi cut in. "Get some rest now Anna, they'll come back after spin-up."

The four of them floated out, Chris, Andrea and Vadim in shock at what they'd just seen and Yoshi resigned to helping Roberto, who at least had a chance. He was separated from Anna by semi-dangling curtain, semi because in the absence of gravity it was doing a poor imitation. Roberto's condition was in stark contrast to Anna's. His skin was reddish, but at least he had most of it; he had an IV, but no bandages. And the only apparent pain he was in was the look of disgust on his face. For whom or for what would remain his secret because he waved them off before they could say a word.

****

Yoshi began the re-spin at zero nine hundred two days later as planned. She was worried about software. Between ADSS, ECLSS, HUMMS, NAV, CWS and DAP, there were seven gigobytes of it, according to Andrea. That meant seven billion locations that the flare could have damaged, seven billion on/off switches any one of which might prove fatal if off instead of on.

"We use four software languages on the C3 and they've checked out clean," Andrea tried to reassure her. "DANYET, INFER and HAL-S+ were virus negative, Z-Base 5 had an apparent positive but I fixed it with DISINFECTANT."

"I don't care about any of that," Yoshi replied testily. "Just tell me I have workaround capability if ADSS goes down."

"You have workaround capability."

It was obvious to Vadim, sitting nearby on the C3 that Yoshi was stretched to the limit, not surprising since she was being asked to double task full time. Save the sick patients while overseeing the spin-up. He'd offer to do the spin-up for her but knew it would be futile. She'd say, "I'm trained primary on it; I've done it and I'm better at it then you." Still he considered offering right down to initiation when ADSS chirped,

"Acceleration and Deployment Spin-up System Ready. Rotational direction input please?"

"Clockwise," Yoshi replied in the usual manner.

It was too late for offers now.

"Reel out Length?" 'ADSS droned in response.

"Two one one point zero meters."

"Center of Rotation?"
"One-one point zero meters."

"Mean gravity gradient?"
"Zero point three eight G."

"Spin-up time?"
"Three hundred sixty minutes."

"Previous time was one niner five point zero minutes. Do you wish to replace the previous value with the new one you've just entered?"

"Yes."

There was a long pause followed by a repetitive clicking noise, a response Yoshi immediately recognized as *out-of-family*, an anomaly. She looked tentatively at Vadim, who returned her gaze.

"Sounds like a hard drive spinning," he said trying to make light of it. She feared he might be close to the truth. She'd heard hard drives spinning like that countless times before. Just before they locked up. But those were on Pentiums running Microsoft Word, not a finicky ADSS spinning a space ship. She hoped, prayed the clicking pattern would change. That would mean it wasn't caught in a loop, that it was still processing. Instead it went silient. Yoshi cursed under her breath in Japanese.

"Perhaps it didn't like the spin-up time," she said trying to stay positive."

"You changed it from 195 to 360 minutes, right?" asked Vadim. "Why not put it back to the original setting, 195."

"I don't want to spin them up that fast."

"Understand, but let's just see if it helps. If it works, you can always try a reset for the longer time."

"Negative," she said anxiously as the silence persisted.

"Why don't you try a hard restart."

They both held their breath as she pushed the *enter*, p and r buttons simultaneosly and held them for ten seconds, hoping for the characteristic 5 chimes reminiscent of the old macintosh computers when they did a factory ram reset. Instead there was silence, its persistence assuring them that ADSS was indeed caught in a loop, locked and inoperative. Andrea swam over with a DVD in her hands, ready for the "workaround" she told Yoshi existed. The DVD contained FMEA (Failure Mode Effects Analysis). It was an anomaly hunter, a program that looked for lockups and proposed corrective actions. After loading it, she prepared for a switchover to DANYET, the first backup code to be used in case one of those 7 billion switches was off instead of on. She never completed it, stopped in her tracks when FMEA spat out its diagnosis:

FMEA INTERROGATION COMPLETE: DIAGNOSIS :

90 PERCENT PROBABILITY OF REEL-OUT FAILURE

10 PERCENT PROBABILITY OF TETHER FAILURE

0 PERCENT PROBABILITY OF SOFTWARE FAILURE

Reel-out, 90; tether, 10; software, zero, the output stared back at her. ADSS wasn't the problem after all. ADSS was software, software they could workaround. This was hardware, and workarounds would be harder. The three of them waited for the next output, the workaround output. It came quickly and rammed the point home:

FMEA WORKAROUND OPTIONS COMPLETE:

NEGATIVE WORKAROUNDS

REEL MECHANISM NOT REACHABLE INTERNALLY OR BY EVA.

TETHER NOT REACHABLE INTERNALLY OR BY EVA.

ACCESS REQUIRES MVAB PROCESSING.

Requires VAB processing. It confirmed Vadim's worst nightmare about the ball and tether system. It could only be fixed back on Earth. He slammed his fist on the C3. He 'd dreaded the fucking thing would fail and now it had!

****

MET = 0124:08:00:00--Night 124.

Day and night meant nothing to Anna. She'd lost her eyesight, just another reason why she decided to take her life. It wouldn't be easy, Roberto was an arms-length away and Yoshi kept checking on her. She'd also have to disable her HUMMS alarm by touch since she couldn't see it. Nevertheless, she'd made up her mind.

The decision to end it had been simple. Her pain had become unbearable, in spite of the morphine. And like the petals of a sunflower wilting in a fast-forward movie she could feel her body coming apart. The last thing she wanted now was for them to waste more medication on her. Someone else might need it. Someone savable.

She'd already executed the first step of her plan, getting the atropine and syringe from the med cabinet. All that remained now was to pick the moment. Fill the syringe, stick it in her IV line and inject. She didn't need eyes for that, she could feel her way through it. It would be simple, it would be quick. And as she lay on her pillow summoning up the courage, she really had no regrets about her life. She'd lived it to the fullest and it was now time to go. She'd become a burden.

Yoshi found the note the next morning, clutched tightly in Anna's hand.

I'm sorry I couldn't see Mars with you.
But I've seen it in my dreams and it's a wonderful place.
I have a favor to ask.
Remember the song at our party,
'Let me Play Among the Stars?'
That's what I'd like to do now if I could.
That's where God's waiting for me.
So put me in the airlock and let me go to Him and them.
And don't be sad for me, it's where I want to be.
Anna

Vadim said the Lord's prayer while they huddled around the airlock the next day. He opened the outer door by remote control and they all watched Anna on the monitor. Her body danced to the rush of the whistling air at first, with her arms and legs slowly swinging. Then she exited gently. Gently and gracefully while she turned. It was a very slow turn. And, as specified by Newton's Law, an eternal one.

****

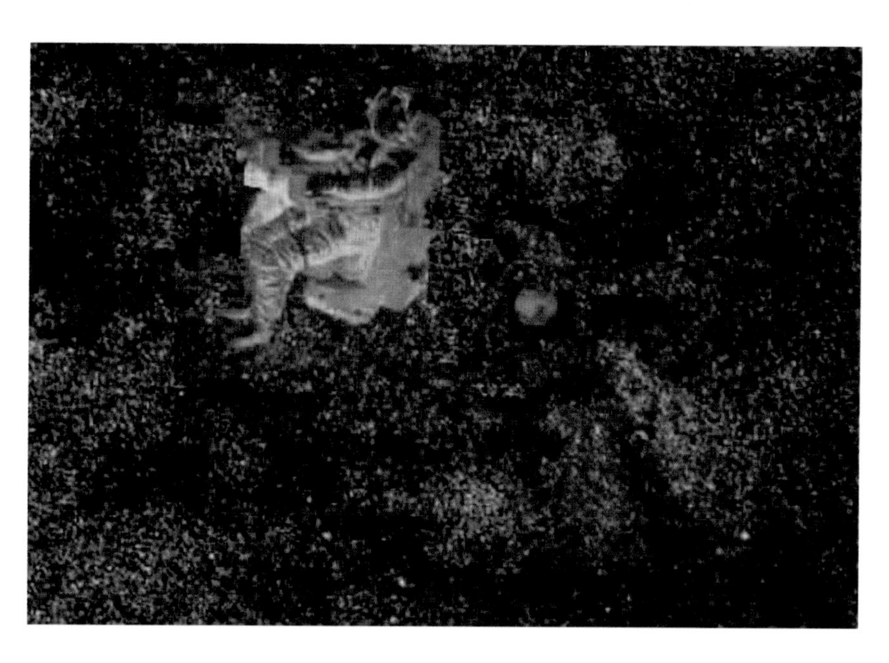

No one noticed Mars as Anna floated off, grapefruit-sized and getting bigger. Without the ship's rotation to obscure it, its features should have been clear but they weren't. An opaque veil had appeared over its red canyons. Whirlpools of dust were encroaching. Windstorms from the south were rushing north. A massive cyclone had begun as they passed the two-thirds point in their journey.

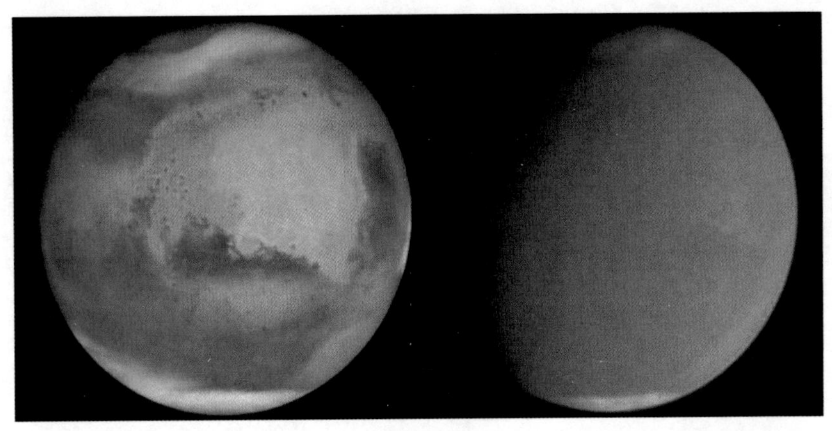

Mars under siege in a planet-wide dust storm

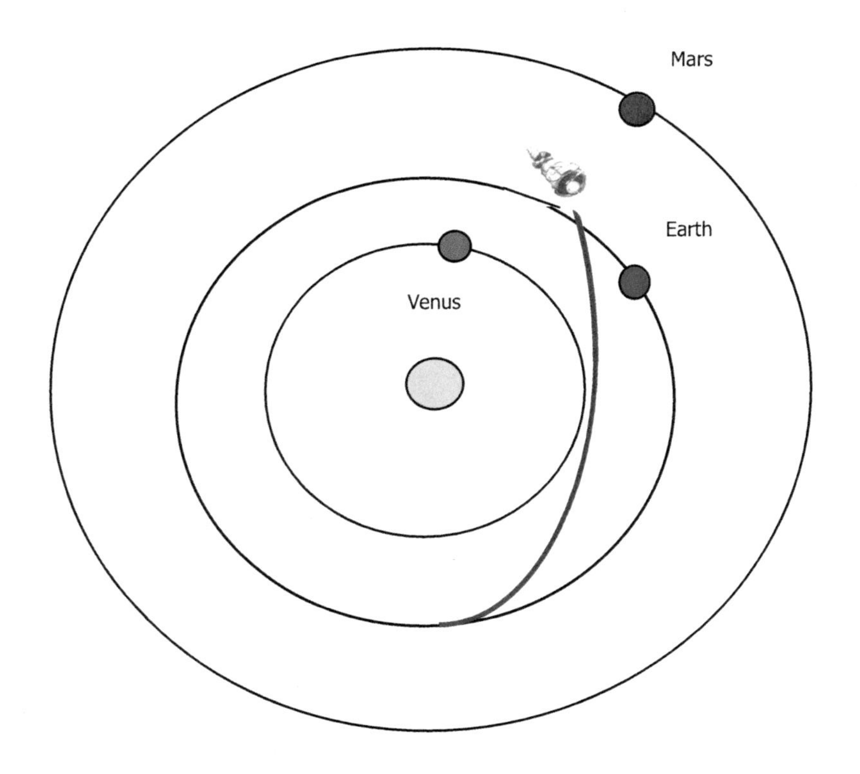

Columbia and Eagle on day 125

Orbits and sizes not to scale

Chapter 19. The Bed

Diarydisk Entry, Day 127 in-transit. Vadim Solodnov

"So much depression here, I don't know where to begin. Andrea can't stop crying and Yoshi's exhausted. Only Chris seems immune to it all. As for me*, shto sdelano mnoy dlya chelocechestva* (what contribution to humanity have I made?) The MOCR knows this of course, and will order us to abort. It's not if but when."

****

Emergency meeting back home:

Thirty-six million miles away, in the MOCR, elliptical lines tracked progress on the wall-to-wall screens fronting H. Buford Stone. FLIGHT, as he was now called (except to his friends, who still called him H), had the best minds in the space program at his disposal, the dozens surrounding him and hundreds more on the loop of the Mars Staff Support Rooms. *Columbia* and *Eagle* were on a ballistic trajectory. If nothing was done, they'd swing around Mars' back side and come back to Earth. It was called a Mode 1 ABORT (or a Free Return since it cost little or no fuel), and would take 18 months to bring them back home. A Mode 2 would cut that down to six but was riskier. They'd have to do an MOI (Mars Orbit Insertion) *retrograde* burn to enter Mars orbit in a hurry; rendezvous with the Backup Fuel Module to transfer fuel and supplies (placed there beforehand for just such an emergency), and do a full throttle *posigrade* burn to pick up enough speed to catch Earth, just ahead of them. H wanted neither as he listened to his Black Team recite alternatives on the 127th day of the mission. He wanted Mode 3, a flipping maneuver to rotate and point their engines towards Mars and fire them briefly. It would slow them down just enough to intercept the Martian atmosphere, which they would then use as an *aerobrake* to ease them into orbit. *Aerobraking* had its own risks. It had never been tried before with humans. But H wanted it terribly. It was the prelude to a landing.

The call for Mode 1, 2 or 3 was his and his alone, H knew, and everyone else knew it. It was the only thing they did know as he polled his team for choices. That and the fact that the last HUMMS scan showed elevated calcium in the crew's urine, the first sign of bone loss. He summed things up with his business as usual brusqueness.

"We got three problems," he underscored. "First the crew. Anna's gone, Roberto can't be moved and the others are stretched tighter than goddamn rubber bands. Next, the ball: we're stuck in zero G without it and that'll cause problems. Finally the flare. It wasn't supposed to happen but it did and there could be more. I want your best inputs on this, all of you. That's why you're here. You first, SURGEON."

Royce Davies, the Chief Flight Surgeon took a deep breath and rose from his console. He ran his fingers over his balding scalp, removed his reading glasses and answered warily. "ABORT 1 will take 18 months to get them home. They'll run out of life support by then."

"Not so," H retorted. We've closed the loop on everything. They get power from the Sun, recycle wastes and grow their own food. It'll be marginal but they should make it. Anything else?"

"Yes, bone loss! They'll lose two percent a month without artificial gravity. Eighteen times two is 36 percent. With that much bone loss you're osteoporotic, fall the wrong way and you're done."

"I hear what you're saying, SURGEON, so what's your recommendation?"

“Mode 2 Abort, FLIGHT. It would cut a year off the return time. They’d be back in six months.”

“What if we got ADSS back?”

“It would help but I don’t see it happening.”

H turned to the contractors who’d built the ball system. "What about that, Lockheed Martin?" he queried, “Can it be fixed?"

A gravelly voice cleared his throat over the comm loop and apologized. "Doubtful, FLIGHT, You just can't get to the reel-out mechanism. We've poured over the schematics, and the only place you can fix it is in the MVAB. It takes tools, jigs, cranes and a horde of technicians."

"Any chance the problem's not in the hardware but software?"

"The data says otherwise. FMEA predicted zero chance."

The strain showed on H's face, he now knew how the legendary Gene Krantz must've felt the night Apollo 13 blew up. Nobody saw him clench his fist and grind his Doc Martins into the antiseptic white floor just then. He took great pains to hide it and the negative vibes he’d always had about ADSS and its 3-ton Rube Goldberg piece-o-shit.

Once again, he wondered why Brandford had ignored him when he’d questioned the system’s robustness, why the only response he'd ever heard back from him was, *‘Changing it will cost two billion bucks and a two year slip.”*

He quickly caught himself. He needed answers not fall guys. Move on, he told himself, and turned to the Environmental Officer. “Okay, the flare. Will there be another one, ENVO?"

"We're dumbfounded, FLIGHT," ENVO answered. "Solar flares just don't happen in Solar Minimums."

"Well, a helluva one just did! How did we miss it?"

"The short answer is it took out SOHO2, our early warning satellite. SOHO2 was a double-edged sword. It was close to the Sun for early warnings but vulnerable to big flares because it's so close. We knew there was risk but thought we'd built it tough enough. Obviously, we were wrong."

"What about a repeat?"

"We've taken steps to compensate, amplifying the downlink sensitivity and networking solar data. Right now, we've got every available resource trained on the Sun, including Hinode, the Japanese satellite."

"Let me repeat, ENVO, what are the odds of another flare?"

"The corona's calmed down, I'd say low. But there are no guarantees."

No guarantees, H mumbled under his breath, just like the fucking stock market. The last thing he wanted was to terminate the mission, he dispised the very sound of the word *Abort*. But everything he'd heard so far was pushing him that way, and when the SURGEON chimed in again, it only got worse.

"FLIGHT, not to belabor it, but time's of the essence. If there's another flare, the shelter may not even protect them. Once their accumulated dose gets to 300 RADs, a normally harmless endogenous fungus like aspergilla could kill them, or a common cold. Your hemopoetic blood-making cells go first, then the cells in the gut, then lymphocytes and T-cells. You lose your immune system in a matter of weeks. That's why we need a Mode 2."

"Don't you flight docs ever have anything good to say?"

"Excuse me, FLIGHT," a female voice with a melodic accent interruped over the loop. It was a voice from one of the back rooms. Back room staff had to act through their MOCR counterparts. This one hadn't. She was out-of-protocol, a no-no. "I may have an alternative," she added tentatively.

"Who is this?" H snapped.

"Kay Loranz, in the Life Support SSR. "What if we use Martian gravity?"

Davies, the SURGEON, rolled his eyes. He knew this Loranz and she was a loose cannon. She'd been nothing but trouble since her first day on the job. He winced as she continued undaunted with, "Mars G is only a third of Earth's, but it's enough."

"Enough for what?" H asked impatiently.

"To replenish them. We can reverse the effects of losing ADSS by landing them."

"Landing them?" Davies cut in disdainfully, "they can't land in the shape they're in."

"That's not quite true, sir," Loranz offered softly. "They've lost some calcium but not much. Except for Roberto, they're actually in pretty good shape. Without AG, it will get worse, true, but I've been working on a solution for that."

Davies had heard enough. Furious, he called H over his private line and ranted, "We don't need some delusional whippersnapper telling us how to save the crew. We need to get them home. Petal to the metal and Mode 2."

“I appreciate what your saying, Royce, but let me be the judge of that!” H replied. He hated negativity and Davies embodied it, as did all the other SURGEONS he’d ever met. They were as predictable as death and taxes, and now a renegade flight doc had embarrassed their leader. He admired that deep down, and turned back to Loranz. “Anything else you’d like to add?”

“Only that I came to NASA because I thought it was a can-do, not a can’t-do organization. “If we abort now, 1 or 2, that’s what we’ll be. I may have a solution, I just need time to work on it.”

“How much time?”

“A day or two.”

“You’ve got twenty four hours,” H replied, “and that goes for all of you. If you’ve got a plan, I want to hear it but ***go through your chain of command, understood***?”

Following the exchange, the Black Team wondered why H had acted so out of character with this Loranz. He normally wouldn’t have tolerated chain-of-command violations for a second but this time he had. Was it because she seemed so disarming? Or because the last thing H. Buford Stone wanted to be remembered for was ignoring Apollo 13’s famous creed: *failure just isn't an option.* It didn’t much matter. The buck stopped with him and it would be his call.

"Twenty four hours," he reiterated once again. "Decisions will be made once I hear y’all out. There’ll be no turning back after that.”

****

Once his shift ended, H did some homework on Dr. Kay Loranz. She was an MD/Ph.D with pedigrees from Dartmouth, MIT, and the University of Pennsylvania Medical School. She'd done her residency in Orthopedics at Mount Sinai and was an expert in Aerospace Medicine like Roberto. Impressive! And like Roberto, she'd gone on to NASA at the Johnson Space Center, but that's where their career paths diverged. He'd become an astronaut, she'd passed on to oblivion.

Or so it seemed, according to Royce Davies, who volunteered the information in a call to H's home that night. She'd been censored and reprimanded for speaking out of turn at meetings, he reported, and going around her superiors; being a loose cannon for the duration of her career. Only recently had she been let out of the doghouse to monitor the mission from the Medical Staff Life Support Room, and now she'd blown it. He'd call for her dismissal immediately. Her behavior was intolerable!

H had a gnawing feeling after Davies' hung up. There was something peculiar about his disdain for her. It was too personal. It also didn't add up that someone so promising would crash with such a thud. Why was Davies really so down on her? He needed to find out but from who? Most of the docs in that Org wouldn't talk because they were under Davies' thumb. To get the real scoop on Loranz, he'd have to go outside Life Sciences, and he knew just where to start: Chris' wife, Tess! Chris knew that Org inside and out and Tess might've heard something by osmosis. And just like Loranz, she'd also gone to MIT. Besides, he owed her a call. She'd heard nothing about Chris since the flare.

Tess was grateful to learn that Chris was healthy, of course, but in shock at the news about Anna. H asked her to keep it in strict confidence.

"What happens now?" she said with concern, "will you bring them home?"

"We haven't decided yet, but you may be able to help us."

"Me, how?"

"By telling me what you know about Kay Lorenz."

There was a momentary silence, then, "What about her?"

"She says she's got some band-aid solution but before I hear it, I need to know if she's a crackpot or a malcontent."

"No on the former, yes on the latter," Tess replied.

"How so?"

"I was ahead of her at MIT, but I'd heard all about her. She was well thought of, worked on artificial gravity in the Human Performance Lab. She had a reputation as a doer."

"What about the malcontent part?"

"That came from her White Paper, but you know all about that."

"White Paper? Don't know anything about it. I never heard of Kay Loranz till yesterday."

"I'm surprised. It really rocked the boat in Life Sciences, Chris and Ed used to talk about it all the time."

"Go on."

"It had to do with *Lunar One Third,* that old Mission Plan, She basically said it was untenable, that it wouldn't protect the crew and in fact it might kill them. That's all I recall. But I'm sure you can get a copy of it. It was a big deal back then. Made it to the New York Times I think."

"Anything else I should know about her?"

"Well....only that everyone wanted to sleep with her...until the accident."

"What accident?"

"Someone spilled acid on her in a lab. It disfigured her, that's all I know."

"Geez, I see. Thanks, Tess, you've been a great help."

"You too. Thanks for telling me about Chris. I was climbing walls."

"No problem."

"Before you go, H, how come you asked me about Kay Loranz? Your people must know a helluva lot more about her than I do."

"I wanted a fresh opinion. Some of my people think she's nuts."

"Would one of them be Royce Davies?"

"How did you know?"

"He was the one who tarred and feathered her after that White Paper. I just remembered."

Tess took a deep breath after H hung up, thankful that Chris was safe, at least for the moment. Then little by little, a world of what ifs began whirring in her head around their conversaton. Connections she hadn't considered turned ugly: Brandford and Ed Cochran; Davies and Loranz; Lunar-One-Third and Andrea Beale. Andrea and Joanna Hewitt. A common denominator connected them all, a nasty one, What was it?

At his end, H went immediately to the web and downloaded Loranz' White Paper. Entitled, *"Life Science Compromises in Lunar One Third."* It was a hundred-page lambasting of the mission plan Brandford had backed so strongly, and within it was a seething condemnation of the ADSS system, its probable failure and suggestions how to fix it. The paper had ***CONFIDENTIAL, DO NOT DISTRIBUTE***, written diagonally in bold red font across every page, and a signature line for Loranz' supervisor on the front. That supervisor had been Royce Davies and the signature field was unsigned. H called Loranz immediately. He asked her to meet him at the Starbucks on NASA Road One. And to bring her band-aid with her!

Loranz was hard to take when she turned up within the hour. It hadn't always been that way, with her Lady Diana demeanor and her fine, curvaceous body. But it was now. The large, owlish reading glasses and long strands of red hair dangling over her forehead couldn't disguise the damage that had been caused by the accident. And though she wore a tight fitting light blue dress to distract attention, it could't compete with the eye patch over her right eye hiding the vacant spot beneath it, or the skin surrounding that patch scarred with reddish brown blotches from her cheekbone to her jaw. She reminded H of a fine Louvre painting, undone by some mindless maniac. He wondered if she'd been undone by one similarly deranged. Quashing the thought, he focused on her good eye, an undisturbed gorgeous deep blue with the fire of intellect still burning inside. That was easier to countenance, at least, and would get easier by the minute.

"Okay, doc, you're up," he began simply to start things off. She was ready for him. She'd been waiting for just such an opportunity for a long time.

"When I was at MIT," she started, "we designed a rotating bed. There were twelve of us in the Human Performance Lab, and we called ourselves the *Gyronauts*. It was basically a human centrifuge, and we'd lie down on it, feet at the center, head on the outer ring opposite and spin around. We'd all try to outdo one another, see who could stay on the longest, and spin the fastest. You know, we were kids. But what we were really after was the optimum duty cycle, how much AG to give and for how long, in order to stop bone loss, cardio atrophy and the other things. Just when we thought we had it, NASA opted for rotating spacecraft, not beds, and our grant ran out. Before it did though, we got enough data to convince me it would work."

"What kind of data?"

"Intensity and Cycle time. For example, 1 G causes problems, 1/3 G doesn't, and 8 hours a day is the minimum exposure time, which is why we opted for sleeping on it, hence a bed."

"And you were able to do that, I mean sleep on it?"

"Indeed. As long as you immobilize the head to stop Correolis forces."

"And if you don't?"

"You vomit. But at least you keep your bones."

The corners of Loranz lips, hardened by the accident into a perpetual downturn, lifted ever so slightly, the best she could do for a smile. H noticed and smiled with her. "Nothing's wrong with a little vomiting," he cracked in sympathy. "Everyone up there's done it by now anyway. But let me ask you, what good's this going to do? Even if it worked, they don't have a rotating bed on *Columbia*."

Her lips hardened again and she looked laser-like at him. "But they could."

"What do you mean?"

"They could build one from parts on C-deck. They'd have to scavenge them from the Versaclimber, bike and treadmill, but they could do it. I could tell them how. I've drawn a blueprint."

Now it was H's time to stare, stare possible salvation right in the face, disfigured as it was. He flashed on Steve Bales, the young backroom guy who'd saved the landing on Apollo 11 when he told Neil Armstrong to ignore computer alarms.

"You know Steve Bales?" he asked absentmindedly, then waved it off. "I need to digest this overnight Kay, can I call you Kay?"

"Sure," she said gulping hard because it was the first time in years she'd been taken seriously.

H couldn't help but notice that her good eye, the deep blue one, had glistenings of moisture around the edge, the beginnings of a tear, which she quickly suppressed. He almost felt like crying himself.

"You look like you could use a drink, Kay Loranz. Can I get you a cup of coffee, that's all they got here?"

"S…sure," she repeated nervously.

When he rejoined her with 2 Grande Lattes, H could leave nothing to chance. He had to see for himself that she wasn't unstable, Tess' opinion notwithstanding. "I need to know what happened between you and Royce Davies," he pushed. Loranz cleared her throat and had trouble getting words out. She was reluctant to talk but proceeded.

"When I first came here, he hit on me," she began, "everyone did before the accident, so it wasn't that unusual. I told him no, nicely enough. Told him I never mixed work with my personal life. I didn't know who he was then, but I found out fast.

Next thing I know, I'm working for him, and he keeps doing it. Asking me to stay late, dropping hints, you know. Anyway, it took awhile before he finally backed off. He never made physical advances, only verbal ones, and they were really gosche, a chimp wouldn't have used some of his lines. Anyway, he had me doing Gap Analysis--tracking things we might have overlooked to protect the crew. I found a lot of them, but every time I did, he'd humor me and reject it. That's when I realized I was just a pretty face to him. And when *Lunar One Third* came down, he ignored everything I had to say about it too, and I got really depressed.

Disrepect does that to you, you know, Mr. Stone? And ignoring someone is the worst kind of disrespect. That's why I wrote the White Paper. I assume you read it or you wouldn't be here talking to me. It was unauthorized and unrequested, true, but it had to be done. It was my catharis. The only way I could get any self-respect back. Once I finished it, I had another dilemma, who to give it to? It couldn't be Davies, I realized, so I asked my office mate what she thought. She said it was too hot to handle and suggested I sit on it for awhile."

"Who was your office mate?"

"Andrea Beale."

He motioned her on to continue. This was getting interesting.

"I decided she was right and tucked it away in my drawer. Two weeks later it was all over the place: NASAwatch, then the Washington Post and New York Times. From there I went into pergatory. They put me in an isolated cubicle doing makework. The parole just came lately."

"Did you ever find out how it got to NASAWatch?"

"No. I called them on it but they refused to tell me. At first I suspected Andrea. I had CDs of the paper scattered all over my desk before I hid them, and we shared an office. It would have been easy for her to grab one and mail it to them."

"Why Andrea?"

"She had motives, I thought. She was sleeping with Don Brandford, and he liked me. She also worried I might compete with her for a seat on the mission."

"So it was jealousy. And leaking that paper was a smart way to bury you."

"Yes, it infuriated my superiors. But in hindsight, I don't think she did it."

"No?"

"Blaming her was unreasonable. Anyone could have done it. Lots of people were angry at Lunar One Third."

"But they didn't share an office with you."

"Listen, I was really paranoid back then, a girlfriend helped me realize it, another astronaut actually. After being in the Core ten years without flying, she became convinced she was being discriminated against because she was small. Sounds ridiculous, I know, but they didn't have small spacesuits back then, and she had to squeeze into ones that didn't fit well. If you didn't fit well, you'd have trouble with the performance tests, which were used for flight selection. Then she found out it would only cost ten million dollars to get suits for smaller women, so she asked management to buy one for her and they refused. That's when she really got paranoid. She was so sure someone was out to get her that she engaged a whistleblower lawyer. She was just about to sue NASA when out of nowhere, she gets a flight."

"And there's a lesson there?"

"Yes, that not everyone's out to get you, that most people are too preoccupied with their own stuff to even think about you. When she realized that, she backed off and it all worked out. She helped me realize it too. That's why I stopped blaming Andrea."

"I look at differently, Kay. Knowing this bureaucracy, I'd say your friend flew because the same dude putting her down got scared of a lawsuit. And I'd also be suspicious of Andrea. She's got a rap sheet around here, you know. That swap for JoAnna, it shouldn't have happened. But tell me, how the hell have you dealt with all this? And what about the accident, do you think it really wasn't one?"

"I'd rather not talk about that, if you don't mind."

"Trust me on this, Kay. I need to know *everything*. It's the only way I can help you."

"You'll have to forgive me, but everytime I've done that, it's come back to haunt me."

"Please."

Again she paused. Whatever had happened had been highly traumatic. And as she struggled again to get words out, H nearly backed down. There were parts of the agency that sucked, he knew, like any big bureaucracy. But the government had its own special brand of assholes: those who stifled creativity; others at the top because of who they knew and hangers on who milked the system because they couldn't be fired. Kay Loranz had endured all of them, it seemed., and now this--he was asking her to relive her own private hell.

"I…I was in the bone lab," she suddenly stuttered, "looking at osteoblasts on the electron microscope. A lab tech was assisting me. It was hot in there that day, normally it's freezing, and I…I couldn't see the image because I was perspiring so much. He got me a towelette, you know, the kind like you get on an airplane, sealed in plastic?

I tore open the seal, wiped my brow and started screaming until I fainted. I don't remember much after that. I woke up in the hospital and here I am."

"How well did you know the tech?"

"Never saw him before, haven't seen him since."

"And this happened about the time you wrote that white paper?"

"A few months later, yes."

"And you're not suspicious?"

"It doesn't matter what I am, it's in the past, it is over. Now about the bed, are you still going to consider it?"

"Yes," he finally said after stifling the anger erupting towards Davies and Brandford. "Of course."

****

MET=0130:16:00 HOU=11:3 CANDOR=22:30 DELAY=06:40

Vadim hated waiting. He hated his life being put in other's hands, he'd always hated it, but especially now, when the next buzz of the comm could terminate the whole goddamn mission. It would be like a knife to his chest when they did it, but what else could they do? Yet Anna had passed 5 days ago and there was still no decision. What the fuck are they waiting for?

He'd done a lot of self-flagellating in those five days, conjuring up every insult he could muster for himself, including the worst, "*Ni v pizdu, ne v krasnuyu armiyu,* (I'm a good- for-nothing ass fucker, not even good enough for the army)!" HUMMS would have a field day with him and his guilt, self-pity and remorse had he submitted to it. That, however, was impossible since Roberto had to administer HUMMS and *look where he is, thanks to me.*

Then suddenly the dreaded buzz *was* there, cutting to his heart. Only instead of Adam Brady, it was H. Buford Stone on the line. Of course! Vadim thought. News like this wouldn't come from a lowly Capcom. Only an Adminstrator or Lead Flight Director would do.

"Good day, Commander Solidnuts," H began, completely disarming him. He hadn't been called that for years, not since H used it on him in the MVAB. If he'd wanted to soften him up for the blow, he couldn't have picked a more curious way of doing it.

"Listen up," H went on, "and don't interrupt, not that you can with a 6:40 lag. First: No action is required of us until MET 0164, 37 days from now. That's the time remaining before we have to fire retrograde for a Mode 2 Abort if we choose to do that. Until then, we have 37 days and we're going to try something.

The blueprint for it is being uploaded as we speak. You don't have to know what it is, just build it! Hopefully it won't be hard. If it works, we'll have another decision to make at MET 0180, which we'll discuss later. For now, notify us when you're done then we'll talk. One last thing, I know, we know, what you've been going through. You're to be commended, all of you. You should be proud of yourselves. We sure as hell are!"

Silence gripped the Bridge, the kind no one wanted to disturb for fear of rocking the boat. They'd just been given a reprieve, short, sweet, and confusing as it was:

"We have 37 days to try something."

Maybe it was his training, maybe it was his ego, but Vadim found himself renewed, wanting to command again, to lead his crew on to better things, great things.

"That's it then," he exhaled deeply. "Let's build this thing, let's get on with it!"

In the hours that followed, it looked crazy, the thing they were making from the blueprint. They disassembled the Versaclimber, the Ergometer and Treadmill first, and scattered the parts over the floor, then added other parts scrounged from every corner of the gym and Med Lab. Another contraption, Vadim started to complain when he saw it taking shape, then stopped. This one might help them, or at least give them a reprieve. But when they took the motor from the Treadmill; the chain drive from the Ergometer and a spare stretcher from the Med Lab and combined them, they all had to laugh. It really *was* a Rube Goldberg.

Yoshi was the first to put two and two together and stop laughing.

"Fantasutikku, suteki!" she blurted out, "incredible!"

From the back of her photographic memory, she'd recalled an article from *Space Medicine*, about a rotating bed some MIT grads had built decades ago. She'd scoffed at the idea of "gyronauts" back then, whirling around at ungodly speeds, trying to sleep on the thing and barfing for their trouble. But what made no sense then suddenly made great sense now. "*Mochiron,* of course!" she chirped at the others. "We're building a human centrifuge."

It took up half of C-deck when they finished, the only place with room enough to accommodate it, and the last thing it looked like was a bed. But a bed it was, 6 feet long and on the stiff side. It cleared a 13-foot diameter circle when they first turned it on, nearly scraping the walls. Vadim mounted it first, surprisingly. Normally, he hated being a guinea pig but for this he'd make an exception. Yoshi read him the instructions:

"1. Buckle the seat belt firmly but not tightly

2. Place your head on the pillow and attach the neck brace to prevent Correolis forces

3. Lower the eyeshades to prevent vertigo

4. Try to fall asleep."

Sleeping, he'd have trouble with, of that there'd be no doubt. Smiling was no issue though as the machine began moving in circles. Being in control again merited a smile. A big smile.

****

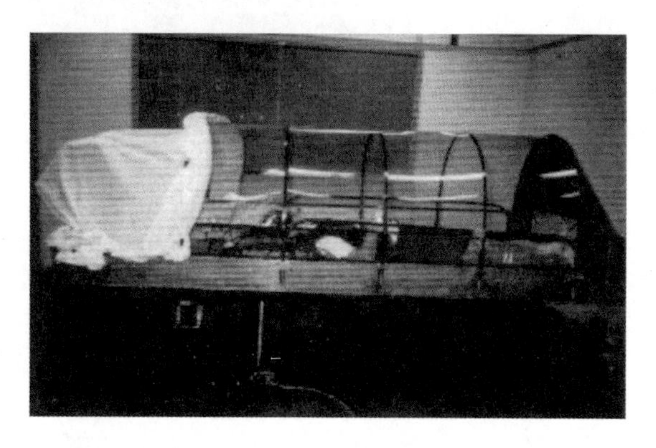

MET=0149:02:10 HOU=21:4 CANDOR=19:21 DELAY=07:24

Three weeks later from 41 million miles away, Chris placed his first call to Tess since the flare. The lag was up to 7 minutes and twenty-four seconds now, and the talk stilted and difficult, Neither of them cared. All they wanted was to reconnect. But with so much to say and so little time to do it in, could they?

When her face lit up the screen, Chris felt like a little kid again, giddy and nervous, just like the first time. What to say, where to begin? After telling her how much he missed her, he decided to start with the bed.

"You lie down, lock in and try to relax," he said excitedly, "and I say try because it's very weird. You feel like a yo-yo getting up to speed, with pressure building from your head towards your feet. Ninety seconds later, you're at 14 RPM and 1/3 g, the same as on Mars. Then gradually the sensations disappear. As long as you stay still, it becomes calming, like transcendental meditation or yoga, or one of those sensory deprivation tanks. But if you move the wrong way, or peek through your blindfolds, it's not pleasant. Instant nausea and upchucking, I learned that the hard way. And though the last thing on your mind is sleep, strangely enough, you do. More amazing than that, it seems to work. According to the numbers, our bone loss is down. The other biomarkers too--T-cells, potassium, kidney function--everything's near normal, even our sperm count. That, they've been watching to see if our DNA's been damaged.

"You're probably wondering why we didn't have this in the first place instead of that bloody ball. It got through the crack because it was such an obscure program, I'm guessing. They wouldn't have chosen it anyway because it's simpler to rotate a single ship than 6 separate beds. But a single bed with each of us on different duty cycles? Who'd have figured that out? I'm on it the least, an hour a day plus one night out of five, about 17 hours a week total. Vadim's on it more, 26 hours and Roberto the most, 37. Speaking of Roberto, his recovery's been nothing short of miraculous. Your salad machine has played a role in it, I'm certain. A steady diet of that thermostabilized, irradiated and rehydratable stuff has to wear on you. At a minimum, it atrophies your tongue. Those spinach salads with all the fresh vitamins are just what the doctor ordered. Roberto's raved about them. We all have.

I don't know if H or Adam told you, but if not, you deserve to know what our options are. They're a bit complex so I'll try and explain them. Our next big decision comes fifteen days from now at MET 0164. That's when we'd have to do an MOI burn for a Mode 2 Abort. I'd be hugging and kissing you 6 months from now if that happens, but the feeling is it won't and we'll press on. We're doing too well. The decision after that comes a month from today near Mars, at MET 0180. We'll either swing around the backside in a Mode 1 Abort home, or do a Mode 3 to orbit, Mode 1 is a free return to Earth, which would take us 18 months. Mode 3 requires an *aerocapture*, which is risky. I think they'll opt for Mode 3 because a lot of things can happen in 18 months, most of them bad. Counterintuitively, we can also get home faster from Mode 3, even though we're wasting time orbiting.

That's because of the BFM, the Backup Fuel Module--our lifeboat. We'd rendezvous with it, take on fuel, do a Powered Return and jaunt home in just 9 months. The best reason for Mode 3 has got nothing to do with any of that though. It's because it would be crazy to send us all the way to Mars and come back without so much as a photograph. We could take a month's worth of pictures before we'd have to leave. Orbital mechanics come into play after that and it's the doomsday Mode. We'd never catch up to Earth. As for a landing, it's out of the question with that storm. It's still raging--the winds hit two hundred mph at our landing site and we lost contact with Candor Base last week. We also lost the landing beacon, which violates a mission rule. So unless it lifts, we're probably Mode 3 for a month, then home. Not that we've given up on the landing. We're even adjusting our body clocks to CANDOR time in case we get lucky--24-hour, 39-minute days, and 61-minute, 44-second hours. Not too different from Earth but enough to make it challenging.

I've got to tell you though, Tessie, it's frustrating knowing we've got no say in any of these decisions, that even if we're healthy, we're at the mercy of that storm. That after all we've been through, it could all come down to the weather, believe it or not. At least we've got our routines to keep us busy, medical tests, timeline reviews, system checks and the like. Know how many filters need changing on this ship each day? Between solenoid, gas coolant, water, CO2, fecal, shower, air inlet, molecular sieve and waste management, there's over thirty. On top of that we've got seals to lubricate, batteries to recharge, urine separators to service, cannisters to swap out, dirt to vacuum and … oh yeah, before I forget, Kay Loranz. I flipped when I learned she designed the bed.

You remember her, she wrote that blistering Lunar One-third critique? Ed and I were sure she'd be management material after that then she disappears. We should've known better. People like her usually don't make it to the top. Nice to see she has, even if it took awhile. Thank her if you see her. Tell her we're all *really really* grateful."

Tess fiddled with her hair back in Oracle as Chris prattled on, running her fingers through long strands flecked gray by time. She'd twist them into braids then flick them obsessivly towards her ear repeatedly, a habit she'd acquired as a kid when nervous or fearful. Both emotions weighed on her as he spoke now. She was ecstatic to see him, and reassured, of course, but it couldn't make up for the guilt she felt over Hosokawa's call. Back and forth, she'd gone--keeping it a secret, punishing herself for doing so, and rationalizing both. She thought she'd finally put it to rest, convinced it *was* a hoax, but that was before H's inquiry about Loranz. With Anna dead, and the mission in jeopardy, she'd changed her mind yet again. There *could* be a conspiracy. The facts backed it up and she'd chronicled them all in a flow chart, her favorite way of solving problems. Someone had bribed Brandford and Davies to push Lunar-one-third. When Ed Cochran and Kay Loranz threatened it, they'd been marginalized. When Lunar-one-third had been killed in favor of the *Columbia/Eagle* plan, Andrea Beale had been swapped for Joanna Hewitt. Brandford and Davies could have orchestrated all of this by themselves. The only question, the salient question was, who would bribe them and why? Hosokawa; someone else; someone she hadn't even thought of? It didn't matter anymore.

She had to tell Chris and **now**. She couldn't even wait her turn to talk. She inserted her chart as an email attachment then hit '**Send**'.

It would take three minutes forty-five seconds to reach him. He'd have it; he'd look at it and then stare blankly at her from 41 million miles away. She hoped he wouldn't be too furious with her. He had every right to be of course. Hiding something she should never have hidden. Unforgivable!

He looked sad, not furious after the obligatory hiatus, and words and tears poured out in torrents when she saw that. When she finished, there was sympathy in his voice, not anger. "Don't jump to conclusions," he said calmly and simply, just like he'd said that night when she'd first ran CASI ahead in time. What he said hadn't mattered, she reflected afterwards. The only thing that did was the way he looked at her. The same way he always had, with love and understanding.

****

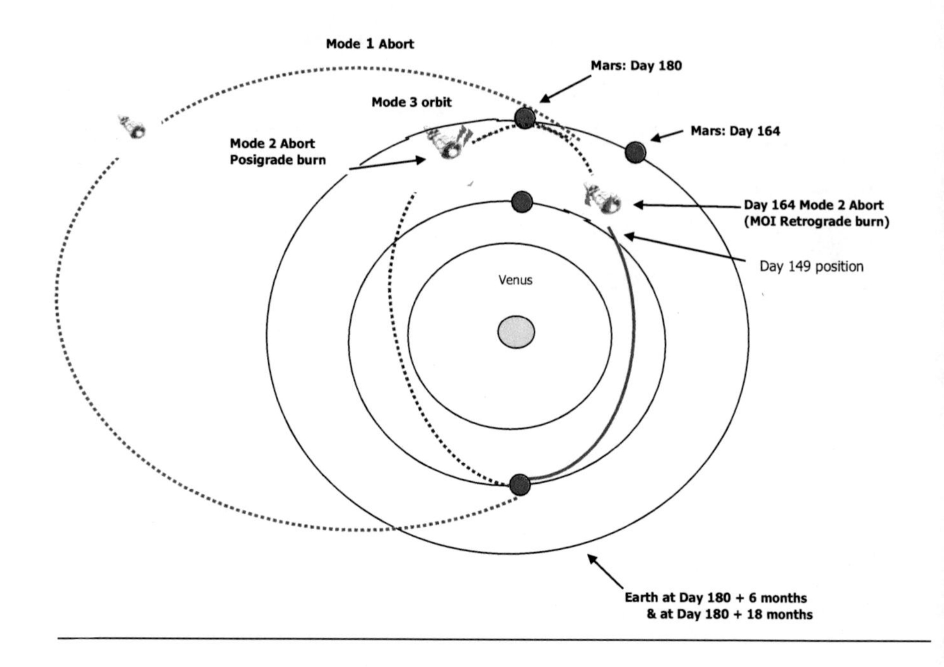

The Options on Day 149

(orbits and sizes not to scale)

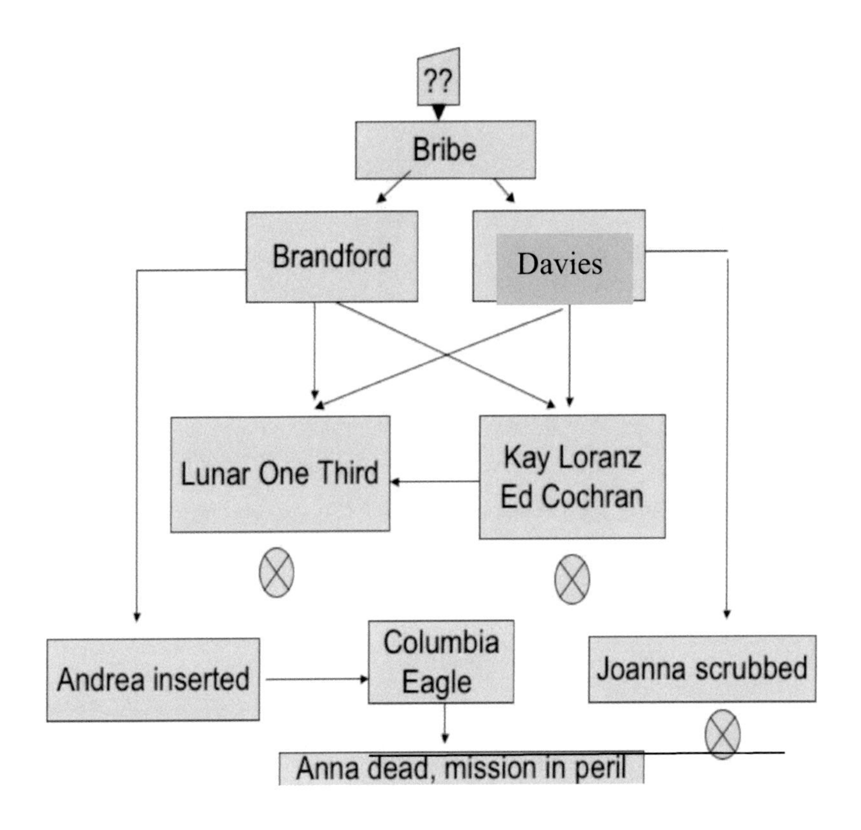

Tess' Flow Chart

MET = 0150:05:00:00. Discussing the call in A-deck the next night.

Chris was in a quandary. The same kind Tess had endured when Hosokawa dropped his bomb on her. Had he done it to cause friction or was he telling the truth? Was the guy just a madman or trying to help? Unlike Tess, Chris couldn't afford to sit on such news, not for a minute, not for a second. For though it might be nonsense, he had to tell the crew. They deserved to know, except maybe for Andrea. If this plot was real and she was in on it, she couldn't know he knew. Vadim, had to though. He was the Commander. He had to be told!

Vadim was livid when they met behind the closed door of Chris' sleeping quarters in secret. At first he shook his head from side to side, muttering, "*pizdui otsyuda, ne pizd!*" (get the fuck out of here, don't bullshit me). But the more Chris talked the more convincing he got, until Vadim finally eruped with, "*huy morzhoviy*?" (who is this walrus prick?)

"He runs FirstEarth!" Chris anwered.

It wasn't what Vadim wanted to hear. He knew all about the crazies in that party. "What do you think of this, what does Tess think?"

"She thinks he's telling the truth, Vadim, I think he's deranged."

"Every time I think it can't get any worse here, it does, *Huyovo!*"

"C'mon, Vadim, I know Andrea! I slept with her! Just because she acts weird sometimes doesn't mean she's a sabateur for Chrissakes. I can make just as good a case for Roberto being one. Notice how hot he was to do that EVA? What if that tile wasn't missing after all? What if he only said it was so he get out there and bust it."

"That's nuts, Chris. He did the repair."

"He said he did. We never saw it, did we?"

"Are you saying he punched out a tile to try and kill us...and himself? Look, I don't like that asshole anymore than I like his HUMMS but he'd never do that, he's a coward. Besides, he's a doctor and doctors take oaths to save people, not kill them."

"My point precisely, and neither would Andrea, who, by the way came up with the bar code idea to save an abort."

"Okay. So why does Tess believe this Horospowa guy."

"It's Hosokawa. Because she worked it out on one of her flowcharts. Brandford, Davies, my old boss Ed, Joanna, Andrea, they're all connected in a way that makes sense to her."

"But not to you?"

"I can make a chart that says I'm related to Stalin if I try hard enough. See where this is going, Vadim? They used to burn people at the stake for this, it was called a witch hunt."

"Okay, okay, so what do we do?"

"Fuck if I know. That's your decision, that's what you get the big bucks for."

"Some big bucks," Vadim complained managing a feeble smile. "I can't even afford a condo in the Moscow ghetto. Ok, never mind. Here's what we'll do, watch, listen and wait."

"For what?"

"A mistake."

"By who?"

"Andrea, Roberto, Horospower, Tess, any of them, all of them."

"What kind of mistake?"

“I don’t know. Maybe this crazy Horsopower will be jump off a bridge, maybe we’ll catch Andrea in the act; maybe Tess will change her mind. We’ll wait, watch, and listen. It’s all we can do.”

****

MET = O165:16:00   HOU=09:37   CANDOR=16:20   DELAY=07:56

Decision Point One

Following that conversation, Vadim watched Roberto and Andrea like a hawk. They made him edgy. So edgy, it was beginning to distract him. Yoshi was the first to notice, and asked him point blank about it. He couldn't tell her of course. Keeping his crew on point was like walking a fine line, or in this case a tightrope. Telling Yoshi would only make things worse. Fifteen days after the revelation he had become so distracted with the RA thing as he called it, that it didn't register at first when the MOCR rang in with their big decision a day late.

"You're go for Mode 3," Adam declared brightly on day 165. "You're to execute the correction burn for *Aerocapture* at MET 180. Fourteen days, twenty three hours from now."

Adam went on to list all the factors in the decision, the rationale favoring Modes 1 and 2, against the single reason for MODE 3, a reason neither Vadim nor anyone aboard had considered. With Anna gone, only 5 would be sharing the life support instead of 6. The mass savings would be multiplied, from food to fuel to power, allowing them to stay in orbit another month if they had to, an extra month for the storm to lift, to reacquire the beacon and possibly land.

"We know it doesn't look good now," Adam admitted, "but things could change in a heartbeat and we want you prepared. That's why we'd like you to start Landing Prep Ops right away Vadim. You and Yoshi are to begin Virtrainer rehearsals immediately; Andrea will fine-tune the Approach Corridor; Roberto will do a HUMMS dump and double your workouts on the Impact Simulator, and Chris should review the *Columbia* hibernation procedures.

We're uplinking a revised timeline to reflect the new schedule as we speak. Following it to the letter's your job. Getting the storm to lift is the Man upstairs'. Let's hope He does His part."

"How long can it last, Adam?" Vadim rejoined quickly. It hadn't even dawned on him that they'd been cleared to orbit.

The answer came back 8 minutes later: "Mariner 9 had a storm like this when it reached Mars in 1971. It lasted three months."

"Three months!" Vadim exclaimed to Yoshi, sitting next to him. "We don't have three months."

"But we have longer than we should have, thanks to Anna," she chastised him.

"Of course," he replied apolgetically.

It finally began to sink in. They'd made it past Modes 1 and 2.

And maybe, just maybe, Anna's death wouldn't have been in vain.

****

MET = 0175:20:00:00--5 days to *Aerocapture.*

The fury of the cyclone clouds had become all too evident now, wreaking havoc on a planet swollen to epic proportions through the windows.

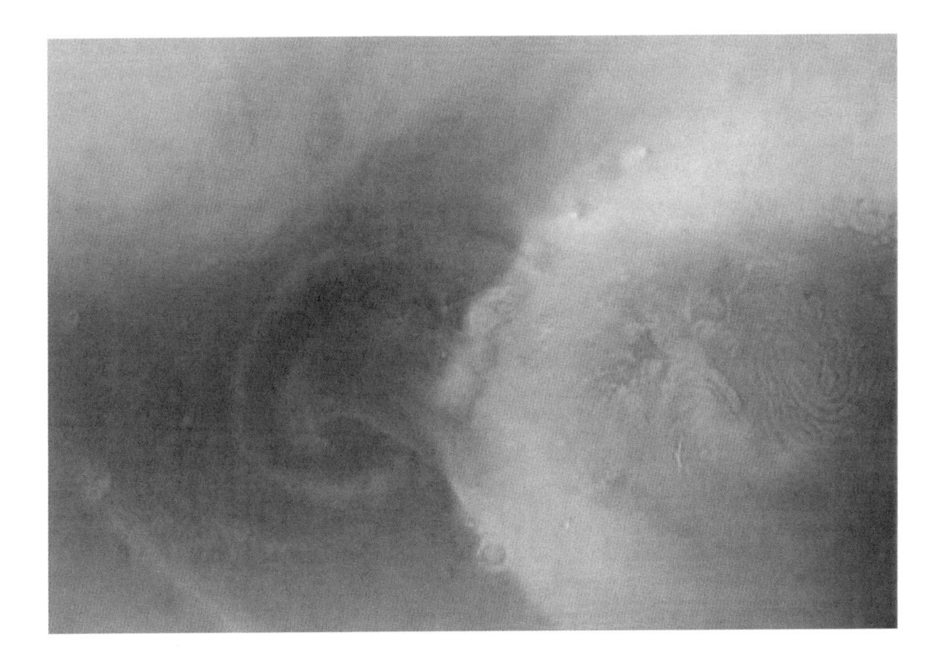

Shades of crimson played on Chris' evergreen eyes as he studied *Columbia's* hibernation procedures. The same way they did when he'd seen the sands of Chryse Planitia for the very first time. He was only 12 then, watching the images on TV. Now here he was, looking at them for real as he boned up on how to put the mother ship to sleep in the remote chance they were cleared for a landing attempt.

Andrea saw the clouds too as she performed the last of her fixes before Aerocapture. Vadim and Yoshi didn't see the clouds however, having shifted to Landing Prep Ops in C-Deck, where there were no windows. Facing a myriad of screens on a console called the Virtrainer (Virtual Reality Trainer), they stared at a facsimile of *Eagle's* EDS controls (Entry, Descent and Landing), schooling themselves over and over again.

"Descent or Aerocapture?" Yoshi requested after donning her helmet display unit.

"Descent," Vadim ordered, "and we need a 99 or better on the Prog score."

"*Shinan, muzukashii,*" she muttered under her breath.

"I caught that, what does *muzku chi* mean?"

Yoshi reset the disc to track 2, pushed the button that engaged the 3-dimensional holographic display and repied, "It's pronounced *muzukashii* and it means difficult. Why don't you just say, perfect, one hundred percent?"

"Okay, one hundred percent then," he snapped. She was actually relieved. He was beginning to act like his old self. Finally!!

Clouds began moving on their faceplates and the artificial horizon rocked steeply as the simulation started. Tiny shapes soon appeared overlaid on the clouds, projected x's, o's and +'s showing where they'd been, were and would be. They conveyed the consequence of each control movement to Vadim and Yoshi, who watched them ever so closely. Their job was to keep a tiny *Eagle* symbol in the middle of a moving band using their joysticks. The band was their Descent Corridor.

There would be six tense-filled minutes of this while they attempted to stay in the center of the narrow target, six minutes of simulated swoops, pitches and rolls culminating in a blinking light that read, ***Parachute Deploy***. It was followed by a scoresheet that popped up with a grade:

PERFORMANCE SUMMARY

A. DEORBIT BURN SEQUENCES--03 ERRORS
1. BURN DURATION
2. ENTRY ANGLE
3. CHUTE DEPLOY
B. SOFTWARE--0 ERRORS
C. DATA ACQUISITION--01 ERRORS
1. UAMS NOT ACTIVATED

DEORBIT BURN--ACCEPTABLE, DIAGNOTICS FOLLOW:

CORRECTIVE DIAGNOSTICS:

BURN DURATION = 22 SECONDS OPTIMUM = 23
ENTRY ANGLE= -15.2 DEG. OPTIMUM= -15.0
CHUTE DEPLOY: 5.7 km@786 m/sec. OPTIMUM = 6.0@700

PERFORMANCE SCORE= 88.3

"88.3," Yoshi whispered, "we pulled the chute out too late.”

“And busted the velocity window, and forgot the data system," Vadim growled. "Let's do it again."

As they prepared for another run, Roberto, across the deck from them, stepped into the Impact Simulator, a countermeasure device that put a piston-like load on the skeletal system. Its purpose was to accommodate their bodies to walking under the influence of Mars gravity while wearing a space suit. It would also be used for Earth Return, when they'd be going through another gravity jump, this one from 1/3 G to 1 G. Return was the last thing on Roberto's mind, however, as he set the tension to 91 pounds, placed the braces over his shoulders and waited for the machine to drive him towards the floor with a force equal to his body and spacesuit weight on Mars combined. His thoughts kept drifting back to Anna. Poor Anna, he thought, poor simple Anna. On the one hand, he was grateful it was her not him who took the hit. On the other he felt responsible. He’d pushed for the EVA she been terrified of. He could have bailed on it.

****

MET=0180:15:00 HOU=08:30 CANDOR=09:30 DELAY=09:03

Aerocapture

Day 180. First order of business that morning was scavenging the decks for loose items. Chris, Roberto and Yoshi battened them down while Andrea got her final fix. As she sighted Rigel in Orion and Regulus in Leo, then did a COAS and Doppler Shift correction, Vadim entered the Bridge and sat down across from her. He stared at her momentarily. She looked determined and purposeful. Aerocapture was at hand. How would she handle it?

The correction burn itself would be benign, hardly a blip of the methox engines. But it would alter their course just enough to make them intercept the Martian atmosphere. Intercept, skip out, and in and out again 4 more times, using the atmosphere as a brake instead of engines. The maneuver saved fuel, weight and cost, but it was also dangerous. Too shallow into the brink and they'd skip into space like a flat rock off water; too steep and they'd fry. How many times had he heard that? Now it was time to do it.

Vadim had no illusions why the MOCR had approved the maneuver. It was because of the AUTO trigger on his hand controller, not his pilot skills. Squeezing it would make the 5 General Purpose Computers take over and run the entire operation. For anything short of an emergency, he was to play a passive role, "*Bud obeziyanoj*" (be a monkey!), Leoniv had ordered him. *Aerocapture* had unknowns, he'd said, the kind wind tunnels couldn't predict.

They'd be using the atmosphere to trade speed for energy the way a skier uses his edges on a mountain. But this was no mountain. The pullouts had to be timed precisely, too precisely for human hands, which is why the GPCs would do it. *Dermo*, Vadim thought, bullshit! His job, as he saw it, was flying the ship, not babysitting computers, contemplating spy versus spy plots and acting like a monkey. Yet that's what he'd be reduced to as Andrea gave him her numbers, numbers their very lives hinged on.

AEROCAPTURE SETTINGS:

NUMBER OF PASSES: 5
ATMOSPHERE INTERFACE: 200 KM
ENTRY VEL: 6.31 KM/SEC
EXIT VEL: 4.90 KM/SEC
INITIAL APOPSIS: 10000 KM
FINAL APOPSIS: 3900 KM
INITIAL PERIAPSIS: 160 KM
FINAL PERIAPSIS: 160 KM
ENTRY ANGLE: 9.8 DEG
ANGLE WIDTH: 2.6 DEG
MAX TEMP: 1446 DEG C
MAX TOTAL Qf: 51.7 KJ/CM2
CORRIDOR WIDTH: 9.0 KM
CORRIDER DEPTH: 48 KM

CAPTURE TIME...3250 SECONDS

Vadim looked long and hard at the numbers: velocities, widths, angles, durations and temperatures. There would be 5 passes through the atmosphere, each taking 650 seconds for total of 3250 or 54 minutes. He looked so hard at her numbers that Andrea had to ask what was wrong with them. She didn't know he'd stayed up all night computing them on his own so he could crosscheck each against hers because he couldn't trust her.

"Nothing," he muttered unconvincingly, then keypunched each, one by one, into the DAP (Digital Autopilot). Only then did it finally hit him that they were entering Mars' lair at last. That the sleeplessness, tension and other bullshit were losing their grip on him, and that one way or another it would all be would over soon.

An update from Adam came next, clearing them for the burn. It said to expect Loss of Signal at AI (Atmosphere Interface), and that they'd be out of contact until their fifth and final exit. Red faded to black through the windows thereafter, as *Columbia's* RCS attitude thrusters blipped, tilting them tail first towards the atmosphere.

When the two big methox engines lit moments later, it was only a short burst, less than a minute and barely noticeable. It would take hours for its effect to be reflected on Chris' screen, five plodding hours where time seemed to slow down in anticipation of the first 650-second ride that would either orbit or kill them. It began with a climbing temperature gauge and a tremor in the Bridge as they met the thin Martian air.

The deeper they aerobraked into it, the more the tremor grew until a red glow appeared out the windows 7 minutes later, from plasma gases stripping electrons. That was Vadim's queue to squeeze the AUTO trigger, his last act of control before the GPCs took over and went to the VOTE mode, where majority ruled on every decision, a majority of integrated, not human, circuits. Having done so, he could only watch with the others while Yoshi read their fate off her screen:

CAPTURE TIME REMAINING: ONE HUNDRED FIFTY SECONDS
VELOCITY: FIVE POINT NINE ONE KILOMETERS PER SECOND
ALTITUDE: ONE NINE NINE POINT NINER KILOMETERS
MAX TEMP: ELEVEN HUNDRED DEGREES C
STATUS: IN CORRIDOR. AUTO CONTROL.

The trembling became a buffeting; the buffeting a pitching, and the plasma red turned pink. White stuff began flying by the windows, Vadim noticed. He hoped that it wasn't tile.

"Max Q in 15 seconds," Yoshi informed them, the Maximum Dynamic Pressure where air would be compressed into a shock wave under the ship. "Ten!" she called out with the buffetting at its peak.

The first pullout came on the heels of Max Q, an automated command from the GPCs. Mashed hard in his couch, Vadim fixated on the Alpha-Machmeter, reading 12 G's at 21 times the speed of sound. The forces were squashing his eyeballs deep in their sockets, and his vision was beginning to grey out.

'We're a toothpick in a hurricane and I'm supposed to do nothing,' he fumed to himself, but the forces soon eased, down to 8 G's, Mach 17, and his vision cleared. The GPCs were supposed to be god, but they'd overcorrected.

There'd be 4 more pullouts lasting 44 minutes and he'd be damned to let this happen again. He'd go MANUAL if it did, screw Leoniv, screw them all. But the computers caught it earlier and backed off sooner on the second pullout. The forces were down to 6 G's and Mach 12, then lower still on the 3rd and 4th pass.

When they exited the atmosphere on the 5th and last pullout, everything suddenly ceased. Buffeting, plasma glow, thruster bangs, and nerves. Everyone heaved an audible sigh of relief, everyone but Vadim. As he unfurrowed his brow, a tiny bead of perspiration crawled over it and around the flared left nostil of his nondescript Slavik nose, then along his angular cheekbone, past the distinctive brown birthmark that bordered wide lips closed over clenched teeth. Orbiting Mars at last, he'd never let on how he really felt.

But Yoshi knew. She'd seen that bead of sweat. She'd seen the fear in his eyes.

****

Aerocapture

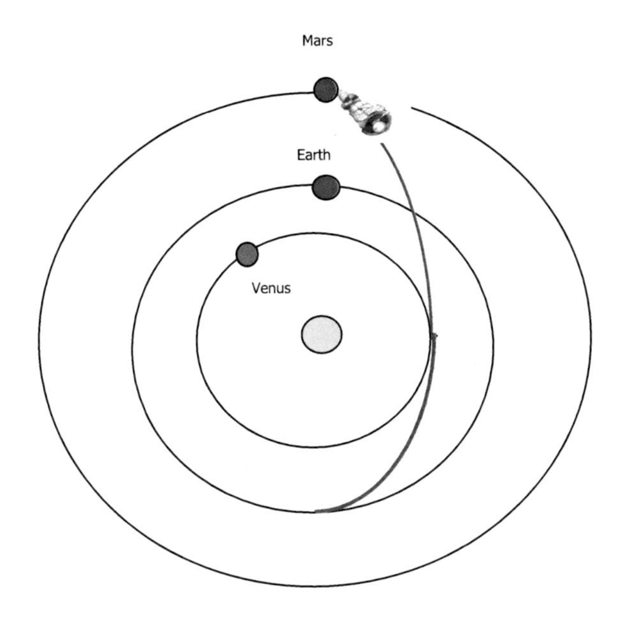

Columbia and Eagle at Aerocapture

(orbits and sizes not to scale)

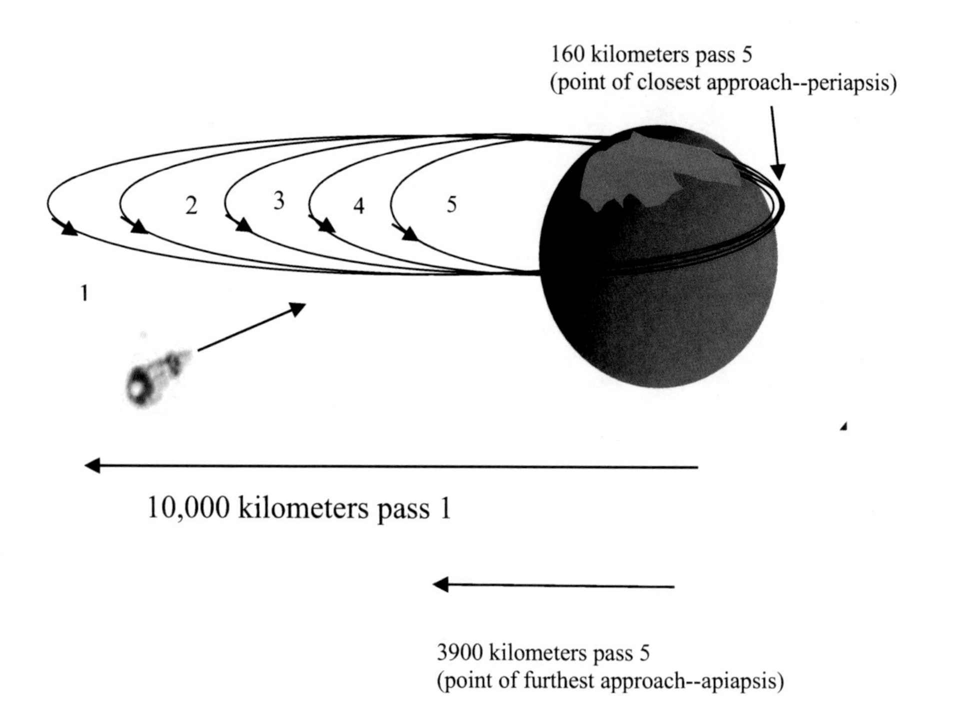

Five Passes: Aerobrake to Aerocapture

MET = 0197:05:00 HOU=22:37 CANDOR=18:18 DELAY=09:5

Aerocapture plus 17

Diarydisk Entry, Day 197 in-transit. Chris Elkay.

How can I describe it? Like the way LA materializes when the Santa Ana winds clear the smog? The Red Sea parting to reveal the sea floor? Yes, that's the kind of miracle we had today when the storm ceased. The clouds have finally peeled away and the view out the window is staggering. The Mars I've known all my life was a mirage. This is the most electrifying sight I've ever seen. Canyons and valleys from one end to the other; an equator bulging from so much subsurface force it looks pregnant; the smallest volcano bigger than the biggest on Earth and so on. Vallis Marineris looks like the work of a mad giant with an oversized shovel, stretching the width of the window as I peer down at it. And right in the middle of it all is Candor Base, our landing site. There's only 13 days left now, we're still healthy, the storm's done and all we need is to get our beacon back. That's not too much to ask for, is it? If there's a God, and there must be, for who else could make something like this, I'll ask Him. If not... if not, I'm just talking to myself.

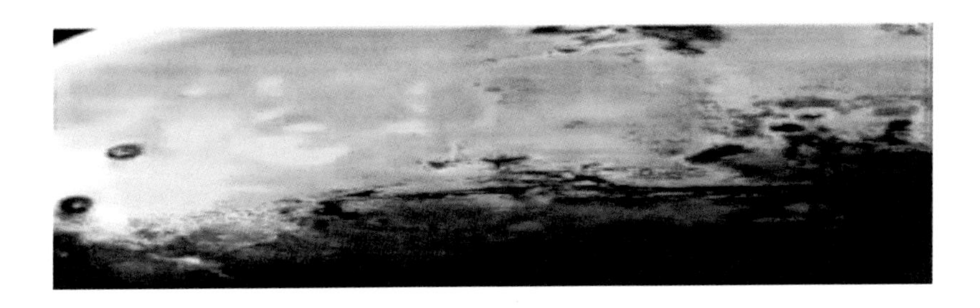

Reacquisition of Signal came on the heels of Chris' entry as if ordained.

"Houston, Columbus Eleven," a startled Vadim announced to all, "we've picked it up. We've got ILS back."

H Buford Stone already knew. He'd heard the signal in the MOCR and was beaming. He also knew what he *wanted* to do next as did everyone else, but wouldn't. He'd go by the book. He wouldn't violate the mission rules. So he went around the horn for approval as required, and then and only then did he feel the creases and folds lifting, the judgment of future history books changing. He glanced over at Kay Loranz, who allowed herself a smile back before he instructed the Capcom to pass the news on to the crew.

"Prepare for Separation," Adam Brady told them with a modicum of decorum. Repeat, Columbus Eleven, prepare for Separation!"

There was hardly time to celebrate.

The checklist of procedures was a long one: transfer supplies; charge *Eagle's* sodium hydride batteries prior to powerup; powerdown *Columbia* into hibernation mode, each with a hundred substeps, any of which could stop them in their tracks. But they wouldn't allow it, they had momentum on their side and the collective will of millions, billions back home. The first problem surfaced at Separation minus 19 hours and they dealt with it quickly.

"Battery won't charge," Chris reported, "*Eagle's* not powering up." They traced it to a popped circuit breaker monitoring the power in from *Columbia*. Snapping it ON fixed the problem but another one surface two hours later, "Helium pressure low," Yoshi alerted, "I'm switching Tank One to the bypass loop."

And so it went until Separation minus 12 hours, which called for a sleep period. Not that anyone could sleep, especially Chris, who had to spend it on the rotating bed. Which made it all the more surprising when he dozed off, and all the more disturbing when his red and green dream resurfaced after months in abeyance. It returned with a vengeance, enigmatic and even more troubling than before. This time he was adrift on a tossing green sea, with red hail pelting him instead of rain. As far as he could see there was nothing but that sea, no airlock door like the last time, no land, no sign of life. Then suddenly he was tossed overboard, being pulled by a vicious undertow to the bottom, towards an abyss, a fissure bigger than Vallis Marineris that would engulf him.

He awoke drenched in perspiration with his heart pounding, and forgot for the moment where he was. Yanking his head from the neckbrace while rotating, the effect was immediate: nausea and regurgitation. Why me, why now, he whined, cupping his hands over his mouth. And what the hell does it mean, this crazy dream? Green for Earth, red for Mars, that was obvious, but the sea, the sky, the raft, the hole?

He joined the others at Separation minus 8 hours, locking lockers, stowing tables and putting *Columbia* on standby while he pondered the dream. But as the clock reached minus 7 he wasn't the only one pondering. Everyone, alone with their thoughts, reflected how they'd gotten here and what they were about to do. Until *Columbia* had been put to sleep. Until she was in hibernation mode and it was finally time to leave her.

They went into her tunnel for the last time at SEP minus 5, carrying transfer bags filled with personal effects, but stopped at the other end to say thanks for bringing them here and to ask for one more favor. They'd have to power her back up after a year and a half on the surface while she orbited alone and powered down in icy space. Like so many other firsts, it had never been tried before. With that request, Vadim motioned the others ahead into *Eagle's* airlock, sealed off *Columbia's* hatch and followed them into the lander.

Eagle's hammock-couches seemed strangely unfamiliar after so many months in *Columbia.* Lying in a circle with their feet at the center, they felt cramped and vulnerable. Four hours to Separation remained, four hours to flip switches, activate systems and wait for the *six minutes of terror* they'd all heard so much about, trained for incessantly and feared. The facts were clear enough. Humans had done EDLs (Entry, Descent and Landings) hundreds of times, but always on Earth or the Moon, never on Mars. Mars didn't have the thick atmosphere that slowed you down so well on Earth, or the 1/6 gravity that made retrorockets perfect for the Moon. Its atmosphere was a hundredth of Earth's, yet still thick enough to cause severe entry heating. And its gravity--though a third of Earth's-- was twice the Moon's, which made excess weight a killer, and *Eagle* was heavy, 81 tons in its stocking feet. All this made Mars a different animal, a very dangerous one. The reality was *Eagle* would fall like a brick from 120 miles high to the ground in just over 6 minutes compared to 40 for a space shuttle on Earth, and the wispy Mars air would only help cushion it for the last 90 seconds.

In those 90 seconds, they would have to slow down from a blistering mile/second to a couple of feet/second, and rockets and parachutes alone couldn't do it unless they were twice the size, impossible given the weight constraints. Something else was needed, another technological breakthrough like ADSS.

That breakthrough was a *Hypercone*, a huge, inflatable donut ninety feet in diameter.The Hypercone would pop open and decelerate them from supersonic to subsonic quickly, enabling them to use lighter and smaller engines and parachutes. If it worked, they'd plummet out of orbit like a skydiver on a dare before "pulling the ripcord" of engines, chute and Hypercone for a soft landing. If it didn't work any better than ADSS, they'd drill a hole in the surface of Mars the size of Meteor Crater.

With 3 ½ hours to go, Chris activated the EDL imaging system, then the UAMS (Upper Atmosphere Mass Spectrometer) that would sample the atmosphere while they descended. Roberto, next to him, engaged the life-support systems; Vadim and Yoshi, the CWS; and Andrea, the NAV computer. Next to her was Anna's empty couch, which she kept glancing at repeatedly. She finally had to force herself to look away as the clock ticked down to SEP minus 2 hours, the unfilled gap beside her growing too large to bear.

As they worked, the only light inside, provided by the harsh glow of fluorescents, was artificial. It would stay that way until the heat shield covering *Eagle's* window was blown off in the descent, which would let in natural light. At SEP minus 1, Vadim began the first crucial series of interplays with Yoshi to make that happen.

"Pressurization check," he announced, beginning the cabin leak-check. Then, "CABIN VENT to CLOSE, VENT ISOL to CLOSE."

"Roger in work, cabin pressure, 14.7 psi and steady."

"02/N2 quantity check?"

"N2, 79.1 percent, 02, 21.1."

From there they went to the arming of the two Main Descent Engines, checking valve positions, fuel quantities and pressures. Next they armed the 16 smaller Reaction Control System thrusters, clustered into 4 pods of 4 to control their pitch, roll and yaw. Starting forward right they worked they way around to aft left until Yoshi finally parroted back her verification, "He PRESS to OPEN, TANK ISOL to GPC; RCS CROSSFEED to OFF. Aft left pod configured, RCS arming complete."

It was SEP minus 30 minutes when they moved to activate the Evaporator and Ammonia Boiler for cooling, turned on the APUs for hydraulics and began loading the descent settings into *Eagle's* computers. Adrenaline coursed through everyone's veins with each step now.

"NH4 to BLR ENGAGE," Yoshi read off at minus 20 minutes.

"APU 1, 2 EXEC in work," at minus 15.

"UNIX 3 to DAP; OPS 303 loaded," at minus 10.

"ADI and AVVI zeroed," at minus 5. *All flight instruments up and running,"* Her voice crackled with excitement.

With 2 minutes to go, the MOCR's, "Go for Separation," clearance finally arrived and Vadim snapped a rocker switch. Two minutes later a SEPARATION GO light flashed, followed by the report of pyrotechnic bolts, and a soft shove. They'd separated from *Columbia.* All that remained now was the final clearance and Andrea's deorbit burn numbers. She read them aloud knowing Vadim would double-check each one. She didn't care. Her senses were ablaze.

"Burn Duration....forty two seconds.
Descent Time...Six minutes, eighteen seconds
Delta Vx...minus 300 meters per second
Entry Velocity...three point five kilometers per second
Velocity at Chute Deploy....six hundred meters per second
Altitude at Chute Deploy....six kilometers
Velocity at Chute Jettison...fifty six meters per second.
Corridor Angle...6.6 degrees.
Corridor Width...5.1 kilometers"

Vadim keyed the numbers into the OPS 303 roll, pitch and yaw program, then waited for Adam's final approval. It came after a ten minute lag that had grown to a gut-wrenching time warp. He sounded even further away than the 200 million miles he was when his disembodied voice rang out with,

"You're GO for deorbit, *Eagle*. LOS will be in 5 minutes 14 seconds; landing in 6 minutes, 18 seconds after TIG. This will be our last transmission before touchdown. Godspeed."

TIG (Time of Ignition) came 30 minutes later at Periapsis--the closest point to the planet on their path around it. A retrograde burn of the descent engines ushered it in, slowing them down with a whining burst that nudged them gently out of orbit.

"Descent Engine Shutdown," Vadim called out 42 seconds later as *Columbia* disappeared from sight. It seemed an eternity before they swung around the backside of Mars and a spike on the UAMS confirmed atmosphere intercept. The *Six Minutes of Terror* was finally underway.

All ears turned to Yoshi, reading off the altitude, velocity and G forces.

"Radar altimeter, 190 kilometers," she reported with buffeting picking up. "Velocity 3.5 kilometers a second, Alpha machmeter, 0.5 G's."

The computers took over, firing *Eagle's* RCS thrusters to hold her to the entry corridor. All 16 of them seemed to report simultaneously.

"Altitude 180," Yoshi rejoined. "Velocity, 2.5 kilometers a second, 0.7 G's, five minutes, thirty seconds to touchdown."

As in Virtrainer practice, the tiny x's, o's and +'s now appeared. They filled Vadim's screen telling him where they'd been, were and would be. There was a huge difference this time around. This was a real entry, not practice.

"150 kilometers," Yoshi alerted him, "velocity, 2.2 kilometers a second, 3 G's, five minutes, fifteen seconds."

At a hundred kilometers high, an S-shaped band appeared on Vadim's screen, a pictogram of the entry corridor with a cross-hair at its bottom and a circle at its top. When the ILS locked on the beacon, the cross-hair would start moving along the S towards the circle. It would be the terminal entry phase, the part he was girding for.

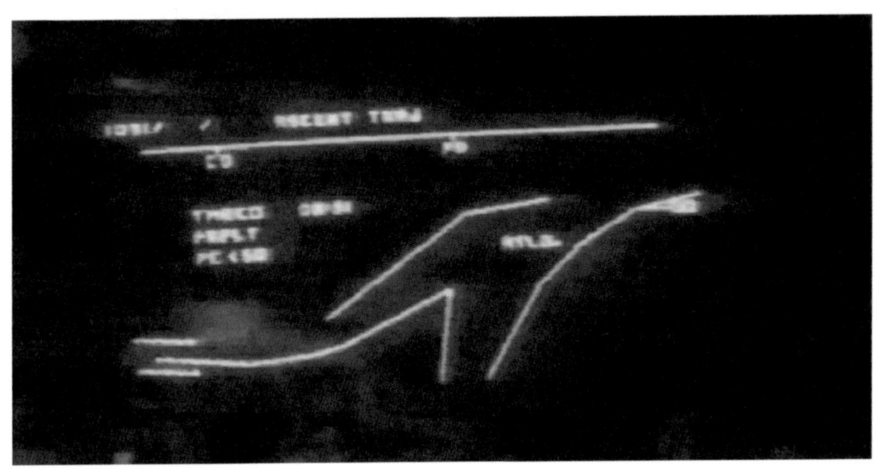

"90 kilometers," Yoshi advised, "velocity 1.9 kilometers a second, 4.8 G's, four minutes, forty five seconds to touchdown. Pitch-up."

The computers were about to pitch them up 14 degrees to ease the dive. It would blunt the heating but push them into their hammocks. It was gentler than expected when it came, but only briefly, followed seconds later by the pitch-down, a pit in the stomach punch from the dive resuming. Andrea checked the NAV numbers. They'd streaked halfway around the equator already.

Patches of red began showing on the descent monitor through breaks in the clouds. They were trading horizontal for vertical velocity with a fury. Falling like a brick at over three football fields a second.

"70 kilometers," Yoshi called out, ".....60....."

At 50 kilometers altitude, Vallis Marineris dominated the screen and they began paralleling it. The descent monitor only hinted at the gape below them where Candor Base hid.

"Altitude, 19 kilometers," Yoshi intoned, "velocity, 1.1 kilometers a second, 1.6 G's, four minutes, twenty seconds. ILS lock. We have ILS lock."

With the radar finally locked on the ILS beacon, the cross-hair started to move, inexorably tracing its path upwards towards the tiny circle. Reflexly, Vadim clenched his right hand around the hand controller, his index finger poised yet resisting the lure of the MANUAL button. *Bud obeziyanoj, Bud obeziyanoj*.

"On corridor, heading in," Andrea reported.

"15 kilometers altitude, four minutes," Yoshi echoed.

Another good sign came when Chris saw the stagnation temperature drop. It meant the heating had peaked and the tiles had held. It also meant it was time to engage the Hypercone. Vadim crossed his fingers, lifted a switch guard and pulled a metal ring. Explosive devices blew the shields off the Hypercone and inflated it at the same time the two big descent engines fired. A vicious yank jerked *Eagle* upwards as the cone became a wing and broke their fall through the atmosphere. A popping sound followed as struts inside *Eagle* sprung spidery legs free to the landing position. Mars was but 12 kilometers below them now. They could taste its dust.

Hypercone Deployment

At ten kilometers high, the descent monitor resolved three canyons: Ophir, Candor and Melas. Candor was in the middle and Vadim began scanning its western edge for the mesa that was their landing site.

Before he could find it, the S-curve drew his attention. The cross-hair was deviating, demanding action. Though his trigger finger itched, the computers were still in control. He could almost feel them voting, pitching the Hypercone, pulling *Eagle* back on corridor.

"7.9 kilometers," Yoshi interrupted. "Velocity, 1 kilometer a second. Three minutes. Coming up on High Gate!"

High Gate, where they'd swing 70 degrees vertically, would be their last No-Go opportunity. Past that point, they wouldn't be able to get back to *Columbia* with their descent engines. An abort would require the ascent engines. They felt the thrusters fire as they crossed the gate and *Eagle's* apex tilted back down again. The heat shield blew off the window, crimson flood the cabin.

"Gate closed," Yoshi rang out, "6.4 kilometers, 780 meters a second. Stand-by for Chute Deploy, two minutes to touchdown."

They were nearing Candor Chasma's yawning rim when more percussive bangs resounded, the report of pyrotechnics jettisoning the Hypercone and deploying the chutes. First the drogues came out, then the huge main chute, 150 feet in diameter. Their shadow swept into Candor's rim. They were plunging headlong into it.

"Six kilometers, 700 meters a second, 90 seconds to touchdown," Yoshi said tersely. They were bisecting the canyon three miles above the landing site now, heading west into a bottomless gulch that could deal death in an instant. Vadim watched riveted but stayed focused. He'd spent half his life on these landmarks: Ares Vallis, Capri Chasma and Shalbatana Vallis. Ghenghis Chasma, Juventae Chasma, Coprates Chasma. He wasn't about to unfocus now.

"Three kilometers, 630 meters a second, seventy five seconds to go," he heard Yoshi announce. "Standby for engine braking."

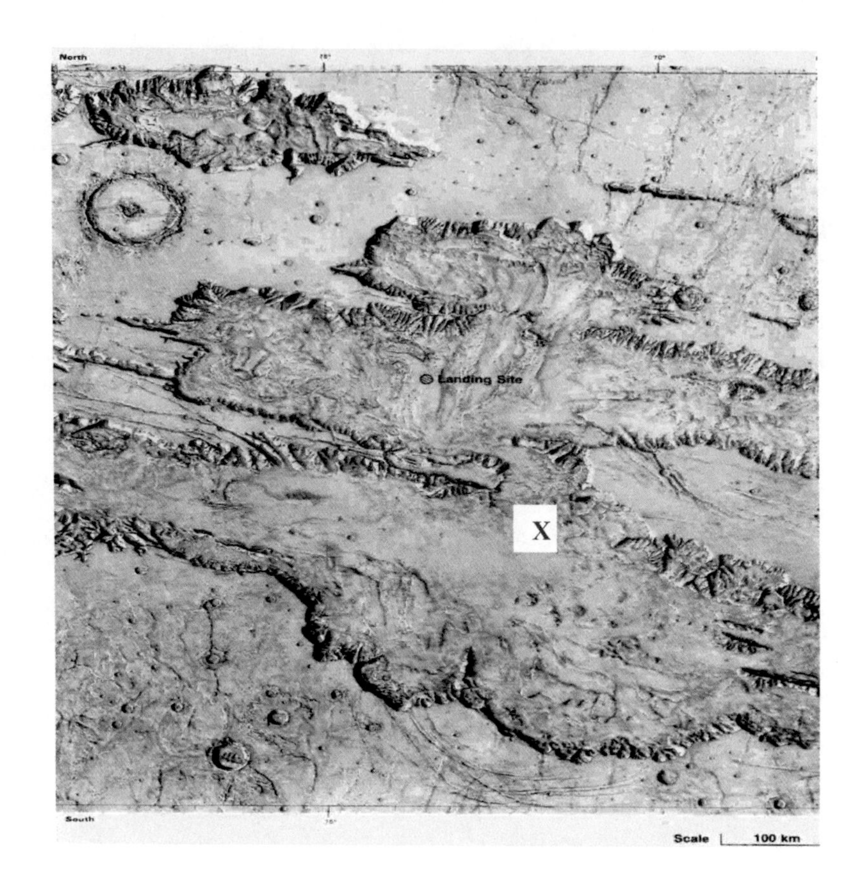

Everything on his S-curve told Vadim they were right on the mark. Every number confirmed it. Yet he felt uneasy when the descent engines lit again to brake the fall. Perhaps it was because the cross-hair had entered the circle but he still couldn't see the mesa. Perhaps there was just some dust below obscuring it.

"Two thousand meters!" Yoshi called out, "vertical velocity 400, 300, 200 meters a second, sixty seconds."

Vadim still couldn't see the fucking landing site. He'd know that mesa if he was blindfolded and he should have seen it by now. Uneasiness became concern when he realized nothing looked familiar. *What is happening,* he thought nervously, his eyes glued to each input like a microscope. Suddenly there was an alert, a yellow blinking light and a warble tone from Andrea's console.

"1201 Alarm!" she cried out, "Program Overload."

Conflicting data was overloading the 5 computers. Their vote had hit a stalemate. If it kept up, NAV would shut down, and they'd lose engine control.

"Override it!" Vadim snapped with an authority that could blister paint.

Override would undo the deadlock allowing another vote. Andrea complied. The light extinguished.

"Landing legs locked, one thousand meters, 45 seconds," Yoshi said cooly. It was a different kind of cool this time, tense and nervous. Another alarm sounded, with more warning wails. Louder ones.

"1202!" Andrea yelled.

Vadim had had enough. "I'm taking it!" he shouted above the din, "I'm taking it."

I'm taking it. I'm taking it!

A boulder the size of Ayer's rock loomed in the window when Vadim finally squeezed the red button. They nearly brushed it as he yanked the stick forward to gain altitude. He realized then he hadn't recognized that rock or anything else in its path. The maps he'd memorized could well have been for Pluto. He eased the stick back to hover, knowing it would cost him fuel. “Methox,” he shouted out to Yoshi, “how much left?”

"4 percent," she responded apprehensively. “Less than 3 minutes.”

Vadim had another decision to make now. They were a hovering above a no-mans land with 4 percent methox in their descent tank, skimming deadly terrain with less than 3 minutes of fuel left. A T-handle with yellow hashmarks beckoned. It was next to Vadim's elbow and *Eagle* would split in two if he pulled it.

Her descent stage would shear off and crash to the surface but her ascent stage would ignite, hurling them back to *Columbia* and safety. Their bodies would survive but not their dreams. Everything they'd worked for would vaporize like exhaust fumes from those engines if he pulled that handle. He knew then he couldn't do it. '*Nyet bud obeziyanoj*, I am not a monkey, I am a pilot, a cosmonaut, an explorer.' Those passions had already taken over, telling him, commanding him to *fly the fucker down*. Just find a flat spot and *fly the fucker down*!

"FUEL, 2 PERCENT," Yoshi gulped,
"TWO MINUTES, LESS THAN A MILE CROSS-RANGE."

As if on cue, a ridge appeared in the window. It had soft dunes near the base of an embankment. It had boulders but small ones, there were inclines but not severe ones. Not perfect but close enough, Vadim decided. He pitched down to line up the landing reticles in the window with the scene below, then told Yoshi to give him range and range rate by the second. She'd been at wits end but his tone instilled new confidence in her. Calm now, she fed him the numbers:

"Altitude, 540, down at 30/second. Down at 15. 400 meters. Down at 9 a second, down at 4, 350. 330, 310. Down at 3 1/2 a second. Pegged on horizontal velocity, 50 meters a second forward. Vadim. 300 meters, down at 3 ½, 47 forward. Ninety seconds fuel. 1-1/2 down. Our shadow's out there now, I can see it. Down at 2 a second, 19 forward. Altitude velocity lights. 3-1/2 a second down, 220 to go. 1-1/2 down, 13 forward. 11 forward. 200 altitude, 4-1/2 meters/second down, 5 1/2 down. 9 forward. Fuel quantity light, Vadim, 75 meters, 6 forward. Landing lights on. Down at 2-1/2...40 meters. Down at 2-1/2, kicking up dust. 30...2-1/2 down. Landing leg shadow. 4 forward....4 forward, drifting right. Still drifting right...45 seconds fuel. 30 seconds...dust. Contact light! Engines stop! Fuel shutoff....."

Suddenly there was nothing but silence.

****

Suddenly there was nothing but silence.

BOOK 3-----ANSWERS

Chapter 21. The Dead Land.

This is the dead land, this is the cactus land,
The eyes are not here, there are no eyes here,
In this valley of dying stars, in this hollow valley.
This broken jaw of lost kingdoms.

T. S. Eliot

July 16, 2034

A creaking.

In the deafening silence after Engines Off, it was the only sound heard besides heartbeats. Vadim spoke first. "*Chertova mashina*," he blurted out, "that fucking beacon. It would have taken us into a boulder."

Yoshi exhaled. She'd never admit it but she'd been terrified. They'd be dead if not for Vadim, all of them. Decisive and unflappable, she worshipped the ground he walked on. "*Irrasaimasu,*" she said gratefully, "welcome to Mars."

He glanced at her quickly, sizing her up like his other instruments. One scan told him everything. No one could have performed better, not Leoniv, not Gagarin. He was glad she was with him through all that.

"Post-landing checklist," he shot back to her stoically. "Engine Arm to OFF; 413 to IN; MODE to AUTO; Fuel to VENT...."

The creaking persisted as she followed his orders, a dull, stretching "claaacckkkkk" from deep within *Eagle's* bowels. The feeling of gravity soon sank in, and with it the sense of a tilt.

"We're leaning," Roberto piped up.

"Inclinometer?" Vadim asked of Chris.

"He's right, Vadim, we're 12 degrees off horizontal."

The creaking subsided as they worked through the shutdown, then picked up again like bubbles from a pop bottle, hissing and fizzing, getting louder then lower then louder until a groan suddenly shook the cabin and it pitched forward. "Jesus," Roberto yelled, before their forward motion jerked violently to a halt. "What the…"

"Okay?" Vadim barked, "everyone okay?"

"What was that?" Andrea whispered.

"I don't know," Vadim replied, "but let's hope that's all of it."

"It felt like a fault shift," Chris replied, "and we're 31 degrees off horizontal now."

"Naturally," Vadim said sarcastically. "We come all this way to land in the middle of a fucking earthquake."

"A Marsquake," Chris corrected, "and we probably caused it."

Loosening his harness, Vadim sought out the cabin pressure guage, reading 14.7 psi--normal, then the ascent engine fuel quantity, 93 percent and dropping.

"That quake tore a hole in a fuel line, he scowled, "what next?" He sent an uplink to the MOCR. They'd be turning blue waiting and would have some advice for him. Twenty minutes later--twice the expected lag--there'd been none. "I can't raise Houston," he appraised the others, "we're on our own."

Everyone inhaled deeply and waited for the next surprise.

Vadim started cranking numbers, whirring out the options of whether to abort home or stay. As for leaving, *Eagle* was already listing at 31 degrees, the launch limit angle that could be too steep to reach *Columbia.* Compounding that was the ascent engine fuel pressure, down to 90 percent now. They could run out of methox before they ever reached her. As for staying, their ILS descent radar had failed and Candor Base could be anywhere. Reading his thoughts, Andrea said,

"I took a Line of Position on final glideslope. We're close to it."

"A line of position's not a point," Roberto countered. "It could be days away."

Vadim kept running numbers. He checked *Eagle's* oxygen quantity, reading 85 percent, enough for two days. If they stayed here that long, all the ascent fuel would leak out. He checked the fuel again and it was down to 87 percent. They'd need to launch within the hour to have any hope of making it. And what if they did? What if they rendezvoused with *Columbia* and made it back to Earth alive, then what? We'd return as failures, not heroes, he concluded. That made it simple: the primary oxygen in their MarsSuits would last 8 hours. In tests back home, they'd walked 10 kilometers in 2 hours in those suits, which translated to 40 kilometers in 8 hours but on Earth. Could they walk that same pace on Mars, was Candor within 40 km, could they find it before sunset when visibility would vanish?

"*Que paso*?" Roberto intruded, "what are we going to do, Commander?"

"It's within 30 kilometers," Andrea chimed in. "I *know* it!"

The choice was clear: Vadim couldn't abandon the mission only an hour after they landed. He rose from his flight couch and looked Chris, Yoshi, Roberto and Andrea in the eye in turn. "I don't know much American history," he started, "but there was this guy Twain who said, 'twenty years from now you'll be more disappointed by what you didn't do than what you did. I believe that so suit up. We're egressing!"

Things got off to a slow start. The MarsSuits were great suits, worlds above the clumsy EVA suits they'd used during the transit. They weighed half as much with twice the bells and whistles including Violet, its voice querying and answer system (Violet stood for Voice Initiated Operator for Life-support and Exploration Tracking). But with *Eagle* listing 31 degrees, none of that meant a thing since they'd have to be donned bass ackwards. It took half an hour instead of ten minutes. More time was lost because only two at a time could squeeze into the airlock. While Andrea and Yoshi waded through the depress sequence first to purge nitrogen from their blood and prevent the bends, the others had to wait their turn. By the time everyone got out, an hour and a half had passed, an hour and a half closer to sunset.

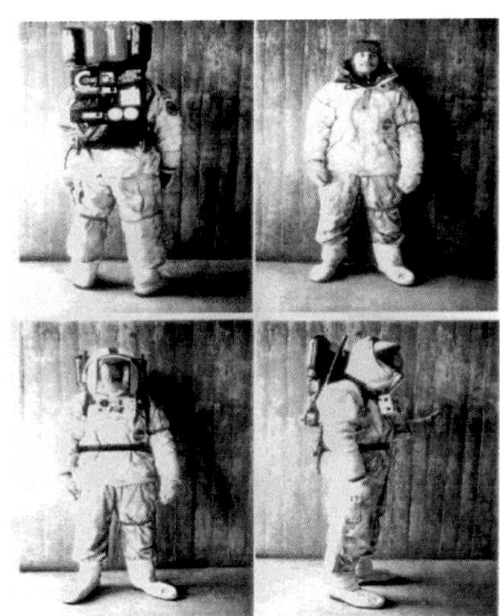

Donning the MarsSuit

It was just after noon when the first human footsteps imprinted the Martian soil. Shafts of strong sunlight blinded the first human eyes as they strained to see the landscape, and as their pupils adjusted, shadows in rust-red appeared, grudgingly at first then in waves. To the left and west, a solitary yellow cloud hung precariously in a salmon pink sky. To the right and east, millions of rocks speckled endless dunes to the horizon. Everywhere else, nothing moved at all. Save for a faded, smoky vapor trail wisping from *Eagle's* engines. They watched it waft skyward, the last vestiges of lifeblood from their fallen craft.

To the left and west

To the right and east

Vadim went to *Eagle's* equipment bay. But instead of the Rover he'd sought for just such an emergency, there was a flag in its place to save weight. He took the UN flag, an inspiration to their successors, he hoped, not a testimony to their failure, like Scott's Base in Antarctica. He moved away after planting it, knowing no more time could be wasted, then glanced back for a second, shook his head, and shouted, "*Smativatsa*, "move out!"

Planting the flag

Walking west along Andrea's Line of Position, they felt only the tug of alien gravity, heard only their own breathing. His crew followed Vadim in single file behind him, Yoshi, Roberto, Andrea and Chris, awestruck by the wonder of the place--the low gravity that made them feel light as feathers; the patches of ice sublimating off the ground; the many shades of red--but it was tempered by a fear of time, the knowledge that if they didn't reach Candor Base within 8 tense filled hours, they'd be history.

Warnings from their suits would hammer home those hours with every step, as well as a hundred other readouts they could either see on their heads-up-display or be told about by Violet, in a sexy eastern European voice.

Those readouts now told them it was cold outside, with a 7-knot wind blowing from the south. It all seemed so Earth-like, except cold in this place was not a few degrees south of freezing but minus 100. The geologist in Chris noted other striking differences, like how the soil took footprints, high-grained and cohesive, yet collapsing on itself like dry sand, a contradiction; or the glistening green maghemite that indicated magnetism, when Mars wasn't supposed to have a magnetic field.

Last in line, Chris pulled the PLSS carrier, a 2 wheeled cart bearing Anna's Portable Life Support System (PLSS). Her PLSS, their buddy breathing system (BSLSS) and their own 45-minute emergency reserve OPS (Oxygen Purge System), provided some margin if they needed it, but would it be enough? As the path up the embankment steepened and the cart slowed his pace, Chris decided to query Violet to try and find out.

"Limiting Consumables," he called out and she responded instantly.

Your limiting consumable is oxygen. You have gone one point six kilometers on a heading of two six seven degrees. Your average pace is one point six kilometers per hour. Twenty-five kilometers remain before life support exhaustion.

Violet's voice was upbeat but her news wasn't. They'd crawled but 1.6 kilometers in the first hour, had 25 to go before their O2 ran out, and west, where they were heading, looked daunting and uninviting. Even if Andrea was right, and Candor was less then 30 km away, they'd never make it at that rate. The irony of it all struck Chris. He'd always imagined this journey in the most grandioise of terms, with discoveries to be made and new planetary perspectives.

He'd even rehearsed the speech he'd make from the surface, beginning with the thank yous.

"The spacecraft which got us here is incredibly complicated," he'd say. "But we had great confidence in it because of our team, the hundreds of thousands who put their blood, sweat and tears into building, inspecting and testing it."

From there he'd describe what the billions back home couldn't possibly appreciate, how everything looked so familiar yet different. How you half expected an iguana to jump out at you from behind a rock until you realized there were no iguanas, or cactii or tumbleweed or anything else alive. And that without a MarsSuit, your blood would boil, your skin would freeze and your lungs would explode in a few heartbeats. He'd finish up with the metaphors and some religion, though he wasn't religious:

'When I consider the heavens...what is man that Thou art mindful of him?'"

He'd often imagined that speech, but not under such conditions, on a deathmarch with noone listening.

An hour later, the crest of the embankment they were scaling was still not in sight. It was 2 PM local time with less than 6 hours of sunlight and life support remaining. Everyone was breathing harder now, sucking oxygen in like water.

Roberto festered inside. 'Vadim's dumb pride will kill us,' he mumbled to himself, 'we should have left'. A voice intruded over the comm just then, Chris', with an observation.

"That fan-shaped debris field below us comes from...uff...talus deposits I'd say we...uff...landed in an impact crater. Probably, uff...very old."

"Why does he give a shit?" Roberto fumed, "We could be corpses in a few hours."

It had occurred to Chris that his passion about Mars and his impending mortality made strange bedfellows but he couldn't help himself. He was who he was. A few minutes later he was rewarded when the peak of the embankment appeared.

A wide plateau lay before them when they crested it, flanked by endless canyons. Vadim knew the area instantly, Texas Mesa. He could finally get some bearings. Turning to his 1 o'clock, he searched for the band of striations that marked Cat-eye crator, an elliptical dune field. If the maps were right, Candor Base would be 16 kilometers northwest of it. He squinted into the midafternoon sun until he found Cat-eye at a heading of 271 on his visor compass, then paced a hundred meters south and took another heading, this one 272. He did the math. Cat-eye should be 6 kilometers west of them, putting Candor Base 22 km away as the crow flies. He was ecstatic, Andrea had been right.

They could make it but they'd have to average at least 5 km/hr. If the terrain held steady, they could do it in the MarsSuits but it would be tight. It would be tighter still for Yoshi and Andrea, who'd burned more O2 waiting for the others to depressurize and egress after them. At the time, sending the two females out first seemed noble, now it seemed stupid, incredibly stupid!

As they moved out again, the group was treated to an unexpected and stunning sight, a thick fog suddenly spilling down the canyon wall to the west of them. Looking like melted ice cream over the sides of a cone, it blotted out the Sun and moved faster than any earthly fog until it reached their feet. It hung low to the ground, barely covering their boots, then cascaded down the embankment where they'd come from. From there it seemed to grow again, foaming up and spreading, until it reached the site of *Eagle*, barely visible from where they stood. It would be the last they'd ever see of her, it billowed up and devoured her. Struck and saddened, they lingered in the moment until Vadim pushed them on. *"Cyobivayemsya,"* he urged, "keep going." Ten minutes later they caught a break. Sunlight poked through again from the west, illuminatiing the path ahead. It never would have happened on Earth, Chris realized, the air was a hundred times thicker, and the fog would have lingered for hours.

"Cyobivayemsya"

From afar, Cat-eye had resembled a lake, with rippling crests and troughs. But two hours later when they finally got there, it became a sea of dunes. Arc-shaped ridges with twin horns punctuated each, pointing away from the wind to the west. The angle between each ridge and the upwind floor was a nearly identical 15 degrees and the downwind sand sloped 32.

Chris knew them at once. These were barchan dunes. But not all the crests pointed west. Others pointed east and were parabolic dunes, U-shaped mounds well known in coastal deserts. Their elongated arms pointed downwind and he stared at them disbelievingly. On Earth their shape was unique, fixed only by vegetation. How could this be, is there water here, is there life? He yearned to know but time forbade it.

Cat-eye

The soil became volcanic as they trudged along Cat-eye, more densely packed but easier to navigate. They could pick up the pace now and pushed harder until they came face to face with another startling sight, thousands of mounds protruding from the ground like trees in a forest. They were conically shaped and varied in size from the scale of an anthill to the height of Vadim, each capped with a circular depression.

"Shield volcanoes!" Chris exclaimed astonished once more. "It's unimaginable they'd be this small."

Again he couldn't stop to look. Time, not science dominated.

Three kilometers later, Violet sent Yoshi a voice alert. "*Leakdown Check, Perform a Leakdown Check*." Violet was asking her to shut off her primary oxygen for 30 seconds then turn it back on again. In those 30 seconds, the O2 Yoshi used would be subtracted from the total drop to compute a leak rate. Her heart sunk when she heard it. She was leaking 500 cc a minute, twice the acceptable rate. Violet followed with, *"Suit Tear Likely, Repair At Once* or *Return to Safe Haven."* She recalled scraping her MarsSuit against an airlock connector, hence the leak, and the nearest safe haven was Candor. She fought back a wave of nausea and thought about telling the others. But what good would it do? It would only slow them down. She moved on in silence.

Five kilometers later, they encountered another tease in topography: teardrop-shaped islets. Signs of flood erosion from an extinct river, they meant water had definitely been here. How much and how long ago was a mystery. Vadim came over the comm loop again, excited. He recognized the area. "We're close. Keep your eyes out."

Yoshi breathed a sigh of relief, exhaling slowly to conserve her O2. She had 90 minutes left of it, she figured. She might actually make it.

Thirty minutes later, the desert changed yet again. The smallish Sun, drawing a bead on the horizon, caused the colors to shift chamelion-like. Reds became auburn and crimsons tan as the salmon sky darkened. The pattern of dunes they'd been seeing, bachan and parabolic, changed as well, to pyramidal mounds with 3 or more slipfaces, all of them radially symmetrical. Star dunes, Chris realized, born of fierce, circling winds. They were telling a story.

Star Dunes

Only a huge force moving in vast circles could have carved this pattern. The storm blanketing Mars prior to touchdown could have packed such a force. It could also have uprooted 1 of their 3 pre-landed radar beacons. Moving only one would have cast off their final approach, causing them to follow the EDL radar down to the wrong landing site. Such a force could also have buried Candor Base. On the other hand, with an atmosphere only a hundredth the density of Earth's, that wind might not have packed enough of a wallop to move a feather. Unless it was hundreds of miles an hour more than expected. The same thoughts occurred to Yoshi, whose anxiety had returned in spades. She had less than 30 minutes left and there was still no sign of Candor Base. Violet began spouting emergency procedures: *Configure the BSLSS, ready your backup OPS.* Yoshi couldn't concentrate. "Shutup," she commanded, "go to visual display mode."

"Split up and fan out!" Vadim yelled out anxiously over the loop now. "Two west, two south, I'll go north. Maintain visual contact and monitor your 02. We'll leave the PLSS cart here. Leave enough time to get back to it if you need to."

'Back to it if I need to,' Andrea repeated. Even in her state of near panic, she was capable of the calculations. She had 50 minutes showing. If they found Candor, it would take 30 minutes to ingress, leaving her with 20. That meant she'd have 10 minutes to find it and 10 to get back to the PLSS cart if she didn't, 9 really since it would take 2 minutes to plug into the cart and activate it.

At her walking pace, 9 minutes would take her less than a kilometer. Four metal cylinders standing 56 feet in the air should stick out like the Eiffel Tower if they were within a kilometer. She scanned west, north and south and still saw nothing. She decided to walk only 7 minutes instead of the 9. The cart would extend her life if she reached it. She wasn't ready to die.

Yoshi had done the same calculations and decided otherwise. The others might rush for the cart but then what? Draw straws for the extra few hours, try to share them, fight for them? Not her. She'd rather pop her relief valve. Take an explosive decompression, go out quickly!

A glint yanked the thought.

Wait a second.

Glints come from things shiny:

Wait a second.

Smooth and metallic:

Man-made.

She yelled into her helmet, "I've found something, I've found something."

"Follow my footprints, follow my footprints."

With no fixed point of reference, the glint could be kilometers away or more. Yoshi and Andrea, on adrenaline, didn't care. They raced towards it and almost passed it in their haste. It came from a small opening in a large mound of sand. The impending sunset, reflecting off the opening had been its source. Lying horizontally and nearly buried, the opening was a window. They'd found Candor Base. Scooping away sand they discovered the Rover Module, not HAB 1 or 2. The HABS, landed to the northwest, were the only source of life support.

They turned to that direction, but the setting sun blinded them and they had to lower their visors. Twin monoliths took form as their Polaroid filters engaged. HABs 1 and 2 were upright. Draped in sand and tilted, but upright!

Yoshi drew a deep and grateful breath. It felt odd, with a strong metallic odor and peculiar resistance. Suddenly her vision fogged and an alarm intruded:

brring **brring brring brring**
brring **bring brring brring**

Violet's voice followed with,
"YOU HAVE THREE MINUTES OF OXYGEN LEFT, GO TO OPS"
The voice was not sexy this time. It was shrill.

"REPEAT: THREE MINUTES...GO TO OPS."

Everyone heard the warning over the loop, but only Andrea was close enough to help. When she reached Yoshi however, she was giving a thumbs-up. She'd found the apple-shaped knob under her chest pack and already yanked it. The rush of pressurized air from her 45-minute reserve tank was flowing. Yoshi kept it to herself that it wouldn't last that long. With her worsening leak rate, she'd be lucky to make 20.

Moments later it was Andrea's turn:

brring **brring brring brring**
brring **bring brring brring**

Andrea gulped and yanked her apple knob. Nothing happened. She managed to get out a feeble call, "Help, no OPS,"before she fainted.

"Stay there," a voice shouted back**. "Don't move. I'm coming."** It was Roberto.

Andrea was prone when he reached her, her lips blue from cyanosis. Yoshi, nearby, was also down with a leaky suit and her 02 reserve nearly gone. Roberto's triage training kicked in. He didn't have the PLSS cart with him but had 30 minutes of O2 left. Sharing it with Yoshi would be a waste of time. She'd leak it out immediately. Sharing it with Andrea would give them each 15 minutes. Vadim was streaking frantically towards them, half a kilometer west and straining against the PLSS cart carrying Anna's backpack while Robetto pondered his decision, Lungs aching from thin air, legs churning from boot high sand and eyes teased by mirages wouldn't stop Vadim now. The strength that had eluded him when he'd failed to save his sister wouldn't elude him now. He wouldn't allow it.

He found Roberto hovering over Andrea when at last he reached the HABs, the Mexican's BSLSS buddy breathing system sharing his life support with her, not Yoshi. Yoshi, his soul mate, lay still and motionless just meters away. Roberto would later tell him it was simply classical triage. Survival favored Andrea. It was in the numbers. But at that very moment, while mating the blue and red connectors of Anna's PLSS to the corresponding ones on Yoshi's suit he hated Roberto. Putting that hatred aside for the moment, he prayed for the first time in his life.

Yoshi lie motionless for seconds that seemed hours but suddenly coughed. Her face, an ashen gray, turned blue then pink in a miracle unfolding before his eyes. In a spacesuit no less.

The Sun, half the size it would be on Earth and crowned with mulithued halos was about to set as Vadim thanked a Spirit he'd never acknowledged before. He helped Yoshi towards HAB 1 while Roberto did the same for Andrea. Debris was scattered everywhere as Chris led the way, and when at last they reached the sand draped ladder, he somehow managed to clear it, somehow, managed to climb it and lumbered to the top rung.

On the top porch and facing the airlock door, he prayed that the mechanism hadn't jammed, the first time in his life he too had really prayed. The X-lever rotated, and the door springloaded open.

****

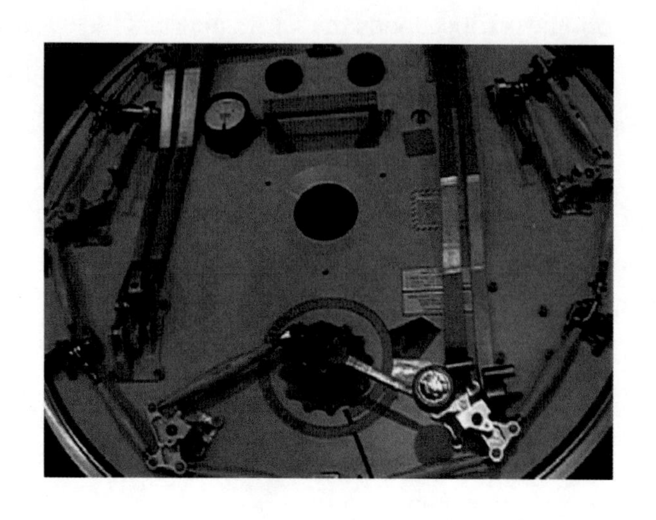

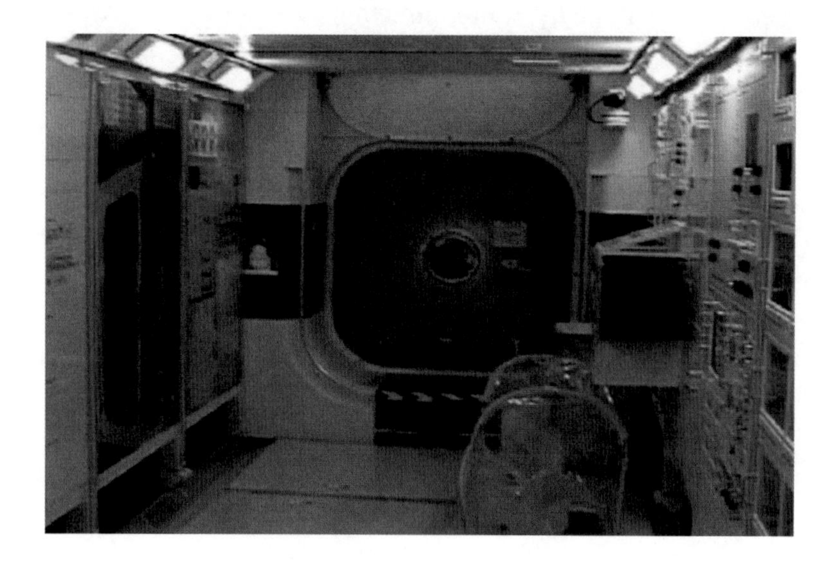

And the door springloaded open

Chapter 22. Hysteresis Loop

Hys·ter·e·sis (n):

A delayed response to changes in the forces acting on an object

A system that may be in any number of states,
independent of the inputs to it,

A system that changes each time through a loop
*with **expanding deviations of consequence***

July 20th, 2034
Oracle, Arizona

Tess was alone on the 49th anniversary of Neil Armstrong's first steps on the Moon when she got the word from Adam. Until it came, she was certain Chris was dead because Adam hadn't called in a fortnight. No news was bad news so she steeled herself. "He's alive, they're all alive," he told her gleefully. He went on to say that they'd made it to Candor Base; the comm was poor and might remain so for weeks. "I wish I knew more," he added, but she never heard that; she was jumping too high from joy.

She wanted to share the news with the spouses of Chris' crewmates but there were none. She was the only spouse: his crewmates were all single. A loner by nature, she had no one to talk to; her parents were deceased and she had few friends."Sorry," she whispered when she finally regained her composure, "it's been hell."

"No I'm sorry," Adam replied sympathetically, "I wanted to call sooner but I couldn't. I know what you've been through. Tell you what, it's Passover tonight and we'd love to have you over. We'll have wine and a ceremony. How about it?"

Tess had never been to a Passover Sedar. She desparately wanted to celebrate. Something. Anything. She quickly accepted.

There were six chairs at the Passover Table when she arrived, one for her, two for Adam and his wife Beth, one for their 5 year old, Betty, and one for Elijah, "the prophet of hope who announces the Messiah," Adam told her.

As the Sedar began, Tess noticed the front door was open. "To symbolically welcome Elijah," Adam added.

Tess' eyes settled on the table, which also had a place setting for Elijah. The plates were filled with appetizers that didn't seem to go together: a boiled egg, a piece of matzo cracker; a stalk of celery and a lonely lamb shank bone. Haroset (a paste of apples and nuts), spicy horseradish, a bowl of salt water and a paper cup completed each setting. The cups were for the wine. They were small but they'd suffice. The Haggadah, a prayer booklet lay next to each.

Adam began by sanctifying the Sedar with a prayer: *"Barukh ata Adonai Eloheinu Melekh ha-olam bo're p'ri hagofin,"* then filled each cup to the brim with Manischevitz a purple, aromatic red wine. Despite being sweet as sugar, it felt good to Tess' palate and she quickly sipped it dry. Do I ***ever*** need this, she thought, where's the refill? Other prayers followed, for the celery (dipped in the salt water); the matzo, the shank bone, the apple mix and the egg, before she got it. Betty, sitting next to her, whispered in Tess' ear that the salt water symbolized the bitterness of slavery, the lamb, ancient sacrifice, the paste, mortar Israeli slaves used to build the Pharoah's storehouses and the egg, the destruction of the first Temple in Jerusalam. Adam filled Tess' cup again, then asked Betty, being the youngest to read Four Questions from the Haggadah booklet.

"Why does this night differ from all other nights?" Betty asked. Tess read the answer in unison with the other adults:

"On this night we eat only matzo instead of other breads to remind us of the Exodus when there was no time for yeast to rise."

"Why on this night do we eat only bitter herbs?"

"To remind us of the cruel way our ancestors were treated in slavery."

"Why on this night must we dip our food in the Haroset twice?"

"To remind us of the hard work our forebears did building Pharoh's cities."

"Why on this night do we eat reclining?

"To be comfortable and remind us that we were slaves, but now we are free."

For the first time in months, Tess' mind, racing in circles with thoughts of Chris and the mission, began to slow down. She found herself immersed in the ceremony and thought, if this is what Judiasm's like, I should convert; until the Haggadah got to the Exodus.

According to lore, by refusing to let the Israelites leave Egypt, Pharoah Rameses 11 brought ten plagues upon his people: the waters of the Nile turned to *blood;* a horde of *frogs* immersed the land; *lice* attacked the people, coming in a mass of gnats; *flies* descended in swarms covering only Egyptians; *pestilence* came to livestock, diseases of extermination; *boils* festered on Rameses' people, causing itching and terrible sores; a *hailstorm* was showered on Egypt, mixing fire and rain and ice; *locusts* invaded the land, ruining orchids and crops and men; the Sun was extinguished in Egypt, with *darkness* prevailing for days and *death* was decreed on the people, smiting only the Egyptian's firstborn.

As the plagues were revealed, Tess flashed on CASI, whose predictions would become today's plagues if they came true: Hurricanes, arctic meltdowns, disappearing rainforests, disappering species, global warming, tsunamis, greenhouse gases, ozone holes, food shortages and death by epidemic.

It dawned on her that the angst she'd been feeling might not be coming from Chris' mission but from her own ten plagues, that like static from the dark matter, they were the background noise of her mind, devouring her, consuming her because they *had* started to come true. If there was time to fix them she knew it was running out. Fear overcame her and she suddenly had to leave. Instead of Elijah entering, she burst out leaving Adam and his family agog.

She went straight to CASI back at Biosphere 2, where her latest polar meltdown predictions were waiting. While others might say they were nonsense, they didn't know CASI like she did. If the temperatures rose in the poles, others said, it would propagate a self-correcting wind shift. The winds would simply blow the warmer air away causing the temperatures to drop back to where they'd been and the ice caps to refreeze. Earth homeostasis, they called it, natural forces at work keeping the climate on an even keel. CASI said otherwise, predicting a hysteresis loop instead, an effect in which temperatures precessed as the wind shifted. Instead of returning to their starting point, they'd get warmer each time through the loop until they finally hit the tipover point. When that happened, the Arctic ice shelf would go first, then the Antarctic. The flooding would be unimaginable. Tess winced when she saw the predictions, prompting her to run another case forward in time. Like all the ones preceeding it, CASI stopped dead in her tracks on February 14th, 2049. "My God," she whimpered, "it's going to happen." Her background noise grew louder.

****

Chapter 23. Digging Out

Diarydisc Entry: Hirumi Yoshioka:
MET: 0211, Day 13 on the surface
Pentad 3

Things got off to a slow start here. Andrea and I acclimatized differently after our ordeal, even our menstrual cycles shifted. The men reported nothing of course, no adverse affects from the low gravity. Isn't that just like men? Roberto teased me with, "maybe you're pregnant." What nerve that man has! I suppose I'm just angry with him for choosing Andrea to save instead of me. Truth is I'd have done the same thing. It was classic triage, as he said. At least we're all alive. Don't tell that to Vadim. I think he'd like to strangle him. But we did recover and we've finally begun working.

Time will be marked by "pentads" here--five instead of seven-day weeks. Our stay time will span a hundred of them, 500 days in all. The first order of business was getting more space. HAB 1, where we'd been staying, had only 3 bedrooms, too cramped for the six of us, so our first EVA was to HAB 2. It went well. Getting it on line gave us 230 cubic meters of extra room including the labs, gym, Telepresence Center and more beds!!

Our next EVA was to the EC (Escape Craft), auto-landed downwind of the Power Modules. With Eagle gone, it's our only way back to Columbia and Earth. Thank goodness it checked out, but it will need fuel when we finally depart which brought us to our 3rd EVA, to the Power Modules.

They hold the Bosch Reactor, Air Extractor and SP-100 Fission Reactor, which act like a medieval alchemist only instead of turning lead to gold, they turn Mars dirt into air to breathe, water to drink, heat, electricity and methox fuel. The methox not only fuels the EC but provides 100 kilowatts of power, 2 megawatts of heat and a year and half's worth of life-support. Our big concern there had been the hydrogen, the feedstock for the factory. It barely exists on this planet, which is why they'd packed 6 tons of it in the PMs. We held our collective breaths when we got to the tanks but again we were fortunate. The original 6 tons had been churned into 107 tons of methox by the automated factory. Waiting for us as advertised!! We had power and fuel.

Tomorrow's EVA will be the Intermodule Tunnel erection. The tunnel will let us walk between modules in shirtsleeves instead of suits, more comfortable and a great time saver. After that we'll do the Rover Extraction, which will not be easy. The three Rovers may be beyond repair after the storm. It knocked the RM on its side and rolled it 500 meters. The force must have been incredible but Vadim says the Rovers are indestructible. We'll see. Then comes the Greenhouse deployment and fresh food I hope. At least we'll have Houston advising us, we finally managed to get through to them. Just thinking about all this work is exhausting, Thank goodness for my very own, big bed for a change. I can't wait to get to sleep. Heaven!

****

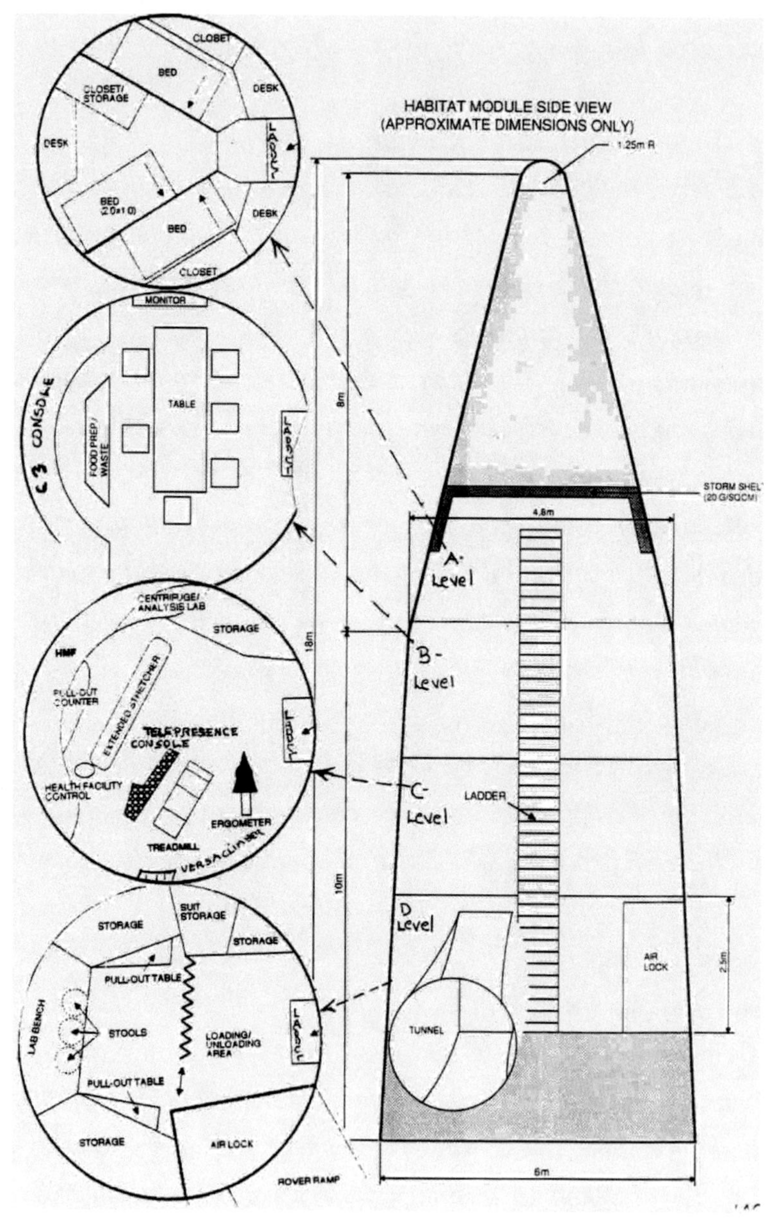
HABITAT MODULE SIDE VIEW
(APPROXIMATE DIMENSIONS ONLY)
1.25m R
CLOSET
BED
CLOSET/
STORAGE
DESK
DESK
LADDER
BED
(2.0x1.0)
BED
DESK
CLOSET
MONITOR
C3 CONSOLE
TABLE
FOOD PREP/
WASTE
LADDER
8m
18m
10m
STORM SHEL
(20 G/SQCM)
4.8m
A-
Level
B-
Level
C-
Level
D
Level
LADDER
CENTRIFUGE/
ANALYSIS LAB
STORAGE
HMF
PULL-OUT
COUNTER
EXTENDED STRETCHER
TELEPRESENCE
CONSOLE
HEALTH FACILITY
CONTROL
ERGOMETER
TREADMILL
VERSACLIMBER
SUIT
STORAGE
STORAGE
STORAGE
PULL-OUT TABLE
LAB BENCH
STOOLS
LOADING/
UNLOADING
AREA
PULL-OUT TABLE
STORAGE
AIR LOCK
ROVER RAMP
AIR
LOCK
2.5m
TUNNEL
6m

Habs 1 and 2

The Power Modules

Pentad 4: Tunnel Deployment.

The tunnel had been packaged in ten 20-meter sections, each weighing 200 pounds, 76 lbs on Mars. Mating them in spacesuits would be hard, even in reduced gravity. It would take 10 EVAs, with Vadim and Chris doing the bulk of the work. Two at a time they moved the coiled sections from HAB 1's D level where they were stored, through the airlock, and down a gangway to the surface. After uncoiling each, they laid them end-to-end between HABs 1 and 2, spliced in the T-joints to mate with the other modules, sealed off the end caps and checked for leaks. A lot of the work was welding, and Roberto watched it with interest from B-level in HAB 1. But his interest turned to disgust prior to tunnel pressurization. They wouldn't be doing it with air as he'd championed. Air was less of a fire hazard than oxygen; not toxic like oxygen and medically safer, he'd told everyone. *But it was an engineering nightmare*, had come the refrain. It needed thicker walls for breathing it instead of the lower pressure oxygen. Thicker walls meant more weight and air's higher pressures meant greater strain on the welds.

The gamebreaker turned out to be none of that, it turned out to be nitrogen. Air was 78% nitrogen and nitrogen was rare on Mars. So rare it would have to be manufactured and doing so would have eaten up 35 kilowatts of every 100 produced, more if there were leaks, and with 1021 square meters of tunnel sealed by only 67 welds, there certainly would be leaks.

Roberto had fought the air versus oxygen battle as hard as he could but he lost. Latinos almost always lost in fights with caucasions, it seemed to him. It had only fueled his anger. Moreso because the engineers hadn't done what they said they would do in the first place. They'd selected Mars' air to pressurize the tunnel instead of oxygen, and chose oxygen for breathing in separate masks. The Mars' air would negate the leaks, they said, since there was an infinite supply of it that could be pumped back into the tunnel from the outside to maintain pressure. It would also avoid the need for nitrogen, prevent the bends and save electrical power. And using oxygen masks would cut weight and help the welds. In seemed reasonable but like ADSS and Hypercones before it, the devil was in the details and they'd skirted a key one: Planetary Protection Rules. Those rules required that Mars bugs (potential alien life forms) must not be carried back to Earth under any circumstances. The conventional was to stop them was with BIG suits (Bacterial Isolation Garments) requiring separate systems for the head and body. The BIGs put back every bit of complexity Roberto had been accused of making with his air plan. But now instead of walking between modules in shirtsleeves, they'd have to do it in those ridiculously ncomfortable BIGS (giant condoms with arms and legs, he called them).

****

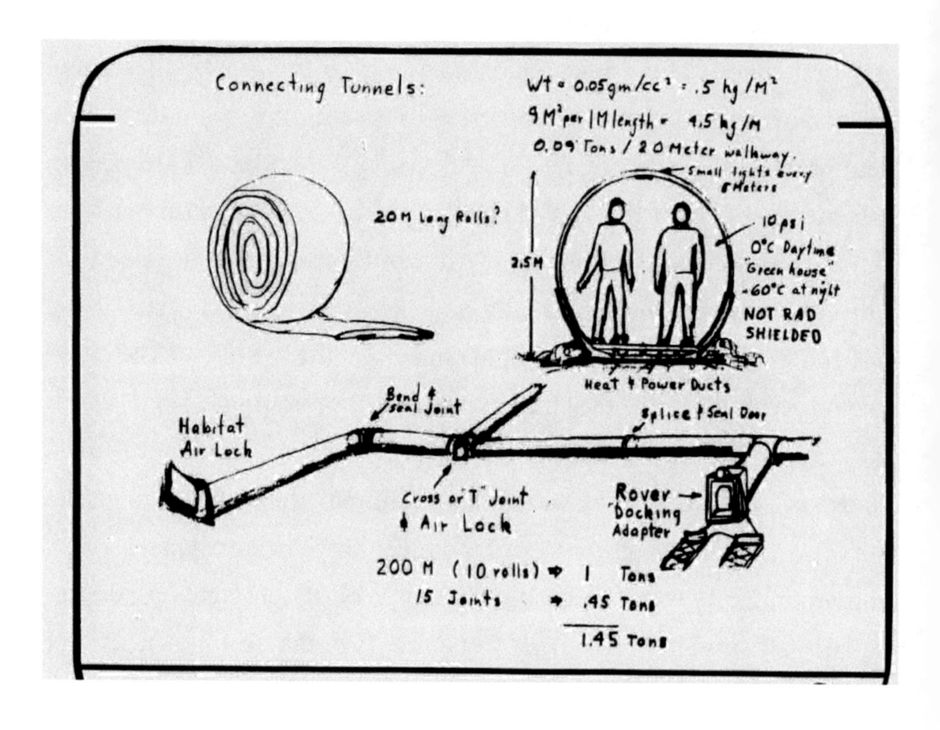

Tunnel Deployment

Pentad 6. Rover Extraction.

Candor Chasm is a cold place. At its warmest, it occasionally hits 80, but 50 below is more the norm. So when Chris and Vadim entered the tunnel for the very first time, they had to exit almost immediately--their BIG suits couldn't handle the cold. The solution was obvious: insulate the tunnel by shoveling Mars dirt over it. But that wouldn't happen without power shovels and they were on the Rovers, garaged but entombed in the Rover Module (RM). Things weren't all bad: the RM had toppled in the only orientation possible to extricate them, with its bay door exposed and facing out. An elaborate plan to extricate them was hatched by the MOCR through email.

It began with an EVA to attach one end of a 150 meter-long cable to the footpad of one of the Power Modules. From there, Chris and Vadim dragged the other end across Candor Base to the damaged Rover Module, entered through a side hatch, forced the high bay garage door open, then snaked the free end of the cable through and attached it to Rover 1's winch. According to the plan, the winch would wind up the cable until it was taut then draw itself and Rover 1 out the door using the Power Module as an anchor. Rover 1 would then be used to pull out Rover 2, its twin, and Crab, a smaller wheeled version used for shorter excursions, then all three would be used to cover the tunnel with dirt. Complex forces were involved in the operation, stresses, strains and centers of gravity. Computed by the MOCR, Vadim hoped they were right as he straddled the seats in Rover 1 ready to start its engines. If they weren't, the Power Module could topple and Rover 1 might never leave its garage. Excursions would be impossible if that happened and the tunnels would be useless as well. The mission would be crippled!

Everyone stood at the ready with the cable in place and the fuel tanks primed with methox: Chris outside the RM, Roberto by the PM and Yoshi and Andrea in HAB 1 waiting to suit up if need be. Rover 1's twin engines coughed before coming to life, giving everyone a scare but soon steadied into a smooth idle whereupon Vadim engaged the winch. It took up the slack in the cable slowly, so slowly that Roberto, 150 meters to the northeast missed it at first, shouting, "Nothing," over the loop until a movement in the sand alerted him. "Motion," he shouted on seeing it, "we've got motion."

Inch by inch, Rover 1 moved out on its side, crawling almost imperceptively until it reached the lip of the RM's bay door whereupon Vadim disengaged the winch. He stopped it to take stock, knowing one of three things could happen once it slipped off the lip to the terrain below, two of them bad. It could fall Stable One (cab up, treads down) and be undamaged; it could fall Stable One but damaged; or it could fall Stable Two, cab upside down, treads up in the air like like an overturned turtle with little hope of righting it. The MOCR predicted that the heaviest part, the treads, would fall first and the Rover would hit the ground Stable One. Weighing his next move, Vadim decided he had to trust them. He'd had issues with them in the past but he had to admit they could calculate. And this was one tough calculation, tougher than he could make. He drew a deep breath from his MarsSuit, re-engaged the winch, pushed the throttles forward and braced for impact. There was a teetering feeling before he hit the ground, then a wicked roll right, a thud and the clamor of treads carrying him forward!

"*Zdor a va,*" he yelled with unbridled joy, "fantastic.

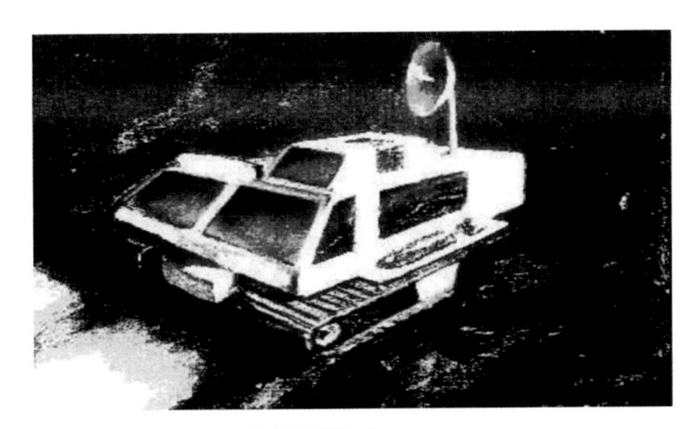

ROVER 1

ROVER 2

CRAB

Pentad 8: Greenhouse Deployment

Progress doubled with Rover 1. They used it to extricate the other two Rovers and used all three to plow through the rest of the timeline. By the middle of pentad 6, they'd covered the tunnel with soil and warmed it; by the middle of pentad 7, they'd pulled the RM vertically to its footpads and deployed its solar panels for more electrical power. All that remained for full base activation was the inflation of Tess' greenhouse, stored in a palate under HAB 1's D-level. It couldn't come soon enough. They'd had their fill of thermostabilized turkeys, irradiated yams and freeze-dried puddings and were ready for real food for a change.

The greenhouse refused to inflate at first, the problem traced to a faulty compressor. Repairing it didn't help. The structure remained limp as a hot air balloon without the heat. The culprit turned out to be a tear in one of the Kevlex composite panels. It was sealed but also didn't fix the problem. Vadim finally lost it when three more tears were exposed.

"*Ni v pizdu, ne v krasnuyu, armiyu* (good for nothing piece of shit)!"

"They warned us the cold would break some things," Chris said, sealing the tears with a glue gun.

"Everything breaks here."

"We have an expression, third time's a charm."

"This is the fifth not the third time, *ot'yebis* (fuck off)!"

To their surprise, the greenhouse popped out of its palate this time, unfolded with a *phisssssssss* and arched upward into a hemisphere. Chris gaped, something about it triggering a long forgotten memory.

He blinked and he was six years old again, riding atop his father's strong shoulders by the steps of the Museum of Natural History in New York on a Thanksgiving eve. It was late, nearly midnight and the Macys Day Parade was tomorrow. His heroes surrounded him, titillating his senses: Iron Man, Spiderman, Darkman and the lot, deflated floats on the asphalt of West 77th Street, waiting to be inflated. As each came to life, they'd done so with the same *phisss* as the Greenhouse did now and he smiled at the memory forty years past and two hundred million miles away. The juxtaposition of past and present brought a sigh of satisfaction at what they'd just accomplished. Candor Base was fully deployed and functional. Ready for science at last.

****

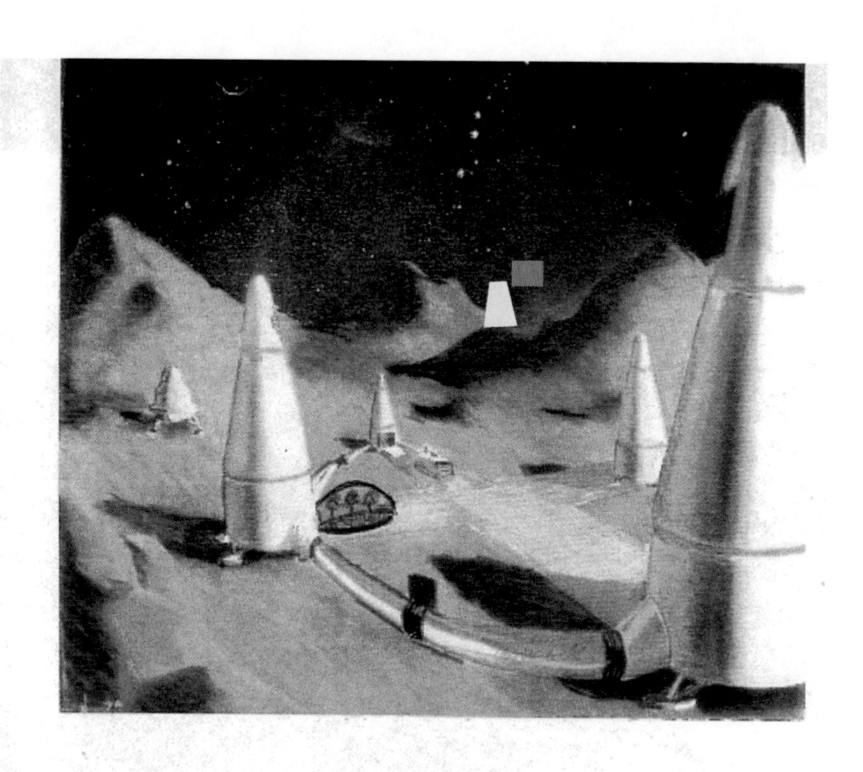

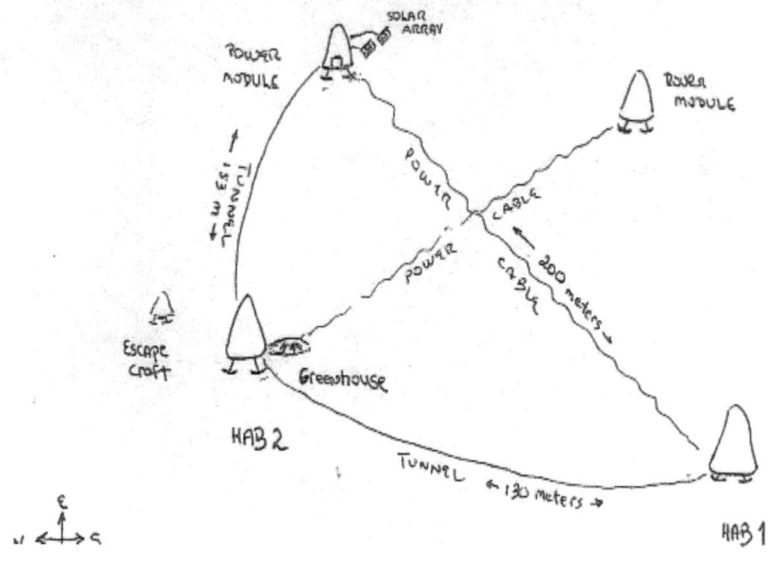
SOLAR ARRAY
POWER MODULE
POWER MODULE
TUNNEL
← 153 m →
POWER
CABLE
POWER
CABLE
← 200 meters →
Escape craft
Greenhouse
HAB 2
TUNNEL
← 130 meters →
HAB 1
E
N
S

CANDOR BASE

View left to right:

Power generators, Rover 1, the Greenhouse and Escape Craft

Pentad 10. Planting Seeds.

Procedures were critical before entering the Greenhouse. Not following them could kill, especially from the *bends*--the bubbling of nitrogen gas from the tissues to the bloodstream when going from higher to lower pressures. On Earth this could happen when rising from the sea floor too quickly in scuba gear. On Mars it could happen anytime they left the HABs because everywhere else *was* at a lower pressure (the HABS were kept at half Earth's sea level, while the greenhouse, tunnel, even the spacesuits were only a third). It wouldn't have been a problem had pure oxygen been used for the breathing gas: nitrogen wouldn't have been in the tissues in the first place so it couldn't have bubbled out. But that wasn't feasible. For while the suit, tunnel and greenhouse did use pure oxygen, the HAB air, where most of the crew time was spent, had to be more Earthlike, with only 30 percent oxygen and the rest, nitrogen. The nitrogen was in the HAB air to blunt the threat of fire caused by too much oxygen. It was also there to prevent oxygen toxicity, a potentially fatal illness caused by breathing too much O2 for too long. But it had two downsides. One was the bends risk, the other was the higher total pressure needed to make the reduced oxygen pressure breatheable. That, in turn, demanded thicker walls to withstand that pressure, tougher suits and so on down the line. Like everything else on the mission, it was a compromise between man and machine, a life and death compromise that avoided death only by following procedures to the T. In this case the T was pre-breathing before entering the Greenhouse: inhaling pure oxygen long enough to rid the tissues of the nitrogen accumulated in the HABs.

It had to be done in the cramped Greenhouse airlock prior to entry, and how long depended on where you'd been; how long you'd been there and where you were going.

The prebreathe time could be cut by riding an exercise bike but it was still over an hour--a "*postavit' kogo" (*pain in the ass), Vadim thought. "There must be a better way," he grumbled aloud to Roberto, peddling furiously next to him on a bike on the first day of Pentad 10.

"There is!" Roberto grumbled back, barely in control of his rising anger, "Use air! I tried to tell them but they wouldn't listen." He felt *El Diablo* surge again, the devil in him that rose from deep within his chest whenever he thought of being ignored. He peddled harder, trying to stuff *El Diablo* back where it came from but it was a dogfight. He'd been fighting it since the day he left Aquas Caliente, since the day he 'integrated' with the gringos. Nearly drained, he unsaddled from his bike after the hour passed and entered the Greenhouse silently.

It looked like one of those inflatable tennis courts peppering Mexico City at first glance. It even sounded like one, with its compressors pumping away to maintain the hemisphere bubble. Only here they were pumping Mar's air against the walls, not Earth's, and together with the low gravity, Roberto wondered what his tennis game would be like. He used to be damn good and had there been nets, balls and racquets, he would have challenged Vadim and beat the *mierda* out of him. At least he could joke about that, he half-smiled.

Midday light poured through the clear roof panels, lacquering the walls with a strawberry tinge impossible on Earth when he sauntered over to join Vadim and Chris in the activation process. Together they began assembling the three chambers derived from Tess' research at Biosphere 2: the Soil Chamber, Hydroponic Chamber and the Terraformer.

They began with the Soil Chamber, where crops would grow in soil, like on Earth, but the likeness ended there. Martian topsoil was sterile, baked into lifelessness by unrelenting ultraviolet unshielded by the thin Mars atmosphere. There was nothing organic in it, nor any nitrogen-fixing bacteria, essential for the seedlings to grow. To compensate, the seeds were to be planted in the subsoil, where hopefully they could survive.

To help them, Tess had created a home-grown magic fertilizer. *Tessmix*, Chris called it, and it had the missing ingredients--organics and bacteria. But it had to be added to the subsoil, which could be a meter or more deep. Hopefully, it was inches not meters away and the *Tessmix* they'd mix with it would power the roots of the seedlings they were about to plant. If it did and they reached down to the deeper organic and nitrogen sublayer theorized to exist, the plants would grow on their own from there. But this was a theory, and it could all go awry, hence the backup Hydroponic and Terraforming Chambers.

Chris thought about Tess as he carried her *Tessmix* to flaps in the Greenhouse floor and unzipped them. Her fingerprints were everywhere, surrounding, coddling and protecting them: her magic mix; her compressors pumping harder as he unzipped the flaps to make up for the leakage through them; her ingenious seal around the flap edges to limit that leakage. The insecure rebel who'd roiled with defiance when they'd first met was history, replaced by the woman he loved so inconceivably. Yes, that was the right word, inconceivable. Inconceivable they'd be working on Project *Columbus* together and inconceivable that he was about to deliver her lettuce, tomato and asparagus seeds to the soil of Mars.

On those rare moments when he was alone, and thoughts of the mission subsided to the background, all he could think about was her alabaster skin; her aristocratic nose, her flowing hair and how he missed her. That was the most inconceivable of all.

"*Chesat' yaytsa, drochit* (stop scratching your balls, you can jerk off later)." Vadim interrupted him goodnaturedly.

He smiled, dropped some carrot seeds in the subsoil he'd uncovered and moved on.

The Hydroponic Chamber came next. The seeds would be grown in recycled water here and the water would come from their urine. As the three of them filled vats of it from the recycler and transferred the contents to the chamber, more thoughts of Tess came to Chris: her blowup at ICES; her tour of the Biosphere; the stars that first night there; her jokes about aliens. None of this would have happened without urine recyclers. They never would have even met without the gizmos. Placing radish, cucumber and cabbage seeds in their respective receptacles, he smiled again. Vadim was too busy wiring the palates that would track the Sun for photosynthesis to notice.

The Terraformer, the most complicated chamber, came last, on the fifth day of Pentad 10. It consisted of soccer ball-sized clear spheres arranged in long rows and columns to form an airtight terrarium. Each contained soil dug from deep below the surface with a core sampler. Theory held that the ancient Mars atmosphere, once thick and ripe for life, had been gobbled up in this deep layer. Never recycled because of the absence of tectonic plating on Mars, it could theoretically be regenerated by heat. Heating the sealed spheres would set free these ancient gases and drive up the pressure inside to a starting point for life.

Given time and enough pressure, seeds, injected in through ports, could sprout and flourish. If they did, and photosynthesised the C02 inside to made oxygen, it would be a blueprint for Earth's twin sister. It might take centuries, perhaps tens of centuries, but if it worked, the red planet could become green. Or so this theory went. Injecting the last seed in the last sphere on the last day of Pentad 10, Chris was struck by all the theories that had to come true to make a simple fruit salad. Roberto was struck by a darker thought: By planting life of Mars, were they trying to play God?

****

Pentad 15.

On Pentad 15, a tiny stem broke the ground of the Soil Chamber and reached for the salmon sky. A newborn carrot had arrived. It was cause for celebration and Chris wanted to share it with Tess. He placed a call by videocom and surprisingly reached her quickly. Delayed though his images were by the lag (6 minutes now), she was ecstatic. Her blossoms had bloomed and there was joy in his face. At last she'd made a contribution, even if it was on Mars not Earth, where she and CASI had grown less appreciated. Ironic. If they didn't believe her theories down here, they could see what she'd done up there. Never mind. No time to be negative, she felt part of his team.

Her Soil Chamber would thrive in the ensuing pentads, bursting forth carrots, lettuce, tomatoes and asparagus. It was as if Mars had been waiting millenia to show off what it could do. Radish, cucumber, avocado, beans, cabbage and lemon followed suit with startling vigor. Wheat, corn, cucumber, grapefruit and other citrus fruits would come out of the Hydroponic Chamber next, a rush of crops so intense it could almost be heard, especially soybeans which could be stored or molded into tofu in a pinch if everything else crashed. Amidst the hubbub, the Terraformer didn't stir, a minor disappointment that portended becoming major.

Pentad 15 was also the pentad of the robots. Thirty probes had been carried by the Columbus 6 unmanned cargo flight and scattered by parachute to the 4 corners of the Martian globe. The size of German shepherd dogs, they'd sat dormant for a Martian year, 668 earth days, but were finally about to be unleashed.

Each had its own obstacle-avoidance system and a built-in electronic map to tell it where to go. Each could motor 5 kilometers an hour, climb 45 degree slopes and explore 70 kilometers a day, and with their 6 wire mesh tires, one meter ground clearance, and cobalt solar arrays, they might have been mistaken for *Spirit* or *Opportunity*, the probes sent to Mars in 2004. But these were far more advanced: Their twin camera eyes, extendable arms, microphone ears, olfactory sensing nose and pressure chip fingers enabled them to see, pinch, hear, smell and touch on a par with most mammels. Taste, radiation, heat, wind and temperature sensing added to the total picture they could transmit back to Candor Base. Anyone donning a Telepresence Jacket there would sense what they sensed as if they were *there* with them.

The jackets were located in the Telepresence Console in HAB 2's C-level. After the robots had been activated, everyone filed in there to try them out and they weren't disappointed. Yoshi gasped when the probe at Olympus Mons took her to the giant volcano; Vadim, his senses rocketed to a polar crevice in the 6 dimensions of time, space, sight, sound, touch and smell shook his head in amazement; Chris, eyes ablaze, sighted the real *Opportunity*, overturned by an outcropping on the planes of Meridiana Plenum. Following his "ride" to Gusev Crater, Roberto tried to act nonchalant but couldn't carry it off. "Madre mia," he exclaimed, "who's going to monitor all this data?" Andrea tried to explain that it was all automated, that they could view it on DVDs at their leisure. But as usual when she spoke to him now, he didn't listen.

****

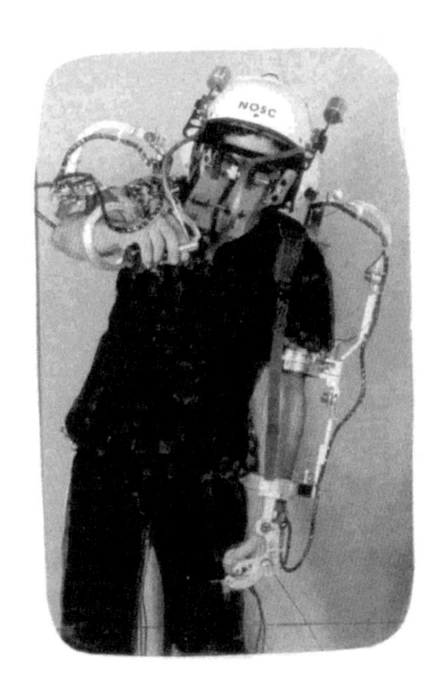

The Telepresence Console

Pentad 17.

The sounds of sex brought wetness to Andrea. Vadim was fucking Yoshi in the next sleeping compartment, just inches away. “Why the **f*&$#@** are the walls so thin and the rooms so close together?” she muttered. She was getting hornier by the minute.

It would help if she could masturbate, at least she’d be relieved, but masturbation was another of those bodily functions she'd had trouble with lately in this Godforsaken place. As the groans grew louder, she wondered if she'd ever feel the warmth of another body next to hers as Yoshi must be feeling now, and if she’d ever have an orgasm again.

She considered knocking on their door and jumping in bed with them, a fleeting notion she quickly dispensed with because they were too straight for that, at least Yoshi was. She thought about Chris, alone in HAB 2 but blind to all but Tess, the crazy man. And she thought about Roberto, sexy but disinterested. What was his problem, or was it her problem? Was she losing her sex appeal, did she have body odor, had she lost her pheromones here?

On Earth when all else failed, she’d call on Mr. VP. Mr. VP, conceived by the horniest minds in Bollywood, India was a Virtual Partner. Movie moguls there had married porn films to AI and taken both a step further. Their laptop sized portable player could select a computer-generated femme fetale (or homme) from a database (theirs or yours), and whip it to a sexual frenzy linked to a vibrator.

God it was good. You could fuck Clark Gable, Marilyn Monroe, your next-door neighbor, or anyone else you saw fit to scan to a JPG.

It was a brilliant idea, worthy of an Oscar if they had such a category, especially if your blood boiled over with desire when no one else was around. Andrea had contemplated bringing Mr. VP, disguising him as a DVD player, but demurred at the end. A monumental fuckup.

****

Pentad 18.

Diarydisk entry: Hirumi Yoshioka
Day (sol) 93 on the surface

The Rover excursions started yesterday! Ddetails follow, transcribed in this log.

7:00 am, local time Candor Base: We met up in the galley for breakfast. All slept well last night except Andrea. She's been looking for organics in the soil lab, working overtime. Still no luck.

7:30- I handled breakfast prep, a menu of scrambled eggs, granola, raisin bran and cocoa. Sounds better than it tasted. The eggs were powdered and the granola stale. The only reason the raisin bran and cocoa were okay was because they weren't irradiated and are freeze-dried on Earth anyway. Grapefruits from the Greenhouse are coming soon, Chris tells us. That will be a treat! Andrea didn't' say a word over breakfast. I worry about her.

8:10- Comm's still spotty but we managed to get the first Rover excursion plan from Houston. Chris and Vadim will traverse to Young's Rill, 40 km to our northwest. They'll take Rover 2 with Rover 1 and Crab on standby in case they break down. Roberto and Andrea will go after them if that happens. If they don't come back, I'd be alone here on Mars. I dreamt about that once, it wasn't a pleasant dream.

10:00- Vadim and Chris got into the tunnel at 9:10, pressurized Rover 2 by 9:50 and got underway at 10:00. Vadim is driving and Chris navigating. Weather's clear and seasonably cool for here-sixty five below if you can call that cool. All depends on your perspective I guess.

10:30- They called in from Ski Ramp, the training area, to cross check the procedures, then did three 7 minute trials--an incline, descent and speed run. They departed for Young'sRill at 10:27.

11:00- Received word they're 3 km west of Candor Base, crossing Terlingua Flats--an undulating plain Chris described as, "littered with chaotic slump deposits."

11:30- Rover 2 now 15 kilometers northwest of Candor Base. Chris reported he saw a volcanic drift of lava tubes that he thinks pre-dates the canyon. He's in his glory with the geology. They're right on schedule, approaching Rose Crater. It's spot on the maps where it's supposed to be.

12:00- We all sang happy birthday to Vadim as he drove. He didn't expect it and mumbled an embarrassed 'spasibo' over the loop. It was cute. He's 54, Diary, and doesn't look or act it, especially in bed! Enough of that! I've got a cake for him when he gets back, baked with cocoa, powdered milk and bread. It's flat as a board because there's no yeast here. Even if we had some, it might rise so fast in the 1/3 g, it could burst like bubble gum. I also can't use candles on the cake since they're a fire hazard. Andrea said not to worry. It's the thought that counts.

12:30- Here's the latest from Japan, dear Diary, courtesy of Asahi Shinbun's uplink. The Yomiuri Giants beat the LA Dodgers in the 7th game of the first truly World Series. Wow! I've been rooting for them since I was 3 years old! There was bad news too: A deep drilling oil platform exploded, killing ten and releasing so much chloromethane that it turned the sea to foam for a hundred kilometers. They were drilling 3000 feet below the Nankai Trough when it erupted out of the deep like champagne blowing its cork. I know there's no oil, but we wouldn't need it if we could use our nuclear power plants. Trouble is EarthFirst won't let us. They're against waste disposal by spacecraft. They're against all waste and spacecraft come to think of it, including ours. Their solution is the Tidepower Matrix, using the ebb and flow of coastal tides to turn mini-waterwheels. Japan's an island, surrounded by coastline, they say. It's a brilliant idea but totally impractical. So instead we get deep drilling. I feel sorry for us.

13:00- Roberto and Andrea just reported in, Andrea from HAB 2's C-level, Roberto from HAB 1's1. She's changing ECLSS filters and he's reviewing HUMMS scores. Our mental profiles are still strong, he says. HUMMS must be crazy. Everyone seems tense here, especially him and Andrea. Maybe they were always this moody and I just didn't notice.

13:30- Rover 2 is at Young's Rill. Ahead of schedule--Super! Their average speed enroute was 13.1 km/hour, better than expected for that terrain. Vadim and Chris starting suiting up for their first EVA, reading the checklist to me and each other. Actually, Violet did it, with that weird mechanical girlie voice of hers. I still can't get used to it. Vadim prefers HAL, he says, the voice from the 2001 Space Odyssey movie.
I think he's teasing me. That voice was spooky. Besides, HAL lost his mind, or "marbles" as the gaijin say.

14:22- Airlock depress and first step out was at 14:03. Young's Rill consists of poorly consolidated, fine grained material with odd white rock chips scattered everywhere, according to Chris. He thinks the Rill is a 2 to 3 billion year old river bed, a good place for fossils if there are any.

14:45- Update from the base: Roberto is now at the Power Module and Andrea is at the Telepresence Console. He'll check the electrolysis cells and add methox to the Rankine Engine. She'll review probe tapes from Pentad 17.

15:15- The first EVA is now in hour 2. They've already completed stops A, B and C and expect to arrive at D within the hour. Chris found "interlayered pyroclastic material" in a tributary at stop B, attributable to volcanic upheaval, he says. When they get to D, they'll install a science station with heat flow probes and seismometers.

16:40- Things went well at D. The station is on line and transmitting good data. Chris and Vadim are now back in Rover 2 heading for Stop E, their last traverse prior to returning to Candor.

17:30- The stop at E was short and Rover 2 is now 25 km northwest of us moving at 17 km/hr. ETA is 18:30. Roberto just called in with news of off-nominal vibrations coming from Water Electrolysis Cell 3. He's investigating.

17:45- Andrea reports Probe #11 inoperative in Melas Chasma region, 238 km southeast. That's our fourth probe loss in 2 pentads. The temperatures must be affecting their collision-avoidance systems.

18:00- Roberto now says he's fixed the vibrations. They were coming from gratings underneath the cell support legs. Odd! Why would anyone mount them that way?

18:37- Rover 2 is back and docked. Vadim and Chris are on their way to the DECON shower to remove and clean their suits. Their samples are in the autoclave and will go to the lab tomorrow. It's been a productive day.

18:58- Sunset: Absolutely amazing. I finally have time to appreciate it. Good thing. We're approaching winter solstice and there won't be many like this. The days will be getting shorter.

19:30- We toasted Vadim and Chris for a job well done-- with tomato juice cocktails, our first offspring from the Greenhouse, delicious. Dinner of thermostabilized ham and canned potatoes was a letdown after that. Vadim's birthday cake dessert was not. He laughed and loved it. We all did. Where have our taste buds gone?

21:30- Reviewed our open items after dinner. The biggest issue is still maintenance. Fixing things is hard in this cold. And it isn't even winter yet.

22:00- Tomorrow's schedule calls for another excursion, system checks, probe monitoring and, of course, maintenance. Chris has left for his quarters to get some emails from Tess. Andrea left me too, with dirty trays in the galley. I don't mind. Vadim will help me. In more ways than one, I hope.

Entry complete

****

Sunset at Candor Base (image from Viking)

Pentad 20.

The timeline dictated two EVAs a day, with 2 people going out and 3 staying in. Those who went would spend nearly 8 hours on the surface, while those who remained would monitor them and work. That work would average 3 hours of science, 3 hours of maintenance, 2 hours of system checks, 2 hours of comm watch, an hour of exercise and a half hour of record-keeping each day per person, split between the Greenhouse, the labs, the Telepresence Center and the other HAB decks. With mealtime, sleep and recreation thrown in, it would fill every minute of Mars' 24-hour, 39-minute day. It was Roberto's duty to organize the time and keep them all motivated. It was also his job to relax them by mixing in days off.

Vadim wondered if he could do it. Roberto and relax was an oxymoron. Still he had no right to complain. Roberto had done whatever he'd been asked to do, and had given him, Chris and Yoshi the duty assignments they'd asked for.

Not so for Andrea. He'd given her few EVAs, and only for routine maintenance. Maintenance was important, but she'd been trained for the meat of the mission, the Rover excursions. Depriving her of them was like punishing her, something he'd been doing consciously or subconciously since the party at Venus. Vadim noticed many things and now this. It was affecting her.

****

Chapter 24--E-mails from Home.

Anyone who thinks the mess we've made isn't our doing is delusional

Anyone who thinks cleaning it up will be easy is daydreaming.

We've been talking about this for decades and doing nothing.

These were Tess' thoughts as she prepared to send Chris emails: the only way she could reach him now since the comm. had degraded so badly. She'd try to make the news rosy; keep her pessimistic side at bay. It occurred to her then that she used to be an optimist. How could she have changed so much?

To: CLK~11@COL.nasa.gov
From: Teliot@Bsphere2.edu

Return-Path: Teliot@Bsphere2.edu.
Received: from r02n06.cac.psu.edu (r02s06.cac.psu.edu [146.186.149.19]
by emin12.mail.nas.gov. (8.6.12/8.6.12) with ESMTP id SAA15540 for
< CLK~11@COL.nasa.gov>; Thu 28 Nov 2012 18:51:36-0500.
>Message-Id: <203512072351.SAA85676@r02n06.cac.psu.edu>
X-Sender: Teliot@Bsphere2.edu: X-Mailer: Windows Eudora Version 1.4.3
Mime-Version: 1.0. Content-Type: text/plain; charset="us-ascii"
Date: Thu 28 Nov 2035 18:52:10 -0500:

Nov 28, 2035,

Hi, Chris. Until things clear up, I'll be sending you e-mails instead of comm, I'm sorry about that. Even with the lag and interference. I'd rather see your face than this empty screen I'm writing on. There is a plus though; I can enclose large files and this one has pix, lot of them. Most are of you, from the papers, the tube and so on. Thought you'd want to see them. You're a hero back here you know, there are models, dolls, books and holovision shows of you and your mates. Fodder for your scrapback if you had one. Don't fret, I'm making one for.you. It's not the kind of thing you'd do, I know!

Things are okay here. I'm well, the Closure's still GO and my work is progressing. CASI's gotten smarter since you've left, exponentially if you ask me. I can almost hear you: *'she was a smart ass before I left and still is,'* right? I won't answer that. You can judge for yourself when you're back. She's gotten so smart it scares me sometimes. Not just me but my peers. They call me a fear monger these days. I call it professional jealousy. Which gets me to the comm. loss.

CASI's take is all that chloromethane is causing it. She noted wind patterns from the Nankai Trough to the Aurora Borealis area and we know it affects comm. Magnetic fields, charged ions, all that stuff, right? I digress. About the file and my pictures; I've enclosed some of me too. In a nightgown and compromising positions. Don't look till you're in bed. Enough for now!

Love you, miss you, can't wait to have you back. ☺ T

To: CLK~11@COL.nasa.gov
From: Teliot@Bsphere2.edu

Return-Path: Teliot@Bsphere2.edu.
Received: from r02n06.cac.psu.edu (r02s06.cac.psu.edu [146.186.149.198]) by emin12.mail.nas.gov (8.6.12/8.6.12) with ESMTP id SAA15540 for
< CLK~11@COL.nasa.gov; Thu 5 Dec 2035, 18:20:38-0500.
X-Sender: Teliot@Bsphere2.edu: X-Mailer: Windows Eudora Version 1.4.3
Mime-Version: 1.0. Content-Type: text/plain; charset="us-ascii"
Date: Thu 5 Dec 2035 18:21:11 -0500:

Dec 5, 2035,

Good news and bad news here, as you've probably heard. The outgassing from the Trench seems to have stopped; maybe the comm will improve. I hope so. It would be so nice to actually see and talk to you for a change.

On the other hand, we've got radioactive drinking water in Tokyo. Rumor has it seeping out of cracks in 3 out of the 6 reactors from the Fukushima Daiichi nulear power plant. The walls on those containment buildings are nearly 2 meters thick so that's' a heck of a breach. It's the second in a month, I hear, the first was at the Tomari plant in Hokkaido. If this is spreading, Japan might have to turn out the lights, the whole country runs on nukes. Better alert Yoshi if she doesn't already know. On second thought, don't. I heard it on the web; maybe it's just a rumor.

Then we had a scare with Closure 4. A Biospherian got sick and we had to pull her out. Jenny, I think you know her--big boobs, curly blond hair, Wellesley girl? I thought we'd have to terminate, it was touch and go awhile, but we got it under control.

Adam tells me things are better at your end, not that I'd know. Big proud boy that you are, you wouldn't tell me if you had a problem. I'd have to find out the hard way like I did on that trek after your landing. Please don't keep me in the dark. It's okay to show some vulnerability; it lets me know you care. And maybe I can help. It keeps me more connected somehow to you. Sorry, I'm lecturing again. I'll try and keep it lighter, starting with another file. This one's got me ... I won't say. Picture's worth a thousand words. Enjoy!!

To: CLK~11@COL.nasa.gov
From: Teliot@Bsphere2.edu

Return-Path: Teliot@Bsphere2.edu.
Received: from r02n06.cac.psu.edu (r02s06.cac.psu.edu [146.186.149.198]) by emin12.mail.nas.gov. (8.6.12/8.6.12) with ESMTP id SAA15540 for < CLK~11@COL.nasa.gov>; Thu 12 Dec 2035 18:49:03>;
Received: from muffin (muffin.me.cau.edu [128.118.183.49]) by r02n04.cau.edu. (8.6.12/8.6.12) with SMTP id SAA85676 for < CLK~11@COL.nasa.gov; Thu, 12 Dec 2035
X-Sender: Teliot@Bsphere2.edu: X-Mailer: Windows Eudora Version 1.5.3
Mime-Version: 1.0. Content-Type: text/plain; charset="us-ascii"
Date: Thu 12 Dec 2035 18:50:10 -0500:
Dec. 12, 2035

Happy Birthday, honey! I'd send flowers if I could but there's no flowers.com on Mars yet, so I'm sending you a dinner recipe instead: Japanese veggy curry, yummm: Maybe Yoshi'll cook it. Hope so!:

Ingredients:

* 1 1/2 Tbsp. plus 1 Tbsp. olive oil
* 1 eggplant, trimmed and cut into 1/4 inch thick rounds (1 cup)
* 2 small yellow bell pepper, cored and cut into bite-size pieces (1 cup)
* Salt and pepper to season
* 1 clove garlic, minced
* 1 small onion, sliced (1 cup)
* 1 medium carrot, peeled and cut into bite-size pieces (1 cup)

* 4 cups water

Preparation (makes 6 servings):
Heat 1 1/2 Tbsp. of olive oil in medium skillet over medium heat. Saute eggplant and bell pepper for a few minutes, or until tender. Sprinkle with salt and pepper and set aside. Heat 1 Tbsp. of olive oil in large and deep pot over medium heat. Saute garlic and onion until onion is tender, about a few minutes. Add carrot and stir-fry with onion for a minute. Add water, stir well, and simmer on low heat for about 15 minutes, or until carrot is tender. Dissolve blocks of Japanese curry roux in the soup and stir lightly. Add fried eggplant and bell pepper in the curry and stop the heat.

Make sure you use fresh carrots, bell peppers and onion from the Greenhouse, not the storage bin or it won't taste as good. I know there's no Japanese curry roux but Yoshi can dream up a substitute. I'm sure she'll cook it for you too. Here's a picture to whet your appetite.

Love you, miss you, can't wait to have you back. :) T

To: CLK~11@COL.nasa.gov
From: Teliot@Bsphere2.edu

Return-Path: Teliot@Bsphere2.edu.
Received: from r02n06.cac.psu.edu (r02s06.cac.psu.edu [146.186.149.198]) by emin12.mail.nas.gov. (8.6.12/8.6.12) with ESMTP id SAA15540 for < CLK~11@COL.nasa.gov>; Thu Dec 19 2012 18:50:30>;
Received: from muffin (muffin.me.psu.edu [128.118.183.49]) by r02n06.cac.psu.edu. (8.6.12/8.6.12) with SMTP id SAA85676 for < CLK~11@COL.nasa.gov; Thu 19 Dec 2035 18:50:37-0500
>Message-Id: <201212072351.SAA85676@r02n06.cac.psu.edu>
X-Sender: Teliot@Bsphere2.edu: X-Mailer: Windows Eudora Version 1.4.3
Mime-Version: 1.0. Content-Type: text/plain; charset="us-ascii"
Date: Thu 19 Dec 2035 18:51:17 -0500:
Dec. 19, 2035

If this sounds panicky, it's because I am. Those rumors about the nuke plants were true; there were cracks in the containment buildings. UNEPA just declared the Sea of Japan off limits, a total, enforced lockout. It was the right thing to do since whatever fish can be found there are either irradiated or dead.

And the Trench has erupted again. CASI says all that methane reaching the atmosphere will oxidize to C02 causing accelerated ozone depletion. As if we haven't had enough. I know you'll say I'm doomsdaying again but I've got her right screen up in the 90's now and I'm really worried. Our entire ecosystem's at risk. I've attached a file of the latest articles if you don't believe me. Hope they're wrong, hope I'm wrong; hope CASI's wrong. Sorry

Love you, miss you, wish I was with you. :(T.

To: CLK~11@COL.nasa.gov
From: Teliot@Bsphere2.edu

Return-Path: Teliot@Bsphere2.edu.
Received: from r02n06.cac.psu.edu (r02s06.cac.psu.edu [146.186.149.198]) byemin12.mail.nas.gov. (8.6.12/8.6.12) with ESMTP id SAA15540 for < CLK~11@COL.nasa.gov>; Thu Dec 19 2012 18:50:30>;
Received: from muffin (muffin.me.psu.edu [128.118.183.49]) by r02n06.cac.psu.edu. (8.6.12/8.6.12) with SMTP id SAA85676 for < CLK~11@COL.nasa.gov; Thu Dec 25, 2035 17:53:17-0500
>Message-Id: <203512072351.SAA85676@r02n06.cac.psu.edu>
X-Sender: Teliot@Bsphere2.edu: X-Mailer: Windows Eudora Version 3.4.3
Mime-Version: 1.0. Content-Type: text/plain; charset="us-ascii"
Date: Thu 25 Dec 2035 17:53:17-0500:

Dear Chris. Merry Christmas. My fondest wish is continued success and good health. If I could send you a present, it would be me but we don't have Transporters yet. Instead I've sent a little Christmas present from Miss Sue's nursery school in Plainview, New York; their impressions of you romping on Mars. I think you'll enjoy them. Sorry about that last email. It was a downer I know. I'll try to control myself from now on. I love you very much, darling. Hard to believe you've been gone nearly a year.

XXXXXXXXXXXXXX :) T

PS…I'll send you a recipe for carrot cake next time.

oxegen
TV glasses
Oxegen Pouch
VCR
remote

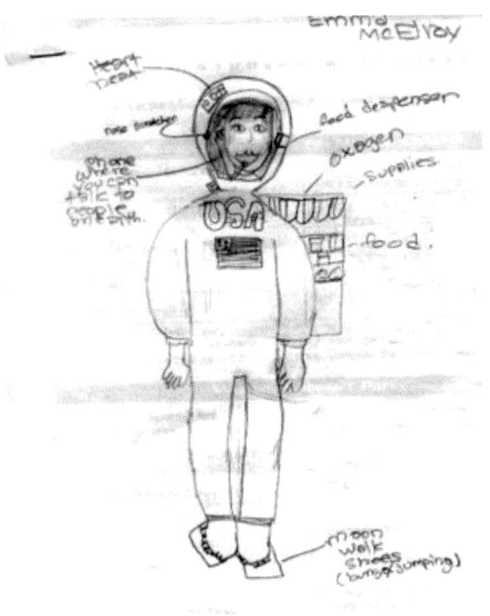

Emma McElroy
food despenser
oxegen
supplies
food.
USA
moon walk shoes

Space ship

Chapter 25: Signposts in the Sand.

Once upon a time, Mars was a warmer, wetter place.

So wet that the Great Lakes could have filled one of its flood plains.

So wet that mile-deep seas may have covered a sixth of its surface.

Today Mars is bone dry.

In 2022, the World Commission on Water for the 21st Century delared:

"More than half the world's rivers are going dry."

On Mars, no one knows why! On Earth we do.

it's us.

Pentad 30.

"The coldest winter I ever spent was a summer in San Francisco."

--- (*attributed (falsely) to Mark Twain)*

A summer in San Francisco was a cakewalk compared to summer on Mars, and would be paradise compared to its winter. The coming icy season at Candor Base would last six Earth months and drive everyone indoors behind closed, sealed airlocks. EVAs would stop; Rover excursions cease and progress would slow to a halt. Winter's onset was 10, maybe 12 pentads away, which made the search for biologics pressing.

They'd explored extinct riverbeds, bedrock and crater bottoms by summer's end; and returned breccias, anorthosites and plagioclase. They'd sifted sands, regalith and rocks by autumn, in search of elusive organics: all to no avail. Chris, ignoring this reality, focused on what they hadn't yet explored, lava tubes and geothermal vents. If life had ever taken hold, that's where it would be, its remnants preserved in fossils. He'd have 50 days at most to find some.

While there'd been no sign of life outdoors, indoors the Greenhouse was full of it. Production had ballooned with logorithmic regularity; and fruits, herbs and vegetables were being squirreled away like acorns for winter.

Though the bulk of the yield was coming from the soil chamber, the hydroponic chamber was doing its part too. Even the Terraformer showed promise, the rising pressure within it providing a backdrop of optimism -- to everyone but Andrea.

Late one night in Pentad 30, dark thoughts surfaced once again as she pondered her role in the mission, and Anna loomed central. “Where are you now,” Andrea whispered to herself? “Floating in the void between Mars and Jupiter? Beyond? At least your pain is over, mine is endless. Why did you have to go die on me, “you were the only one who made me smile.”

It was then that she glimpsed Mars’ tiny moon Phobos through one of HAB 2’s windows. It was a captured asteroid not a true moon, she recalled, so small that it didn't even have enough gravity to keep its own dust from escaping to space. The sight of this otherworldly apparition, resplendent with majestic yellow halos only drew her deeper into depression, it’s beauty a facade for the real Phobos, a fractured, broken place, smitten by multiple mpacts. She knew just how it felt!

A rustle of footsteps surprised her. It was Chris, coming down from his quarters to use the electron microscope. She attempted to wipe away the tears streaking down her cheek but wasn’t quick enough.

“Hey?” he queried.

"Come see Phobos," she deflected, pursing her lips in feigned fascination.

"Come on, what is it Andrea, what's up?"

She’d been hoping someone would ask that question, and Chris was as good as anyone. Better actually, since they’s had a history.

“Why are you all doing this to me?” she suddenly lashed out.

Startled by her intensity, he knew to shut up or he’d make things worse. He didn’t need that, the mission didn’t need that.

“Doing what?” he asked softly.

“Keeping me inside, depriving me of excursions. Why do you all hate me so?”

He thought for a moment, it was IDS again, and the delusions that could manifest but soon realized she could be right. All of them were guilty, each with their own reason for mistreating her. It had started with the Johanna switch; then taken on a life of its own. They’d all trained with Johanna for years and liked her. Anyone swapped for her right before launch would have been resented, that was obvious; Andrea just happened to be that someone. The sabotage thing hadn’t helped, especially with Vadim. What was it he’d said? *“Maybe we’ll catch her in the act... We’ll watch, listen and wait.”* That was six months ago and she’d been a model crewmate since. He himself had had suspicious history with her; the one-night-stands; the lipstick on the mirror; Ed Cochran’s accusations. And Roberto was probably the worst, labeling her an outight distraction. On the other hand she’d guided them to Mars with precision, and even Vadim had to apologize for accusing her of steering them into a boulder during EDL when it turned out to be the ILC beacon moved by the storm.

"No one hates you," he started to say, but Andrea wasn't buying it, regurgitating a littiny of grievances, each like a sledgehammer.

"Do you know what Roberto told me at our party?" she emphasized for finalityi n the midst of her surging tears.

Chris' jaw sagged at the tale of transsexuals, transvestites and cheap thrills. "None of that's true. He said it for his own sick pleasure."

Roberto had gone too far, he agreed. They all had, but especially Roberto. His job was to use HUMMS to prevent IDS and depression, not cause it.

Dueling emotions surged within Chris: sympathy for Andrea, anger towards Roberto. For the former, he formally apologized to Andrea, marshaling the most heartfelt emotion he could muster. He would never be confused for the touchy feely type, Tess had told him a hundred times, but this demanded a supreme effort and he delivered. Andrea stopped crying, and thanked and hugged him. As for Roberto, he'd confront him in the morning.

Roberto denial was immediate: "She's got IDS," he shot back emphatically.

"Then treat it, Roberto. The I in IDS stands for ISOLATION, doesn't it? Humor me, get her outside, give her a Rover excursion. That's what she was trained for."

"*Verdad*, *mi amigo*, but understand the risks--she makes mistakes. She ran out of oxygen on the trek from *Eagle* because she failed to fully charge her OPS. I could give you a dozen examples. Yes it's my job to assign excursions; but it's also my job to protect crew health. With Andrea that means protecting her from herself. Anna was enough. I won't have another loss on my watch!"

"'And Yoshi agrees with you on this?"

"I'm the primary physician; I don't need Yoshi's approval!"

Chris stared at Roberto, not knowing what to make of him. Part of him concurred. Andrea could be a loose cannon; she'd had IDS in Antarctica; had links of some sort to FirstEarth; had an aggressive sexual appetite and so on. But she'd helped pioneer their mission plan and had guided them flawlessly with NAV. And when it came to Roberto's dealings with her, they smacked of overreaction. He softened his tone and repeated his request for an excursion.

"Look, Roberto, I know you feel terrible about Anna, we all do, so let me propose a compromise. Send her out with me. I know your concerns and I"ll watch her like a hawk. Anything happens, I'll take the blame and you can shut her down till Earth return."

"OK, Chris, it's against my better judgement but I'll do it."

"I appreciate that."

"*De nada*, but I'm disapopointed."

"Why?"

"Because I gave you more credit. I thought you'd see through her."

In the solitude of his quarters later, Chris started to waiver. What if Roberto was right, what if something did go wrong, what if she lost it? His alter ego countered with, "what the hell are you thinking. You've all been impeccably chosen and trained ad nauseum to deal with danger and emergencies to the point of it being a reflex. Andrea can handle it!

As he drifted off to sleep, he thoughts bounced back to Roberto. He hadn't always been such a hard ass. He used to be kinder and gentler but he'd changed. Maybe they all had. Maybe Mars was causing this. He flashed on how the Apollo astronauts had been changed by their missions: Neil Armstrong becoming reclusive; Buzz Aldrin battling depression; Jim Irwin searching for Noah's Arc; Edgar Mitchell championing UFOs and aliens.

Prior to this mission, Chris had never known a nightmare. Now they were pervasive. Were they Mars' doing, an omen of worse things to come? He couldn't shake the fear that the red planet wasn't finished with them yet.

****

Pentad 33.

Andrea's first excursion, a two-week jaunt to the Valley of the Quedemans, was still a month away but like night and day, it made all the difference in the world. She felt part of the team again; a contributor. She owed it to Chris. She owed a lot to Chris; he was the only one who respected her. Roberto didn't respect her; he tolerated her. Vadim cared only that she didn't fuck up. And Yoshi seemed distracted and too distant to notice her at all. Was it Mars, as Chris alleged, or was she micromanaging her emotions? She would talk to Yoshi, she decided; do some fence building as Chris suggested. Yoshi at least was a woman; the other two were hopeless. Yoshi used to be sensitive. Perhaps she could be again.

"Can we talk?" Andrea whispered outside Yoshi's door after knocking softly one night. The voice inside sounded hesitant, almost in pain. "Of course… come in."

The two women stared silently at one another for a moment, an uncomfortable silence in which they sized each other up. "I've uh, been meaning to talk to you too; about your uh, cycle," Yoshi started.

"Which one, circadean, temperature or bi…as in bicycle?" Andrea replied trying to break the ice with a joke. Yoshi didn't smile.

"Your menstrual cycle," she went on seriously. "Have you noticed any changes?"

"None since the first few pentads. You could set your clock by me now."

The look on Yoshi's face and the gravity of the question said this was a smokescreen, not about Andrea but about her. There was a veil of resignation and Yoshi's eyes clouded over.

"I missed my period, Andrea, "I was hoping..."

"I had too? "

"I think I'm pregnant." She didn't know whether to laugh or cry.

"Are you sure?"

"As sure as LH, HCG and progestrone spiking tells me."

"Couldn't that come from stress, low gravity or…"

"It happens if you're pregnant."

"On Earth."

"Yes but…"

"This is Mars, anything goes. Have you told Vadim?"

"No, I'm scared."

"Do you want to have a baby? On Mars, I mean."

"I don't know. It might not be possible."

"How far along are you?"

"Two months, maybe three."

Andrea realized she was pushing too hard and backed off.

"Don't worry," she said, "it will be okay. We'll decide what to do. Together. Both of us."

The veil that had come to Yoshi's eyes exploded in a torrent of tears. "What am I going to do?" she cried openly. "What do I do?"

Andrea, sobbing herself now rushed to Yoshi's side and caressed her. What was wrong with this picture: proud Yoshi, in-control Yoshi, crying like a baby in her arms?

Andrea had always been jealous of her, of the ease with which she did things; of the admiration and power she had over men that she herself could only get by sex. That jealousy, a barrier between them now melted away with every tear. Yoshi would need her now. More than she'd ever needed Yoshi.

****

Pentad 35. HAB 1, C-level Exercise Area.

"What do you mean you *think* you're pregnant?" a stunned Vadim asked incredulously.

"It could be false, we're on Mars, I'm not sure," Yoshi whispered, barely audible.

"You either are or you're not: *Kak ty mog etove ne znat? F#$%#$#$*(@. Ty shto - s pizdy svalilsya* (how could you not know, did you just fall out of a pussy)?"

"You're the man," Yoshi replied testily. "You should have used condoms. They were in our kits."

"I have too big a rod, a *huylo*, remember. They intended them for dwarfs."

She had to laugh. He did have a big one. Her smile broke the tension.

"Why did you wait so long to tell me?" Vadim asked more softly now.

"I was hoping it would go away; and frightened of what you'd say."

"Frightened? What did you think, that I would throw you out the airlock?"

"I didn't want to upset you."

"Jesus, what do you think I am, *huyovina, huy morzhouiy, huy mozhoviy* (a worthless, marinated walnut prick)?"

"I don't know what that means, but I've talked to Andrea..."

"Yadrona mysh (that one? She'd fuck a mouse she's so horny)."

"Please, English. This isn't funny to me!"

"Okay, why her?"

"Because she's a woman. That's enough reason."

“And what did she say?”

“That I should search my soul deep down.”

“For what?”

“To decide if I want to go through with this, to have this child.”

"And what about me, am I just a limp *huy* in this?"

"I want this, Vadim, you can be with me or not."

"This isn't Earth, Yoshi, and we’re not conducting a medical experiment. We don't have incubators, bassinets, pablum, or diapers."

"We have diapers, from the female UCD (Urine Containment Device). As for the rest, we'll make due."

"The MOCR would shit if they knew about this."

"I don't care about them.”

“What do you care about?”

“This baby.”

“Is that all?”

“I still have the greatest confidence in the mission.”

“So did HAL.”

“Of course I still love you, Vadim, with all my heart. But I just don’t know if you’re fit to be a father. You’re like Peter Pan with your adventures, and you would have to change. Can you?”

"I guess we'll both find out."

****

Pentad 40.

They were 290 kilometers northwest of Candor Base crossing the Valley of the Quedemans when they came face to face with the Rainbow Zone. Piloting Crab, the smaller, 6 wheeled Rover, named for the way it could move sideways, Andrea spotted the zone on her very first excursion, and while Chris didn't say so, he was impressed. All of his reservations about her were peeling away quickly.

He'd seen the Rainbow Zone before through the eyes of Probe #4 in the Telepresence Center. *"Intermittent bands embedded with rainbow-colored flecks of blue, red and yellow,"* he'd noted at the time. But now as they approached it along the foothills of a pass that cut through to the highlands, the bands stood out brilliantly, spanning half the facade of a cliff they'd nicknamed Half-Dome. Like the rings of a prehistoric tree trunk, it could be a snapshot of ancient history; a record of the way Mars used to be--its Rosetta stone. After a pentad of driving, they began to get excited.

The sun was setting over the summit when they arrived, too late to explore, that would come tomorrow. But as he steered Crab towards a protected alcove to overnight, Chris noticed some of those odd clouds in the sky again, yellow with a hint of gray. They were something never seen before, one more thing to make him feel like a kid again. All else paled next to that feeling. It was the reason he'd come to Mars; the reason he could hardly wait till tomorrow. There'd be more to learn tomorrow, he sensed.

After stopping and leveling in the alcove, they configured the systems for overnighting. It was easier in Crab, more comfortable than the Rovers. Crab was also more energy efficient, running on batteries not gas; and had its MarsSuits mounted on the outside with access through an internal suitport to eliminate pre-breathing and prevent dust transfer. Comparing Crab to the Rovers was like comparing Porsches to tanks, Chris thought, and was glad they'd taken it despite its untested reliability. It also had a better galley, which Andrea appreciated as she prepared the meal trays for dinner. As it had since the bombshell, the conversation wound its way back to Yoshi's condition after they sat down to eat.

"You think she'll be okay?" Chris asked.

"Women have been giving birth in strange places long before doctors and hospitals," Andrea replied. "In caves, street corners, the back seats of cars. Since Adam and Eve."

"But Mars?"

"It's just another place."

"You agree with her decision then."

"Chris. If Mars is to be colonized, people will have to have children. Someone's got to be first and she wants to do it. I admire her."

"Vadim thinks there'll be hell to pay if we keep it from the Surgeons."

"Why is he even thinking about this; his future is now."

"Maybe he's trying to sort out his feelings, prove something to himself."

"We all are. Yoshi wants to be a mother; you want to solve the mysteries, Vadim and Roberto? Who knows what they want?"

"What about you, Andrea, what do you want?"

"I just want to get laid."

He shared a smile with her but said nothing.

The wind was whistling through the onboard sensing system as they locked themselves into their sleep restraints, louder then they'd ever heard it.

"It reminds me of a wind organ," Andrea whispered.

"What's a wind organ?"

"Different length pipes they place in the ground with holes to catch the wind. We had one in Toulouse, where I grew up and it sounded like flutes or violins depending on the wind speed."

"It just sounds like wind to me."

"*Bizarre que cela puisse paraître*, use your imagination, Chris."

"You spoke french then, Andrea, you almost never do, why not?"

"I…I don't know."

"The others let fly with all kinds of stuff. Vadim with his russian expletives, Roberto, even Yoshi now and then."

"I suppose its because I would like to pass for a native in the US or the UK someday; go unnoticed, so I practice English."

"You, unnoticed? I don't think so."

"I take that as a compliment. "

"It was."

Neither said a word for what seemed like the longest time until Andrea murmered, "Ever think about that time we made love in the shower, Chris?"

Of course he had, and the mere thought of it made him rock hard. He lay there not responding for a minute, pondering what was surely another invitation to make love to her. So far he'd resisted, this time he couldn't.

"Shhhh," he demanded, unharnessing and climbing in with her, "don't say a word."

"I don't intend to," she answered finding his mouth and probing his tongue with her own. He reached gently for her breasts and started stroking her nipples until her eyes closed and she began purring.

"I'm so wet," she moaned when he mounted her; "you won't stop, will you. Promise?"

"I thought you weren't going to talk,"

"Can I moan?" she asked, moving ever faster on him, matching stroke for stroke until her face turned crimson, until he knew she was about to come and he with her.

They rested awhile, how long he wasn't sure, somewhere between sleep and awareness that she was grabbing his cock again. Tentatively at first then sensing no resistance, she arched the curve of her backside against him and said, "You're big, aren't you, I can tell. I'm not even going to look. I'd rather use my imagination, it's better that way, don't you think?"

He felt far too aroused to disagree. Moreso when she placed his forefinger tip deep inside her and massaged it against her clitoris. They both came so hard the second time they thought they'd faint.

"I'd tell you I didn't want to do that but I'd be lying," he said.

"What would Tess think if she knew?" Andrea panted in her velvet accent.

"She does know," he said. "If the chance presents, I won't resent. Just don't fall in love." That's what she told me before we launched. She knew it would be hard for me, no pun intended."

"Think you can keep that promise?"

"I like you Andrea, but yeah, I think so."

"I'm not in love with you either, don't worry. But if you get horny again, keep me in mind."

He laughed, getting back in his own bed. "Can we sleep now?"

Hours passed with each in deep and restive sleep until a loud bang suddenly pierced the night followed by a crackling, percussive flash. Stunned, they lifted the Rover's shades to reveal a surreal sight, lightning and thunder!

Impossible, Chris erupted, as another brilliant flash lit up the sky in the multicolored shades of a prism splitting light: blues, ambers, greens and reds. Andrea clung close to him, frightened and amazed until a thunderclap shook the very ground beneath them, followed by a low steady rumble. It lasted only a minute but during that minute, Chris scrambled in a frenzy to hit the driving lights and saw what he knew he shouldn't, couldn't be seeing.

Rain: the timeless unmistakeable patter of rain. How could it be, the pressure's too low for that, liquid water on Mars should sublimate away, boil to a vapor instantly. And then a paper he'd read long ago rambled to the forefront, a paper so controversial he'd never taken it seriously.

There were places on Mars, it speculated, that straddled the right condition, a condition called the Triple Point. In such places, water could be solid, liquid or gas; ice, rain or vapor, depending on temperature and pressure. Half-Dome must be one of these places, he marveled and watched with awe as the storm moved past them to the east. Andrea smiled. It felt good to share this with him; a sight no other living being in the universe had ever seen.

The smallish sun gazed down through a cloudness pink sky the next morning, with no discernable trace of the prior night's fireworks. Chris kicked himself at first for not taping the storm, but it couldn't dampen the sky-high way he felt. There was rain here, liquid water here and with water comes life. Refreshed and renewed, he'd rededicate himself to finding it starting today, at the Rainbow Zone.

Seeing Half-Dome in the flesh instead of on holotape, its sheer wall gaping skyward, told a story of extraordinary forces. Whether by quake, fissure or collision, it owed its creation to a pressure buildup in Mars' core. The monumental explosion to relieve it had cleaved off a face of Half-Dome, leaving a mound of rubble at its base and revealing its interior. Nestled in a break between the exposed facade was an enigma of color in a sandwich of rust: the Rainbow Zone. Before they could get to it, however, there'd be preliminaries to attend to--getting contingency samples and a media opportunity with Earth, if the comm held out. It would all be a first for Andrea and she was thrilled.

Her suit, mounted outside but ingressed from the suitport within, had green stripes around the shoulders and legs to ID her (Chris' had blue). Unlike the heavy in-transit suits, it was more like a ski jacket with 6 layers of "smart materials." The first, the Thermal Control Layer, automatically controlled body temperature using chilled or heated water pumped through her liquid cooled long johns; the second, the pressure bladder, inflated to protect her against the thin Martian atmosphere; the third, the restraint layer, used a metallic sheath to keep the bladder from puffing out like a balloon; the fourth, the radiation layer, used a reflective film sandwich to keep radiant energy at bay; the fifth, the insulation layer used hollow-fibers to keep the cold out; and the sixth, the protective layer, had a triple weave of plastex, steel and nomex to give her micrometeorite tear, dust and germ protection. Together with her lifeguard *Violet*, it was a technical marvel but she was wary of it. She'd nearly died in it on the trek from *Eagle* and didn't know why. Still her eyes danced with anticipation as she unhinged the entry port from within Crab, climbed in the exposed lower torso and sealed the port behind her. She breezed through the expedited depress protocol, stood up to release the suit from its external mount; lowered her EVVA sun visor to cut the morning glare and stepped off Crab's platform to the surface. Her image reflected off Chris' visor when he followed and she took a picture of it with her helmet cam before they scurried off to take their first samples from the Zone moments later.

They worked together as they'd been trained to do--quickly and efficiently. Andrea held one end of a hollow aluminum core sampler tube while Chris extended the other. When he'd pulled it out fully, she handed him a drill bit to attach to the end and rotated the tube into the ground by rubbing it between his gloves until it reached the one-meter penetration mark.

He then retracted the tube and ejected the sample into a teflon collection bag Andrea held open for him, which she sealed and labeled, “ONE”.

From there they moved to a nearby rock, which Chris hammered until it split apart like banana peels. Andrea scooped up the pieces into another bag, which she sealed and labeled, "TWO", then looked for and found pebbles that had the red-rust signature of iron oxide. They filled a third bag with them and a fourth with a layer of topsoil. Other samples followed: browns with glassy flakes; berries of iron hematite; purple chips from outcroppings.

They used the gnomon while doing it, a tripod with a free-swinging plum line to measure sun angle, combined with a camera to record size, reflectance and hue.

They were five year olds in a candy store as they hurried from sample to sample, bagging, labeling and placing each goody in a vacuum box for posterity, having so much fun, they forgot about the call from the MOCR. It was time for their dog and pony show, the long awaited, oft postponed, salute from their fellow Earthlings.

The comm held as they received homage from UN Secretary General Molic-Barer. His words, twenty minutes old and echoing, were still riveting. *"Chris and Andrea," he began, "and Vadim, Yoshi, and Roberto back at Candor Base, this has to be the most historic call ever made. I'm sure I speak for everyone on Earth when I say how proud we are of what you've been accomplishing. You've opened the heavens and made them part of our world."*

As he went on to say how they'd inspired harmony and tranquility, Chris wished he was looking more regal, but standing there in his MarsSuit, nature was calling. He started rocking back and forth because he had to pee. Thankfully, Andrea took the pressure off, by panning the TV camera to the horizon for the audience while he voided into the UCD (urine containment device) attacheed to his thig

"I don't know if the TV does it justice," she said, "but we're in a 5 kilometer-deep canyon under a clear, pink sky. Yesterday, we saw yellow clouds with thunder and lightning and rain, a supposed impossibility. Winter's nearly here and the temperature will get desperately cold soon, minus 150, even though we're on the equator. Because Mars takes takes twice as long to orbit the sun as Earth, the winter will last twice as long as ours but our days are nearly the same, only 39 minutes longer than Earth's, so our sleep pattern's quite normal.

The one thing that isn't is normal gravity. It's only about a third of ours, which is good news for us girls, I only weigh 46 pounds here. It would be a great place for the Olympics too; you could polevault thirty feet and run a hundred meters in five seconds if you didn't have to wear these suits. Anything you'd like to add, Chris?"

"Speaking of the suits, they're wonders," he began more relaxed now, then bent down to touch his toes. Taking off in a jog, he added, "They're fast too. The legs are easy to accelerate, and skipping is better than running. Violet, my computer, says I'm at an 8 kilometers an hour clip and I'm nowhere near topped out. Only trouble...uff, is slowing down. Inertia sneaks up on you, it takes three or four steps to stop, kind of like a football player."

His suit demo done, he stood silently for a moment and blew a kiss to Tess, who he knew would be watching.

"That's for my wife. I'd also like to thank everyone who helped get us here, especially Ed Cochran, who's no longer with us."

With that, he reached into his upper leg pocket and grabbed the vial he'd been carrying with him for over a year. "This is for you, Ed," he said, loosening the lid and scattering Ed's ashes. They faded in the 7-knot breeze and disappeared into the crimson background. He hoped Ed and Millie would approve.

After their show and a lunch break back in the Rover, they recharged their suits and began their second EVA by setting up a science package to measure heat flow, magnetic field and seismic vibrations before proceeding to the base of Half-Dome. It was filled with chaotic debris and they hoped some might have fallen from the Rainbow Zone above it. None had--there were no colored flecks anywhere-- so they had to go to plan B, *Cliffhanger*. *Cliffhanger* was a robot that could scale walls and take samples but it failed to come to life after they retrieved in from Rover 1. The Zone was nearly a hundred feet above them and they had no way of reaching it.

"Let's just throw rocks at it," Andrea half joked. "Maybe we can chip some samples off."

"It's too high to reach, even in the 1/3 g," Chris said.

"Then how about using the pyro charge in *Cliffhanger*?"

"Too dangerous. Any other bright ideas?"

"You're tough to please, Dr. Elkay. OK, try this. The geophone charges we use to set off seismic vibrations, we could fill a core sampler tube with some, use nuts and bolts for projectiles and fire them up there. Make a gun in other words."

"That one I like. Got it admit it, Andrea, you're smart."

"That's why they picked me, not because I slept my way here."

“I’m starting to believe that.”

It took the rest of the day to fashion the device, and they didn't get to test it until the next day. When they did, the first bolts tore into the facade but missed the Rainbow Zone. The next got closer and the third closer still, until they were reaching their target consistently.

They wouldn't have an inkling of what the samples meant for nearly a pentad after they returned, and when they did, Chris had to scratch his head. The flecks showed oxides under the mass spec. "But not just any oxides," he told the others, huddled with expectant eyes nearby. "The previous samples we've tested were formed from crystallizing lava, probably 4 1/2 billion years ago when Mars was formed. I won't know till I’ve dated them but these are much younger, by at least a billion years.”

"Mars was ripe for life then," Andrea noted.

“Another mystery, isn’t it?”

“At the rate we're uncovering them, let’s hope we can solve the old ones."

Chris pondered the paradox of Andrea. She came with baggage, yes, but with assets that made up for it.

****

Chapter 26: The Meat Guzzlers

One day we'll realize that the murder of animals...
is the same as that of human beings.

Leonardo DaVinci

Pentad 44 on Mars; March 16, 2035 in Oracle, Arizona.

"We're so lucky to have your fabulous fresh vegetables, Tessie, but not everyone agrees.Part of the problem is boredom. They gripe about everything now, and soybeans are an easy target. Roberto's the worst but Vadim's not far behind. They'd both love a T-bone

"A T-bone?" Tess cringed back in Oracle. Decades of research had gone into her vegetables, and they want a T-bone? She had zero sympathy. She couldn't recall the exact moment, but she'd been a vegan most of her life. Perhaps it started when her granny told her pigs felt pain and cows cried as they were being led to the slaughterhouse; or that fish, birds and whales moved in coordinated turns that could only be attributed to intelligence; or that lobsters, honeybees and octopii were sentient beings that 'talked, danced and loved.' Or that the connection between eating animal protein and disease had been firmly established in the old China Study.

As much as she knew these things, the interaction between all of these species and the planet itself had all but escaped her until CASI began connecting the dots. With each fractional jump in accuracy, she came to know the real meaning of interdependence and symbiosis; the quantitative, not the qualitative meaning. That it wasn't too many fish in a fish tank that caused a fishkill, but 8 Blue Tang mixed with 4 Queen Triggers. And the more she came to know this, the more she feared for Earth. CASI was pointing to a point of no return, an event horizon just on the horizon. Was the planet in real peril or was this just Earth's way of sustaining itself, its homeostasis mechanism? She wanted to believe the latter so desperately that while others might question the meaning of life, she joked it was all about plastic.

Earth required it, couldn't grow it and had evolved humans for the express purpose of making it (it was an old George Carlin joke her father once told her). We'll be discarded like the dinosaurs soon as we made enough of it, she'd add, and would have sent her joke to Vadim and Roberto, but they needed motivation, not jokes. Meat was an addiction, like cigarettes or alcohol, and drastic measures were required to wean them off it. She rifled through her files until she came upon a yellowed article she'd saved from The New York Times dated January 27th 2008. The statistics jumped out:

The world ate 71 million tons of meat in 1971 and 284 million in 2007.
By 2050, it will rise to 570 tons.

Americans consume 15 percent of the total, twice the world average, about 8 oz/day per person or 200 lbs of beef, chicken and fish per person per year, up from 50 in 1957. That's 110 grams of protein a day, when only 30 is required. The excess is tied to cancer, diabetes and heart disease.

Roughly 30 percent of the Earth's ice-free land is involved in making meat.

It's supported by a relentless growth in livestock and generates nearly a fifth of the world's greenhouse gases: more than factories, cars, power plants or heating oil.

Eating 2 lbs of beef makes as much C02 as driving a car 155 miles and uses the equivalent energy of lighting a 100-watt bulb for a month.

Meat guzzling drives up grain prices and consumes croplands intended for other food production. Though nearly a billion people are staving or malnourished, most of the world's corn and soy feed pigs, cows and chickens, not people.

Ethanol made from corn is no savior. It wastes calories from the land and pollutes the air. Cutting meat guzzling by 20% is equivalent to driving a Prius instead of a Chevy.

She grimaced at the litany of old statistics, now far worse. She'd once used them against anyone who disagreed with her but no more. And to volatile meat eaters like Vadim and Roberto they could surely backfire, the last thing Chris needed. She filed the article away.

****

Pentad 47.

Winter didn't sneak up on Candor, it pounced on it like a hellcat, blanketing the Base with hellish temperatures and howling gales. First to go were the Rovers. The excursions stopped when their hydraulic fluid turned to mush and steering them became like twisting the helm of a rusted ship. The EVAs came next, stopping when the finger heaters in the gloves couldn't keep pace and frostbite loomed. Faced with confinement for 6 months or more now, their ability to get along would be tested. With nothing but each other to stave off IDS, Chris worried if they'd survive but recalled the polar seas of Antarctica and the geothermal vents in the depths of boiling caudrons. Extremophiles had survived, even flourished there. But those were extremophiles and that was Earth, they were humans and this was Mars.

No training, Antarctica or otherwise could have prepared them for this. In Antarctica they'd had continuous comm; here they were lucky to get it at all. They'd also had daylight there; here fierce sandstorms squeezed all remnants of it from the sky. In the midst of this, Vadim, Yoshi and Roberto became frantic caretakers, fighting to repair failing equipment while Chris and Andrea remained glued to the only meaningful science anyone could do...finding some meaning to the Rainbow Zone.

The work was laborious, each sample had to be documented and fed into hoppers for pulverizing or scorching. The pulverized ones went to the GCMS (Gas Chromatograph/Mass Spectrometer), which zapped them with electricity into ionized gases then read their signature. The scorched ones went to the XRMS (X-Ray Fluorescence Spectrometer), which bombarded them with X-rays to form fingerprints on a chart. After weeks of isolation, they finally had some conclusions.

"We've found oxides of copper, iron, aluminum, silicon and magnesium," Chris told the others. "Most formed from volcanic cooling like I thought, but there are some," -- he held up the samples from the Rainbow Zone-- "that look different, like they've been out in the sun too long."

"The kind of thing you see when something's exposed to oxygen," Andrea added.

"I know that sounds crazy," Chris resumed," but there's more. The levels increase the higher up the zone you go, until they they disappear altogether near the top."

Everyone looked dumbfounded; then the questions started.

"How old is this zone?" Vadim asked.

"Older at the bottom, younger at the top, I'll let Andrea explain."

"Like any sediment, newer layers build over older ones. Where it starts at the bottom is 4.1 billion years old while at the top it's a billion or less."

"So you're saying not only was oxygen here, but it lasted 3 billion years?"

Chris smiled. "I find it hard to believe too but that's what the data says."

"And why does the zone disappear?" Roberto asked.

"It doesn't just disappear, it ends in a line, a sharp line. It marks the end of whatever process created it. I've no idea why but it happened quick, at least in geologic time, less than a million years or so."

"Like the extinction of the dinosaurs, eh?" quipped Roberto. "Next you'll be saying there were little green men."

"There's some error in the process," Andrea chimed in -- the decay of argon 40 to argon 39, and contamination of course, but we were careful."

"And who handled the samples?" Roberto said looking at Andrea pointedly.

"I resent that," she snapped, "you don't have the..."

"Stop acting like children!" Vadim cut in. "All he's saying is we can't make outrageous claims…"

"Without outrageous evidence," Chris added, "we know that. That's why we'll keep pushing till there's no doubt."

As the meeting broke up, he wondered what other evidence he'd need to prove oxygen existed here. Or lightning, thunder and rain. Together they were a notion as crazy as Tess' doomsday. But if he found it, the ingredients for life may have been on Mars for eons. And while some said ingredients meant nothing and only the roll of the dice leads to life, others claimed it was the path taken, not the starting point. Einstein believed that and it was also the basis of Chaos theory. Could there have once been a Camelot here, one violently extinguished by a cataclysm? He doubted it. But immersed in the question, he flashed again on Tess and her doomsday scenario. He used to say it was crazy; now he wasn't so sure.

****

Pentad 50.

Yoshi wanted no concessions entering what she guessed to be her second tri-mester. "I'll do my usual duties until I can't," she insisted.

That changed dramatically when she caught a cold. Did she get it from an Earth-borne bug that might have stowed away? That kind of thing Roberto could deal with. But an IUO, an Infection of Unknown Origin, made him nervous. That kind of life form could penetrate all defenses. And while alien life had yet to be found, if it was an IUO, he'd be in trouble. He'd barely passed obstetrics on Earth and the prospect of treating a pregnant Yoshi on Mars was too much, especially with the loss of Anna still tormenting him. Violating chain of command, he decided to email the MOCR for help.

Vadim caught him in the act just as he was sending it. "Don't take matters into your own hands again," he exploded. "We're a team here or we're nothing, haven't you learned that yet?"

"It's you and Yoshi who've learned nothing," he shot back.

But if he'd hoped for the MOCR's support he'd be disappointed. Their reply had only the vague promise of assistance. There were no primers about neo-natal care in space. The e-mail ended with a congratulatory note to the "happy couple". He'd be on his own, he realized soberly.

****

Pentad 55.

When Earth and Mars moved into *Opposition* (opposite sides of the Sun) in Pentad 55, the comm lag between the two planets reached a peak -- 21 minutes one-way; 42 round-trip. Together with the dropouts, contact was getting worse. It made the news from Japan all the more startling when a wayward email from Adam Brady managed to get through.

Date: Monday, April 29, 2035 11:54 AM
From: adam.brady-1t@nasa.gov
To: "vadim.solodnov@Columbus.nasa.gov; hirumi.yoshioka@Columbus.nasda.ja; andrea-beal@ESA.fr; chris.elkay@nasa.gov>Roberto.diaz@Columbus.gov

Subject: NASDA JL cancellation:

"The Japanese Consul has just informed us that NASDA will be leaving the alliance. Their space budget will be redirected to Japan's nuclear program. They'll support one more mission, Columbus 12.

The SLSD FACB will be conducting a joint meeting SORR/CoFR and review of this announcement tomorrow May 1, 2035 10:00am. The CoFR for each Division should stand ready to address the issue. All Divisions shall submit an ISS backup plan presentation consistent with the above. Please submit to the SA CM Receipt Desk by 8 am tomorrow."

Yoshi had a troublesome rash and was on antibiotics when Vadim delivered the news. *"Kamisama,"* she coughed through her mask at him, “my god. Those people who sabotaged Shizuka knew exactly what they were doing. They knew what it would do.”

It was worse that that. Japan, with no fish in its seas; dwindling power in its reactors and a severe recession was on the brink of chaos. If they withdrew, ESA and the others might follow and history could repeat itself. Columbus would die from the weight of indifference the same way Apollo had.

****

Pentad 60.

Yellow lights would blink on the Telepresence Console if a probe malfunctioned. It had already happened 13 times: 5 freezing up in the cold; 3 trying to navigate hillclimbs and 3 from computer failures. Only 17 of the original 30 still functioned, prompting Chris to turn up the fault alerts on the survivers. This would save some of them but increase the odds of false alarms. The alarms could come from anything now, spikes in temperature, pressure, movement and other things. They could be real or borderline, setting off warnings like the boy who cried wolf.

Everyone who took probe watch knew this and took each alarm seriously. Yet when #18 flashed yellow on the console, Roberto continued sipping coffee nonchalantly and.didn't report it until two days later. Chris was furious when he found out.

"Why the hell didn't you log it immediately?"

"It was an oversensitivity error."

"How do you know?”

“It was obvious, amigo, I could tell.”

“I’ll be the judge of that! Don’t do it again!”

"Okay, okay. Chill out man."

Roberto was probably right about the sensitivity error. Then again, he could be wrong so Chris went to the Telepresence Console ASAP to find out. At the point in the holotape where the blinks had begun, he saw that #18 had been stopped not by wind, sand or weather but by a thick viscous, black fluid. With the cessation of flowing lava, there were no viscous fluids there, at least none he’d ever seen.

It could be a visual anomaly, an illusion or desert mirage, but he didn't think so. Excitement rising, he let his imagination to run wild and donned the Telepresence Suit. He was that kid in the candy store again.

Hoping the probe was still responding to commands, he hit the DISPLAY mode on the console and the black mass instantly came into view on his helmet's heads-up display. The stuff looked thick as mud. Next he hit the SLAVE mode, then lowered his head and extended his hand. Capturing his every movement, the Telepresence Suit transmitted it thousands of kilometers away, where #18 duplicated his motion, lowering its camera head to the mass and placing its metal fingertips into it.

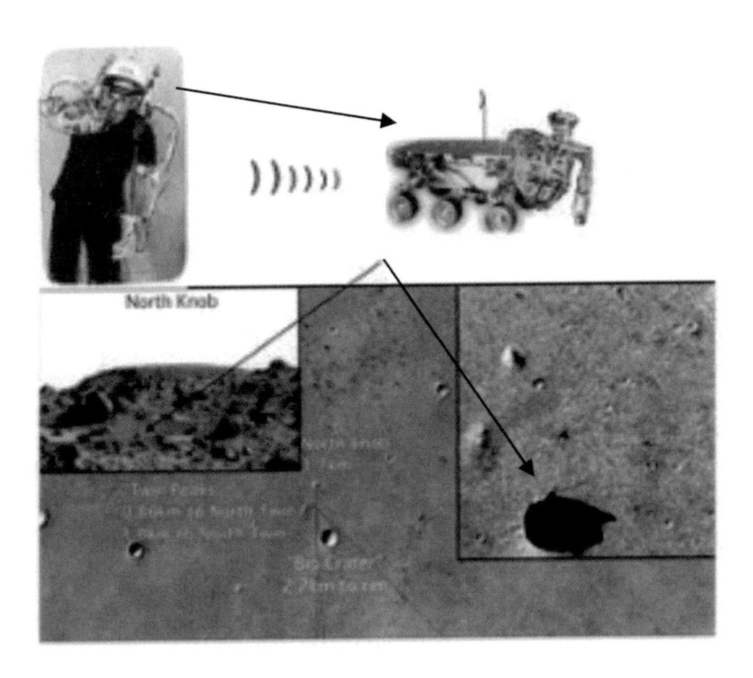

He next clicked SENSE, and felt the coolness and stickiness in his own fingertips, and began moving his glove in a stirring motion. The faster he stirred the thicker it felt, until there was so much resistance, he couldn't stir at all. Andrea soon joined him, her jaw dropping at the scene.

"Goodness!" she exclaimed.

"Can you get the location for me? To the centimeter if possible."

"I'm on it, as you say."

"130 west by 15 north in Sector MC-9 near Olympus Mons," she reported after pulsing the Mars GPS positioning satellite that traced the site. By then it was too late. The look on his face said it all: he'd lost the connection.

"I'll never know what that was now," he said forlornly.

"But the data's on holotape," she reminded him brightly. "You can pass it to our mass spec, maybe it can ID the mass."

“You’re brilliant Andrea,” he smiled. “Has anyone ever told you that?”

“Only you and you’re married.”

“It’s moments like this I wish I wasn’t!”

Neither was prepared for what came back from the instrument so quickly; a match that lined up the spikes in the vapor analysis to a known substance in its library precisely; an exact match.

"There must be an error!" Chris howled, “It says that stuff is tar. It did kinda smell like asphalt through the sniffer in the suit, but this is ridiculous.”

"Tar is the remnants of living things, is it not?"

"Yeah. It's basically accummulated hydrocarbons.”

“You think we’re imagining all this, Chris, the rain, the zone, now tar? You think we’re seeing this because we want to?"

“I don’t know what to think anymore.”

“If it’s real, maybe there are fossils in that sector. The LaBrea Pits in LA had tar and it turned out to be from dinosaurs.”

"And maybe I’m from planet Krypon. For Chrissakes, Andrea.”

It was obvious to her he was getting testy. Who could blame him, with so many clues but no answers? He stared at the results as if in trance, a tug of war between sanity and fantasy before announcing a plan minutes later.

“We’re going to send another probe there. Are of them close?”

“#12 is 300 kilometers south.”

"It would verify #18; give us another data point.”

"Ok, but what if it gets the same result? Çouldn't we still be accused of human error, a computer glitch, whatever. You know the old saying, extraordinary claims require… "

"Extraordinary evidence, Carl Sagan. I'm sick of it already. I know we need a slam dunk which is why we're gonna send 12 to Sector MC-9, grab a sample of that stuff and bring it back to us."

She gulped and swallowed hard. That was halfway around the planet at the foot of Olympus Mons. "Excuse me, Chris, but that's a 3000 kilometer trip."

"I know that."

"And we're down to fifteen probes, half what we started with."

"I'm aware of that too."

"Then you also know #12 won't have a chance."

"Maybe. But I'm going to send it anyway."

****

Pentad 67.

Be it from cabin fever or Yoshi's delicate condition, Vadim was climbing the walls. He began to think he'd made the wrong decision going along with her on the baby.

The reality of it all had come painfully slow to him; him with his ironclad self-image of the great explorer/astronaut. "Women are like wine," he loved to tell friends. "When the bottle's finished, you move to the next." As for children, he would joke:

"They're shriveled raisins when infants; screaming brats till 12; drug addicts as teens and money pits afterwards. And your reward for nursemaiding them through this? Sunday visits when you're old and funeral arrangements when you're dead...if you're lucky."

None of this jived with who he thought he was. Until he saw Yoshi's belly grow and the unexplainable illogical bond that grew with it. Once it started, he had no way of stopping it and soon found himself fretting over her every need. He especially worried about the strange rashes now covering her body and the idea of Roberto treating them. He didn't trust the bastard; never had; never would. Surprisingly, Yoshi defended him.

"I'd prescribe the same antibiotics myself," she tried to reassure him.

"Then why is your cold getting worse? And those open sores?"

"I don't know; probably because we're on a different planet."

"I'll say. And he's got no idea what the gravity, or even the air here does to you."

"No one does, Vadim, now stop it. I'll be fine."

"You better! That boy needs a mother."

"What about a father? And it could be a girl!"

"That too, I've been thinking about it. Having Mars as a birthplace we can't help, being born out of wedlock we can."

"What are you talking about?"

"That I think we should get married!"

Yoshi's eyes opened wide and she squinched up her nose, a sure sign she was perplexed. "It would offend my family," she mumbled. "They treat ceremony seriously. And even if we wanted to there's nobody here to perform it."

"I can do it. I'm the Commander of a ship."

"A captain can't marry himself," she giggled at him. "That's silly."

"I'm authorized to do it and I will. We will."

Chris and Andrea were witnesses and even Roberto got into the act, toasting the couple with fresh grapefruit juice from Tess' garden and wishing them well. And for the moment, they all forgot where they were.

****

Pentad 72.

Each passing pentad seemed to take out another probe. Since sending #12 on its suicide run, Chris winced as he watched each of its brethren fell by the wayside: #9 on a volcanic ridge in the central planes; #27 in the cratered Argyle region to the south; #14 in the Kasei Vallis flood channels; #4 in a sandstorm at Hebbe Chasm; #2 in a crevice at Gusev crater, and four others for unexplained reasons. By pentad 75, only six of the original 30 were left standing but #12, miraculously was one of them. Its OAS (Obstacle Avoidance System) was crippled and it had to be manually steered, but it hobbled on.

As it neared Olympus Mons and the black mass, Chris noted the debris, sediment and dessication in its path. They smacked of places on the fringe back on Earth; fiendish places where things called extremophiles lived: Halophiles in salt ponds, Radiolarens in nuclear reactors; Thermophiles in boiling hydrothermal vents; Bacillus Infernos at abysmally high pressures. If they could survive in those living hells, something could survive here too, he believed with all his heart, and who besides him could find it? Yes, the Columbus 12 crew was scheduled to lift off in less than 30 pentads; and yes they would touchdown at Olympus Base (pre-landed a month before their landing by the foothills of Olympus Mons) and scour the area by the black mass. But as Probe #12 crossed 125 degrees west by 12 degrees north, all the years of spirituality he'd practiced succumbed. His high-handed ideal that it didn't matter who made the discoveries faded and the pressure on him to make them ramped up. If there was any life here at all, only he could find it, noone else.

Besides with Japan now out of the alliance, Columbus 12 could be the last mission; there might not be another chance.

Andrea's reality check reverberated: Even if Probe 12 got to the mass and scored a sample, it would never make it 3000 km back to Candor Base. She was absolutely right! An idea suddenly grabbed and shook him, absurd yet fantastic. He could pull Rover One's passenger seat out, swap in a second fuel tank to double its range and bring the tar back himself. He actually considered it until he realized it would only get him halfway there with no way back. Was he going nuts? It struck him then that he'd been having a lot of crazy thoughts since his red and green dream resurfaced.

****

Pentad 77.

It was Steve Del Cardayre's voice, not Adam Brady's calling Candor Base on Pentad 77. Adam had come down with Eye-Ray, he explained, the disease of the New Millenium. Unheard of prior to the 21st century, Eye-Ray was a play on EIRA or Electromagnetically Induced Retinal Atrophy, a blistering of the retina caused by UV bombardment through the ozone hole. Everyone was dismayed at the news about Adam. He was not only the "Voice of the Mission" but would be the Commander of Columbus 12. He'd taken many detours before getting that seat, trying Flamenco guitar, eastern religion, sculpting, acting, teaching, even accounting.

"Need something to wear?" he would tease Vadim, who lived in his blue flight suit. "I've got wardrobes for everything from all my career changes."

His illness was all the more surprising because he was a near perfect physical speciman near the bottom in risk factors. He hadn't lived near a nuclear reactor, toxic waste dump, chemical plant or high voltage tower; he was below average in X-ray accumulated dose; he'd never owned a cell phone or holoplayer with type 16 circuitry; hadn't smoked, drank or did drugs and was an exercise freak on a calorie-restrictive diet. When the hole started opening over Houston, he'd even donned wraparound purple lenses to protect himself from even the remotest possibility of Eye-Ray. He wore them everywhere except in the MOCR where the walls were thick enough to block any UV. Down in the MOCR, he wanted to see everything on console in big, bold letters. Now he couldn't see at all.

Del Cardayre, his backup, tried to minimize the loss but couldn't. He told Vadim and the others that a retinal chip implant might help Adam, but not in time for the mission. Adam was gone; he was now the Columbus 12 Commander and he was ready. It didn't provide solace. They all felt terrible, not only for Adam but for everyone else back home. Was there no place on Earth that was safe now?

****

Pentad 82.

They'd hardly gotten over the shock of Adam when Yoshi went into premature labor and aborted. Roberto suspected GCRs, the Galactic Cosmic Rays that poured through the thin Mars atmosphere and the lack of good shielding to stop it, especially on the MarsSuits. He recorded the details on HUMMS' medical log with a voice he couldn't keep from shaking:

HUMMS entry, Day 429 on the surface: Roberto Diaz

Dr. Hirumi Yoshioka went into labor at 16:00 and la cosa (the thing) that came out (no other word can describe it) was delivered stillborn at 17:61. It had a stump for a head--no eyes, no nose, no mouth, and webbed fingers and toes. It was also anencephalic, ie, the brain never developed and it had only part of a cerebellum and medulla. There was a strange grey color internally, presumably connected to similar colored pustules on the skin.

This has jolted me. We knew before we left that we'd be esposed to a career dose of GCR radiation on this mission, enough to raise our cancer risk to 1 in 10. We also knew that we ran the risk of some memory loss from the continued exposure to these heavy particle galactic cosmic rays but we signed up anyway. What we didn't know was it how it might effect a pregnancy. Now we do, at least I think I do. Would Dr. Yoshioka have signed up anyway knowing this? Of course. But that was a hypothetical. This isn't!.

The question now is how to treat her. I will take a blood sample, centrifuge it to concentrate the T-cells, then inject it back in intravenously to boost her immune system. After that we'll see.

I've had a premonition about Mars, that we've no business here. Something evil is lurking, and there's an awful truth we're about to find out. Whatever squashed the life from this place is trying to do it to us too. We were warned. Earthfirst warned us.

****

Chapter 27. The Grapefruit Juice Incident

Morale couldn't sink any lower after Yoshi's miscarriage. But at least she was alive and recovering, albeit slowly. As winter lingered long past spring solstace, confinement at Candor Base only added to the gloom, which extended all the way to Earth and Tess, whose only word from Chris came in the disembodied anguish of his last e-mail. His best chance to make a contribution had ended with the dramatic dropout of Probe 12. It had stopped sending signals. She didn't need to be near him to know what he was feeling; the dread of unrealized dreams from a project burdened by outlandish expectations. It had always been too grand a project, doomed from the outset, and she knew that feeling because oscillations were threatening Closure 4 again and she was in the same boat. Last time, she'd handled them, but then they were much smaller. Now they were bigger and her moment of truth would soon be at hand. CASI's twin DNA processors and every theory behind them, her life's work, would be tested. She feared that she'd fail.

In the midst of it all, a bizarre new project came across her plate: blight in Central Park. The mayor of New York had pulled strings to get her to the City and stop it. His reelection hinged on it, he'd promised it in his campaign.There was an implied threat that if she didn't drop everything and hop a plane to the Big Apple ASAP, funding to Biosphere 2 would cease, and he was a big enough fundraiser to carry out such a threat.

It was the 87th pentad on Mars when she got the message and considered how absurd her life had become, a tragicomedy of Mars, Central Park, fish kills, Closures and CASI's rolled into one. Shakespeare couldn't do it justice. But while loss of funding was an abstract, Closure 4 was not. If the Closure went under while she was playing in a park, she'd never forgive herself. Fuck the mayor, she told her management. He'll just have to wait in line.

****

Pentad 88.

The first sign of spring on Mars was subtle; not like on Earth where flowers bloom, shadows lighten and groundhogs stop running from their shadows. No, on Mars, it was just the barest perceptible lessening of the ubiquitous nighttime scirocco; evidenced by the faintest drop in the wind's pitch; a shift from an A sharp to an A flat at the high end of the scale when the winds were at their peak; a shift only someone with perfect pitch could discern, someone like Yoshi who immediately began to smile and rise up. It happened on the 88th Pentad and it was followed on the 89th by a rise in barometric pressure, yellow-white clouds in the sky and permafrost vaporizing.

The change lifted everyone. Yoshi got out of bed; Andrea got mischievous and Vadim even patted Roberto on the back. He had to acknowledge that the Mexican had probably saved Yoshi's life. And that he might have been wrong about him all along.

****

The veil seemed to lift for Tess back on Earth as well. Miracle of miracles: Closure 4 self-corrected without her lifting a finger. It struck her then that perhaps she'd been taking herself too seriously; that maybe, just maybe she wasn't the *dues-ex-machina* she thought she was with CASI. That maybe like George Carlin had said, Planet Earth only needed us for plastic. It could do fine without us, thank you.

****

Pentad 90.

Though the others felt uplifted, Chris remained troubled. The unanswered questions, punctuated by his jarring red/green dream were wearing him down.

"You look like a zombie," Andrea told him with concern.

"Probe 12," he just mumbled back, "the key's in that fucking probe."

The tone of his voice; the use of expletives like *fuck*; and obsessing on a probe: these were all out of character for Chris. He was scaring her. Could he be losing it, the most stable of them all; was she the only one noticing? She thought about telling the others but decided to wait a pentad. By then they'd be at 91, only 9 from departure; by then with just 45 days left, maybe he'd come to his senses. Or not. If he spiraled down further he could do something rash, then what? It became moot when he knocked on her door late one night.

"It's back," he whispered, "it's back!"

She didn't bother asking how he'd resurrected Probe 12; she simply followed him down to the Telepresence Center, donned the Telepresence Suit and watched it come back to life before her eyes: the remote vision of its own eyes; its audio; auditory; touch, heat, wind and pressure sensors, all of them, but none so strong as its RAD counter; the telltale click-click-click of a radiation source.

"It was nothing I did," Chris informed her, "other than hoping and looking. It came back on its own, heading southeast towards Pavonis Patera."

"But that's opposite where it was supposed to go. The tar is northwest!"

"I know but I've got a theory on that," and with that, he flipped off the RAD HOME switch on the sensor console, whereupon Probe #12 promply wheeled about and began tracking northwest.

"I don't get it," Andrea began to say until he flipped RAD HOME back on again and it reversed course again, southeast. "It's tracking a radiation scent, isn't it?"

"Yes. Radioactive methane. When it came back on line, the GPS was disabled and it lost track of the tar. It's been using RAD HOME instead."

"But why?"

"Dust in the circuits, who knows?"

"What about the tar?"

"It never would have made it there; you were right. And this is just as interesting, more interesting. Life forms generate methane."

Over the next two sols, they became riveted to the Telepresence Center and the slow, meandering progress of Probe #12. Its herky-jerky motion mesmerized them as it treked, caused, no doubt, by the undulating strength of the mysterious radiation source. But as it moved southeast, the source strength grew greater, and it seemed to thrive on the energy. Together Chris and Andrea watched it negotiate a lava field, leaving treadmarks of red in its wake; then it criss-crossed a white outcropping and a glass-streaked ancient riverbed. From there, came a gradual incline which it forged slowly up until the view jerked to freeze frames. It took awhile to see why: slippage on ice caused by permafrost beneath 12's treads. Too much of that would put it in *Safe Mode*, causing its systems to shut down.

A lightbulb went off: that's why it shut down in the first place. And since *Auto Reboot/Restart* followed *Safe Mode* after a time delay, that's why it had come back on line. Mystery solved, but how to keep it from happening again?

The easy fix would be the Sun; the higher in the sky it got, the warmer the ground temps. Would they get warm enough to melt permafrost and stop the slipping? Maybe. While minus 50 at night, at the peak of the day near the equator where 12 was, the ground would heat up quickly; it might even hit plus 80 in the thin air. Moving 12 during noon to sunset only then putting it to sleep at night would be the strategy and it worked, until the next obstacle surfaced: a mesa where pebbles became rocks and rocks morphed to impassable boulders. They searched for a detour until darkness drove them dizzy.

"We should stop," Andrea intervened. "A good nights' sleep will help us in the morning."

Maybe you, Chris thought, not me, but he agreed to try. And though his red/green dream didn't return that night, the threat of it alone kept him wide-awake and fitful.

Bleary-eyed the next morning, he stumbled down to the Telepresence Console, where Andrea was already waiting. She had a surprise for him: a possible detour past the boulders through a narrow crevice that appeared with the rising sun. He hit #12's zoom lens to highlight it; then scoured the opening through bloodshot eyes.

"Maybe," he mumbled before donning the Telepresence Suit. "Maybe."

He'd have to wait hours before daring to wake the probe at noon to try it: hours that would pass like glaciers moving. There wasn't a damn thing he could do to speed them up but wait, drink coffee and think about Tess and Andrea; his life on Mars and back on Earth; about leaving empty-handed; the thoughts circling madly until noon grudingly came. The probe awoke routinely when it did, unexpectedly almost, and he engaged its SLAVE mode.

It followed him obediently, snaking its arm and torso in response to his then moving closer to the crevice. Almost as an afterthought it passed through the gap with all the fanfare of a sloth. And though he heaved a sigh of relief that this had been been much ado about nothing, other roadblocks soon followed, each a bigger dilemma. At one, the view through Chris' helmet pitched, rolled and yawed and his stomach rolled with it to nausea.

"I feel sick," he whispered to Andrea, who once again rose to the rescue.

"Toggle the cameras to pan, not close-up," she shouted, "you're getting motion sickness." When he did so and the nausea cleared, he chastised himself for ever doubting her. None of them should have, especially Roberto.

The probe's route rarely wavered after that as entrenched, they both watched it: until the last sol of Pentad 91 near Pavonis Patera when the tenor of its clicks changed to beeps. It happened at dusk where it was hard to see details and Chris hesitated. Dare he go on with nighttime encroaching, and risk a possible shutdown and delay till a reboot?

The source was around the bend and he might find it in minutes. And though it was dark in the visible range, he might be able to see it in the infrared. Okay, he decided, and toggled to IR.

A pale green glow instantly appeared in his visor from an outcropping just ahead. If he waited until morning, it might disappear in the daylight. A few minutes more wouldn't hurt so he pressed on.

The glow grew in size by the outcropping as he cut 12's tracking speed and it seemed to be coming from under a rock. It was an odd shaped rock, small enough to be clasped within the metal fingers at the end of 12's robotic arm so he extended his gloved hand to pick it up. The virtual image when #12 followed suit show pits, rinds and phenocrysts on the surface but he was suddenly diverted by the sound of bubbling gas. It was seeping through the ground on the soil where the rock had been, and he knew without doubt that it was methane.

He put the rock down and had #12 inch forward to an undulating dune field where its beeps seemed to crest. There were more of the funny rocks there, and geysers of glowing gas, some so bright he had to look away until his pupils could readjust. Something circular, symmetrical and stunning in the dunes shook him then, a something not fashioned by nature. That at least was his first inclination, until he recalled Fibonacci. Fibonacci's numbers and the *golden mean* derived from them proved that nature could produce perfect patterns too; in the leaves of an artichoke, turns of a nautilis shell and twists of a pine cone. If that could happen on Earth, why not Mars?

But this pattern was different. It defied the familiar with its smooth and whitish outline, like a crop circle etched in sand instead of grass. The nearer Probe 12 got to it, the faster its RAD count rose, until the beeps started fluctuating madly. When they became a warble—something he'd never heard before--Chris shifted his attention for less than a second. But in that second, sand started caving in around 12's treads and by the time he noticed, it was too late. A balance alarm went off; the view through his helmet lurched upwards and a flicker of red light flashed.

One sensor after another died on #12 then, all but the warbling wail of its RAD tone. He would have cursed aloud had he not been speechless. Shapes in a subterranean cave, unnatural, unreal, astonishing!

Though blind, deaf and helpless now, #12's warbles carried on. If someone could track them, they might lead to what he'd seen. To do that however, he'd have to shut off 12's power. It might never come back on but at least there'd be a chance.

Andrea looked at him oddly after he'd done that. Why wasn't she as agog, agape and amazed as he was? And then he remembered only had was wearing the Telepresence suit. She'd seen nothing, felt nothing, touched nothing and heard nothing other than his shouts of disbelief. Het attention had already shifted to the other active probes. Only 5 remained now, none of them near #12 or #18, dead, buried and gone as far as she was concerned.

****

Pentad 92. Departure Minus Forty Days

Though Vadim had called a truce with Roberto, he couldn't bring himself to like him. And though he'd been okay since spring broke, following orders and not undermining him, that changed in a heartbeat the morning of the grapefruit juice incident; the morning Vadim's mouth caught fire after he drank the juice Roberto had squeezed; the same juice everyone drank but didn't seem to notice.

"What the fuck," Vadim cursed, "What the hell did you put in this?"

"Citric acid; grapefruit juice to you."

"*Dermo, mierda*, bullshit," Vadim shot back. Taste it!"

"*Ay caramba*," Roberto yelped after a sip he promptly spat out.

"Where did you get it from, when did you squeeze it?" Vadim interrogated him.

"I don't like what you're suggesting, amigo."

"Answer the question!"

"I got it from a grapefruit of course."

"Where did you get the grapefruit?"

"Same place I always do, the ripening bin."

Vadim turned to Chris, his usual ally in this battle of wills. And though Chris' eyes were glazed over, and his thoughts still immersed in the probe, he shot to attention from the tone in Vadim's voice. "Get down to the bin with him and test this," he demanded, "I want to know what's in it. I want to know now!"

Chris couldn't fathom why Roberto would want to spike Vadim's grapefruit juice—a senseless and stupid act from someone who was neither. If he'd really wanted to poison Vadim, there were far better ways to do it.

By the time they entered the tunnel, he began to wonder if Vadim, not Roberto might be the problem, overreacting over one bad grapefruit in a harvest of plenty. And as he prepared to waste what precious little time he had left on another wild goose chase, he started to resent Vadim. For in lieu of sending him out to find tar or subterranean caves, he'd relegated him instead to be a taster, tester and chief bottle washer.

Roberto, silent as they transited the tunnel in their polymer suits, became livid in the confines of the greenhouse airlock. Prebreathing pure oxygen had a tendency to do that.

"Fuck him!" he unloaded on Chris. "Next he'll put me in irons. "

"Take it easy," Chris replied sympathetically. "He just wants to know what happened."

"Why am *I* always the *cabron*?" Roberto persisted, "why is he always on me?"

"You bring a lot of it on yourself, Roberto. The way you handle Andrea, those crazy sex operation stories, the ... "

"Those weren't stories," Roberto shot back. "And it's still my opinion that Andrea needs…"

"I'm not interested in this, okay, and you're wrong about Andrea. Look I just want to get this overwith."

But as they moved to the bin where the grapefruits were stored, he found it harder to maintain neutrality. Roberto might be an asshole but Vadim was pissing him off. This was a waste of time.

"I suggest we test the rinds from the waste bin first," Roberto offered, "then the batch those fruits came from and the trees the batch came from. And we should test other crops besides the grapefruit. Tomatoes, oranges, broccoli."

Reasonable, Chris thought as he retrieved the rinds from the waste bin. If Roberto had it in for Vadim, why would he make such suggestions? Still, how could the Mexican have missed the pungent, overwhelming odor of the rinds he soon began testing. The plummeting pH meter, together with the oxygen bubbling past the platinum catalyst after he'd added sulfuric acid and other reagents confirmed it. Ammonia--NH^3! The juice had been laced with ammonia. Roberto's explanation: a deteriorating sinus condition. A sense of smell so congested, he couldn't tell roses from methane. It was logical but far-fetched.

The plot thickened as they moved to the batches and trees. Most tested negative, but some came back with the same perplexing result, in different degrees and intensity. It held true for the oranges, tomatoes and broccoli too and Chris soon roiled with concern. How had they missed this, how much had they swallowed? On the edge of panic now, he decided to query ECLSS.

The ECLSS computer tracked every crop in every chamber from the time it started life as a seedling. From watering cycle, sunlight exposure and nutrients to size and weight of each fruit, it recorded every nuance. If patterns could be found, ECLSS would find them.

There were none in the hydroponic chamber or the terraformer, but there seemed to be a clue in the soil chamber, traced to harvests post-pentad 85. Each type of fruit had similar yields prior to it, while everything following was smaller. Ammonia would do that, Chris surmised, but where the hell would it come from? It had two types of atoms: Hydrogens (3) surrounding Nitrogen (1). They were rare on Mars, like platinum, gold and diamonds on Earth, yet here they were.

“I’m at a loss to explain this," Chris reported to Vadim later. “I put some of the soil through our mass spec and emailed the findings to Tess. Maybe she can help.”

“Yeah, if she gets them. Meanwhile, how’s this for an explanation: the fucking Mexican. If he screws transsexuals, he’s capable of anything."

****

Pentad 93.

To: CLK~11@COL.nasa.gov
From: Teliot@Bsphere2.edu

Return-Path: Teliot@Bsphere2.edu.
Received: from muffin (muffin.me.psu.edu [128.118.183.49])
by r02n06.cac.psu.edu. (8.6.12/8.6.12) with SMTP id SAA85676 for
< CLK~11@COL.nasa.gov; Tue 9 Nov 2035 14:19:59-0500.
>Message-Id: <201212072351.SAA85676@r02n06.cac.psu.edu>
X-Sender: Teliot@Bshphre.edu: X-Mailer: Windows Eudora Version 1.4.3
Mime-Version: 1.0. Content-Type: text/plain; charset="us-ascii"
Date: Tue 9 Nov 2035 14:20:54 -0500:

Nov 9, 2035,

Chris! That's not just nitrogen and hydrogen atoms in the tracing you emailed, there's a lot more: methyl and ethyl groups, pentanes, hexanes, benzene rings: all kinds of stuff. They're all bound up in some complex molecule I'm guessing. Perhaps contamination of some sort, the kind of thing you might see in a chemical spill. The nitrogen can't be coming from my *Tessmix*, there's just not enough of it. You store chemicals in the Power Module, don't you? I'd start there, maybe some are leaking.

Another possibility is that this stuff occurs naturally in a deep soil layer; and that it got into the chamber's root system after the crops grew down into it. I wouldn't bet on it. That kind of chemistry is not in any of our models. It flies in the face of everything we know about Mars. Just to rule it out though, I'd dig down to the roots and run samples. E-mail me the traces and I'll try to make some sense of them. Wish I could do more but I've got my hands full myself. Closure 4's gone tipsy again and NY's mayor is driving me crazy.

Miss you; love you; counting the minutes till you're back here.

(: < T.

Pentad 95.

Be it in the ground naturally or leaking from the Power Module, Chris eschewed both possibilities. The first meant they were monumental bunglers; they'd missed the very essence of Mars itself. The second was even worse. Following Tess' advice, he went to the Power Module and found no leaks. The only way to get chemicals from there to the greenhouse then was for someone to have taken them there. Sabatoge theories again, that would be hard to stomach. Yet everyone had access and anyone could have done it. He preferred the third possibility, that he could have missed something fundemental, adn decided to start from the beginning. Gather up more root samples and do another mass spec run.

The greenhouse went into freefall before he got that far. The crops in the soil chamber began withering before he could get to their roots. By the middle of the 95th pentad, they were reeking from ammonia and inedible. Fortunately they'd stored enough food to last 5 more pentads or they might've starved to death before they ever left Mars. Unfortunately all signs still pointed to sabotage. It can't be, Chris kept repeating over and over to himself, until he realized how to rule it out, or in. The soil in the Terraformers came from 2 meters below the surface--the same depth as the contaminated roots in the soil chamber. He'd taken great pains to collect the Terraformer soil himself from random sites around Candor Base, and he'd been the only one to do it. He'd also been the only one to place the seeds in that soil and seal them in each plastex sphere. If the seals were unbroken and ammonia could be found, it had to be occurring naturally. But if the seals were broken and ammonia was within, only sabotage could explain it.

The seals *were* unbroken; and NH^3 *was* detected!

“Impossible,” Vadim bellowed when Chris told him, “you’ve made a mistake.”

"If you don’t believe me, I can prove it on a Rover traverse.”

"What can you learn that you haven't already in the 17 months you've been here?"

"That ammonia’s omnipresent."

"If so, you should have seen it in the Rainbow Zone. It was tens of meters deep and you didn’t detect it."

"That’s because it was layered rock, not soil."

"I’ll ask you again, is there any way Roberto could have done this?"

"No. Come with me on an excursion if you doubt it. See for yourself what’s in that dirt."

As Vadim pondered the offer, mutinous thoughts ran rampant in Chris’ head: Was Vadim’s dislike for Roberto undoing everything, could either of them be trusted? His choices were growing more complicated. Decisions had to be made soon that had nothing to do with grapefruits.

"I’ll probably be sorry,” Vadim finally responded, “but I’ll go with you. We’ll take the Crab. Be ready at 0700.”

****

The samples they took the next morning clinched it. Taken 2 meters down, they matched the soil in the spheres. And just like Tess said, there were methanes, hexanes and other organic compounds in Chris' GCMS run; all bound together in a molecule like...

"Blood?" an astonished Vadim erupted.

"It's not blood, but the molecular structure's similar to it. Every sample we took has it, Vadim; it seems to be pervasive. That's why the soil chamber failed when its roots reached 2 meters; why the Terraformer never worked. And it's why the hydroponic chamber, which uses water instead of soil, still works."

"Those dreams of yours are getting to you, Chris. I'm no geologist but I know the red color here's from iron, not blood."

"Iron is in blood, Vadim, in hemoglobin."

"Blood in the ground, you're crazy."

"I didn't say it was blood, it just resembles it."

"You've been here too long, Chris. All of us have."

****

Pentad 96

To: CLK~11@COL.nasa.gov
From: Teliot@Bsphere2.edu

Return-Path: Teliot@Bsphere2.edu.
Received: from muffin (muffin.me.psu.edu [128.118.183.49])
by r02n06.cac.psu.edu. (8.6.12/8.6.12) with SMTP id SAA85676 for
< CLK~11@COL.nasa.gov; Tue 9 Nov 2035 14:19:59-0500.
>Message-Id: <201212072351.SAA85676@r02n06.cac.psu.edu>
X-Sender: Teliot@Bshphre.edu: X-Mailer: Windows Eudora Version 1.4.3
Mime-Version: 1.0. Content-Type: text/plain; charset="us-ascii"
Date: Thursday 25 Nov 2035 14:20:54 -0500:

No point wasting words darling. Hosokawa was just arrested for the nuke incident and under questioning admitted the sabotage thing was a hoax. He never met Andrea or Roberto, only knew them through the media and made the whole thing up. I'm so sorry for putting you all through that craziness, like there's not enough things on your plate. Please ask Vadim, Yoshi and especially Roberto and Andrea to forgive me and not be too angry. I was just trying to protect you. I know there's not much time left but hopefully this news will help calm things down there and you can do some real science before you come home. I'll be waiting with open arms.

(: < T.

Pentad 98.

Sabatage was no longer on the table but other issues were: Lightning and rain; the Rainbow Zone; the tar; methane; a radioactive cave; ammonia and now a bloodlike molecule. These were questions at the forefront; no doubt there were more. And though answers had become an obsession to Chris, the crew of Columbus 12 would have to get them. *Constitution* and *Intrepid*, their Transit Craft and Lander were already at *Alpha* waiting and they'd be launching from the Cape soon to meet them. Three months from now, both missions would cross paths, Columbus 12 on their way to Olympus Base; Columbus 11 on their way back to Earth. The 12 crew would be focusing on their countdown right about now, while 11's remaining tasks were packing, fueling and leaving. Chris had ten days left on Mars, little time for the discoveries he'd come to make.

Dark thoughts intruded as departure neared, thoughts about his future. He'd never see Mars again, that was a given. And with NASDA pulling out of the alliance, he doubted anyone would after Columbus 12's mission. What would he do with the rest of his life? Go on tour, make speeches, write books, be an elder statesman? Or would he spend his dotage as the typecast ex-astronaut, signing autographs and parroting canned answers to stupid questions like, what was it like, what did you learn, would you do it again? Whatever he did wouldn't top what he'd done--another given. The instant *Columbia* lit her engines, his life would become a replay.

His malaise escaped no one as the clock ticked on. First Andrea, then Vadim tried to snap him out of it.

"No one expected us to solve all the riddles," Andrea said brightly over dinner at T-9 sols, "but look at what we did: grew our own food, made oxygen, prove self-sufficiency, survived. My God, we've survived!"

"That may be enough for you," he said sourly, "but I wanted more. I wanted answers to real questions. Instead all we got was some interesting geology. No one gives a shit about geology. What carves canyons and makes volcanoes or yellow clouds doesn't do it for them."

“What does then?” Vadim cut in.

“Life, Vadim, life: is it here; was it here; can it be here?

"We didn’t come here for that," Vadim shot back. "Our job was to lead, to pioneer. We've done that, we're in the company of giants: Ponce de Leon, Leif Erikson, Perry, Scott, Armstrong and Aldrin. They planted flags; we planted flags. We’ve even outdone our namesake Columbus, you should be proud."

Roberto, who’d been sitting silently suddenly erupted, his voice dripping with sarcasm.

"Let me tell you about Columbus," he burst out. "He fucked the New World the same way we'll fuck this one. He pillaged its treasures; ruined its crops and murdered the native Indians. Listen to the words of the Mayan prophets passed down to the people of my village:

The coming of the whites will bring burning.
The coming of the whites will break bones,
He takes the life of our beaver.
He takes the life of our buffalo,
Soon he will take Mother Earth.
Soon there will be nothing at all.

"That's who your Columbus was," Roberto finished. "That's who we all are. That's why I'm glad we're leaving and why we should never come back!"

****

December 11th, 2035:

There were 8542 magnitude 3 to 5 earthquakes on Earth in the year 2000; and 13484 in 2007, a 50% increase. By 2035, the number had risen to 25000, but the number of magnitude 7s hardly changed at all over those years: until the night of December 11th when....

Simultaneous quakes stuck planet Earth. Their epicenters, 30 miles south of Okushiri Island in the Sea of Japan and 56 miles east of San Juan, Puerto Rico, both registered 7.8 on the Richter scale. They occurred within minutes of each other. But in a year of firestorms, floods, tornadoes, power outages and heat waves leaving millions of people dead, hurt or homeless, it was just another environmental disaster. "Expect aftershocks," the experts warned.

By then, mountain sized tidal waves had already struck out from the epicenters, leveling everything in their path as they steamrolled towards land. One plowed through Cuba while the other smothered the coastline of Japan before setting sight on Russia.

It was morning in Cape Canaveral when the Launch Director turned her wary eyes eastward, almost the same moment her counterpart at Baikunur Cosmodrome looked south. It was the week before Columbus 12's scheduled launch and they both had decisions to make, the same kind of decisions.

At the Cape, the new Space Shuttle *Artemis* was on Pad 39B in final checkout before ferrying the Columbus 12 crew to ISS and their waiting transit craft of Mars. But if it didn't get off the ground before the storm surge hit it would be a sitting duck. According to predictions, the tsunami would strike north, 300 miles away at the Keys. The fringe of its great arc would be spent before reaching the Cape -- unless the predictions were wrong.The prudent thing to do would be to roll *Artemis* back, to the VAB, the Vertical Assembly Building, built to withstand nature's worst catastrophies. But rolling her back would close the launch window. If it stayed closed a month, the next one wouldn't open for 18; ending for decades, the grand humans-to-Mars experiment. Considering the cost, effort and stakes, the Launch Director didn't want that. Neither did her counterpart or anyone else associated with Project Columbus. It was enough to make her pause before making her decision, a decision that hinged on a 3-mile race. That was the distance from Pad 39B to the VAB. And while *Artemis* could orbit at 18,000 miles an hour in space, it could only make 1/2 mile/hour on the ground on its Mobile Tractor. At that snail's pace it would take 6 hours to cover those 3 miles and reach the safety of the VAB, about the same time it would take for the effects of the tidal wave to reach the Cape after it struck the Keys.

Hundreds of miles south in Key West, the wave was about to make landfall. It's advance guard was a blinding rain, followed by a storm surge that toppled the seawall. As Key West became part of the Atlantic, Category 4 force winds descended on Miami, setting off a hail of glass, wood and metal splinter-bullets, the remains of what used to be homes and buildings.

North, up the coast in Lauderdale, boats were tossed from their moorings like footballs, then dropped from the sky like raindrops.

Decades of hurricane warnings had made the populace jaded. More often then not, they'd been overhyped with false alarms and by the time they realized this wasn't one, it was too late. Their last minute dash crammed millions of cars in gridlock. Seeking high ground they were sucked out to sea by the tens of thousands.

The Launch Director watched all this with growing alarm from KSC's Firing Room. It was now a snail vs hare race; the snail that was Shuttle *Artemis* vs the hare of the storm. The hare had already wiped out Vero Beach, was descending on Daytona and would soon make haste for Melbourne. The race would be close. They would reach the VAB within minutes of each other.

The sky was black when the barometric pressure took a nosedive at Cocoa Beach. The Sun Coast Tower condominiums toppled over from a surge of churning water. Fourteen miles to the south, someone threw a lever at KSC and a grinding noise shook the VAB. It was the sound of the high bay doors closing. The snail had won; Shuttle *Artemis* was inside and safe. The Launch Director exhaled deeply then ran for cover as fast as she could. For while the VAB could withstand the onslaught, the Firing Room might not.

When the fury finally hit, its huge windows imploded like paper, passing in rain, silt and projectiles. And though the Launch Team survived, their consoles did not. Neither did the 3-mile tractor path from the VAB back out to the launch pad, now a quagmire. Nor did Pads 39A and B, lying twisted and toppled, or the Launch Complex at Baikonur, destroyed by similar aftershocks. Nor would the Columbus 12 mission, which had no way of reaching Alpha now.

****

Pentad 100: Last night on Mars

Mars would soon be alone again. This was the thought haunting Chris on D-1, the day before departure. Nothing could stop that thought; it would tease him throughout the Closeout Checklist. He packed data and computer files thinking it, and holotapes, lab, soil and rock samples. It toyed with him while he helped fuel the Escape Craft with 24 tons of methox and mocked him when Vadim send the signal to awaken *Columbia* from hibernation, the very last step before putting Candor Base in permanent deep freeze. He did all these things in the trance of defeat, repeating. *Candor Base will be gone soon*, the earworm in his repeated incessantly, *buried in sand as if it never was*.

He turned in that last night hoping sleep would purge the thought, but fearful his red/green dream wouldn't let him. He'd stay up all night if need be, but like victims in Invasion of the Body Snatchers, his massive fatigue scuttled that vow. The dream started out with same roiling sea but sequeyed to something entirely different this time; encompassing him with the pleasant smells and hues of a flowering Candor Base. It had been been excavated and turned into a museum. Under a blue, not a red sky; on green, not red hills, parents waited in line with their children, wearing normal clothes, not space suits. Inside the museum was a statue of him astride *Crab*, lifelike and ready to go. The parents pointed at his statue, telling their children, "That's the Great Daddy, the One who started it all," whereupon Crab erupted in a whine of treads. The whine grew deeper and throatier in his ears, a pounding drumbeat until it suddenly exploded into red and green vapor trails and he awoke. Knowing at long last what the dream meant, and what he had to do.

Unlike Chris, Vadim felt vibrant when he awoke that morning. He'd squeezed everything from life, he believed, what more could he have done? He grinned broadly as he began packing his personal effects for Earth, what to take, what to leave? His gaze gravitated to the framed photo of Yuri Gagarin that he'd spirited away two years earlier at launch. "My hero stays here," he declared. "Martian children will want to know about my hero, and me too, someday."

His next order of business was preparing the suits. He would take no chances for this final traverse to the Escape Craft. He had set his alarm early to insure that, waking before the others to fully charge their tanks with oxygen. Nothing could go wrong on this last and final trek. But a discomforting feeling intruded as he descended down the ladder towards D-deck. It turned to astonishment when he got to Chris' locker. The locker door was wide open and his MarsSuit was gone. In its place was a note.

Vadim, Andrea, Yoshi, Roberto,

By the time you read this, I'll be too far away for you to do anything about it. You can't follow me; I have both Rovers and Crab.

Don't attempt to call, I won't answer.

Leave on schedule, it's your only choice.

I'd come to find answers but didn't.

Now with this scrub Columbus 12 won't either.

That made my decision to stay easy.

I'm heading for Olympus Base, their destination.
There's food and life-support to last years there if I make it.
Don't worry, I'm not delusional.
I know the odds are slim of making it there.
But I have a fighting chance with both Rovers and Crab.
I worked through the night pulling the passenger seats,
and stuffing extra fuel tanks, meal trays etc in their place.
If I'm lucky I can go a month and 3000 kilometers maybe more.

Whatever happens, don't feel sorry for me.
I'd have been a useless fool back on Earth.
Without my answers; without the thread connecting everything.

Tell the MOCR I'll contact them if I can,
qssuming the solar wind lets the comm. get through.
Tell Tess I love her, and tell her I'm sorry.
I hope she understands.
I hope all of you do.

Good luck you guys, C

Chapter 28. Four-leaf Clover.

The Mountain Pine Beetle likes Pine trees.
It devoured 32 million acres of them in British Columbia in 2007.
The beetles die off in winter, reproduce in summer
and are sensitive to temperature change, very sensitive.

.

As temperatures inch up from global warming, reproduction increases,
and the beetles more Pine trees.
The trees release C02 as they die, adding to the greenhouse effect.
This causes higher temperatures, more beetles and so on.

It's called a positive feedback loop and at some point,
photosynthesis will be affected.
No one knows when, where or by how much.

The only thing we do know is that photosynthesis makes oxygen,
and that's what we breathe....

December 21st, 2035: Earth, Biosphere 2:

The Indefinite Closure was on the brink again. After 7 years of waves, Tess thought she'd seen them all, but as the oscillations grew, this one looked worse. Tess retreated to her lab and CASI for the fight, the same fight she'd been fighting since MIT, and as she did so, it occurred to her that her life had been a ruse; a deception of thousands of equations buried in CASI that only she understood (and even that was a stretch).

Never mind the awards and accolades, the recognition and publications. Never mind that CASI's DNA solution matrix had pulled off miracles before. The thought of another fight exhausted her. And mixed in with everything else brought her to the brink of tears. But at least Chris was.coming home. Eight months from now, he'd be in her arms again and that should have fortified her.

But it hadn't.

It was not what he'd said in his last email that sent her spiraling, but what he hadn't. Not a word about missing her, no mention of the future. It was not what she needed as she steeled herself for the fight.

Nor was the videocomm call that followed from Houston.

****

Rover 1 strained against the slope of the terrain and the mass of *Crab* and Rover 2. Its engines weren't built to tow a train like this. Could they take the pounding? Fear of them ungluing kept Chris riveted to the manifold pressures, cylinder temps, methox quantity and so on. They were all in the green now, in the middle of their arcs. Would they stay that way?

He knew Vadim, Andrea, even Roberto would try to change his mind and he'd be tempted. But despite wanting to shut the comm off he couldn't. He had to keep listening, if only to make sure they got off.

"Come back," their voices kept hammering, "You still have time."

"Get on with it, " he whispered to himself, "the window's closing."

In his minds eye, he could see them pulling out all the stops, maybe even patching in a shrink from the MOCR to talk him from the edge like they do with a madman on a skyscraper. That might be a good on a skyscraper, he flashed, but not on Mars with a 40 minute lag time!

The comm squawked continually with their pleas, voices that gradually went from desperate to resigned before growing silent, followed several minutes later by one last burst, the voice of Tess. Through the void and the static, it rang true, steeped in a mixture of shock and sorrow,

"Come back. I beg of you," she beseached him. "Don't do this to us. Please."

From a quarter billion miles away, the voice pierced his resolve. He'd falter if she kept it up and he couldn't allow that. Not after the planning, the note and the unanswered questions. He clicked it off.

He kept the comm off until the last possible minute, until the window was nearly shut and Vadim's voice replaced Tess' with the final countdown. It was flat as steel as it read off the checklist to Houston.

Chris wheeled the Rovers about towards an overlook, a bluff with an unobstructed view facing east where he could see them off, and wish them well. The cabin was pin-drop quiet after he killed the engines, a quiet broken only by Vadim's voice echoing "ten," and "nine," and "eight," and "seven." Chris strained his eyes to the northeastern sky at "five, and tensed at "four, three, two, one," looking for the cloud of ffire and methox.

It rose like an arrow in the distance, chased by a roar he couldn't hear for 60 seconds. They were 13 kilometers away by his reckoning: the distance sound travels in a minute in Mar's thin air. The trajectory veered north, pointing the way towards *Columbia*. He imagined their thoughts as they rose higher and faster, arching their way back to Earth. Roberto would be glad; Yoshi would be sad and Andrea and Vadim would be in shock; stunned by his choice to stay on a dying planet instead of returning to a living one. Madness they'd say, and they'd be right!

He watched them as they faded to a dot in the pink sky, first blending, then vanishing into it. And as their exhaust contrail scattered in the winds, the parallels to his life became inevitable; once so straight and narrow, now scattered by obsessions. Obsessions so burning they'd overwhelmed his love for Tess. With cravings so maniacal, they'd condemned him to death or desolation.

He started to cry in great heaving spasms; spasms that shook him so violently he started to gray out. They were the same spasms his red/green dream had portended, a future without love for there'd be noone to love.

He was barely aware of the engines as he started them and headed west. Gloom pervaded everything; a gloom born of the life he'd just abandoned; a life he could have shared with Tess on the farm she'd always wanted; with the children she'd secretly yearned for. And in the midst of this gloom, he finally realized who he was: a scientist first, a husband, lover or father second. Everything else had been bullshit and bravado, pretending and posturing for the sake of his mother, his father, his friends and finally Tess. "Enough!" He shouted as if someone could hear. "Enough!

Tess wondered how she'd make it without him, not that losing him hadn't occurred to her. She'd often pictured his oxygen running out or his spacecraft exploding. But staying behind? Never.

She was surprised she hadn't thought of that one. After all, she knew him better than he knew himself. She knew he'd apply for the mission before he did; knew he'd be picked when he'd dismissed it and knew he'd be miserable without his answers. He was too much like her in that regard: a scientist. Science first, people second; it's the way it had to be with them, the only way they'd worked.

Tell Tess I love her, and tell her I'm sorry. I hope she understands.

The words pounced like mortar shells. Of course she understood.

The display read 2670 kilometers to go when he checked again. To make it in 30 days, he'd have to average 7 km/hr for 13 hours a day with 7 hours for sleep. The first leg of the journey would take him to Hebbe Chasm, 200 kilometers northwest, where landslides had separated the canyon walls and stacked up talus deposits. The deposits would be his bridge to the highlands if such a bridge existed. He'd have to cross the canyon floor to get to it, then climb two kilometers up along a 30 degree incline for nearly a week to get to datum (sea) level. The Rovers would have to mount boulders; the engines would have to work perfectly and he'd be slave to the same titanic forces that had reduced Mars to rubble.

Later that day, he rolled into Snake, a linear depression that forked upwards to the horizon. Buckets of stone rained on the treads as the Rover train traversed unstable avalanche chutes and he prayed for minimum havoc and passable gaps. Serpentine-like he scaled the gorge slowly, meandering with it, twisting and turning and dodging until dusk when he found a protected alcove that leveled off.

He ate a makeshift meal from a tray he couldn't heat; then set up the bunk thinking of the physical demands ahead: one hand on the throttles, the other on the yokes; one foot on the brakes, the other on the fuel cutoff; one eye on terrain, the other on the gauges. They'd already taken their toll, slowing him from 7 to 5 km/hr that first day. He'd need ten more days to get to Olympic Base at that pace, ten days he might not have.

After a fitful sleep, he decided to eat on the run to save time instead of stopping. He'd cram meal trays under the seat each night; eat whatever he grabbed in whatever order, breakfast for dinner, dinner for breakfast, cold, on the move, with his fingers. No time for utensils, no time for food heaters, no time for niceties like dining with a view. Likewise for the toilet. In the back of the Rover, it took 5 minutes of prep time, 5 minutes he couldn't spare. From now on he'd use suit fecal bags, quick and dirty. Dirty he could live with, minutes wasted, he couldn't.

A tweaking of the ocean syatem saved the day this time. It was CASI's new AI logic but Tess didn't understand how or why. That's how sophisticated it had become. She'd won the fight to keep the IC going but not really. The inanimate box artificial intelligence had handled the threat on its own and on its own pace. It could handle any threat, Tess now believed, but if its pace didn't conform to hers or the critical one it could all end badly.

Nevertheless, the effort had an upside to it. She hadn't thought of Chris. But with the Closure rolling again, she felt his pain, her pain, so intense now that only another diversions could numb her to it, a diversion like the Central Park thing!

The park, occupying nearly a third of Manhattan, was devoid of its usual denizens when she arrived. The stockbrokers, fashion moguls, artists, and musicians were gone, as were the skaters, sunbathers and models. The joggers, jugglers and mimes weren't there; nor the hansome cabs, baby-watching nannies or dogsitters. The park had persevered through the worst New York could heap on it for centuries, a green oasis in the city's heartland. But in the harsh afternoon shadows, it was eerily empty now and everywhere Tess looked, she saw decay: Naked branches falling to the ground and ash-black meadows. There was a stench in the air and not a living thing moved as she gathered up samples to take back to Oracle. Just her and dead leaves, rustling off the Great Lawn from an ominous, foul-smelling wind.

Sunset came later than usual and caused a mirage at the horizon, on the bridge to the highlands. A summit appeared, winding above Hebbe Chasm, but was it real or imagined? The incline became gentler now and the road smoother, with an unfettered trail ahead that was suddenly inviting. The highlands were still formidable, with the Tharsis Montes mountains rising to 27000-foot high peaks. But this was no mirage. Suddenly all things seemed possible, and the journey less daunting.   Over the next 2 days Chris piled up 200 kilometers through channels carved by prehistoric floodwaters. The sights teased him with their oddness and peculiarity: teardrop-shaped islets with more strange striations; statuesque sand-cones springing from nondescript flatlands, and tortuous tributaries branching and complex. But his thoughts kept returning to #12, and the strangest sight of all—strange shapes in a subterranean cave. He'd seen them for just a split second, by the dunefield with the undulations, but sensed they held his answers, his long sought Pandera's box.

The land transitioned on the 9th day out. He'd been crossing Solis Plenum, a featureless, flat plain, when craters gradually loomed beyond them. The craters, infinite in number and set amidst lobes and gullies, belonged to the southern hemisphere; so incongruous to the north it had been given its own name, the *hemispherical dichotomy*. The pockmarked south looked more like the moon and theories for the difference ran the gamut, from bombardments by the asteroid belt to selective volcanism and atmospheric dissipation. He didn't care what the reason was or what it was called as he veered northwest to avoid it. He was relieved not to be going there.

The going got even easier over the next half day, easy enough to switch Rover 1 to Autopilot, the first time he'd had such a luxury. He kept it there until grooves under his treads began crisscrossing, an erosive effect from the collapse of ground ice. He flinched when it happened, and paused to take stock.

It was during that pause he saw Vallis Marineris in his rear view mirrors. Four thousand meters below him now, it was staggering in its majesty. He could hardly believe he'd been there, explored there and lived there for a hundred pentads at Candor Base; or that he'd climbed out of its depths.

A fuel quantity light flickered as he began to move out again. It might have been flickering for hours and he'd failed to see it but it hardly mattered. It would either extinguish (bad guage) or go steady (low fuel) and it went steady. He redid the calculations: only 500 km on the first tank of methox not the 750 he'd hoped for. As he switched to tank 2, and resumed his advance on the Tharsis Bulge, he'd have to slow down again, trade speed for mileage or never make it.

On the morning of the 12th day, 900 kilometers out with 1800 to go, he perceived the Bulge. The Tharsis Bulge was unique in the solar system, protruding from the Martian equator like a tumor on the side of a basketball. Building pressure from Mars' molten core had blasted it 5 kilometers above datum level, deforming a quarter of the planet's surface. Easy to see from space, it was harder to discern from the ground because it sloped up so gradually. And while Rover 1's instruments couldn't detect it, the horizon itself was the giveaway, dotted with vent volcanoes. By the end of the 13th day, they dominated, not dotted it: Ascraeus Mons, Tharsis Tholis and Ceraunius Tholus to the north; Arsia Mons, Biblis Patera and Ulysses Patera to the south; and Pavonis Patera and Jovis Tholus in the shadow of Pavonis Mons to the west. These were the shield volcanoes of the Bulge's central vent. Yet as impressive as they were, they were only a minor prelude to the greatest volcano of all, Olympus Mons.

Besides the soil samples she took home with her, Tess also took terrible thoughts. Visions of Earth's demise played ping-pong with flashes of her husband's. She imagined a New York choking on its fumes, while Chris suffocated on his in his space suit. She pictured the park's ashen blight spreading west, while his blood vaporized in the atmosphere. She envisioned humanity entombed while he shriveled from starvation or decompression. What the MOCR told her when she finally got through to them only made it worse.

"No word," they said tersely, "but we're still trying."

On the 16th day out, 8 km above datum level on the Tharsis Montes range, the port engine quit and the starboard soon followed. He'd been hoping to make the summit then coast the downhill passage but would fall short. He computed the mileage: 550 km from Tank one, 750 from Tank 2, 1300 total. With 1400 to go, it would be tight. But he drew comfort knowing he'd be going downhill most of the way, and that he'd taken Crab.

Crab didn't need fuel (it used batteries); could turn on a dime; had suitports with quick-don spacesuits and two extra weeks of life support. On the other hand, it was slow and untested in very rough terrain, its batteries vulnerable and questionable. He hoped he wouldn't need it; that Rover 2 would hold out—but he was very glad he had it.

He released the coupling holding Rover 1 to Rover 2 and crawled aft to don his MarsSuit. He knew he'd have no help as he squeezed into its multiple layers, no one to catch him if he screwed up, not now, not ever. It made him doubly aware of his solitude. Emerging from the airlock he felt tense and impatient, but the Tharsis Chain changed that.

The Vista of Titans had been imposing enough through the windows, but face-to-face, it was heartstopping. Pavonis Mons, to the west, was marked by long lava flows, levees and ridges; Arsia Mons, to the south, by its puckered caldera; Ascraeus Mons, to the north, by curving, complex craters, and Ceraunis Tholus, east, by a sinous fork on its flank. Interspersed between these bigger volcanoes were countless smaller ones extruded by the forces of millenia. And in the distant horizon loomed their King: Olympus Mons.

Given time and enough life-support, he'd have studied the volcanoes for years. But he had hours, not years, and moved on reluctantly, checking that Rover 1's coupling arm had indeed disengaged from Rover 2 and that Rover 2's was still holding Crab. Satisfied, he moved towards Rover 2's airlock to ingress when something kicked up dust to his right.

Dust devil, he thought first, until another bit the soil and a "phhtttt" noise came through his helmet. Too late he realized he was in a freak micrometeorite shower.

Too late he realized it was a freak micrometeorite shower.

A searing pain suddenly raged through his arm and the MarsSuit reacted -- his neck dam inflated, compressors whirred loudly and Violet wailed, *"Suit puncture,"* – all trying to stem the tide of oxygen loss by inflating his torso with Mars' air from outside.

The countermeasures would compensate if the puncture was small enough (and he didn't get hit again). But if not, he'd be dead in seconds.

"7.5 psi, 6 psi, 5 psi," Violet droned, *"suit pressure dropping, you must return to airlock."* The voice seemed detached, indifferent.

As he struggled with the airlock door, the voice returned with, *"4 psi, 3 psi, 2 psi, return to airlock" H*is vision began greying.

He closed his eyes and held his breath until his lungs felt like bursting then Violet raised her decibel level,

"Tachycardia imminent: 215 BPM. 224."

On the doorstep of unconsciousness, he heard as if through a fog, *"2.5 psi, 3.4 psi, 3.5 psi."*

The pressure was returning.

He rasped and sucked desparately, the kind you inhale at the end of your limit. Only after his breathing and vision returned to a semblence of normal, did he became aware of his arm, cold and wet from blood, the next major crisis. This one his MarsSuit couldn't stem. This one would kill him if he didn't act quickly.

Time slowed down again as he attacked the problem: stop the hemorraging, get in the Rover, peel off the suit, treat the wound.

First step, turniquet, or something similar to stop the bleeding. But there were no turniquets out here or in the Rovers, so he'd have to improvise, use ice, or better yet, permafrost, ubiquitous on Mars. He kicked some soil away using the heels of his boots and exposed a clump of the white stuff, gathering enough to fill a pocket.

The rest was a blur as time sped up again, ingressing Rover 2's airlock, locking the door behind him, pressurizing and doffing the suit. Only later—after pressing the permafrost hard against the wound until it all melted and the bleeding stopped— did he realize he'd survived a micrometeorite hit. Someone, something *had* to be on his side. Or could it be he was just being set up for the next fall, the final fall?

With no time to ponder this, he spun up the magnetos; engaged the throttles and pulled away from the expired hulk of Rover 1.

The samples from the park lay in wait for Tess at her lab now: from the Sheep Meadow, the Reservoir and Delacote Theatre; from Wollman Rink, Strawberry Fields and the Zoo; from the Boathouse, the Bandshell and the Conservatory. Air and soil samples in test tubes begging for answers, answers she hoped would stop the blight from spreading north, south and west. She tried to forget Chris as she set up her instruments, what might be happening to him, or what might already have happened. No one had heard from him since his crewmates left and that was 3 weeks ago. She'd have to face it, he was probably dead. But what if he wasn't, what if he was alive, then what? Back and forth, back and forth the thoughts went, like an ear worm with no end to it.

No time for this now, she imposed on the worm.
The samples: GET TO THE SAMPLES.

Rover 2 had an easier time of it with Rover 1 jettisoned. Forging downhill, the engines squeezed 800 kilometers from Tank One this time. Only 600 remained to Olympus Base and Chris began to imagine the unimaginable: he'd make it. But as he slid down the remnants of a hard-packed alluvial fan southwest of the Jovis Tholis vent, the trail turned twisty, to tongues of rocky lava.

Swells of it led to landslide sediments obstructing the way and forced him into another V-shaped gorge. Uneasiness returned as he looked for a way through or around it. It took most of the day to find one, a cut through the sheer walls just wide enough for the Rovers, another stroke of luck. He looked back at the brilliant colored gorge and shook his head in near disbelief.

The impassable gorge

And incredible luck

Tess tried a trio of tools on the samples from the park: the GCMS, which broke things down to parts; the Laser Microscope, which scanned those parts in close-up; and the Magnetic Resonance Imager, which gleaned their atoms in 3-dimensions. The task was laborious--pulverizing, vaporizing, centrifuging, and digitizing, but after mistakes and miscues, she managed to unmask a suspect: a four leaf clover-shaped molecule.

Each leaf of the clover held a globular protein--an amino acid chain linked by peptides. Each protein chain was arranged like DNA but in a single (alpha), not a double stranded helix. And at the center of each cloverleaf was an iron atom--held in the middle of a heterocylic porphyrin—a 5-sided ring. The molecule resembled Hemoglobin--the oxygen-carrying component of blood, and words from a recent email loomed.

"Something underground here looks like blood," Chris' email had said in an email she'd filed and forgotten. She rushed to retrieve it with the tracings he'd sent with it and stared at them, convinced she'd gone crazy. The tracings lined up peak for peak and valley for valley with hers from Central Park.

There had to be an error, some baldfaced fucking error!

On the 24th sol of the journey, with just 450 kilometers to go, Chris felt buoyed enough to try Olympic Base's homing beacon. The 1.4 GHz warble reverberated through the cabin like the fine, sharp tones of a Stradaverius. He could hardly contain himself.

On the 25th sol, he rolled onto the gateway of Olympus Mons! Soaring 30 km in the sky, it dwarfed everything around it. But though it loomed like a giant before him, its foothills were deceptively flat. And in the midst of those foothills, hidden from sight by its majestic surroundings stood Olympus Base, gettimg nearer by the hour.

On the 26th sol he stopped twice, first for a fleeting shadow that crossed his path, the shadow of Phobos he guessed.

The shadow of Phobos

Next up he recognized the fluted triple crater of the Biblex Triad from the maps. He would use them for a navigational fix, he decided, by lining the Triad up with his compass and triangulating it with the heading from the 1.4GHz homing beacon. Having done so, he computed the distance remaining to be 250 km. Barring mishap, he'd be there in a sol or two!

The terrain became even more agreeable after that, solid and hard packed, with the sights growing ever more spectacular. Upswellings reminiscent of the Australian outback appeared, Uluru and Kata Tjuta. Or were they just his imaginings, his mind playing tricks on him? Like the wongawangawangaring of the digari-do he swore he heard in the background.

Minutes later he heard another sound and knew he'd been teased yet again--the crack crack thump of a piston seizing. And in the icy dead silence that followed, he kicked himself for being an optimist on a planet bent on burying him.

With this latest bubble burst, he sat motionless in the gloom and lost track of time--until he remembered Crab. Rover 2 might be dead, but he still had Crab.

Repeating the mantra he used leaving Rover 1, he left Rover 2 and entered Crab sinking deep in her command chair, flipping switches, activating systems and crossing his fingers.

Everything hinged on the batteries, icy, untouched and unused for months. An amber light illuminated then turned green. So far so good. Other gauges pulsed, turned green and Crab powered up. Just like that. Could somebody up there be liking him finally. He unlinked from Rover 2 and moved the throttle forward.

Crab's unobstrcted canopy fielded a wide-angle view of Oympus Mons. From the moatlike skarp of its foothills, it was spectacular. He guessed the Base to be but a day's drive away. The gloom and doom since the start of this impossible journey began to lift. That's when he whiffed the scent of Andrea, remnants of her L'Air du Temps that marked her comings and goings be they on Earth or Mars. The last time she'd been here they'd made love in the rain, another impossible event. The image completed the transition from malaise to excitement and he pushed the throttle ¾ forward. And there, amidst the whirr of Crab's electrics, he smiled for the first time in a long time.

Tess was grasping at straws; certain she was losing her mind. Had she swapped her tracings with Chris', or somehow cross-contaminated them? It was the only sensible explanation as she recalibrated her instruments, checking them against known controls then retesting and retesting. The result was the same: Whatever this thing was, it was in the soil of Earth and Mars. And identical!

She'd spent a career answering questions that many thought unanswerable but this staggered her, an alien in the White House was pedestrian by comparison.

At wits end in the middle of the night, she summoned Leslie Forbes, the woman who'd first hired her, smart as a whip and a skeptic by nature. With Chris gone, she was the only one Tess could trust and they hadn't spoken since her Central Park trip. She sequed in by focusing on the blight first, and how it was spreading to Pennsylvania, Connecticut and Massachusetts. Then she folded her arms and waited.

"I assume you didn't drag me out of bed to tell me what I already knew Tess?"

When she told her of the molecule, she was silent then incredulous.

"Are you suggesting this...this thing Chris dreamt up on Mars is here?"

"I don't know what I'm suggesting. The only thing I do know is that the tracings match up."

"How much sleep have you had lately?"

"It's got nothing to do with sleep, Leslie, GCMS's don't sleep and its signatures don't lie. I've double, triple and quadruple checked them."

"Assuming you're not delusional, and I'll give you the benefit of the doubt, have you thought about using the Synchrotron?"

"The Synchotron? Don't we need it for Closure 4."

"Closure 4's stable now, I can spare it, use it!"

A giant welcome mat seemed to have been laid for him as Chris sailed towards Olympus in the still of the Martian night.

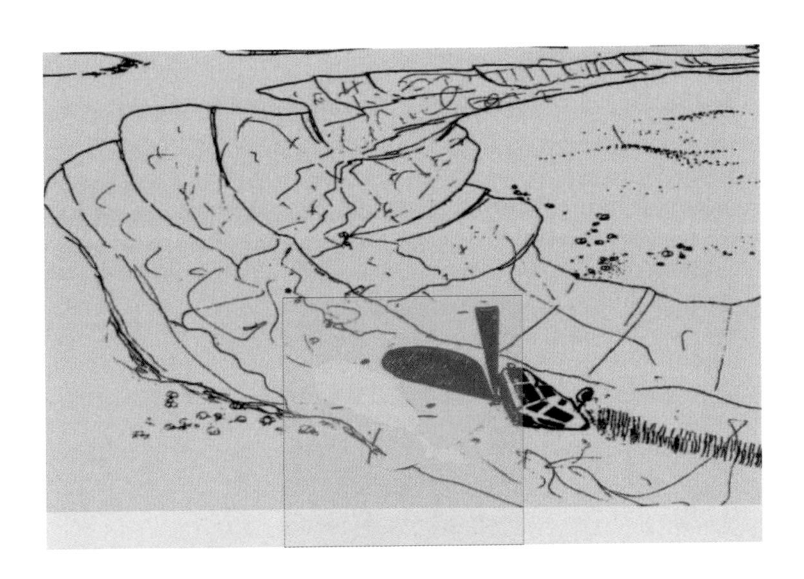

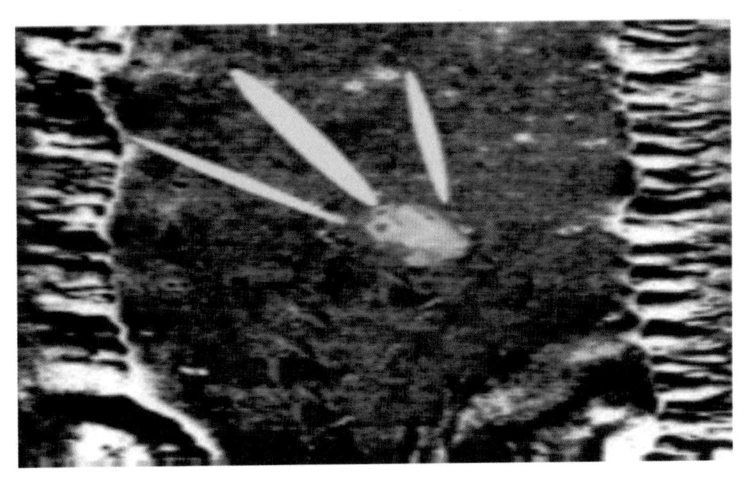

Yellow beams played off impacted terrain crushed by primorial forces into this red carpet highway but it smacked of another Mars setup, so near yet so far--the Mars way. Would treads roll to a halt just short of their goal; would his MarsSuit fail at heaven's gate; would he have a heart attack? And then his thoughts shifted to Tess: what might she be doing this very moment? And back to Andrea and why he'd been obessed with her, and then to his future on Mars and all the ways he could die here. One disconnected stream of consciousness thought after another, like a ping pong ball until just like Oz at the end of the yellow brick road, 5 mighty monoliths appeared in the midst of the red carpet. He wept at the sight of them. Pausing Crab in her tracks he wept unabashedly.

He'd seen the two HABs, Power Module, Rover Module, Escape Craft and Storage Modules before of course, in Houston, Antarctica and Candor, so familiar, yet different; the house the same but the views so unlike. He knew that house like the back of his hand. But this one, Olympus Base, was the one he never expected to see. The one he'd yearned most for.

The house he never expected to see

Chapter 29. The Plate and the Door.

Would we not, when glancing heavenward,
On a star so silver fair,
Yearn and clasp the hands and murmer
Would to God that we were there?

Alfred, Lord Tennyson

Gaining entry was easy. Chris had life-support to spare and there was no piled up sand like first entry back at Candor. As he waited in HAB 2's airlock for the pressures to equalize, he considered his next moves: turning on the Rankine engine, snapping on the circuit breakers, scaling the ladder, then calling Tess. Yes he would call Tess as soon as he possibly could!

Climbing the stairs towards the C3 console later, the lonely echoes of his footsteps reverberated through the empty walls and dismayed him. Could he survive here alone, even with supplies to last a lifetime. Could anyone? He drew solace from the C3, his lifeline to Earth and Tess. It would join them, their pixels and voices, if only electronically. They'd lived most of their marriage like that anyway. It was almost normal. Almost.

"Houston, Olympus Base," he trumpeted over 8.4 gigahertz on X-band. "Have arrived here safe and sound. Repeat, have arrived safe and sound."

The DELAY clock on the wall read 21 minutes when he sent the message. And it would take another 21 for a reply if there was one; enough time for a shower, a hot one; his first in a month. He'd worn the same clothes so long they could salute, and he yearned for that shower. He looked rank and wanted to look good on video for Tess, or anyone else if they answered.

Each bit of road grime draining down B-level's shower was a catharsis, and he suddenly found himself looking forward to, even savoring the days ahead. Especially the day he'd try to find Probe 12. The very thought titillated him. With the reply a mere 20 minutes away, he stepped from the shower, put on fresh coveralls, then climbed down to C-level to the comm console and waited. Would Tess appear first or would it be a Flight Director, Capcom or bureaucrat? He appreciated the fact that what he'd done was newsworthy; astounding, even unbelievable, at least that's how the media would label it. If so, they'd go for the bureaucrat first. But if they gave a shit about him as a human being, they'd find Tess, wherever she was, and get her on the line first. They would do that if they gave a shit, if they were even half human!

Thoughts of her kept firing in his cortex as he waited, about what an angel she was, with hardly a wrinkle after all these years, her body firm as ever, still with that dancer's grace, those wonderful freckles, that long, silky hair. The ebb and flow of Andrea interspersed among those thoughts embarrassed and shamed him. How could he have allowed it, how could he have consented to it. Never again, he vowed in his mind, never again—an absurd and nonsensical thought, he had to admit, given where he was and his future.

"Enough." he hissed at himself, just as the 42-minute mark arrived. He straightened at the incoming signal, attempting to look healthy, happy, professional, grateful and alive. Most of all alive.

But when the image unfurled, it wasn't Tess's that greeted him. Nor was it a Capcom, Flight Director or bureaucrat's. Nor was it Vadim's from *Columbia,* which was closer and could have responded as well.

No, the image that unfurled was just jibberish, accompanied as it was by the usual crackling hiss, plunging through the void with an utter and total contempt.

In the eyes of Tess' lesser tools, the molecule looked like *Hemoglobin*, the complex protein that carries oxygen in out blood. It was even shaped and twisted like it too, but under the scrutiny of the Synchrotron, there were differences. The Synchrotron bounced x-rays off its atoms to form diffraction patterns and the patterns had exposed those differences. Instead of binding oxygen the way *Hemoglobin* does in the bloodstream, this molecule sought out nitrogen and did it in the air and soil. She decided to call it *Nitroglobin*, and its meaning began to unravel.

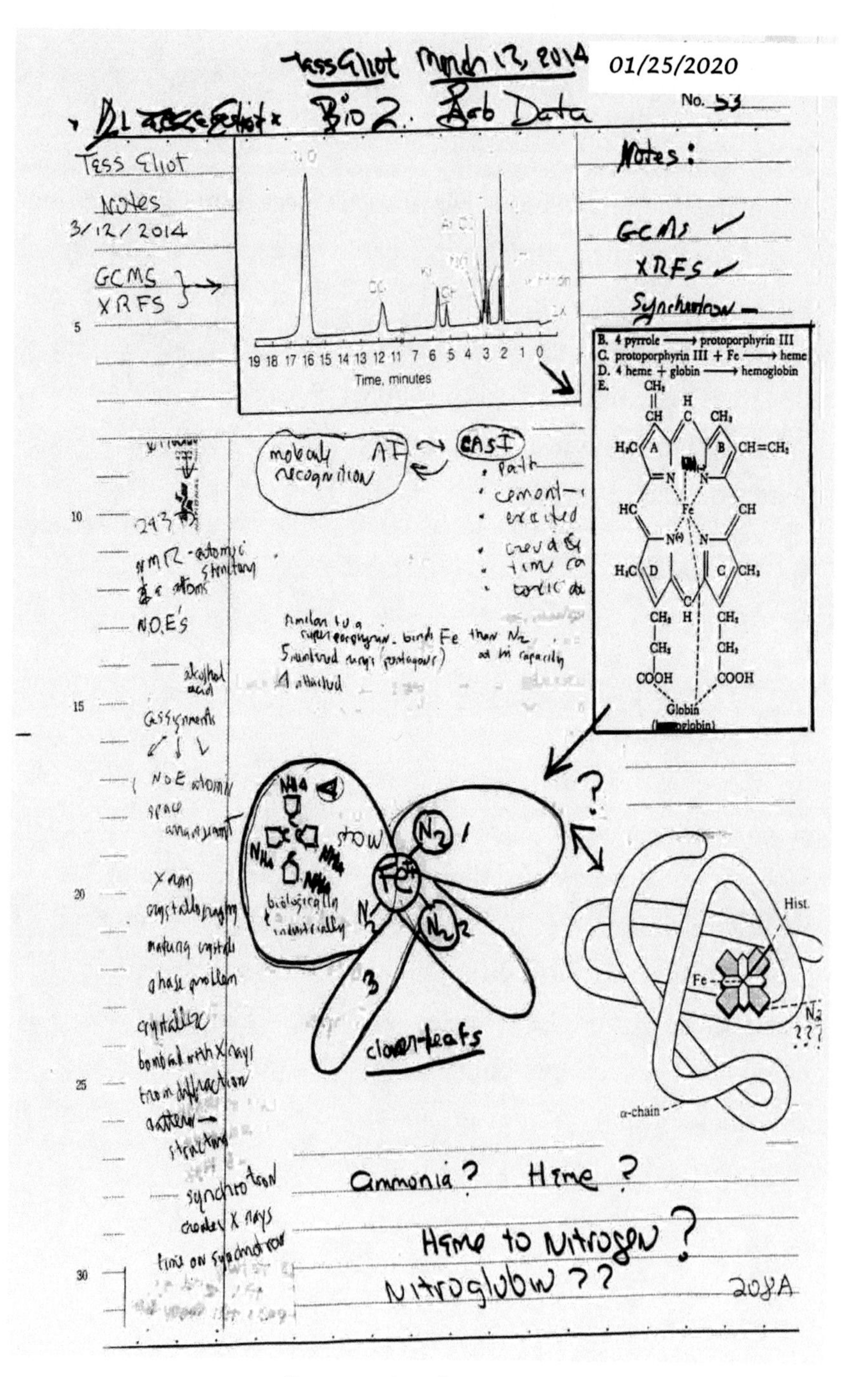

Its meaning began to unravel.

Chris tried to raise the MOCR again the next day and the next. He tried on X-band and C-band; 8.4 GHz and 2.6; high gain and low gain, all for naught. Maybe it's the solar wind; he started speculating, or a faulty relay satellite. His frustration began to mount until it dawned on him how early he'd arrived at Olympus Base, weeks earlier than anyone could have imagined. "That's it, they're not expecting me," he consoled himself, "they're training all frequencies on *Columbia*."

Still at any givne time, there had to be multiple antennae pointing at Mars. Everyone from SETI to amateur astronomers scanned the heavens regularly for supernovae, ET or some other form of intelligent life, and Mars was always high up on that list. Somebody out there must ***surely*** be looking for him. Unless they were convinced he was dead. Or that he'd lost his mind and was incapable of communicating—a conclusion his actions of late might warrant.

He suddenly felt hungry, a sharp, ravishing kind of hunger. The pangs struck often, born from days on the road until he could no longer stand them. All he could think of was a piping hot meal so he climbed down to B-level and the food bins, extracting trays of scrambled eggs, lamb chops and vegetables then laserheating and devouring them as if he'd been raised on peanuts and beans—not far from the truth over the last month. Then he began examining his options.

He could continue to try and raise Earth but that would be a waste of time. They'd reply on their schedule not his. He could try and construct the tunnel so he could walk around unsuited. But doing it solo would take planning and effort and there was no urgency. He could go to the PM for more methox fuel but he had enough on hand for a pentad. He could set up the greenhouse to grow fresh greens and vegetables but that wasn't urgent either and it could fail like at Candor anyway. Without answers to his questions, everything would fail, which made planning easy:

He'd go to HAB 1's Telepresence Center first, where he'd switch on Probe #12's batteries. If he got its signal, he'd triangulate; if he got its position, he'd recharge Crab and set off without delay. He *had* to have his answers before any of the other things. That, after all, is why he'd come in the first place. And why he'd stayed behind.

Tess was obsessed with answers too, but unlike Chris, she needed them quickly. The air and soil from the park were changing fast but science didn't work that way. Science solved questions on its own schedule, not hers, and those answers might came slowly, like a fogbank lifting over a mountaintop. But at least the Synchrotron gave her a fighting chance. It was telling her not only that Oxygen was plummeting; Nitrogen was being sucked from the air to the ground and Carbon Dioxide was replacing it but how fast those changes were happening. Her first air samples had been normal (21% oxygen, 78% nitrogen and 0.03% C02) and her last, alarming (17% oxygen, 74% nitrogen and 8% CO2).

Central Park was like no other place on Earth. It was heading in a Martian direction.

Experience had prepared her for the marathon ahead. Her desk, armed with a terminal to CASI's brain, aspirin and coffee, would be her fortress; her only armament against the molecule. A reminder from her youth resurfaced, the refrain she'd lived with so long:

Soups of pollution are stirring. Unspeakable things are being formed.

She tried hard not to cry, there'd be time enough for crying in the days and nights ahead. She began programming the molecule's atomic structure into DNA code suitable for CASI. Only CASI could tell her the extent of the damage and if anything could be done about it. Only CASI could sort out this molecule.

This molecule named *Nitroglobin*, this telegram from hell!

The beeps started strongly when Chris switched on #12, but began losing steam as its batteries trickled down. The air in his telepresence helmet became stifling and if he didn't get a fix soon, he'd lose the probe forever. The signal strength vascillated as he dialed in the radio compass, its tracking needle fluttering wildly. A last second tweak before signal death held steady -- 223 degrees Southwest.

He drew a 223 Line of Position on an image map, tracing it over another line of 338 he'd taken earlier from #12 at Candor Base. The two lines crossed in the foothills of Pavonis Patera, 176 kilometers away. The trail would be narrow, according to the image map, but wide enough. Crab with its slithering, slip-sliding, sauntering motion could make it, only Crab. It would take 2 days to get there and 2 to get back, leaving a day or so at Povonis. He'd have to average 6 km/hour and it would be dangerous there. There'd be radiation. I better bring a lead vest, a RAD counter and dosimeter patch, he reminded himself.

Tess thought of her career as she readied CASI for the fight, a career spent in the closets of Artificial Intelligence, Chaos Theory and DNA computers. Like her, CASI was ready, she had an accuracy to be proud of now, a number nobody could dispute, better than a 90 percent correlation coefficient with the past. But that was the past, this was the present and pressing CASI ahead in time would be the future. The sheer knowledge of knowing she could do this was exhilerating. She could finally come out of that closet but it was scary. That's what made her hesitate before pushing the "RUN" button. Still she had to push it. She would always have to push it.

And just like that first time, the flat lines appeared like the EKG of a dead man. But unlike that first time, those prediction lines came sooner -- in 2041, a mere 5 years in the future not 105.

She stared at the endpoint not wanting to believe it. And considered a rerun, a code change, a respite, then stopped. She believed it to be true. 2041? She knew it to be true.

Words poured forth furiously from her pen to her lab book in the hours that followed. She wanted them from a pen, not a computer or a printer. A computer couldn't convey feelings; a printer couldn't capture fear. Words from a pen, on the other hand, could tremble, and she wanted that. She wanted posterity to know exactly how she felt. If there was going to be a posterity.

Chris chatted to himself while garnering provisions; he talked to the consoles, tunnels and walls as he prepared Crab. Talking to himself didn't seem as outrageous as it might have once; he liked his own voice bouncing back to him. It never disagreed.

There was a full complement of methox at the Base the morning he embarked. The Power Module could churn out enough to last forever at the paltry rate he'd be using it. He decided to calculate just how long forever might be after pressurizing Crab and rolling out. It would be a nice diversion to start of his trip.

A year and half's methox for 6 people should last one person 9 years, he figured. A year and a half's meal trays for 6 could last him 12 if he skipped lunch, a lot more with the greenhouse deployed. As for water and oxygen, they'd last decades if the greenhouse didn't fail. If it did he'd cut commode flushes, limit EVAs and showers. That would give him 7 years minimum he calculated just after noon. Seven years might be long enough for NASA to mount a rescue mission. Assuming they knew he was alive or cared.

Crab was making good time as it adroitly skipped around on Autopilot. It was forging a tick over 7 km/hr giving him extra time to rethink his strategy when he arrived at Pavonis.

Probe 12 had been lost in an undulating dune field, swallowed up by a large unseen sinkhole. He could be swallowed too. To avoid it, he'd use Crab's sonar, displaying a hundred meter depth map on all sides of him. When he got to the dune field, he'd go to Part B of his plan: stop at the periphery and hook a cable from Crab's winch to his MarsSuit. Anything he might fall into he could pull himself out of with that winch. A simple touch of its remote control would engage it, pull his lifeline and yank him out. To reduce the risk of collapsing sand, he'd go to part C: the juryrigged snowshoes he'd brought with him. Only these were sandshoes and they'd keep his boots from breaking through the thin, sandy crust as he walked.

It was a good plan but it had its flaws: the thickness of the crust; the size of the sinkhole, the power of the winch, the strength of the cable, the intensity of the radiation. Most of them were wild ass guesses.

To whom it may concern
February 1, 2036
From: Dr. Tess Eliot
Senior Climatologist, Biosphere 2

For the last two centuries we've been conducting an uncontrolled experiment; putting things in the air we didn't know about. From our smokestacks and chimneys; motors and generators, car and plane exhausts these things mixed in unfathomable ways. In the presence of ozone-depleted sunlight and enzyme-abetted air, they've now formed a hideous molecule, this thing I call *Nitroglobin* (see my lab notes). It's ironic that it's shaped like a four leaf clover, a symbol of luck. But this molecule, with iron at its center and ammonia on its wings is anything but lucky. It digests nitrogen from the air and replaces it with C02. The rising C02 will make up 10 percent of our air within 5 or 6 years and people and animals start having trouble at 2. We can't last very long in this air, but Earth's plants might. Some can actually thrive in the high CO2 to inherit the Earth, but an escalating greenhouse effect will drive up the temperature and eventually kill them too. *Nitroglobin* works in exponential ways, and the greenhouse effect is just one of them. There are many others. It goes like this: As the ozone hole gets bigger, it lets in more UV, increasing the rate at which *Nitroglobin* is formed in the air. The more made, the more nitrogen it snaps up, the more C02 it generates and dumps.

That's just the start of the cycle. The molecule--heavier than air—then settles to the ground and penetrates the biome's root system where it mutates green leaf chlorophyll. This subverts photosynthesis causing green plants to make less oxygen. Without 20% oxygen we''ll soon have trouble breathing.

It gets worse. Oxygen is used to make ozone in the atmosphere and less means the ozone hole will grow faster, letting in more UV and creating more *Nitroglobin*. It's called a positive feedback loop, a vicious cycle in which the molecule grows like a cancer until the integrity of the atmosphere is compromised. We won't have to worry about that though because the rise in C02 and greenhouse gases will escalate the sea temperature, melt the poles, surge the oceans and obliterate our coastlines. If that doesn't kill us, hypoxia and disease will.

The evidence for *Nitroglobin* is chronicled in my lab book, along with chemical analyses and math model projections. If you are unconvinced, the planet Mars can supply more evidence. Mars is an object lesson never heeded. It had nitrogen once, oxygen once, a thick atmosphere once, running water once, and, I suspect, plants. There may even have been a civilization there once that brewed *Nitroglobin* as surely as we're brewing it today. You only need look beneath the surface to see the consequence.

Pray for us.

It was dark when Chris rose after a fitful night's sleep, too dark and hazardous to resume the trek to Pavonis. He thought about Tess while he waited for the sun to rise; about her CASI and Earth and its uncertain future; about Andrea and the others hurtling towards that Earth; and his own uncertain future. He filled the dragging hours dallying over breakfast; a tasteless oatmeal pack from the food stores. He wanted it to be hot but didn't dare use the laserheater because it sucked the batteries big-time. He could see the headlines: *Last man on Mars Chooses Hot Oatmeal over Safe Return and Perishes* – only there were no headlines or newspapers here. Besides him and the windblown sands, there was nothing even moving.

When the sun finally did rise, he set off to the southeast again and soon saw Pavona Patera in the distance, its ridged flanks unmistakable. The terrain became familiar, the same terrain he'd seen before through the eyes of #12's camera back at Candor: the cinder cones, curvilinear ridges, crevices and interweaving channels. And as the end of the second long day neared, he paused by the red-brown tinge of an undullating dune field and turned on the RAD counter. It beeped a warning tone. He was close.

Following his plan, he next switched on Crab's sonar to look for subsurface sinkholes. Yellows on the screen meant they'd be 20 or more meters deep; red, 10 to 20 meters deep; orange, 5 to 10 and blue, 5 to 0 (surface). The screen was blue where he'd stopped but peppered with smatterings of red and orange just ahead. "Watch it!" he whispered aloud, "there'll be sinkholes about."

The smallish sun would soon be setting over Pavonis Patera so he decided to camp out here for a fresh start in the morning. No sense taking chances, no sense doing anything stupid now. Small as it was, the sunset was breathtakingly beautiful and provided a temperary respite from all the stress. He fell into a deep and trance-like sleep shortly thereafter, dreaming about his tomorrow.

It was a breathtaking sunset of unimaginable beauty

It was dawn when he awoke, refreshed but anxious to proceed, feeling this was the sol when questions would finally be answered. The instruments indicated 70 degrees F outside—warm enough on Mars for him to need an LCG for cooling. He donned one and scanned the other items he'd need from the checklist he'd prepared and grabbed them too: the sandshoes, the lead radiation vest, the toolbelt of accessories and the winch's remote control, then moved towards the Suitport hatch. He swung it open, slipped into the MarsSuit's lower torso, then the upper torso and closed the hatch behind him. Outside now, he tugged upwards on the locking plate to release the suit but it wouldn't move. He swallowed hard. The damn thing only weighed 26 kg on Mars and he could barely budge it. Was he losing his strength in the low .38 gravity, a warning from Roberto he'd repeatedly ignored? He could still hear the Mexican's voice, "Get to the Countemeasure Gym, you pussy or you'll flab out and die." Would he pay the piper now, stuck in this suit till his O2 ran out? He swallowed hard, gathered his energy and pushed off his boot heels with all the strength he could muster. The locking plate clicked and the suit lifted free. Another bullet dodged he gulped but sure as hell not the last.

Ambling down the ramp to the surface, he thought about Roberto and his crewmates, where they might be and if they were safe. He hadn't thought of them in weeks, he realized.

Like the waves from a splash in still water, the undulating dunefield spread out as he tied his boots to the sandshoes and prepared himself. It was strangely familiar after so many sessions in Candor's Telepresence Center and he was ready for it, whatever IT was. He secured Crab's winch line to the suit and proceeded.

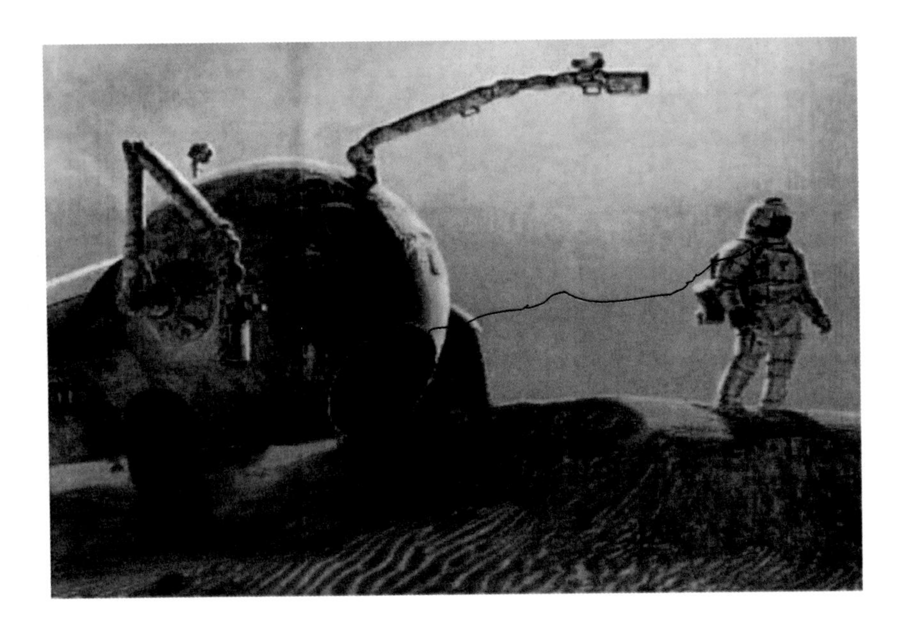

Whatever IT was!

As the cable unfurled behind him, he plodded slowly ahead to the rhythmic clicks on his RAD counter. Violet translated them to: ***"Four hours max dosage,"*** then followed with another warning, this one relayed by Crab's sonar: ***"Red underfoot, 5 to 10 meters deep."***

Sideslipping, he was awash in low morning glare and could barely see until he lowered his EVVA visor. Even then there were precious few features other than the ubiquitous swirls of shimmering ridges in infinite patterns of crimson.

Gradually he came upon a lighter outcropping and saw geysers of a gas disturbing the shimmering dunes. Bubbling from below, Violet's auditory sensor ID'd it as Methane. Something else protuded from the dunes in the distance. He squinted in escalating disbelief just as Violet interrupted with, ***"Three hours max dosage. Orange underfoot, 10 to 20 meters deep."***

The picture defied logic, just as it had from Candor's Telepresence Center the first time he saw it. The perfectly formed cylinder in the sand ahead didn't belong. It was not fashioned by nature. He had little time to process the shock of the first evidence of intelligent life other than Earth when Violet's audio tone rose with,

"TWO HOURS MAX DOSAGE."

His heartbeat raced and his lifeline tugged back in fear:
"Turn back ..get the fuck outta here."
He thought he'd have a day or 2, not 2 hours!

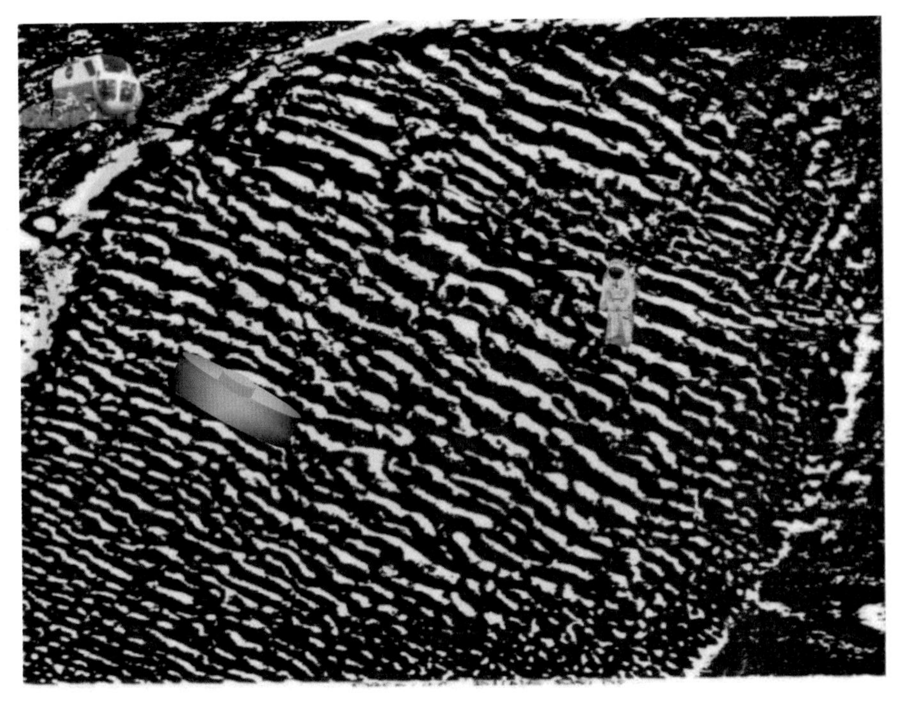

Ignoring the obvous, he moved tentatively towards the thing, testing the surface beneath his sandshoes like eggshells until he fronted it. The cylinder was lavender-white, deliberately made from the same stuff as its surroundings no doubt. Its protruding circular top was roughly 3 meters in diameter with the rest of it descending to an unknown depth beneath the sand. The top itself appeared seamless and pristine as if it had been made yesterday and at its center was a smaller, grayish cylinder. His brain screamed questions that his mouth couldn't contain, "What the fuck is this, who built it, when?"

With less than 2 hours of safety remaining, it was time to act, not speculate, so he decided to hedge his bets by taking a sample--a chip off the thing for testing in the Base before skeedaddling back. But hard as he tried, with a chisel, hammer and mini-drill, it wouldn't chip or crack. Mindful of the time, he moved to find Probe #12. He wanted to see what it had seen when it tumbled beneath the sand, an image still fresh in his mind. It was close, very close to the cylinder.

There were 98 minutes left when he got to the place he thought #12 fell but nothing seemed out of the ordinary. The dunes were undisturbed except for two unusual moguls at his 2'oclock, one small, one large. Drawing him forward like a moth to a flame, he went to them, the sand beneath his sandshoes still firm underfoot. He stepped over the smaller one in a single measured bound but the larger would take in two. The first came easily. The second never did.

As the sand began collapsing, he could feel himself being sucked down and every muscle tightened. The cable nearly tore his neck off when it snapped against his backback, then everything went black.

It was still black, save for an eerie pink glow above him when he opened his eyes. Am I in heaven or hell, he wondered until the hum of his suit fans let him know he was still alive. The glow was Marslight, its distinct pinkish hue peeking through the sinkhole and, slowly illuminating the scene.

He was dangling in a chamber of some kind, its ceiling 10 feet above him; its floor 40 feet below. He flipped on his helmet light to see more of it when it hit him:

"You're trapped under the Martian surface, asshole!

"The remote," he flashed next, *"where's the fucking remote?"*

He groped his left leg pocket frantically for it, then his right as sweat poured from his brow. It nearly blinded him before his LCG caught it and cooled him off. The cold water flushing over his body had a calming effect. He suddenly remembered where he'd put the remote, in an elbow pocket, the left one. The floor moved closer when he squeezed the unwind button, first with a jerk, then more smoothly. And after holding his breath for what seemed like forever, he finally exhaled.

He was touching the ground!

The chamber was larger than he thought and Probe #12 was lying just a few meters away. He'd fell through near where it had and he walked towards it. It lie face down with its camera eyes shattered. He contemplated extracting its memory stick but there wouldn't be time so he moved on. There were more important things to see.

On close inspection the chamber walls weren't as impervious as they first appeared and a Stalactite descended through a crack in one above him. It was kissing a budding stalagmite from below, indicating water. Methane gas trickled through another breach he noted, triggering floods of other questions:

From what: living or dead things?

From where: the chamber or the planet's core?

It dawned on him that given enough oxygen, the methane could ignite, and that's exactly what he was exhaling. He could go up in flames if he lit a spark so he moved away quickly.

Another breach revealed a maze of complex passages when he trained his helmet light through it. He briefly considered squeezing through when Violet reminded him it would be suicide:

"FORTY MINUTES MAX DOSAGE."

He ran the numbers. It would take 15 minutes to extricate up, leaving 15 to explore and 10 minutes margin. The only task he'd have time for now was inspecting the cylinder, where it penetrated, how deep it went and so on.

Precious minutes passed before he got to it, switched on his recorder and illuminated the scene with his helmet light. It was deeper than he thought, descending 50 feet from the surface to the floor where he stood and penetrating below, far below, its purpose another conundrum.

"THIRTEEN MINUTES UNTIL MAX DOSAGE."

Fuck it, he thought. I can leave now with nothing, or stay another 5, take a hit and hope for the best. It was an easy decision. Like the frog carrying the scorpion, he would risk getting stung. It was his nature.

He placed his gloved hand against the cylinder and felt for vibrations, movement, anything, then placed his MarsSuit helmet against it listening for sounds. There was nothing. He switched his helmet light to high intensity and began circling the perimeter, following the curvature of its surface. It was unbroken. seamless and pristine like at the surface. Nuclear storage, like for waste or maybe power, he wondered? What else could cause the fast RAD counts?

“No time, gotta go,” he told himself when something stopped him, something disturbing the curvature. There was a hairline recess on the surface facing the back chamber wall that barely caught the lightl and below it, an opening. In the pitch black time crunch, he’d have missed it completely in another second. Reaching inside and down, his light caught a dusty capsule of some kind, resting on a pedestal as if it had been delibeately put there in hope that someone or something would find it; someone like him. Someone who’d traipsed halfway across the cosmos. It occurred to him then it could be booby-trapped.

He reached for it anyway.

If he had to die, this is how he wanted to do it.

If I have to die, this is how I want to do it.

No bombs went off when he grasped the capsule. It was unattached and light to the touch. He brushed off some dust and it seemed translucent. There were curious things exposed inside -- artifacts, devices, and a strange metallic plate. He couldn't take his eyes off it until Violet chastised him:

"OVERDOSAGE OVERDOSAGE!!"

Five minutes later he was dangling under the hole he'd come through, clutching the capsule tightly to his chest while Crab's winch pulled him upwards. An hour later he was rolling towards Olympus Base checking his dosimeter patch. It was brown-- sub-lethal. He might get sick but he'd survive.

The closer he got to Oympus, the more certain he was that he'd found his Pandora's Box. The things inside that capsule were:

'*Wonderful Things*,' as Carter had said to Canarvan.

The most significant things in human history.

He'd shout it on X-band or C-band or any other band he could find when he got back. But all he could raise was the empty and vacuous hiss of nothing. He wouldn't wait for the MOCR's guidance, he decided, or for Tess' or anyone else's. He'd waited long enough for this moment, a lifetime. He would open the capsule himself.

It had survived pristine for so long, he expected it to be hard to open, very hard. Which made it all the more surprising when it came apart so easily. As if it had been programmed to do so.

Most of its contents were undecipherable: tablets written in an alien hand, devices whose functions were ungraspable. But the metallic plate was different; the etchings on its surface seemed familiar; unsettlingly familiar.

The symbol at its base was a cylinder, ***the cylinder***. Etched above it was a large ***gold-filled circle***. Surrounding the circle were 11 concentric ellipses varying greatly in diameter, the smallest being nearest to the golden circle, the largest, the furthest away. They were orbits circling a sun he was sure. Our Sun? Most astonishing was the curved line pointing inwards from the 4th ellipse to the 3rd.
A trajectory??

The unthinkable emerged. The plate wasn't an artifact, it was a map. The ellipses were the orbits of 11 planets in our solar system, 8 known and 3 unknown that had been speculated about for decades. The cylinder hadn't held nuclear waste, but fuel for a journey. And the writings on the tablets were the last will and testament of a long dead race, a race whose legacy had been a molecule. A molecule that had ruined this place leaving red dust in its stead.

In that singular moment, Chris Elkay understood that humanity had come full circle. That whoever made that trip from Mars to Earth countless eons ago had survived. But hadn't learned their lesson.

Tess had aged ten years in ten days--puffy lids over colorless eyes, disheveled hair against bleached and haggard skin. All the crying had made her unrecognizable but she'd never cry again. Not for Chris, not for Mars, not for Earth, not for anyone.

Although her mind and body ached terribly, she still knew what she had to do. Summoning her last vestiges of strength, she went to the liquid nitrogen bath, retrieved the vial with Chris' sperm and placed it in a dewar flask. Then she started walking towards the airlock of Biosphere 2.

Visions played havoc as she approached the airlock. Jacob and his ladder linking heaven and earth; Moses in fear before the Ark of the Covenant; the shepherd in the valley of the shadow of death.

Then she thought of Closure 4 and all the progress she'd made. How CASI now handled the fluctuations so well; how the fruits and vegetables were blossoming; how the animals and insects were flourishing. And how the eight humans inside, the Biosperians, got along so well. So well they'd hardly object if another joined them, perhaps even two: her and the first true Biospherian, her child.

When she got to the airlock she hesitated. What if Biosphere 2 can't keep the molecule out? What if a seal is breached by a pinhole or a tiny break in the glass? Lines from T.S. Eliot's *Wasteland* came to mind again, the same T.S. Eliot she'd been named after.

The eyes are not here
There are no eyes here
In this valley of dying stars
In this hollow valley
This broken jaw of lost kingdoms

There was a hazardous waste bin by the foot of the airlock door. She stared at it for minutes that seemed unending; then at the dewar flask in her arms and then back at the bin. Before clasping the flask tightly to her breast and stepping through.

The End

Acknowledgement

Thanking everyone who helped shape this book is a difficult task but here goes:

To Dr Debra Johnson for guidance, support and patience
To Kazu Tajima, Hagi and Yoshi of the Phenix Co, Japan
To Ling and Steve for the Challenger Memorial and *Nitroglobin.*

To my colleagues and friends at NASA and its contractors:
Dick Johnson, Ed Smylie, Aaron Cohen, Jim Correalel
Walt Guy, Wilbert Ellis & Crew and Thermal Systems Division
Dave Cook and the math modelers of Lockheed Houston
Jim Waligora, Chuck LaPinta and the docs of space medicine
Mathew Radnofski and Doctor Fred Dawn
Randy Stone and the Mission Controllers

The spacecraft builders at the Cape, notably:
Kenny Kleinknecht   Sy Rubinstein
Dan Brown   Jim Berry

The NASA-JSC CSD Test Team:
Jack Mays, Frank LeBlanc, Howard Green, Reagon Redmon, Marion Lusk, Gordons Chandler and Spencer, Lou Casey, Jim O'kane, Manny Rodriguez and Harold Battaglia

The spacesuit makers at NASA Ames: Vyk and Bruce Webbon

SPECIAL THANKS ARE DUE TO:
Astronauts Story Musgrave, Tom Stafford,
Deke Sleyton and Alexi Leoniv

Neil, Mike and Buzz

The Secretaries: Phyllis, Juanita & Donna

The Office buddies: Hudkins, Scheps, Melgaris and Ayotte
Seamons and Proctor; Stan Fink and Joel Leonard

The images that shadow the novel come courtesy of:

Carter Emmert and the space artists for sketches of suits, bases and spacecraft.

Kerry Joels for images from the Mars One Crew Operator's Manual

NASA PAO for photos, data and support.

Special thanks are also due to:

Professor Bruce Lusignon for the Stanford University mission design.

Luvichkin Association of Russia for *Columbia* and *Eagle* renderings

Bob Zubrin for Mars Direct and the methox fuel factory

Dr. Steve Delcardeyre for the structure of nitroglobin

Kenny Kleinknecht, Wilbert Ellis and Nello Pace for the education

Ed Smylie, Jim Correale and Walt Guy for leadership

Mars Scientists Chris Mckay, Carol Stoker, Owen Gwynne, Geoff Briggs, Larry Lemke, Robert Zubrin

Thank you all for the inspiration.

FREQUENTLY USED NASA ACRONYMS

ADSS. Acceleration Deployment and Spin-up System.

AI. Artificial Intelligence

AOS. Acquisition of signal. Resumption of communication via deepspace network.

Apiapsis. Furthest point in an elliptical orbit of Mars

Apogee. Furthest point in an elliptical orbit of Earth

ARED. Advanced Resistance Exercise Device. A system of bungee cords used for weight and muscle mass maintenance

BSLSS. Buddy breathing Secondary Life Support System. Umbilicals for connecting two spacesuits

Capcom. Capsule Communicator. The only person in the Mission Control Center authorized to talk to the crew directly, usually an astronaut from the previous or next mission.

CEVIS. Cycle Ergometer with Vibration Isolation System, ie, exercise bike

Chasm. Canyon

C3. The Command, Control and Communication System console.

CWS. The caution and warning alarm system.

CRT. Video monitor, usually cathode ray tube but can be liquid crystal or flatscreen

DCM...Display Control Module. Computer keyboard/display on spacesuit chestpack

DAP. Digital Autopilot. Keyboard for entering thruster pitch, roll, yaw and main engine commands into flight computer.

DEXA. Dual X-ray Absorbtiometry, a tool for measuring bone density.

EC. Escape Craft. Backup launch craft to get from Mars to *Columbia*, the mother ship, orbiting it

ECLSS. Environmental Control and Life Support System.

EI: Entry Interface. First contact with the atmosphere upon reentry

EMU. Extravehicular Mobility Unit. A spacesuit plus its related equipment (helmet, gloves, backpack, boots, etc)

EVVA. Extravehicular Visor Assembly. Gold-coated sun visor that slides over an EMU helmet to keep glare and UV out.

GCRs. Galactic Cosmic Rays. Very high energy radiation originating outside the solar system, perhaps from the explosion of stars. Consists of very high energy particles such as protons, helium nucleii (alpha particles and heavier nucleii, as well as electromagnetic radiation (photons, x and gamma rays). Energy intensity can exceed 10^{18} electron volts

GUIDO. Guidance and Navigation Officer.

HAB 1. The 4-deck Habitation Module containing sleeping quarters for 3, life support, command, communication and control consoles, the recreation area and galley, the greenhouse, storage and other facilities.

HAB2. Similar to HAB 1 but with labs, gyms and medical facilities.

Hypegolics. Rocket fuel and oxidizer that ignite on contact. Nitrogen tetroxide and hydrazine for example.

HUMMS. Human Medical Monitoring System. A computer that did medical diagnosis, designed by Roberto Diaz.

IDS. Isolation Dysfunction Syndrome. The disorder of "aloneness", symptomized by depression, fatigue, lethargy, hostility, migraines, hallucinations, anxiety, miscommunication and impulsive behavior.

ILS. Instrument Landing System. A beacon that the can be electronically followed down to a landing.

IMU. Inertial Measurement Unit. The "brain" of a spacecraft used for navigation. Though the IMU is attached to the spacecraft structure, the platform it is mounted on can maintain its position and direction in 3 dimensional space. Position and velocity change is sensed by gyroscopes and accelerometers on this platform, then used to fire the engines to maintain course heading and attitude. The gyroscopes and accelerometers themselves are mounted on gimbols, each capable of movement in only one of the 3 spacial directions.

IUO. Infection of Unknown Origin

LCG. Liquid Cooled Garment. Long-johns with cooling tubes for circulating chilled water.

LH2. Liquid Hydrogen fuel

LOS. Loss of Signal. Loss of communications with a spacecraft due to electrical disturbances, orbital obstructions (heavenly body between transmitter and receiver) or other interference.

LOX. Liquid Oxygen fuel

MOI. Mars Orbit Insertion, a maneuver whereby the spacecraft's engines are pointed in the direction of travel to slow down.

NAV. Navigation computer

OPS. Oxygen Purge System. A 45 minute, open loop emergency oxygen supply delivered at high pressure

Periapsis. Closest point in an elliptical orbit of Mars

Perigee. Closest point in an elliptical orbit of Earth

PLSS. Portable Life Support System. The backpack worn on a spacesuit. Contains oxygen, batteries, water and 8 hours of primary life support
Posigrade burn. Firing engines in the direction opposite to the direction of travel to accelerate.

PM. Power Module. The Base module containing the Bosch Reactor extractors and SP-100 nuclear reactor. Together they form the fuel factory that makes methox fuel from hydrogen and Mars gas, water and oxygen as well as electrical power.

QC. Quality Control.

QCT. Quantitative Computed Tomography. A tool for measuring bone density.

RCS. Reaction Control System. Sets of opposing thrusters used to change a spacecraft's attitude by pitch, roll and yaw firings. Results in small translation and rotation movement.

RM. Rover Module. The Mars base garage holding the three Rovers and mechanical facilities.

Sol. A day on Mars or 24 hours, 39 minutes on Earth

SPE. Solar Particle Event. High energy particles emitted from the Sun during peak sunspot activity. Also called a solar flare, they occur roughly once every 11 years. The emitted particles are primarily protons (hydrogen nucleii), alpha particles (helium nucleii) and heavier nucleii. Intensity may be 200-300 million electron volts per hour, or hundreds of RADs, equivalent to over 300 chest x-rays per hour. Exposure to an SPE in unprotected space would be extremely dangerous, probably fatal. Intensity drops off sharply within hours or days flare subsidence.

RAD. Radiation Absorbed Dose. A unit of radiation corresponding to the absorption of 100 ergs per gram by any medium. Exposure to 550 RADS or more is usually fatal 100% of the time; exposure to 350-550, fifty percent of the time

REM. Radiation Equivalent Man. A unit of radiation exposure to tissue.
Retrograde burn. Firing engines in the direction of travel to decelerate.

TEVIS. Treadmill Vibration isolation System. Treadmill system isolated from floor to prevent vibrations

TIG: Time to Ignition. Minutes to engine ignition on a rocket

Vallis. Valley

VAB. Vertical Assembly Building. High bay where Space Shuttle is assembled and stored

Dr. Lawrence Kuznetz

Lawrence H Kuznetz is a 40-year veteran of the space program with advanced degrees from Columbia University and the University of California, Berkeley. His PhD thesis, a computer model of human thermoregulation in spacesuits, was used to protect and guide astronauts on the lunar surface during the Apollo Program when he worked at NASA's Mission Control Center and is still in use today. During his tenure with NASA at the Johnson, Kennedy and Ames Space Centers, he participated or directed projects as diverse as water and life on Mars to education outreach to talking spacesuit design. His publication list includes a white paper used by Congress to evaluate research aboard the International Space Station, one of the first journal articles to demonstrate that liquid water could be stable on Mars and a novel and children's book about space. His first exposure to the Space Shuttle Program came as part of the elite "Build Team" tasked with completing construction of Columbia, the first Space Shuttle, and he later directed the Challenger Memorial Project, a full scale interactive memorial to the Challenger crew built by the efforts of over 1000 student volunteers and 100 corporate donors. In addition to his NASA experience, he has taught extensively at UC Berkeley, MIT, and other universities; has been an independent consultant to private industry; holds 8 US patents and has appeared on the Tonight Show, Good Morning America and CNN. He is a licensed Professional Engineer and Private Pilot and enjoys lecturing aboard cruise ships as part of their public enrichment programs. In his spare time, he plays keyboard in piano bars.

Made in the USA
Las Vegas, NV
09 January 2025

16138035R00335